8/25

FORGOTTEN DREAMS

Sierra

Who do you think you are?
I thought I knew until I accidentally discovered my adoring parents' biggest secret on my twenty-fifth birthday.
I am adopted.
Part of me is missing, and I set out to find it.
Trying to figure out the past piece by piece, I bought a little fixer-upper in the small town I was given up in.
Old lies will come out. Secrets that everyone is trying to keep buried.
Who am I really?

Caleb

When I needed a clean slate, I moved to Montgavin to start my own construction firm.
Slowly, I built my crew after my success with the bakery renovation.
When the newcomer in town wants to restore her house to its former glory, I trust no one but myself.
Sierra looks lost, slowly putting her life together, with her dedicated room complete with a whiteboard.
Something calls to me to protect her and her secrets.
Someone wants her out of the town.
But now they have to get through me.

BOOKS BY NATASHA MADISON

Dream Series
Shattered Dreams
Forbidden Dreams
Buried Dreams
Stolen Dreams
Forgotten Dreams

Meant For Series
Meant For Stone
Meant For Her
Meant For Love
Meant For Gabriel

Made For Series
Made For Me
Made For You
Made For Us
Made for Romeo

Southern Wedding Series
Mine To Kiss
Mine To Have
Mine To Hold
Mine To Cherish
Mine To Love
Mine To Take
Mine To Promise
Mine to Honor
Mine to Keep

The Only One Series
Only One Kiss
Only One Chance
Only One Night
Only One Touch
Only One Regret
Only One Mistake
Only One Love
Only One Forever

This Is
This Is Crazy
This Is Wild
This Is Love
This Is Forever

Southern Series
Southern Chance
Southern Comfort
Southern Storm
Southern Sunrise
Southern Heart
Southern Heat
Southern Secrets
Southern Sunshine

Hollywood Royalty
Hollywood Playboy
Hollywood Princess
Hollywood Prince

Something Series
Something So Right
Something So Perfect
Something So Irresistible
Something So Unscripted
Something So BOX SET

Tempt Series
Tempt The Boss
Tempt The Playboy
Tempt The Hookup
Tempt The Ex

Heaven & Hell Series
Hell and Back
Pieces of Heaven
Heaven & Hell Box Set

Love Series
Perfect Love Story
Unexpected Love Story
Broken Love Story
Mixed Up Love
Faux Pas

Copyright © 2025 Natasha Madison. E-Book and Print Edition
All rights reserved. No part of this book may be reproduced or transmitted in any form or by any means, electronic or mechanical, including photocopying, recording, or by any information storage and retrieval system, without permission in writing.

This is a work of fiction. Names, characters, places and incidents are the product of the author's imagination or are used factiously, and any resemblance to any actual persons or living or dead, events or locals are entirely coincidental.

The author acknowledges the trademark status and trademark owners of various products refer-enced in this work of fiction, which have been used without permission. The publication/ Use of these trademarks is not authorized, associated with, or sponsored by the trademark owner.

All rights reserved

Cover Design: Jay Aheer

Couple Photo: Wander Aguiar

Editing done by Karen Hrdicka Barren Acres Editing

Editing done by Jenny Sims Editing4Indies

Proofing Julie Deaton by Deaton Author Services

Formatting by Christina Parker Smith

Forgotten DREAMS

DREAM SERIES

NATASHA MADISON

One

SIERRA

I PULL UP to the house I've grown up in my whole life and turn off the car. Getting out, I look across the street to see Mr. Jackson outside, watering his potted plants. "Hey there, Sierra," he greets me, looking up once he hears my car door slam shut. "How are you doing?"

"I'm good." I smile at him, holding up my hand to say hello.

"How is the new age treating you?" He turns off the water to make sure he's not wasting any while talking to me.

"So far so good." I shrug. Today is my twenty-fifth birthday—a quarter of a century old.

"If it makes you feel any better"—he smirks—"I don't feel a day over seventy."

I tuck my phone in the back pocket of my jeans and laugh. "I'll be sure to remember that," I say, turning and looking at the house. "I have to get in there. My parents get really upset if they aren't the first ones to wish me a happy birthday." He nods and turns the hose back on to continue to water his flowers.

I walk up the pathway to the five steps to the front door. I turn the doorknob, trying to push open the door, only it doesn't budge. I touch the keypad and enter the numbers two, four, nine, one. I hear the lock turning to open before I push the door open. "Hello!" I shout. "Your favorite and only daughter is here." I make the joke because I'm an only child. I toss my keys on the brown side table at the door before stepping into the house that holds so many memories. I walk straight past the staircase to the kitchen, where I would normally find my mother, but it's empty and spotless, of course. "Mom!" I holler her name as I walk toward the front door and start up the steps to the bedroom.

The wall is filled with memories throughout the years. In the middle is a picture we took when my father finally became a judge. He was a lawyer for twenty years before he was elected to be a judge. I still remember how proud he was when he told us. My mother made such a big deal about it. I swear, there were never-ending parties for a good month. That's what you get when your father is a big deal. He was friends with everyone, and it didn't hurt that my grandparents were very wealthy and involved in politics back in the day.

It's a painted portrait that we sat posed for not just a snapshot, that would have been too easy for my mother. Nope, she wanted it like they have the royal families have it. It was something my mother had longed for, for so long. My father, being so in love with my mother, made sure she got everything her heart desired. So he did it without even a grumble. My mother sits on the chair in a pink gown. Obviously, she needed a gown. I'm surprised she didn't insist on us getting tiaras. Her hands are on her lap while my father stands proudly beside her on one side, and I stand on the other. My own pale-blue gown drapes to the ground, hiding the fact I am wearing flip-flops. The smile on our faces lights up our eyes, and I can remember it like it was yesterday, not almost eight years ago.

Next to the grand portrait are pictures of our family through the years—from the first day they brought me home to Christmas last year. Twenty-five years of memories on one wall is crazy, yet every time I catch a glimpse of one, I'm immediately taken back to said memory.

"Mom!" I shout when I get to the top of the steps and see the four bedroom doors open. I'm about to go to their bedroom at the end of the hall when the phone rings from my back pocket.

Pulling it out, I see it's my mother calling. "Wow," I answer without saying hello, "I'm home, and you're not here."

"I know. I know. I know," she pants, and I can hear people talking in the background as she hustles. "I had to pick up a couple of things, and my car didn't start this morning, so I had to drag your father out with me," she groans. "Happy birthday, my angel," she says softly. "Am I the first to say it?" she asks eagerly.

"Um," I start, "you texted me at midnight, like on the dot, and then at four o'clock and another one at seven thirty."

"But those don't count," she retorts. "I knew I should have called you this morning, but I was going crazy, and your father said I would wake you," she grits between clenched teeth. "Good going, dear," she mutters to my father, who is probably walking beside her, "worst parents ever."

I roll my eyes. "That's a little extreme, don't you think?" I laugh. "I mean, ever is huge."

"We have to pick up a couple of things, and then we'll head home," she explains. "Don't talk to anyone or answer the phone until I get there and wish you a proper happy birthday."

"Got it," I tell her. "But can you hurry up? I'm starved since you told me not to eat."

"You can go into the kitchen and have one cupcake," she whispers like someone is going to hear her, "but only one."

I smile as I listen to her whispering as if it's going to be a secret from everyone else in the world. "You are too kind."

"Bye, angel," she says. "I love you."

"Love you too, Mom," I reply, hanging up the phone. I turn to walk downstairs when I remember I wanted to get a special picture from their wedding for their anniversary coming up in a couple of months.

I walk into the spare bedroom on the side, grabbing the white stepladder from the closet before going to the attic stairs. I open the ladder and have to climb up to the third rung before I can reach the latch and pull it down. I step off the ladder and move it to the side to climb the wooden ladder built into the door.

Moving up into the attic, I duck my head until I'm standing inside. Looking at the right side, I see the Christmas decorations ready to go in four months. Taking another step in, I see blue bins stacked on the left-hand side, all with my name on them. Mom's kept pretty much most of my outfits since I was born. I take a couple more steps in and see she has all my school stuff in white bins. It's only three bins. Thankfully, she didn't keep all my art projects. But they are condensed and labeled by school year. I shake my head as the phone rings again, and when I take it out, I see it's Lilah calling.

"Hello," I answer, putting the phone to my ear and smiling. Lilah and I became friends when we were both sixteen years old, and we joined a fan fiction group for our favorite author, Cooper Parker, who writes cozy mysteries. We would comment on the same post and then quickly started chatting in private messages. To this day, the minute Cooper Parker puts out a book, we take the day off work and read it cover to cover on FaceTime, discussing it by chapter. It once took us fourteen hours, but it cemented our friendship, and when she got kidnapped last year, I rushed to be by her side. Even though our friendship is mostly online, she's my best friend.

"Happy birthday!" she shouts out with happiness as she proceeds to sing to me.

I laugh. "Thank you," I say, taking a couple more steps in and trying to spot the box I'm looking for. I see things that are my dad's when I spot a box with wedding written on it.

"What exciting things are you doing today?" she asks as I stop in front of the box.

"Right now, I'm"—I look around the attic—"in my parents' attic, looking for a picture from their wedding day so I can get it painted to match the other portrait."

"I love looking at old photos. Okay, I have to go, but I just wanted to make sure I called you and told you I love you."

"Love you more," I tell her. "And tell Lucy I got her birthday video this morning, and it's the best video I've ever gotten in my whole life."

"She wanted to call you this morning first thing when she looked at the calendar on the fridge, but I pushed her off by filming her singing to you. She'll force me to call you tonight." She laughs. "I'll speak to you then."

"I can't wait." I smile, thinking of Lucy, her stepdaughter, and the infectious happiness she brings into your life with just one conversation. "I'll talk to you then."

I hang up, putting the phone back in my pocket, when I get on my knees and pull open the brown box. The white book on the top has my mother's and father's names, Marian and Joseph, on the cover in elegant cursive writing in the middle.

I smile, taking it out and opening to the first page, where my mother's writing appears. She wrote their names and the wedding date as if they would forget such a momentous occasion like that. I flip the page and start reading the well-wishes people had written. Some are just the names; others are advice for a marriage. I laugh out loud when I see one of my uncles wrote, "If she asks you what twice, don't repeat it the third time."

I close the book and put it beside me on the floor, taking the newspaper from that day with their wedding announcement in it and placing it on the other side of me. I grab the next item in the box, a white envelope. I open the flap, seeing it's little flower petals. Putting it aside, I grab the brown envelope under it that has wedding vows written on the top. I put it with the newspaper article before I go back and see the photo album and mumble, "Yes." I pick it up and spot a gray lockbox under it. I pick up the silver handle, and it weighs almost nothing. I look and see it needs a key and wonder why the fuck it would be in this box. Putting it aside, I open the photo album, taking out the picture I was looking for. It's the one where she's facing the camera, but my father is looking at her. The expression on his face is between he's the luckiest guy in the world and he would die for her. It was always one of my favorite pictures. She always took it out of the album when I was younger, and we would flip through it. I place everything back in the box except for the newspaper clipping, their vows, and the gray metal box. I hold everything in one hand as I grasp the ladder with the other.

I walk down the steps to the kitchen and the drawer where my father keeps all the keys. The ring of keys has about twenty keys on it from the padlocks around the house to extra keys for the shed and then the pool house. There is even a couple for the garage door and the two side doors to the garage. I look on the key ring, searching for a small key. When I see it, I slide it in and turn it to the left before pulling the top up.

The first thing on the top is a newspaper article. I open the folded paper that was once white and is now tinted a soft yellow. "Hours-old Newborn Left on Fire Station Steps." I gasp out as my eyes scan the article, putting it to the side. My heart speeds up faster than it should, as if my body knows something is about to happen, but my head doesn't.

Two pictures are in the article. One is of a fireman squatting down in front of a cardboard box with a baby wrapped in a white blanket sleeping inside of it. The other is with a nurse in a rocking chair giving the same baby a bottle. I put it to the side, seeing two Polaroid pictures that must be the same baby in a wicker basket. I lay them down softly and only then do I see a white folded paper. I pick it up at the same time I hear the sound of car doors shutting. I look at the side door leading to the mudroom right off the garage.

Turning back, I'm about to unfold the paper when another Polaroid picture slips out and lands on the counter in front of me. It's of my mother sitting in the same chair the nurse was sitting in, with the baby in her arms. The wicker basket sits on the hospital bed beside her as she looks down at the baby in the blanket. My hands tremble when I unfold the triple-folded white paper.

Both of my hands shake when I see the top of the paper. "Certificate of Adoption."

I don't know why it feels like the room is spinning around me like it does in movies. My eyes scan the paper when I see the name Jane Doe, and the birthday is today's date, just twenty-five years ago. The gasp that comes out of my mouth echoes in the room. My hand goes to my mouth as I see teardrops falling onto the paper, not realizing they are coming from me. My eyes scan down to the next line where it says Birth Mother's Name: Unknown and the same for birth father's name.

I move down and see the line for the child's name after adoption. There, in bold letters, is my name:

Sierra Rose Davidson.

I hear my mother's and father's voices coming into the mudroom. "You are going to tangle the balloons," she scolds him as they walk into the room.

The smile on her face falls when her eyes go from me to the box. My father takes a step toward me. "Is this true?" I hold up the paper, my heart shattering in my chest, making it hard for me to catch my breath. "Tell me." My voice rises. "Is this paper true?"

Two

SIERRA

MY HANDS GOING into fists, my fingers gripping the white paper in my hand so hard the sound of it crinkling fills the room, as well as the sound of my breathing. Or maybe that only echoed in my ears, along with the thumping of my heart.

I see the tears rolling down my mother's face as she tries to take a step toward me, and I snap, "Is this true?" I hold up the paper, my heart shattering in my chest, making it hard for me to catch my breath. "Tell me." I'm shouting, and I don't even know it. "Is this paper true?"

"Sierra," my father begins calmly, his arm around my mother as she sobs, making her body shake.

"I asked you a question." My voice never wavering from before.

"Perhaps we should sit down and discuss this." My father doesn't raise his voice.

"Discuss this?" I shake my head from side to side.

"Discuss this?" The air suddenly leaves me, and I have to fold over to catch my breath. "Discuss this?" This time, I shake my hand with the paper still in it.

"Sierra." My father is now by my side, his hand rubbing my back. "Breathe, honey." I look up at him and move away from his touch. The man who would make sure nothing hurt me, who used to kiss my boo-boos away. The man I said I wanted my husband to be like. The man who taught me how to ride a bike. The man who taught me how to hang up a shelf by myself so I didn't need a man to do anything. The man who lied to me my whole life.

"I—I—" I stutter and try to breathe in and out before I literally have a full-blown panic attack. I have never had one, but I'm pretty sure I'm about to have one. "I don't."

"Please sit down." My father pulls out a chair at the breakfast table, where I had breakfast my whole life, starting in a high chair. The pictures are in my baby book. From me being on my knees since I wasn't tall enough to finally being able to sit on my behind without hitting my face on the table. "Sierra, please, we will tell you everything."

"Why should I believe you now?" I ask, and I can see the hurt all over his face. "You've lied to me my whole life. Why should I believe you now?"

"We have never lied to you," my mother says softly, coming to stand next to my father. "You were—are—loved with everything we have."

"Don't you think me not being your child is you lying to me?" The words come out of my mouth in anger, and my mother looks like I slapped her across the face.

"You are my child." She puts her shoulders back. "You will always be my child."

I shake my head and look down at the paper in my hands. "This says otherwise." I hold it up, my voice in a whisper. "Those other papers." I point over at the counter. "Those say otherwise also."

"Before you say anything else you can't take back," my father says, "at least hear us out."

I think about what he's saying, and I know they are the only ones who will have the answers to my questions. I don't even know if I'll ever not have questions. I step toward the chair and sit down. My father looks over at my mother and motions with his chin to go to the chair in front of me. She walks over as if she's walking the plank and will be pushed into shark-infested waters. She pulls out the chair as she sits down and my father walks over to the counter, taking the article in his hand—along with the picture that fell out—before he comes over and pulls out a chair next to my mother.

I put my hand, still clutching the paper in it, on the table, my mouth suddenly dry. "Do you want something to drink?" my father asks, and I shake my head instead of nodding. He takes a deep breath before he starts talking. "We tried for five years before we thought about going the adoption route." I listen to him, my chest rising and falling as if I just swam for an hour without stopping. "We tried everything, even two rounds of IVF, when we found out that nothing we could do would result in us having a child. Basically, we could have children with other people, just not with each other." I look at him, then my mother. "We just couldn't do it together." He puts his arm around my mother, pulling her to him and kissing her temple. "And there was no one else I wanted to share my life with, so we decided to go the adoption route."

"Because your father was in family law, he had contacts." My mother now takes over from my father. "We wanted to make sure that when we adopted you, it would be private." She puts her hands on the table and fidgets nervously with her fingers. "Which is why we moved here when we had you—"

"So no one would out your secret." I cut her off and shake my head. "A secret everyone in my life kept."

"We got a call one night; I can still remember the exact time. It was five thirty-seven in the evening, and we had just gotten home with Chinese food." My mother looks at me and puts one hand on her stomach. "We didn't know anything about you except you were abandoned."

The gasp comes out of me without me even knowing. "From what we could find out at the time, you were dropped off at a fire station"—he puts the article on the table—"in the middle of the night." I swallow down the bile that is rising up my throat. "They didn't ring or anything. You were found when one of the firemen heard crying." I close my eyes. "You were in a brown box and a hospital blanket."

"They called the police right away, and you were rushed to the hospital. The only thing they could tell us was you were a couple of hours old. You were also dehydrated and had a bit of jaundice." My mother helps him with the story.

"They put the story in the paper, hoping someone would have information or come forward, but no one did," my father continues. "They called us the next day. It was a miracle." He wipes away the tears from the corners of his eyes.

"From the minute I got that call, I knew you were mine." My mother's voice quivers. "Then we got there, and I held you for the first time and had this overwhelming sense of love that you can't explain. I looked down at you, blinking your eyes and looking around, and said, 'Hello, angel,' and you squawked at me as if you were telling me hello." She holds the picture out to me. "This was taken right after."

"I called my father right away and made sure we got everything we needed in order to make sure you were ours," my father says. "We moved here a month after you were born. No one knows that you aren't biologically ours. We also made sure the adoption was sealed."

"But you kept these and those." I hold up the paper in my hand.

"We never wanted you to find out like this, never," my mother admits. "We thought maybe when you turned sixteen that we could tell you, but then it just didn't seem like the right time."

"When did you think was a good time to tell me everything I thought was real was a lie?" I ask. "You should have told me when I was younger so I could grow up always knowing. Not keep it locked up in a box."

"We did what we thought was best," my father says, and I push away from the table, standing.

"You mean what was best for you." I fold the now semi-crumpled paper and put it in my back pocket. "You did what was best for you and—" I stop before I say Mom as I shake my head. "I can't be here." I turn and walk out of the house. I run down the steps to my car, getting in and driving away with tears pouring down my face.

I don't know how I do it, but I make it home, then walk up the steps to my house in a daze. Unlocking the door, I collapse on the couch. I pick up my phone and call the only person I can think of. Lilah. "Happy birthday," she says again with a cheerful voice.

"Lilah." My voice breaks. "Lilah," I sob.

"Sierra," she says my name in almost a whisper, "what's wrong?"

"It's a lie," I blurt between sobs, trying to catch my breath. "It's all a lie."

"What is?"

"My life." I close my eyes. "I just found my adoption papers." Her gasp fills the phone.

"I'm on my way," she states, disconnecting.

Three

CALEB

"OKAY, I'M OFF." I walk out of my office and head toward the front door, seeing my business manager, Mikaela, sitting at her desk with her coffee cup. She self-appointed herself that title, which is just another title for receptionist/secretary/accounts payable and receivable/assistant, but she likes to call herself the business manager. I would have agreed to any title she wanted to give herself, because I know without her I can't run my business.

"Good," she mumbles. "I was wondering when you would be leaving. When you're here, I can't do what I want."

"Like what?" I ask, my eyebrows pinching together.

"Like call my friends and talk smack about my boss." She smirks and winks at me as I roll my eyes. The first person I hired was Mikaela when I decided to open this place, and she is worth every single penny.

"I have two meetings." Now it's her turn to roll her eyes at me.

"You act like I don't have your schedule"—she puts her cup down—"or that I do your schedule." I don't answer her. "Tomorrow, we have the weekly meeting," she reminds me, "at eight o'clock. A couple of things need to be moved around on the schedule." I look over at the big whiteboard she keeps on the side with every project we have going on and who is at what project. She used to do it on her Excel sheet, but then my father came into town and said it would be easier for everyone to see it. So she gave in, and now it's there front and center.

"Sounds good." I nod. "I'll see you tomorrow."

"It's your turn for coffee and donuts," she calls out right before I walk out the front door.

Slamming it shut behind me, I walk down the four steps and then turn right to go to the driveway where my truck is parked. The CW Construction logo is on the side of the black truck in orange writing with my phone number beside it.

Pulling open the door and getting in, I toss my keys in the middle of the console where the cupholders are, then place the phone down in the other cupholder before starting the truck. The minute I pull out of the garage, my phone rings, the display showing me it's my father calling. I press the green button and wait to connect before I say, "Good morning."

"Hey, son." His voice fills the truck. "How're you doing?"

"Good," I reply. "I'm on my way to Charlie's to quote

him for the barn he wants to fix up and add on to."

"Oh, I saw the project in the folder. It looks like it's going to be a big project."

"If we bid properly," I say, "I think it'll be great for the business."

He chuckles. "You are already over the projected numbers that we thought you would be at after two years, and you did it in less than a year."

"Well, it helps that the Cartwrights fucked everyone over with their bullshit, and no one wanted to work with them. Plus, when the news came out that their old project was crumbling, it was the perfect time for a new person to come in and start their construction business." I laugh. "It's a good thing I'm the one who took Everleigh's phone call when she called."

"It's a good thing," he repeats my words. Almost a year ago, Everleigh's mom's bakery was torched, and she needed it to be rebuilt. The last people she would have turned to were the Cartwrights because of their bad history together. From the gossip around town, she was in the car Waylon Cartwright drove the night he was drunk, killing two bystanders plus the two people who were in his truck. That was when the Cartwrights' house of cards slowly started crumbling. Even though they tried to hide it, they found out that Waylon was wasted when he was driving. But being the narcissists they are, instead of pointing fingers at their son, they pointed at everyone else around them. "Let me know if you need me to send any of the crew back down."

"I will, but I have a good bunch of guys working for

me here now. I should be thanking the Cartwrights for that," I joke, knowing the last thing I'll ever do is talk to them. It was bad enough that they fucked over Waylon's girlfriend, but then they also tried to fuck over Waylon's best friend, Brock, who was also in the truck that night. He also worked for them as an architect, but they fucked him over. They stole his plans, and the greedy sons of bitches modified them without even working with the structure to make sure it was reinforced and nothing was up to code. And because they had everyone in their pockets and bribes out everywhere, no one said anything. That is until the buildings literally started to sink into the ground. Now there are class-action lawsuits everywhere, and no one wants to do business with them. It'll only be a matter of time before the Cartwright name is erased from Montgavin's memory.

"Okay, well, I have about five guys here itching to come up there," he shares, and I can't help but smile. When I first started here, we thought it would only be the bakery, and then I'd go back and work with my father. I don't know what it was, but I felt in my bones this is where I was meant to be. So I took another job while doing the bakery, and then they just kept coming in. There were so many times that I talked to my father about fronting me money to start my own construction company. I started CW Construction, and now I have my own team of twenty, which is crazy when you think about how fast we grew.

"It's because I'm fun to work with and for," I tell him, and he groans.

"I'm fun too," he snaps.

"Dad, you stopped being fun when Mila"—I mention my sister—"started dating one of the workers," I remind him. "I believe you said, 'I'm going to bury him under a slab of concrete if he puts one finger on her.'

And what did that do?" I ask.

"Your mother and I had words," he admits. I may be two states over, but I can feel the glare directed straight at me.

"And…" I egg him on, knowing exactly how this turned out. It's the single most joked about thing at all our meals together.

"They got married," he grumbles, "under my protest."

"You walked her down the aisle." I laugh. "And they have two kids." Two children who my father worships. He even took a step back from work to spend time with them while Mila went back to work. He says it keeps him young.

"I have to let you go," he blusters. "You're annoying the fuck out of me."

"Love you, Dad." I laugh.

"Love you too," he responds. "Proud of you."

"Thank you," I say, and he hangs up. Then I see a text come through from him.

Dad: Call your mom. She's worried about you.

I roll my eyes as I pull into the parking lot of the ranch. I park and then grab my notepad from the passenger seat before snatching my phone and tucking it in the back pocket of my blue jeans.

Running a hand through my hair reminds me I should

get a haircut this weekend. I look over when I hear galloping to see the horses being let out of the barn. Walking toward the glass door and pulling it open, I see Lilah sitting behind the desk. She looks up and smiles at me. The two of us dated a while back. To be honest, dated is a stretch since we technically went out a handful of times. Each time, it felt like I was sitting across the table from a best friend, not someone I wanted to take home and have my way with. In the end, it made sense to just stay friends. Besides, she's engaged to Emmett now, who she had been secretly in love with. "This is a nice surprise," she says.

"Hey," I greet. "I have a meeting with Charlie." I look over to the side when I hear the sound of boots coming closer to us.

"And me," Emmett interjects, walking into the room and going straight to Lilah.

"Hey, baby." He bends, kissing her lips.

"You know I dated her first, right?" I tease him because it's so easy to do.

"Yeah, but I'm the one she ended up with, so who is the winner?" He puts his hands on his hips.

"Definitely not her." I motion to Lilah with my chin, who snorts.

"Stop bugging him." She points at me. "And you." She points at him. "Did you come in here just because you saw him arrive?"

"Yes." He doesn't even care that it's not the right answer to tell her.

"You are incredible," she huffs, picking up the phone.

Then I hear her voice on the intercom.

"Charlie, Caleb is here and Emmett is also here waiting," she announces before she hangs it up.

It takes a full thirty seconds before Charlie walks into the room. "Did I miss it?" he asks, and I look over at him, confused. "He goes all barbarian when a man comes in and talks to Lilah."

"I do not go barbarian," Emmett scoffs at the accusation. "I'm just making sure she's safe."

"Is that what you're going with?" Charlie asks, trying not to laugh in his face.

"Yup," Emmett clips. "Should we head over to the new building, or are we just going to stand here discussing shit we shouldn't be discussing?"

"I vote for discussing when Lilah and Caleb were dating." Charlie puts his hand up.

"Let's go." Emmett doesn't pay any attention to him before he strides away.

"Sounds good," I agree and follow them out to the back where the barn is.

"We'll take the golf cart," Charlie states. I get in the back and look around as we make our way over to the very far end of the property to a red barn that looks like it's about to fall down if the wind blows too strong.

"What in the…" I say when I see it even closer up. "Is it even safe to walk into?"

"It just looks bad," Emmett says. "It's rough around the edges."

"Yeah." Charlie parks and gets out. "Like him." He points at Emmett, who walks over to the barn door and opens one side before walking over and opening the second. I walk next to Charlie as we step into the darkened barn, and the only light comes from the missing pieces of the roof.

It's completely empty. The concrete on the floor with caked-on mud has been there for what feels like decades. "So what do you think?" Charlie asks.

I take a look around. "We'll have to take the whole roof off and then probably reinforce the sides. Depending on what we find when we take the roof off, it will give us a better idea." Emmett nods. "Then what are you going to do with it?"

"We want to make this a rehabilitation center for the horses until they are ready to be put out with the population." He explains to me about the ranch that he is running now. It's been in his family for a long time. They do equestrian therapy, and deal mostly with soldiers who come back from war and suffer with PTSD and domestic violence survivors. "So we are going to need stalls on both sides, and then in the back, we'd like to have an open area for the foaling pens."

I nod. "It's going to be a lot of work," I tell him. "We'll have to get a couple of cranes to come in and take apart the roof."

"We know," Charlie replies, "but it has to be done."

I nod at him. "I'll get you the quote by tomorrow, and you let me know." I'm about to say something else when my phone rings, and I look down to see it's Mikaela. "Excuse me," I say, turning and walking out of the barn.

"Hey." I put the phone to my ear. "What's up?"

"Hey," she says quickly. "You know that Victorian house you were eyeing for the past month on Preston Street?"

"Yeah."

"Well, it's just been sold, and the real estate agent just called us to ask if we would be willing to meet with the new owners."

"Fuck," I hiss, "I was thinking of buying the house and fixing it up."

"You don't have time. Now you can just fix it up, and everyone wins," she returns happily.

"Yeah, okay," I agree, and then she doesn't talk. "What's wrong?"

"Well," she sings out the word, "the new owner is really keen on moving in right away."

"Okay," I reply, not knowing where she's going with this.

"She said she'll pay extra." I start to groan. "I know the list is long, but if we move some things around…"

"We can't do it," I tell her, shaking my head. "We already have a waiting list."

"This is your dream job," she reminds me. "It's going to be a huge undertaking, and you're the only one who can do it justice."

I hold the bridge of my nose. "I'll have to call in some men from home."

"Already on it," she says, and I look up. "What would you do without me?"

"Fine," I huff out, "tell her I'll take the meeting."

Four

SIERRA

THE PHONE RINGS from beside me on my desk, and then it rings on my computer screen, showing me Lilah is FaceTiming me. I move my cursor to the green accept button in the corner of the screen, waiting for it to connect before I say, "Hello."

Her face fills the screen with a huge smile, and I see she's at home. "Hey," she says, her hair piled on her head as she leans on her elbows on the island.

I smile when I see Emmett come in and stand behind her, probably not knowing she's on the phone, before hugging her and then kissing the side of her face. "Hi, Emmett."

He looks at her phone, shocked. "Oh, hey, Sierra." He looks at Lilah. "I'll leave you two be," he says, turning to leave but not before he smacks her ass.

She just shakes her head and watches as he walks away. She literally sighs before she looks back at me, and I can't help but laugh at her. "Do you need to call me back?"

She closes her eyes and laughs at herself. "No, I'm fine." She giggles. "I get him all the time anyway." Looking over to where Emmett must be standing and winking at him.

"Good to know." After all the time she's been in love with him, I'm happy that the feeling is returned.

"How're you doing?" I shrug my shoulders at her question. It's been two weeks since my life was turned upside down. Two weeks I've felt like I've been living in a fog of sorts. The only thing I've been consistent in has been my work. I've been working all hours of the night when insomnia catches up with me. Which is why I now set my alarm clock for eight o'clock because I'm sleeping until noon and then staying up until four o'clock in the morning. It's time to get my ass back into a routine.

"About the same. I don't know what to think." Lilah was the first person I called once I left my parents' house. She didn't understand a word I was saying and literally talked me through the sobbing. She was calm, and three hours later, she was at my door with a packed bag.

"I finally got a therapist." Her eyes go up. "It's been a week."

"Is that helping?" she asks softly.

"I think the shock is wearing off," I admit. "I need to call my parents and talk to them."

"How do you think that's going to go?"

"I have no idea. I understand they love me. I love them. I just—" I take a deep breath. "It's the fact it was such a secret, like they were ashamed of it."

"They were not ashamed of it because then that would make them ashamed of you, and we both know they worship you." I nod because it's true. "Maybe they were scared to tell you."

"I would have preferred to be told and not find out the way I did. Would I have been shocked? Yes, yes, I would have, but fuck, I don't know."

"I'm happy you are talking about it with your therapist," she says, "and I'm here if you ever need to vent."

"Thank you." I take another deep breath, and she tilts her head to the side and looks at me.

"What's with that look?" she asks me quizzically.

"Well," I start, "I was thinking."

She shakes her head. "The last time you did that, we spent the week 'hiking,' and you forgot that it gets cold at night, and we almost froze to death."

"We checked into a Four Seasons hotel six hours later," I remind her, "and you slept in the robe they gave you." I point at her, and she rolls her eyes. "I was thinking of maybe moving."

She gasps, "Move away?" I nod. "There is more to it, isn't there?"

"There is," I admit and ignore the way my heart speeds up. "I was thinking of looking for my birth parents." Her eyes go bigger.

"I don't know if you should do that." Worry fills her voice.

"I feel like I don't even know who I am." Just saying

it out loud to someone other than my therapist feels both scary and good at the same time. "Like, I know who I am, obviously."

I look up at the ceiling. "But why didn't they want me?"

"Listen, I'm all for finding out where you came from but, Sierra…"

The tears come to my eyes. "I know. I know. It's stupid and they literally threw me away."

"They didn't throw you away." She tries to make me feel better.

"They put me in a box and left me outside, wrapped in a blanket." My voice gets higher. "They didn't even, like, ring the bell or, I don't know, contact an adoption agency." The tear escapes. "Like, who does that?"

"Assholes," she retorts. "But you also don't know why they did what they did."

"Was I a secret?" The questions that have been going through my head nonstop for the last two weeks have been wild. "I literally dream that I'm walking down the street, and everyone is a stranger to me and staring at me. I walk up to random people and am like, 'Are you my birth mother?'"

"Sierra," she says my name, and I feel like she's about to hug me through the phone.

"It's crazy. I shouldn't even care since they didn't." I lean back in my work chair. "But I fucking do."

"It's only normal," she agrees with me. "So where are you moving?"

"Somewhere I think I could have support and still

have a fresh start. Sort of in the middle of where I am now and where I was left."

"Have you been looking?" Of course she would know I have already started this plan.

"I have," I tell her, then I click on my emails and send her the listing I found late last night or, better yet, in the middle of the night. "I just sent it to you."

She clicks on her phone, and her face disappears as she looks at the link I just sent her. "Sierra," she says my name and reappears on the screen. "Okay, one." She holds up her finger. "This is here." I nod and smile. "Two, this house—"

"I know." I tap my desk. "It's utterly perfect."

"It's run-down, girl." She laughs. "I think I've driven by there and thought it was going to fall on top of my car."

"You've really gotten more dramatic now that you've hooked up with the love of your life."

She scoffs. "I've always been somewhat dramatic. Just not in front of him because I was being all 'in your face, I'm a tough girl, but then I want you to push me against the wall and kiss me. And then do all kinds of dirty things to me.'"

As if he has been waiting for her to call his name—"You rang?"—Emmett pops back up behind her, wrapping one arm around her stomach and the other around the top of her chest, pulling her to him. She holds his arm with both of her hands.

"Guess who is thinking about moving?" She looks over her shoulder at him. "Sierra." She doesn't even give him a chance to answer. Having met Emmett a couple of times, I'm going to go out on a limb and say he has no idea nor does he actually care to play this game.

"Oh fun," he says, saying whatever he needs to in order for her to smile.

"It's more than fun. We can have book clubs together in the same house, and she can come over for dinner." Her eyes light up. "We can have girls' night at the bar." He groans. "Isn't that going to be fun?"

"Baby," he says, his head going back, "it's not going to be fun. It's going to be the opposite of fun." I can't help but laugh at him. "But it's fine."

"See?" One hand lets go of his arm and holds his cheek. "Told you it'll be fun."

"I can't wait," he mumbles.

"Okay, I have to go," I tell them. "I'll keep you posted."

"I'll call you later," she replies and quickly hangs up.

I spend the rest of the night working on some contracts I have going on. I've been a graphic designer for the past four years, graduating with a bachelor of arts degree. I got a job as soon as I graduated with a commercial real estate company. I would design all of their spaces, and slowly, I branched out doing jobs here and there on my own, building my portfolio. I went from creating brand logos to creating billboards in Times Square. When I finally had enough clients under my belt, I left, and now I work for myself. I have all types of clients, from restaurant designs to corporate companies who need brochures made. Being able to create things is the best, and I've been good at it since I was twelve, when my parents let me have my way with my bedroom. I thought for sure I would go into interior design, but this was much more fun for me. Sometimes I even get to do both of them at the same time. Those are my favorite projects. I have a couple of builders who have the houses all ready to go, and all I have to do is design the catalog with furniture and all.

I'm closing down my computer by 8:00 p.m., which is a new record for me this week, when the phone pings. I grab it from my desk and look down to see my mother texted me.

Mom: It's been a while. I'm trying to give you space. Would like to hear your voice. I love you.

My heart tightens in my chest at the same time as my stomach lurches. It's been over two weeks since I found out the truth.

I don't know why, but I take the phone and call her instead of ignoring it. She answers after one ring. "Sierra," she says my name as if she's never said it before.

"Hi," I reply, closing my eyes as I hear her softly sob.

"Um." She clears her throat. "How are you?"

"I'm okay," I answer softly, "just"—my own tears start now—"I needed some space."

"I know, your father said you would call when you were ready."

"I think we should talk," I repeat the words my therapist has had me practicing for the last week.

"Of course, name the time and place."

"How about we meet for coffee?" I suggest, not really

wanting to go back to the house just yet. "Tomorrow morning."

"That sounds fantastic. I'll text you in the morning."

"Okay, I'll see you tomorrow."

"I love you, Sierra," she states, and I close my eyes.

"I love you too, Mom." The minute I say the words, she cries even harder.

"I didn't think you would ever call me that again."

"I'm sorry I stormed out," I tell her. "It was a shock."

"I know."

"We'll talk more tomorrow," I assure her.

"Will do," she says. "See you then."

I hang up the phone and head upstairs to slide into a bath. After the past two weeks, I need to pamper myself.

I HEAR THE soft bells of the alarm, and my eyes fly open. I'm on my side in the middle of my king-sized bed with five pillows surrounding me like a cocoon. I slip my hand out from under my head to grab the phone and turn it off. Before closing my eyes again, my eyelids feel like they weigh over a hundred pounds.

It takes a minute of me telling myself that I have to get up. My eyes slowly open and close before finally staying open. I toss the covers off myself, getting out, and slipping on my pink slippers before grabbing the long gray cashmere robe.

I finish in the bathroom before grabbing my phone from under my thick plush white duvet and walking down the stairs to the kitchen. I open the shades in the back before starting my coffee. The smell fills the small kitchen before I walk over to the fridge and grab the milk. Pouring the milk in the frother, I press the button and then put the milk back. I contemplate making myself something to eat, but I close the fridge. I head over to make my coffee, making sure the milk is hot enough before adding it to my cup. I bring the mug to my lips as I look out from the kitchen window, seeing it's gloomy outside.

Heading to the couch, I curl up in the corner of the L-shaped couch and grab a throw blanket, putting it over me.

The phone rings in my hand, and I see it's Rebecca. "Hello," I answer, putting it on speakerphone.

"Sierra," she says my name cheerfully, "did I catch you at a bad time?"

I close my eyes. Considering it's after eight thirty in the morning, what the fuck could she think I've been doing? "No, just having coffee," I say. "What can I do for you?"

"I have good news," she chirps, "the offer on the house was approved." I sit up, putting the cup on the coffee table. My nerves get the best of me. "The house is yours." I close my eyes. "And I spoke with my girl at the top construction company in the area, and she is going to talk to her boss about squeezing you in."

"Wow," I blurt, "this is happening faster than I expected."

"That's a good thing. Welcome to Montgavin."

Five

CALEB

I PULL UP to the house and park on the street, looking out the window at the house. It really is a beautiful house, but fuck, does it look like it's going to fall down. I grab the clipboard along with my phone while getting out of the truck. Looking down at my steel-toed boots as I walk up the paved pathway that has seen better days. Weeds and grass grow out from between the joints. I walk up the three steps, the whole time, the building creaks, and if I didn't know better, I would think this is a sign to get the fuck out of here.

The deck has to be sanded and resealed. I put that on my notepad before I pick up my hand to ring the bell, but the doorbell is hanging, and the wires look like something has chewed through them. I pick up my hand and knock on the glass part of the door. Shockingly enough the door looks to be new, or at least it was replaced in the last ten years. I can see someone walking to the door, and not wanting to seem like a Peeping Tom, I look down at my boots until I hear the sound of the lock turning and the door is pulled open.

I look up and see her blondish-brown hair blow back. "Hi," she greets, her voice soft, her blue-green eyes lighting up with a smile. "You must be Caleb. I'm Sierra," she says, and for the first time in my life, I'm left speechless. She's hands down the most beautiful woman I've ever seen. She extends her hand, and mine moves on its own as it slides in her soft one. I watch her hand in mine as if it's the first time I've ever shaken hands with someone. I awkwardly move her hand up and down for what seems to be over a year before she slides her hand out of mine and it falls to her side. "Please come in." She moves to the side to give me a chance to walk in. I make the stupid mistake of letting my eyes roam down her outfit. A long-sleeved, rust-colored, V-neck crop sweater falls just about the waist of her blue jeans, which are tight in the hip area but go loose on the way down to the floor.

"Thank you." I finally find the words, stepping into the house and into the foyer. She closes the door behind me. "This is a beautiful home," I tell her when she comes to stand in front of me. The dining room is on the left with a chandelier hanging in the middle of the room. To the right is what would probably be the living room, but the house is bare of furniture.

"I wouldn't use those words." She laughs, folding her arms over her chest. "But I think that it could be"—she looks around—"in time and with the right person."

I look at the crown molding which looks like it is original. "This is true. Why don't we talk about what you want done, and I'll let you know if we can do it or not." I turn to her and she nods.

"I'd like to take the wallpaper off," she says of the old wallpaper that is peeling down in the corners of the room, "and I'd love to have built-in shelves from the floor to the ceiling." I look over at her. "Maybe have those ladders that move side to side." She takes a deep breath. "I want this to be a library." Her voice goes higher. "I can see big, cushioned couches," she explains her vision, but I'm lost in the way her eyes light up even more talking about it.

"You want a ladder like in the movie *Beauty and the Beast*?" She looks at me, shocked. "It was my sister's favorite movie," I fill her in, and she just nods. I make a note on my pad, trying to focus on writing and not how she smells of lavender and vanilla. "What do you want to do about lighting?" I ask and look up at the ceiling, seeing there isn't one fixture. "I'm going to guess there is no wiring to put in some spotlights."

"Yeah, I'm guessing they had lamps all over the place. Which is also what I'm going to have, but I'd love some extra lighting when I have girls' night." She does a circle in the room, and I can imagine she's picturing what those nights would look like. She then moves to the corner of the room and points to the side. "When you walk this way, there are these French doors." She shows me the doors that look like they are going to fall off the hinges if they're moved. One even looks like it's scratched the wood floor from being opened and closed so many times. I bend to touch and see how deep it goes, happy it is pretty much just the surface. "I would like to keep them." I stand back up and move into the room. Looking to the right, I see it has a bay window. The sunlight streaming into the house is almost ethereal.

"What do you want to do with this room?" I ask. She walks over to the window and looks outside before turning to face me.

"I want this to be my office. I would like to have built-in storage." She motions to the wall under the windows. "There, I can have benches." I write the note, thinking how kick-ass it would be. "When I have kids, this could be their playroom."

My eyes quickly go to her hands to see if she's wearing a ring. My heart feels like it's stopped in my chest until I see her hands. I literally sigh in relief when I see her hands free of any jewelry. "Are you married?" The words come out before I can even stop them.

Her head tilts to the side as she takes in the question that even I know is inappropriate. It doesn't fucking matter if she's married or not, but I have to hear the words. "Not at the moment."

I nod. "Boyfriend?" I inwardly cringe at the question.

"Not at the moment." She tries to hide the smirk, but it comes out in full force. "So, for now, it would only be an office. Then, in the future, when I get a boyfriend, then get married and have kids, this would be a nice playroom."

"It would," I agree with her.

"Are you married?" I look back at her and shake my head. "Girlfriend?"

I smirk. "Not at the moment." She stares at me and tries not to laugh, but she can't stop herself as she turns and walks out of the other set of French doors on the opposite side of the room.

"Good to know." She moves to the side. "Now this," she starts as I watch her ass. When she looks over her shoulder, she catches me, but I quickly look away, and I can see her smirking. "This is where I want to keep the moldings and everything in almost the exact way it was built." She points at the ceiling. "But I want to bring in some modern."

"How so?" I ask her as she points at the far wall. "I love the fireplace"—her hand comes out to touch the red brick of the mantel—"but like maybe paint it."

"We can try." I nod. "What we can do is maybe put other stones here." I walk over to the fireplace. "Depending on what color you're going with, we can use bigger stones. Very old but stylish at the same time."

"That sounds so good," she agrees. "Much better than my idea."

She moves over to the side where there is a bathroom with no window. The only light is from the room outside. From what I can see, the whole thing has to be gutted, and the plumbing has to be redone. When we get to the kitchen, I see that the cabinets are from the middle of the room to the ceiling and have crown molding all along them. "What do you want to do here?"

"Gut it," she states, and my eyes go big. "I know it's

extreme, but I want to open it up." She points at the two walls that divide the dining room and the kitchen. "I want to knock down these two walls." She walks over to the walls that separate the kitchen and the dining room. "Have one big space but with a huge island in the middle, with under-the-counter stools on one side, a sink on the other, and I definitely want electricity in the island."

I walk to the wall and knock on it, hearing the hollowness. "If there isn't a load-bearing wall, it'll be an easy fix. If there is, you would have to put a post and a beam."

"We have to do that since I already have a vision for this room." She leans her hip against the counter. "If you do end up doing the work—"

"Oh, I'm going to be doing the work." I don't give her a chance to finish that sentence even though I know that taking this on will be a huge project, and I will have to call in extra men instead of saying no or putting her on the list.

"You're a little sure of yourself, Caleb." She raises her eyebrows. "We aren't even sure you'll have the best bid." Now my eyebrows go up. "I'm sure you know how this works by now. I have to get more than one quote."

"Oh, I know exactly how these things are done, Sierra. But, considering I'm practically the only one in town who can do this work, I'm going to go out on a limb and say I'll have the best quote." She chuckles. "Unless you bring out people from the city." I shrug as I look around. "That will probably cost some big bucks, considering they will have to bring in their men and have them holed up at the motel while they get the work done."

"Surely, more than one person in this town does this kind of work."

"The only other option is the Cartwrights, and with all the court cases against them, you won't want them to do the work." I hold up my hands when she thinks about arguing with me. "The last development that they did is now sinking into the ground. I don't think you want someone like that working on your house." I wait for her to counter with me.

"Well, then the second part is"—she puts her hand on the counter beside her, her nails clicking on the marble as she taps them—"it will also depend on when you can get the work done." She crosses one ankle over the other.

"When do you need it done?" I mimic her stance as I lean against the counter across from her. I don't know why I'm enjoying this so much, but I am.

"I'm moving in," she says, taking a huge breath, "next week."

"Sierra," I say her name, laughing, "there is no way that can happen. Even if we work around the clock. Seven days a week with three crews." I shake my head.

"What I'm hearing is that you can't get it done?" She eggs me on.

"I have to bring in electricians and the plumber, and that is an easy fix, if you don't have to get the house rewired. I know you're aware that we don't even know what we are dealing with until we open the walls."

"Okay." She nods, giving in. "Can you at least get my bedroom done? I can live here while you guys do the work. I'll only bring in my bedroom and a desk so I can work."

"I haven't even seen upstairs yet," I remind her. "I don't like to make promises and then break them."

"Well then, let's go." She pushes off and walks past me, and I follow her up the stairs. "These might have to be reinforced or something." She looks down at the worn-out stairs.

"They might have to," I say, trying not to laugh. "I think I can see down to the basement through this crack alone." I point at the crack on the third step. "They are not safe at all," I tell her. "But that can be a quick fix while we work on the house."

"Great." We head up the U-shaped staircase. "I'd love to have this a dark mahogany with white spindles, but I haven't decided yet."

"I would have to see everything you plan to do with the house before I agree to that."

"Well, it's a good thing you don't own the house and work for me," she quips when we get to the top of the stairs.

"I may work for you, but I'm not going to defile a house because you get a bee in your bonnet." She turns and quickly walks toward the bedroom.

"Is that the polite way of saying if I don't get a wild hair up my ass?" My eyes make the mistake of literally looking at her ass.

She spins around and my eyes quickly move back to hers. "Yes, that is the polite way. My mother would knock me on my ass if I was rude."

"Good to know." She walks left and opens the two doors that are closed. "This is my bedroom."

The room is bare, and the floor looks to be in need of sanding and varnishing. "This doesn't look too bad." I look around, seeing the ceiling has plaster crown moldings that have to be handled delicately, and I know exactly who I'm going to call. He's retired, but for this, I think he'll come out of it. "Where is the bathroom?"

She points to the side, and when I walk in, all I can say is, "Oh my."

"Yeah," she adds from beside me. "I mean, I guess if you were in the fifties and oozing money, this would be like a wow, but I'm not sure I need a gold tub. I'm also not sure how I feel about Pepto-Bismol pink. I mean if I was eight, this would have been my dream instead of the Barbie Dreamhouse, but now, not so much." I laugh as I look around at the bathtub that sits right under the bay window. Gray and pink drapes hang on each side, held open by a gold-tasseled silk rope. I walk to the closed door, opening it and seeing just a toilet, and closing it back up. "I'd like to add a shower in the room."

"In that corner," I suggest, pointing to the side that has an empty space with a linen closet right next to it. "We'll have to do it all glass, so you don't cover the window." She smiles at me.

"I like the way you think." She takes a deep breath. "So the main question is…" I wait for her to ask the main question. "Can you do this in a week?"

"It'll be hard, and I'll probably have to get two sets of crews to come in." I look at the two rooms, tilting my head. "But for you, I'll make it happen."

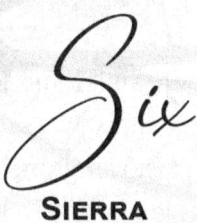

Six

SIERRA

"ARE YOU SURE you will be okay with me staying with you guys for the night?" I ask Lilah as we walk out of the house, followed by Emmett. "It's not a big deal. I could probably get a hotel in town."

"Don't be silly," Lilah returns. "It'll be fine." I look back at Emmett, who doesn't say a word. We just finished dinner, and Lilah brought up us hitting the bar for a drink. I didn't really pack anything to go out, so I'm wearing my tight blue jeans and a tight, long-sleeved light-beige shirt that goes off the shoulder. I pair that with the only pair of heels I brought with me. Heels I didn't even know why I was packing, but luckily, I did.

"Is it okay with you?" I ask, and he sort of grunts, but not before he grabs her hand and brings it to his lips.

"Whatever she wants," he states, opening her door as she gets on her tippy-toes and kisses his lips before touching her little baby bump that is barely visible.

"You say that now, but then I ask for something, and you say no." She gets into the truck, and he gawks at her.

"Like what?" He practically screeches out, putting his hands on his hips.

"I asked if we could make me a library," she retorts, and he rolls his eyes, "and you said no."

"I did not. I said who is going to use that, and you never answered me." He points to her, waiting for her to remember the conversation.

"It was a no." She reaches out for the handle of the door and closes it in his face. He turns to look at me.

"I didn't say no to her." He holds up both hands as if he is surrendering to the fight.

"But you didn't say yes." I open the back door and get into the truck and slam the door. Knowing that with me saying this, he'll turn and give it to her to make her happy. Fuck, it wouldn't surprise me if he built her a whole new wing for it. "You are going to get the best library anyone has ever gotten," I mumble, putting on my seat belt.

"I know." She claps her hands as she watches him walk around the front of the truck. I can see his mouth mumbling probably curse words. "And he's going to get the best blow job of his life."

"Eww." I fake vomit. "It better not be tonight."

She laughs as he gets into the truck and starts it. I look out the window, seeing the trees as we pull away from his house. From the moment I visited Lilah, something about this town just made me smile. I don't know if it's because every place I went to it felt like I belonged there or the fact that everyone in the town seemed so friendly. Whatever it was it felt like a big hug after a long day at work. It could be because I liked the people so much. It could be because it was new. It could be a thousand things. All I knew is I felt somewhat settled here. It was the strangest experience.

I don't have much more chance to think about it before he pulls in the parking lot. The minute I get out, I can hear the music coming from inside the bar. "This is going to be so much fun," Lilah says again as she slides her arm in mine, and we walk into the bar. The sound of my high heels on the paved parking lot mixed with the clunk of her boots fills the air. Emmett is on her other side, holding her hand before she lets me go and disappears past the open black doors.

I look up and see the sign for Thatcher's Bar before walking in and stopping dead in my tracks. It's utterly fucking gorgeous. As I walk into the bar area, the ceiling opens up, and I take a look around at how pretty this bar is. The exposed red brick around the bar pops out against the dark metal cladding surrounding it. It's a rustic feel but almost modern at the same time. The big brown square bar area is in the middle of the space, with the square metal rack suspended over it with different glasses all hanging in their place, ready to be used.

Old wooden barrels used over time also help with the decor. Dark brown leather stools surround the bar, while little round tables scatter against the outer wall area. "This is fabulous," I admire, turning around as Lilah walks farther into the bar.

"Oh look, there is Brock and Everleigh," she points out, grabbing my hand, and she follows Emmett as he zigzags through the tables. Stopping beside a table that seats about six but only two people are sitting there.

"Where is our daughter?" he asks the couple, seated beside each other. His hand is draped over the back of her chair, and her head is leaned close to his.

"She's with my mother and Oliver," Everleigh replies, ignoring the hissy fit that Emmett just pulled. "Hi, Sierra." She moves her head to the side, eyeing me. "Excuse the brute," she says, "I'm Everleigh." I smile. "We met when you came down last time." She looks at Lilah. "But there were so many new faces, you probably don't remember."

"You brought the donuts," I say, walking beside her. I pull out the chair, sitting in it, and she smiles at me. "I have to say, I've been dreaming about them since I left. I brought six home with me and even my parents said they were amazing. I had to ration out the leftover ones, and then one night I had a nightmare they would go bad, so I ate them all for breakfast the next morning."

The smile on her face is from ear to ear. She tosses her long black hair over her shoulder. "Tell me more," she jokes. "I'm kidding. Maybe." She rolls her eyes. "This is my husband, Brock." She motions to the man sitting next to her. His black hair is pushed away from his face, his dark eyes looking at me as he nods and picks up his beer before he takes a pull of it. Not saying a word to me.

"Nice to see you again, Brock," I tell him. "You have a little girl, right?" He nods. "Saige?"

"That would be her." He turns to look at the server, who comes over to take our order.

"Excuse him," Everleigh says. "He's not fit for company."

I give a short snort as I order myself a dirty martini. "I think it's a common theme with the men in this area." I pick up my hand and do a small circle of the table, making the girls laugh. Lilah sits beside me, with Emmett between her and Brock.

"What are you doing in town?" Everleigh asks me. "Are you visiting again?"

I smile as I look over at Lilah who sits down with the biggest grin on her face. "No. I just bought a house here."

Everleigh gasps out while Lilah claps her hands soundlessly with glee. "No way. Where?"

"On Preston Street," I tell them and I hope they know where it is, because I wouldn't even know in what direction to tell them to go.

"Oh, that's near Brady," she says and I look over at Lilah.

"He owns this bar." Lilah fills me in on who Brady is. "He's Charlie's brother-in-law."

"Got it," I say of the mention of him. I'm sure I met him the last time I was here but I can't picture him.

"Well, that's exciting. When do you move in?" Everleigh asks as the guys exchange about five words to each other.

"Next week," I answer her as the server comes over and places the glass down in front of me. At the same time, my eyes move to the door, and I see him walking in with four other men. He is laughing at something one of them said, and my heart literally speeds up. Caleb is wearing dark jeans and a light-gray hooded sweater, the sleeves pulled up to his elbows, showing off his thick, tanned arms. He lifts his left hand with his silver Rolex on it and runs it through his dark brown hair. He must sense me staring at him because his eyes find mine, and the smile on his face gets even bigger. His eyes go up as he nods his chin toward me.

"Oh, Caleb is here." Brock pushes away from the table. "I have to speak to him about the crane he was looking for." He gets up and makes his way to the bar where Caleb and his four friends are.

"I have no idea what they are going to talk about," Emmett says, getting up and bending to kiss Lilah, "but I'm sure it will be better than listening to you girls gab."

I can't help but laugh at his directness before I bring my glass to my lips and take a sip. "So you guys know Caleb?" I ask the table and see Everleigh hide her smile as she reaches for her glass of whiskey, then she looks over at Lilah.

"Oh, she knows him more than anyone else does." She motions to Lilah, who is blushing but shakes her head and looks down at her lap. The flutter I had in my stomach from seeing him literally plummets down to my feet. "Isn't that right?"

"Oh, good lord, it's not as interesting as it sounds. We dated," she shares, and the dirty martini tastes like acid in my mouth. "How do you know him?"

"He is the one who is going to renovate the house." I try not to say anything more. I especially don't share that he handed me his business card and wrote his personal cell number on it.

"Oh, he does fantastic work," Everleigh praises. "He rebuilt the bakery when it burned down." I'm trying to listen to her, but my head is spinning that Lilah and Caleb dated. "He moved to town after that I think." She takes a sip. "And then he dated Lilah." Pointing over to her.

"Dated is a stretch," Lilah now says. "It was a couple of dates, and it just…" She looks over at the bar, and I make the mistake of looking over to see Brock leaning on the bar with his elbows while he talks to Caleb, who is leaning with one elbow on the bar. His body is turned toward our table. "Even kissing him felt weird." Lilah shakes her head and takes a sip of her drink. "That should have been my first clue to stop dating him."

"How long did you date for?" I ask, but the sound of my breathing, or better yet panting, is now the only thing I can hear.

"It was a couple of months," she says, and I feel like the air is taken from me.

"You never mentioned him," I reply.

She shrugs. "It really wasn't that big of a deal." I wait for her to ask me if I like him. Or ask me why I'm so interested in knowing more about him. But she doesn't. She just takes a sip of her drink before looking over and pushing away from the table. "I'll be back," Lilah says, getting up as I grab my martini glass and bring it to my lips.

My eyes go to the bar, straight to him, as his head goes back and he lets out a laugh that feels like it warms your soul on a cold day. Like the hug you need at the end of a shitty day. I exhale as I take a sip of my drink. "You're into him?" I blink quickly and look back over at Everleigh.

"No." I shake my head. "No." I try to think of the words. "I just met him. Literally today less than three hours ago."

"Well, that's how it usually goes," she quips. "By the way, he's a thousand percent single."

"Yeah, but…" I start to say, as my hand goes to the stem of my martini glass. I turn it with my fingers and look down at it. "There is a girl code that says you don't date your best friend's ex. The whole bros before hos but hos before bros." I don't even understand why I'm so bothered by this. Fine, he was good-looking, he made me smile, and his humor made me laugh, but seriously, I've known him for a whole hour.

"I mean, for sure," she counters, pushing away from the table, "but does it count if she was in love with someone else the entire time she was dating him?" She picks up her glass. "Talk to her and tell her how you feel. I'm sure she'll tell you it doesn't go against the girl code." She walks away from the table, leaving me by myself.

I watch Everleigh walk over to Brock and wrap her arms around his back before he looks over, and she gets on her tippy-toes to kiss his neck. I look over and see that Lilah is plastered to Emmett's front as he looks at her, saying something, pushing her hair over her shoulder before smiling and kissing her through his laugh.

"Funny running into you here." I hear his voice and blink once before looking over to see Caleb sitting next to me. His musky smell invades my senses as I fight to put my shield up.

"Why is that?" I ask.

"I didn't know you and Lilah," he says, and I smile tightly, "knew each other."

"Yeah," I reply, keeping the conversation short.

He puts his arm on the table, leaning forward. "Good news." He looks at me with his golden-brown eyes. "We start work at the house tomorrow," he informs me, and my eyes go big.

"I have a group of guys coming down, and we're going to be finished by the time you move in." My hand goes out, and I squeeze his bicep, feeling the softness of his sweater under my fingers and the tightness of his arm.

"Are you serious?" I ask, and he nods.

"Very serious." He smiles at me, my hand feeling the heat from his arm. "We start tomorrow morning at eight o'clock. Someone has to be there to let me in."

"Are you ready to go?" Lilah asks, and the minute I hear her voice, my hand flies away from him.

"Yeah." I nod, pushing away from the table. Standing up, I pick up my glass and finish what's in it before placing it back down. "Ready," I confirm as I move away from Caleb, the palm of my hand itching to touch him again. "Thank you." nodding to him and turn to walk away.

"Bye, Caleb," Lilah says, and I look over my shoulder at him as I walk away.

His eyes are fixated on me as he does a chin up, and my mouth waters. "See you soon, Sierra."

Seven

CALEB

"WE ARE GOING to be there in five minutes," my cousin Theo tells me when I pick up the phone. He was my right-hand man when I was back home. I mean he was technically my right-hand man since we were in diapers, but we lived two hours away from each other. Until he decided to move near me after college. Ever since, we've been attached at the hip. When I decided to move here, he thought about coming with me, but he wasn't sure just yet. In the past couple of months, he's been back here every other week to help me, and I know this job is perfect for him. It'll keep him in town long enough to allow him to make the biggest leap and come join me. Or at least that is what I'm hoping for.

"Sounds good," I say, getting into my truck and putting on my aviator sunglasses. The sun is so bright today with not a cloud in the sky. "I should be there at the same time, maybe a couple of minutes later."

"We'll start to unload things until you get there." This is why I need him to be here and working with me. He would do things without me telling him to do it. Also, he's the only one who would be able to tell me to my face that things can't be done like I think they can.

"See you then." I disconnect the phone and pull out of my driveway before making my way over to Sierra's house.

My head goes back to seeing her at the bar, sitting there with Lilah with her hair tucked behind her ear. I stood at the bar and tried not to look over at her when Brock was talking to me, but I pretty much failed miserably when he said, "Are you fucking listening to a word I'm saying?" While he was going on and on to me about the crane I needed for the roof of the barn, I should have been paying attention to what he was saying. Instead, my head was in the clouds, thinking about the woman sitting not too far away from me.

I tried to stay away from her, but when everyone was chitchatting at the bar, I made the mistake of going over and sitting down with her. I told myself I was doing it so I could update her that we would be starting on her house. In reality, I just wanted to talk to her. She was standoffish right off the bat. Totally different from when I met her at her house a couple of hours before. I thought there was a flirty vibe at her house, but at the bar, it was a straight this-is-never-going-to-happen vibe.

Now I'm pulling up right behind Theo's truck as I see him, Frankie, and Nino unloading all their equipment. Frankie and Nino have been with us for a couple of months and are young, so going out of town is a treat for them. I grab my phone and the keys before jumping out. "Hey," I say to Frankie, who is grabbing his tool belt in one hand and his toolbox in another.

"No one is here yet. Door is locked," he explains, then looks back at the house. "Is this place even safe for us to be working in?"

I look up at the house. "She looks worse than she is," I tell him, and he nods, walking away as Theo comes to stand next to me.

"I don't know what the fuck you just signed us up for," Theo accuses, just as a car parks behind my truck, "but you owe us big-time."

I look over, seeing the car door open. One brown high-heeled boot comes out of the car before she steps out, closing the driver's side door while I take in her whole outfit. She's wearing black jeans with a thick, loose-knit, long-sleeved brown sweater that goes past her hips but is tucked in on one side. The sleeves look like they are rolled twice. She looks at me before coming to me, the sound of her heels getting louder as she gets closer. "Morning," I greet with a smile, and she turns to look at the guys waiting at the front door.

"Am I late?" she asks, pressing the button on her phone and seeing it's a bit before eight. "I thought you said that you start at eight."

"No," I tell her, wanting to get closer to her and see if her lips are as soft as they look. The wind blows her blond hair in front of her face, and she turns her head to get it away from her. "The guys just got here."

"Okay," she replies. "Do I leave you the key?"

"That depends," I say, and she looks up at me.

"On?"

"If you trust me or not?"

"I don't know you well enough to answer that question." She doesn't miss a beat answering my question. I don't know why it suddenly feels like we aren't talking about the house but about something else.

"Well, you can either come here every morning at eight to let us in and then come by to lock up"—I look back over at the guys now standing together talking—"or you can leave me the key, and I can let them in and out."

"I'm leaving as soon as we are done here," she shares, and I have the sudden urge to ask her where she's going. "I'll be back next week."

"For good?" It's so wrong for me to ask her this and so unprofessional. There is no reason for me to know this answer, yet I can't help but ask it.

"That's the plan." She smiles, pulling the key from her back pocket and holding it out to me. I reach out and grab the key from her hand, my fingers grazing hers. I want to let them linger, but she pulls it away quickly. "If you need anything"—she tucks her hands in her back pockets—"you can call me."

I tap the key in my hand, trying to prolong our conversation. "Oh, I will," I assure her as she dips her head and turns to walk away. "Drive safe, yeah?" I tell her, and she opens her door and gets in without saying anything else.

I watch her drive away before I make my way over

to the door. "Fucking finally," Theo grouses. "I was wondering if we would have to disappear in a puff of smoke while you were doing the mating dance."

"What the hell are you talking about?" I retort, walking to the door and sliding the key in.

"I'm talking about you looking like you were going to pounce on her." Theo laughs. "And she was looking like she was going to stab you in the eye if you did anything."

"How could you know that from here?" I unlock the door and push it open.

"The whole time you were talking to her, you didn't move, not an inch," he elaborates, picking up his stuff to follow me inside. "Jesus Christ." He looks around. "You fucking lied." He drops his stuff by his feet and the noise echoes in the empty house.

"How?" I put my hands on my hips and look around, knowing exactly why he's freaking out. I might have fudged a little bit when he asked me about the house. A smidgen.

"A little work," he scoffs, taking a look around. "A little work?"

"Do you think I would have called you all the way from home if it was a little job?" I turn to walk out to grab my own tools. "That was your first mistake." I shake my head. "It's like you don't even know me anymore."

"You are totally right," Theo grumbles. "I should never, ever trust what you say. A little. A little my ass."

"Didn't you call me the other day asking me…" I remind him. "No, begging me to let you come back here?" He rolls his eyes, walking to the stairs. "The stairs need to be reinforced before anything," I tell him. "The wood is in the back of my truck."

The three of them groan, putting down their things before following me out to my truck. Each of them takes a plank of wood before the trailer gets here with the tools we'll need for this job. Dominic parks the truck with the trailer in the driveway. "Good morning, boys!" he hollers, opening the back of the trailer. We help unload the tools we need, taking the table saw first, putting it in the living room, and walking to grab a couple of other tools. By the time I walk back in, Theo already has five pieces of wood cut for the steps while Frankie is nailing them in.

I walk back out, seeing Dominic taking the last of the tools out, when my phone rings, and I look down, seeing it's Mikaela. "Hey," I say, putting it to my ear, "I'm unloading—"

"Okay, I'll make it fast," she cuts in. "I hired a new one today. His name is Owen. He comes from the Cartwright crew, so he has experience."

"That sounds promising. Send him to work with David for now." I mention the guy I hired when I got into town. He's been with me the longest and is almost finished doing a remodel. "He will assess him and let me know. They are starting a small job tomorrow that David was going to do by himself but now with the extra hand he'll be able to really see what he can do."

"Already done. Also got the quote for the house on Preston Street."

"Yeah, and?"

She whistles out and I can hear the creak from her chair that she's in. "It's pretty fucking steep."

"Send it over to me so I can check it out, and I'll call and discuss it with her," I tell her, and she snickers.

"Since when do you call clients to discuss things with them?"

"Are we done?" I ask, and she doesn't bother answering me. Instead, she hangs up on me.

I get back inside, and they're already working upstairs. Walking up, we decide to start in the bathroom since it will be the most work to demolish. The dumpster arrives as soon as we rip out the toilet bowl. "That tub," Theo says, "is impressive. I don't think I've ever seen a gold tub before." He laughs. "I'm going with we are tossing this shit out and not keeping it."

"We are tossing that shit out," I tell him right before he takes the hammer and demolishes it.

I take a picture of the before and after while the electrician comes in and starts opening the walls in the bathroom to see what is inside. I don't see the time click by, and when I walk out of the house with Theo beside me, both of us are covered in white dust. "Where are you staying?" I ask.

"Got a house not too far from here," he answers. "Renting it for a month."

"You could stay with me," I tell him, and he shakes his head.

"What if I want to bang a girl?" I stop in the middle of the street and laugh.

"What girl?" I look around. "Where are you finding

this girl to bang?"

"I don't know, but if I do find her, I want options, and I don't want her to feel uncomfortable about my roommate hearing her while I'm banging her brains out."

"You are such a romantic," I joke with him as he flips me the bird getting into his truck. Frankie and Nino are long gone. The two of them are staying at the hotel close to the highway.

I get in my own truck, head home, and take off my boots in the mudroom before making my way to my bedroom to take a shower. I put on shorts, then head to the kitchen and grab a beer before I look at what to cook for dinner. My options are either a frozen pizza or frozen burgers. I opt for the pizza, putting it in the oven and then taking my phone out to check my emails.

I spot the quote at the top and open it before I dial her number. The phone rings once before she answers it. "Sierra Davidson." I can't help but smile when I hear her voice.

"Sierra Davidson," I repeat her name, "it's Caleb Walker." I take a pull of the beer, leaning back on the counter.

"Caleb," she says my name, shocked, "is everything okay?"

"Yeah, I was calling to discuss a couple of things with you." *And to ask you why you are moving to town. How long are you going to stay? Also, what is it going to take for you to go out with me?*

"Oh, okay." She hesitates, and I hear her moving on her side of the phone.

"Did I catch you at the wrong time?" I ask, but what I want to ask is "What are you doing?" Is she on the couch watching television? What type of shows does she watch?

"No, it's fine." She doesn't give me anything. "What can I help you with?"

"I wanted to let you know that we've demolished the bathroom." I tell her everything we did today. "The electrician is going to start downstairs tomorrow to see what he's working with, but he thinks you should rewire the whole thing."

"Is it safer to do that?" she asks, her tone worried.

"I would if I were you," I answer her honestly. "We don't know how old the wiring is, but we can assume it's from when they built the house. It's probably not even up to code."

"So we'll do it. Do you need me to send you guys a deposit or anything?"

"I'm going to look over the quote and see what I can do on my end," I tell her. "You can also do this in sections if it's too much for you."

"Send it over. I'll take a look at it, but I'm thinking we do everything at the same time and get it over with."

"Sounds good," I reply and then don't say anything else.

"Is that all?" she asks me after thirty seconds of silence.

"Yeah," I say even though that isn't all. I want to spend time on the phone talking to her. "That's it."

"Thanks for calling, Caleb." She hangs up the phone,

and I look down at it.

"What the fuck are you doing?" I ask myself because there is no one here but me. "You should focus on growing your business, not the new girl moving to town." I take another pull of my beer. "Send her the email and move on. She's obviously not interested in you." I look to the side when the oven beeps, smirking when I think of her. "She's not interested in you yet." I smirk. "Challenge accepted, Sierra. Challenge fucking accepted."

Eight

SIERRA

I HANG UP the phone and look at it for a whole two minutes before I put it down beside me on the couch. My heart races when I close my eyes and see him standing in front of me wearing his fucking sunglasses, looking like he's a *GQ* fucking model instead of a contractor. Sure, he was wearing worn jeans and a gray T-shirt that molded to him with his steel-toed boots. His dark brown hair pushed back, and you could see where his fingers went into said hair. My eyes went to the tattoos on his arms, trying not to ogle them too much while telling myself that he's off-limits. He's also way too good-looking to start anything with. You just know a guy that good-looking must have a trail of broken hearts behind him. I have enough shit going on in my life. I don't need to take on Caleb Walker.

I pick my phone back up when I hear a ping coming from it and see I have an email from CW Construction. I open it up and see he just sent it to me.

From: cw@cwconstrucion.com
To: SD@sdgraphic.com
Subject: Quote

Sierra,

As per our telephone conversation, here is the quote. Please let me know if you need to discuss anything further.

I've also attached a couple of pictures I took today of before and after.

Caleb

I open the attachment and cringe when I see how much it's going to cost me to fix up the old house. Then I thank my grandfather for leaving me an inheritance substantial enough to cover the cost of the house and the renovations, and I'll still have some left over. It's a good thing my investments are paying off.

I open the pictures, and my eyes almost bug out of my head when I see how much work they did in one day. I put the phone down before getting up and heading to the kitchen, seeing the boxes that I've already started to pack. Tomorrow is going to be a big day.

My alarm goes off at six, but I'm already making coffee in the kitchen. The nerves in my stomach are going crazy since I know today is going to be a rough day for me. I get dressed in sweatpants and a sweater before going over to my childhood home.

Getting out and walking up the steps, I take a deep breath before I ring the doorbell. I've never rung the doorbell before, but walking in to me seems strange. The door is pulled open by my father, who is already dressed for the day in slacks and a button-down shirt. "Sierra," he says, shocked, "why on earth are you ringing the doorbell?" He moves away from the door, giving me access to the house.

I step in at the same time he comes to kiss my cheek, and my mother peeks her head out from around the corner where she is in the kitchen. "Who is it?" she asks, and then her eyes light up when she sees me. "Sierra." Her voice is filled with happiness. "I didn't know you were coming over this morning." She comes to me wearing her long gray cashmere robe. She opens her arms to give me a hug, and I walk over to her, hugging her, closing my eyes tight as my stomach clenches with nerves. Only when she's let me go does she look at me. "Did you forget your key?"

"Yeah," I lie to her, but when I look over my shoulder at my father, he puts his hands in his pockets and smiles tightly at the lie he knows I just told, but he doesn't call me out on it.

"Come in, come in," she invites me, wrapping her arm around my shoulder and walking me more into the house. "I was just making breakfast." She lets go of me as she walks toward the kitchen, and I follow her. "Do you want pancakes or waffles?" she asks me of my go-to breakfast when I'm at home.

"I think I'll just have coffee," I tell her, too nervous to eat anything. I feel like I'm going to vomit and the last thing I need is to put food in my stomach. I am so nervous, almost like I'm a kid who knows that I have a bad report card coming in and I have to break it to my parents how bad it's going to be.

She turns, and I can see the worry on her face now. "Is everything all right?"

I nod. "Yes, everything is fine, Mom. I just wanted to talk to you guys." Her hand comes up to close the top of her robe, and I can see her fisting her hand so tight her knuckles are going to turn white soon.

"Oh," she says, and my father walks past me and heads to the coffee machine. "Okay." She pretends that she's fine. I walk over to the coffee machine and make myself coffee. Meanwhile, my father tries to pretend nothing is happening as he goes about making himself two pieces of toast, and my mother goes to the fridge to grab her tub of yogurt and granola that she usually has for breakfast. "I have fruit already cut up." She puts the fruit down on the counter as my father butters his toast and looks over at her.

"I'll have some of that," I say to try to get her to relax, knowing what I'm going to tell her is probably going to kill her. Also knowing I have no choice but to do what I need to do.

It takes about ten minutes for us to all sit at the table in the kitchen. My mother nervously eats the parfait she created even though she barely puts anything on her spoon. "Okay, so what is this meeting about?" She finally gives in, not willing to have another minute go by.

I pick up my cup of coffee to take a sip, since my mouth feels suddenly dry. "There are a couple of things, actually," I say, putting my mug down. "The first thing is, which is kind of the biggest thing." I take a deep inhale before I say the word. "I'm going to be moving." The minute I say the words, the gasp from my mother fills the room and I look over to see her holding her chest, like she was just stabbed in the heart. "I think it's a good idea to just get away for a little while." I try to soften the blow, but my father reaches out and puts his hand on top of my mother's.

"That sounds like it will do you good," my father responds, and I look over at him, not able to gauge his look at me. "Where do you think you'll be going?"

"I bought a house in Montgavin," I state, and now it's my father's turn to look shocked.

"You bought a house?" He sits up straight. "Without consulting us?"

"It's a fixer-upper house, and I got it for under market price. I had someone go out there and do an evaluation before I even signed the papers." His eyebrows go up since I would have normally gone to him for all of this, but I couldn't this time. "It happened really fast." At least that is the truth; it really did snowball. The offer was accepted in twenty-five minutes without a counter. The house was in a trust from their grandparents, and ten people wanted the sale to close. None of them wanted the house.

"A fixer-upper." He shakes his head. "Do you know how much work that is going to be and going to cost? You didn't even think about it for even one second, you flew by the seat of your pants, and then in a month or two, you will regret it, and then what?" His voice goes higher as the sentence goes on.

I try not to let his words sting. "Then I'll have a house I can turn around and sell for profit." I leave out that I will have to wait for the construction to be finished before I do all this, but he doesn't need to know all the details. I don't think he would be too happy about it anyway.

"What are you going to do about the house you have here?" He lets go of my mother's hand to put his on the table, and I can see his index finger tapping the table nervously.

"I haven't decided, to be honest," I tell him. They bought me that house as a graduation present. Both of them making sure that everything was perfect before handing me the brown box with the keys tied to a white ribbon.

"For now, it'll just sit there, and I can always come and spend half the time here when I—" I stop, not ready to say the rest just yet. Needing to have a little bit more courage for that. I suddenly wish I had taken maybe a shot of tequila before coming here.

"At least you'll have Lilah there for you," my mother offers softly. "She's always been such a good friend to you."

"She has, and it's about twenty minutes from her, so that will be fun. Especially with the baby on the way," I agree, picking up my coffee again when my mouth feels like it's getting dry. I brace for the impact of my next words.

"Well, we can't wait to visit," my mother says, looking over at my father, who is still just looking at me. "Right?"

"Yeah," he agrees and smiles over at her, "I can't wait." He picks up his cup of coffee.

"When are you moving?" my mother asks me, finally taking a spoonful of her yogurt.

"By the end of the week," I relay, and her eyes go big.

"So soon?" she says when she swallows. "That's so fast." She blinks furiously, and I know she's fighting back tears.

"I have a break in my schedule." Another lie. I had to email everyone and ask for a couple of days' extension. I'll be doing most of the packing at night, but I know I'll have to take a couple of days off to get to the house and then unpack some of my stuff. "So I thought I might as well do it when I'm not on a deadline or anything."

"That makes sense." She smiles. "But still, it seems so fast. Do you need help packing?"

"Not really," I tell her. "I'm just going to pack my bedroom and stuff, and then see how I settle in before I move the whole house there." She nods.

"That makes sense. What if you don't like it?"

"No, making sense would be testing it out before buying a whole-ass house," my father snaps. "That makes sense. Buying a house out of the blue does not make any sense."

"Well, it's done, and I got the keys, so we can agree to disagree on this part at least." I try not to snap at him. "There was also another thing I wanted to talk to you guys about." My mother puts her spoon down as I avoid even looking at her. "Ever since I found out that I was…" I take a deep breath in. "I've had a thousand and one questions."

"We wish we had the answers to give you," my mother states, her voice filled with sorrow.

"I know." I finally look up at her and then at my father. "I know if you knew the answers, you would, without a doubt, share them with me." Neither of them says a word. "So I was thinking of looking for my birth parents." I can tell the minute I say the sentence and the words, my mother's heart breaks. "It has nothing to do with you or how I was brought up, or any of that." I try to make her feel better. "It has nothing to do with you, and everything to do with me."

"You are who you are"—my father tosses the white linen napkin he had on his lap onto the table—"because of the way we love and adore you."

"I know that." My heart speeds up nervously. "I know all of that," I repeat breathlessly as my own tears itch at my eyes. "It's just something I need to do."

"Whatever you need," my mother assures me, her voice higher than normal, "is what we will give you. Whatever it is, whatever you need." I have to say I didn't expect her to be so strong. "I want to meet the woman who gave me the biggest gift I've ever gotten. I want to thank her for doing the most selfless thing a person can do." She picks up her own linen napkin and dabs the corner of her eyes. "I don't know how she had the courage to do it."

"She put her in a box and dumped her off at a fire station." My father's voice is tight. "She didn't even have the decency to set up something with an adoption agency."

"I thought of that also." I try not to let his words get to me.

"Did you ever think that maybe she doesn't want to be found?" he asks. "Did you ever think she did what she did because she didn't care?"

I swallow down the lump. "You are going to open Pandora's box. What do you expect out of all of this?"

"I don't expect anything," I admit. "I just want to know where I come from."

"I think you're making a big mistake." He pushes away from the table and stands. "Before you start this, ask yourself, are you okay if she wants nothing to do with you?"

I swallow at his question. "I'm going to have to be." I put my shoulders back standing straight, "But what if she's waiting for me to contact her? What if—"

"What if she isn't?" he asks. "It's not all fucking roses, Sierra."

"That's enough!" my mother snaps, slapping the table. "She wants to do this, and we are going to support her in any way we can." I close my eyes. "If all the negative happens to her and she finds out her birth mother doesn't want her, we are going to be there to hold her up and make sure she feels loved." She shakes her head. "It isn't about us," she tells him. "You're scared of losing her. You don't think I'm just as scared?"

"Mom," I say, the tears running down my face. "Dad." He looks at me, and I can see the anguish all over his face. "You guys will never lose me."

"But what if we do?" my father asks. I get up on my feet despite my weak knees and go over to him. "What if we lose you?"

"You can't ever lose me." I grab his hands. "I'm your daughter." He takes me in his arms, and I hug his waist. "I'm your daughter," I repeat.

"I love you, Sierra. You'll never, ever understand just how much we both love you." He kisses the top of my head. "Never."

Nine

Caleb

"WHAT DO YOU think?" I ask Theo when the painter finally leaves the bedroom and heads out and we step into the room.

"I think I'm going to spend the weekend sleeping for forty hours," he huffs as he walks into the room. "I didn't think we could finish this in less than seven days."

"Ye of little faith, my friend." I smirk at him, and he rolls his eyes.

"I have all the faith in the world. I'm just not as faithful as you, then. I never thought we would get it done. Fuck, you must have worked eighteen hours a day to make sure it was done." He looks around the room, seeing the chandelier I got rushed in for this room. It's an antique French cage style. The crystals hanging have a rainbow effect when the sun hits them, and when it's turning on, it looks white. It's all golden brass, and it looks like it was hanging in here the whole time. She didn't even approve it, but with the grandness of the room and the way the ceiling molding was, this was the only light that would do it justice. I just hope she likes it, and if she doesn't, I'm going to have to hide it in my garage and hope no one ever notices. "What time is she set to arrive?" he asks, and I take out my phone and look down, seeing she's about half an hour late.

"Thirty minutes ago," I tell him, and he nods.

"I'll get out of your hair, so you can woo her with your brilliance." He picks up his tool chest.

"I'm not wooing anyone." I watch him smirk.

"You kept taking pictures every fucking hour of the work we were doing and sending it over to her."

"So?" I put my hands on my hips. "She's a client. I was keeping her informed." It is the truth; I obviously didn't tell him that she never got back to me every time I sent her an update.

She got back to me twice in the last seven days. Once was to choose the color of the paint she wanted for the room and the bathroom. Even though she was going with white for now, she went with the soft tone of white, not the white you see in sterile environments.

The other time was to let me know when she would be arriving since I was the only one with her key and she didn't have an extra one.

"Whatever lets you sleep at night, man." He turns and walks out of the room. "I'm leaving this in the kitchen since I'm going to be here on Monday," he tells me, and I nod as he walks down the steps toward the kitchen. A couple of minutes later, I hear the front door slam shut, and I look out to see him walking to his truck. He gets in at the same time I see her black Audi arrive at the house. She reaches into the passenger seat to grab her purse before leaving. I take a minute to take her all in. Her blond hair is loose and down, blowing softly in the wind.

She's wearing a pair of blue jeans ripped in the knees and frayed at the bottom. She wears a tight white shirt, her neck and the top half of her chest exposed. A long-sleeved, thick sweater hangs to her knees, open down the front. Her cuffs are rolled once, the sweater the same color as the little booties she's wearing. She walks up the pathway and must sense eyes on her. She looks up and I smile down at her. She gives me a soft smile and a nod before disappearing on the stairs.

I hear the front door open, and a couple of seconds later, I hear her footsteps coming closer and closer as she walks in the open double doors. "Hi," she says, and all I can do is look at her. "I'm really glad it was you looking down at me and not a ghost."

I can't help but throw my head back and laugh. I'm trying to get my heart rate to a normal pace and not elevated because she just walked into the room since I've been looking forward to this moment for the last seven fucking days. "Not the ghost-friendly girl?"

"I'm friendly with ghosts who don't live in my house," she counters, looking around the room. Then her eyes go to the chandelier, and I pray to everything when I hold my breath, waiting for her reaction. "What is this?" she gasps and points up to it when she gets in the middle of the room and stands right under the fixture I had put in.

With the way the sun is coming into the room right now, you can see spots of blue and even pink.

"If you don't like it, we can switch it out," I state, trying not to get my feelings hurt.

"No." She folds her arms over her chest. "It's perfect." I breathe a sigh of relief when she says the words. "I didn't know what type of lighting I wanted for this room, but this is perfect. Even better than I could have imagined." She gives me a side smile, and I think *it was all worth it*. She looks at the floor. "I can't believe the floors look so good," she gushes over the original flooring that we sanded and then varnished.

"I sent you pictures." I wait for her to give me an excuse for why she didn't get back to me, but she doesn't even acknowledge that she got them. She just nods as she looks over to the side where the bathroom is. Her feet now move toward the bathroom. "So she doesn't even try to deny she ignored every single message I sent her."

She looks over her shoulder, probably shocked I'm calling her out on it. "I wasn't ignoring you, there just was nothing to say."

"Wow." I walk toward her as she stops before going into the bathroom. "Is that what you're going with?"

She turns to me. "I'm not going with anything." She pretends she has no idea, but I can see she's fucking with me. "I have no idea what you're talking about." She tilts her head to the side, and it's taking everything I have inside me not to bury my hands in her hair, fisting it and keeping her head exactly in that position when I kiss the ever-loving shit out of her. "Now, can I see my bathroom, or are we going to stand here and talk about you being butthurt that I didn't fawn all over your messages and stroke your ego?"

She turns and leaves me with my mouth hanging open. My fingers itch to grab her hand and yank her back to me. She steps into the bathroom, and I hear her gasp out. "You did not send me these pictures!" she shouts, sticking her head back out. "And you did that on purpose."

"Did I?" I point at myself. "I don't know what you mean. I mean, if you wanted to get pictures of the bathroom, all you had to do was ask me, and I would have sent them to you." I did in fact not send her one picture of the bathroom. I sent the before pictures from the demolition but didn't send her another one. I sent her a picture of the marble I was putting in and the faucets I chose. Other than that, she hasn't seen anything.

She glares now and I can't help but think, even with the glare, she is hands down the most beautiful woman I've ever seen. "Well played, Mr. Walker," she retorts, turning and walking back into the bathroom and my dick goes to half-mast. "Well fucking played."

I put my hands on my hips, giving myself a little bit more time to get my dick under control and not go into her bathroom with my cock straining to get out of my pants.

"This is gorgeous!" she shrieks. I finally walk over to the bathroom and see her standing in the middle of the room, right in front of the tub that took six of us to carry up the stairs. They cursed me and all the saints they could think of, including a couple who weren't even saints but became saints to them. I worked my ass off to make this bathroom come to life like it was in my head. She looks over at me, and her hands are covering the smile and shock.

"This tub," she says of the tub sitting on a piece of white marble with light-gray veins, right in front of the bay windows that are stained glass with gold trim. The handles to open the windows are brass, which match the faucets to the tub. "It's like it's in its own room." She walks over to the side of the wall, touching the molding I put up as I made the wall arch, the illusion making the ceiling above the bathtub is higher than the rest of the room. But the ceiling is all the same height, it is just the arch that makes it seem that way. "I never thought that wood would go in a bathroom," she says of the brown mahogany wood floor I had installed between the shower and the bathtub.

"If you don't like anything," I tell her, "we can always change it." I follow her as she looks around the room. Hands down one of the best bathroom remodels we've ever done. I've taken a couple of before and after pictures, and I can't wait to add them to the portfolio I've started for the company since we've been here.

"No," she rebuts, turning around in a circle and then stopping to check out the shower that has glass all around it. "I like how big it is without the linen closet," she compliments. "Nice touch with the seat." She tries to hide her smile, but when she looks at me, the smile on my face is ear to ear. I stare into her eyes, silently telling her

I picture her sitting on that naked. She clears her throat when her cheeks get pink, and I'm wondering if she's thinking the same thing or even if she's added me into the image in her head. "Do you work with a designer?" she asks me and I shake my head.

"No." I walk into the bathroom to stand in front of her. "It's all me. I drew it up one night." That's all I give her, hoping she'll ask me about it, but she doesn't. Nope, not Sierra, she makes sure she avoids asking me anything that is personal, and I fucking hate it.

"You're a natural, then," she praises, looking up at the ceiling.

"If you want to add a light fixture here, it will be easy enough." She looks at me, then back to the ceiling. "I'm going to head out," I say, even though I don't want to go anywhere.

"Sounds good." She nods.

"Do you need any help with anything?" I ask her, and she shakes her head. Of course she doesn't, I'm not surprised by this, but it does piss me off a bit more than it should. "Have a nice night, Sierra." I want to know all about her, yet she wants to know nothing about me. I should take that as a sign she's not interested in me, but something pulls me to her, and I can feel what she is telling me is different from how she feels. I guess it means I will have to work harder to get her. *Challenge fucking accepted* is the last thing I think about before walking out of her house.

Ten

SIERRA

I HEAR THE front door slam shut, close my eyes, and take a deep breath, which is a mistake since all I smell is his musky scent, and it makes different parts of me tingle. Different parts of me that shouldn't be tingling because he's off-fucking-limits, I remind myself. But my feet are moving on their own to the window to watch him walk down the path to his pickup truck at the curb. I watch his ass in his worn jeans, my mouth literally fucking salivating as I check out his legs, all the way to his construction boots. Then my eyes roam all the way back up, stopping again at his ass that fills out those jeans phenomenally. I keep ogling, going up to his black T-shirt that pulls at the shoulders, and you just know he must have an amazing body.

    He looks up at the window, and I don't have enough time to duck for cover. He smirks at me, like he knows I was checking him out. I fold my arms over my chest and shake my head. I'm saved by the moving truck pulling up to my house. I point at the truck to let him know I was waiting for it when he throws his head back and laughs, and I wish I could hear it clearer. It makes my pulse speed up as I turn away and head down to the front door to open it for the movers. By the time I get down there for the movers, his truck is gone. "Hi," I greet the guy I was with not too long ago when they packed up my bedroom and office. "Right this way." I motion with my head as he walks into the house.

"Wow." He takes a look around. "This is an old house."

"Yeah," I reply, "probably lots of history in here. Only one room is done, so you can bring everything upstairs to my bedroom."

"Got it." He turns and heads out to the truck, where he and two other guys start bringing in my things.

It takes them three hours to unload the truck and assemble my bedroom furniture. They place the bed on the wall opposite the windows. For now, I opt to put my desk in front of the window. I grab the box with bedding written on it, opening it and unpacking it.

It's another three hours before my bed is done, and my computer and stuff are all ready to go in the morning.

I turn on the side table lamp before heading to the bathroom. I smile when I look at the bathtub, and instead of taking a quick shower, I opt to soak in the big tub. Looking out the stained-glass window at the stars in the sky, I close my eyes, finally able to relax after this week. It was a week to end all weeks. Telling my parents I was leaving was one of the hardest things I think I've ever done. Seeing my father in pain the way he was cut me off at my knees. I had no idea what else was going to happen, but I'm happy nothing did. Last night, I was at my house, and my parents came over with pizza. We spent the night together. My father told me he would swing by several times a week to ensure everything was okay. My mother was quiet, no doubt wondering how long I would be gone and probably wondering how our relationship would change. I was determined not to let anything change.

Getting out and finally slipping under my covers, I turn off the lights as I listen to the house in the dark for the first night. The streetlights come into the windows, but I'm having the shades delivered next week. I toss and turn and the last time I look at my phone, it's a little after 2:00 a.m. I've never slept so light in my life. Every single creak made my eyes fling open as I listened to hear if it was followed by more noise. I was being overly dramatic, to say the least. No one in their right mind would break into a house that was almost falling down. Even so, when I roll out of bed at eight o'clock this morning, I have the name and number of someone who I'm going to call about installing security and doorbell cams.

I rush down to the front door, open it, and see it's Theo. "Sorry, hope we didn't wake you."

"No." I shake my head. "I was up." I walk away from the door. "I'm going to have a copy of the key made today for you," I tell him as he heads to the kitchen area, and my eyes go straight to the cup of coffee in his hand.

I groan, jogging back up the stairs and head to my closet, when I hear the front door open and then hear the sound of a couple of the guys coming. Tiptoeing to my bedroom, I close the door before heading into the bathroom and my walk-in closet. Out of everything, it was the easiest part to unpack since everything was on hangers in the boxes and then just hung up. I walk over to my jeans hanger, grab a pair of dark blue jeans, then put on a white lace bra before choosing a long-sleeve, white knit sweater with side slits. Putting it on, I slip on a pair of suede booties before heading out of the room. I hear voices coming from the kitchen. Not wanting to be in the way of them organizing their work, I slip out the front door and head to town to grab coffee and breakfast.

I step into the bakery at the same time Everleigh comes out from the back with a tray in front of her. "Sierra," she says with a huge smile as she fills the display case with fresh donuts.

"Hi," I return, walking up to the counter. "I'll take two dozen donuts," I order right away and see the shock on her face.

"I have workers at my house, so I thought it would be nice to give them a little bit of a treat."

"Oh yeah." She walks over to the side, grabbing a box as she fills it in. "What else can I get for you?"

"I will have an everything bagel with cream cheese and an extra-large coffee." I smile. "I don't have a kitchen yet, so I need the extra to last all day."

"Ugh, you could do yourself like a little coffee cart to keep upstairs if you want." She suggests, "We just bought Saige one of those little fridge things so she can keep snacks in her room. She saw it on social media and just had to get it. It's not half bad. You can store some milk in there."

"That's a fantastic idea," I tell her, opening my phone and ordering everything I need for the coffee cart I'll keep in my bedroom or even in my closet at this point.

I walk out of the bakery with my hands loaded with two boxes of donuts, along with my bagel, coffee, and a bunch of snacks that Everleigh told me to have for later.

I pull up to the house and walk in, hearing the sound of hammers and someone shouting as I make my way over to the kitchen. I sweep the room, checking for Caleb and not seeing him anywhere.

Theo looks up at me and smiles. "Looking for someone?" he asks, and I shake my head.

"Nope," I lie. "I brought donuts for you and the guys." I show him the two boxes in my hands. "I just don't know where to put them."

"I'll take those for you." He comes to me, grabbing the two boxes out of my hands. "We'll try to keep it down as much as possible."

"No worries," I assure him, turning and heading back upstairs. I'm at the top of the stairs when I see my bedroom door open, and I know I shut it before I left. I walk into the room. "Hello," I call and walk to the unmade bed. I stick my head toward the bathroom when I see someone walking out of my closet.

"Sorry," he says, walking past me, "thought I left something." He doesn't finish. He just closes the door behind him.

I put the coffee down on the desk, taking out my phone and calling Caleb. He answers after one ring. "Hello." I don't know why, but I can see him smiling through the phone. "What can I do for you, Sierra?"

I roll my eyes and look around the room, feeling uneasy. "Hey, can I just ask that no one come in my bedroom?"

"I'm sorry, what?" he asks, confused. I close my eyes and put my hand on my forehead, wondering if maybe I'm making a big deal out of this. I walk to the bathroom and see the towel I used last night is still hanging where I left it. As I walk toward my closet, I see one of the top drawers is slightly open.

"I just got home from getting coffee and found one of your guys in my bedroom. I get it's a construction area and all that, but can they not come into my bedroom?"

"I'm sorry, Sierra," he replies, his voice tight. "No one should be in your bedroom. Especially since that part is done and completed."

"Oh," I say softly.

"Do you know who it was?"

"No clue," I answer. "He was dressed like you."

"Like me?" I can hear the snicker. "Like I was dressed yesterday when you were checking me out?"

"You mean when I was looking at my moving truck?" I close my eyes and pull out my office chair. "Anyway, this chat is great, but I need to call someone to hook up a security system."

"I have a guy," he says, and I literally groan.

"Of course you do."

"Yeah." He chuckles. "It'll cost you, but I'll send him over."

"What is it going to cost me?" I ask, not sure I really want to know, but then again, I probably need to know.

"You'll know when I collect on it," he teases. "I'll take care of it." I'm about to interrupt him when he says, "I have to go. Theo is calling me back." He doesn't even wait for me to answer before he hangs up the phone.

"Rude," I blurt when I look down and see that he hung up on me. I put the phone down and finally take a sip of my coffee. It's literally heaven on my tongue as I turn on my computer and start my work.

The day flies by, and when the phone rings beside me, I look down and see that it's Lilah. I smile. "Howdy, neighbor," I answer the phone, smiling and hearing her laughing.

"Howdy, neighbor yourself." She finally stops laughing. "What are you doing?"

"I'm about to go and have hot sex with Chris Evans." I lean back in my chair. "Why?"

"I was going to tell you to come and have dinner with us, but Chris Evans…" She trails off.

"I can be there in twenty minutes," I tell her. "I'm sure Chris will be fine. Besides, I heard he got married, and I just can't do that to his wife."

She snorts. "See you soon," she says, hanging up the phone. I grab my keys and my purse and head down the stairs. The house is totally quiet as I walk out and lock the door behind me.

I drive toward Lilah's house with the windows open, the breeze coming into the car and whipping my hair around as I put one of my hands out the window and move it with the wind.

I pull up to the house, getting out of the car at the same time the front door opens. She steps out of her house with a huge smile on her face. "Hi," I say, tucking the phone in my back pocket.

"I don't think I'll ever get used to you being so close." She walks down the steps and comes to me, giving me a big hug. "It's so good. How's the house?"

"So far so good." I let her go. "I have a bedroom and a bathroom."

"Better than sleeping on the floor," she quips, making me laugh. I see her eyes go over my shoulder and I look over to see a golf cart coming from out of the field. My eyes go to the guy who is sitting in the passenger seat. He is looking over at Emmett, talking as Emmett looks straight ahead at us. It takes him a couple of minutes to look forward. I try to look away when he spots me, and I see a slight smile on his face. Then I wonder if it's for me or maybe he's still harboring feelings for Lilah.

"Oh, they are back already," Lilah notes from beside me.

"Back from?" I ask her.

"Caleb is renovating the new barn. They had to go over and talk about a couple of things." She shrugs and moves over to the fence area, and I follow her. The golf cart stops by the fence. "Hi," she says to Caleb, smiling big at him as he gets out of the golf cart, and I ignore the way I'm drawn to look at him.

"Dad." We look over to see Lucy running out of the barn. "I need your help."

Emmett looks over at Lilah and holds out his hand for her. She takes a second to look at me.

"I'll be back in a second." I nod at her as the two leave Caleb and me alone.

"Hi," he greets, getting out of the golf cart and coming to me with a clipboard in his hands. "I didn't expect to see you here."

"Well, here I am." I try not to let my voice be tight, and he knows it bothers me somewhat that he's here.

"Good, saves me a phone call." I tilt my head to the side and raise my eyebrows. "We fired the guy who was lurking in your room." I gasp.

"That's a little extreme."

"Not extreme enough, he's lucky I wasn't there to beat his ass for making you feel weirded out." I put my hand to my stomach to hold on to the flutter that happens without me wanting it to. "Randy, the security guy, is going to be over tomorrow to get an alarm system going."

"Um, thank you," I say softly. "You didn't have to do all that. I could have called him."

I look down and then mistakenly look up and into his eyes. "Have dinner with me."

"No," the answer flies out of my mouth. I almost flinch at the way his face looks, the disappointment apparent, but he doesn't say anything else.

He just nods. "Then I'll be heading out," he states, and my chest feels tight. "Have a nice night, Sierra." I watch him walk back to his truck, his back to me, as my heart beats what feels like out of my chest. I don't think I've ever had this emotion with another person. The way I'm pulled to him is a force I can't explain. However, knowing Lilah dated him and that it's a line I won't cross, it's about to kill me.

I watch him drive away without giving me a second glance. I should be happy since this is what I wanted to begin with, but it nags at me. Lucy comes over and hugs me before jumping into the golf cart with Emmett and heading over to Charlie and Autumn's, where she and Saige will have a sleepover.

The three of us enjoy a quiet dinner. After dinner, Lilah begs Emmett to go out for a bit. He glares at me, blaming me as we walk out of the house and head over to Thatcher's. The Friday night crowd is going at it when we get there. The music plays while a couple of people make room next to their tables to dance. I smile as I take it all in. Following Lilah and Emmett to a table, I pull out an empty chair beside Lilah, who introduces me to Nicholas, a new ranch hand who just got to town.

"Nice to meet you, Nicholas." I extend my hand to shake his. His light-brown hair pushes back to the side, and his light-brown eyes light up.

"The pleasure is all mine," he replies. "Can I get you something to drink?"

"That would be great," I say. "I'll have whatever you are having."

He smiles even bigger. "A girl after my own heart." He puts his hands to his chest before getting up and heading to the bar. I listen to the music as Emmett and Lilah talk to each other. I see him leaning in and whispering something in her ear, and she puts her hand to her little baby bump as she smiles.

I look around, seeing a couple more people getting up to dance. Nicholas comes back over, placing a drink in front of me while he sits down in the chair beside me, holding up his glass. "To living in Montgavin," he toasts with a smile.

I hold up my hand with my glass in it. "To living in Montgavin," I repeat, clinking my glass to his and smiling at him before taking a sip, then looking over to the front door with two eyes staring straight at me.

Eleven

CALEB

I REALLY DON'T want to fucking go out tonight, I think to myself as I get out of the truck, meeting Theo in front of it. But it was my turn to drive, and after he busted his ass last week to make sure Sierra's house was done in time, I owed him one. I can hear the music from the bar in the street, and I hope it's not a long night. I'm fucking exhausted, and I'm also fucking pissed that Sierra shut me down again. It's like I'm a glutton for punishment regarding her. The more she tells me no, the more I want her.

It's almost as if the universe is fucking with me when I walk into the bar, I quickly sweep the room, and my eyes find her. She's holding up a glass to a guy. He must be someone new that works with Emmett since they are sitting at a table with a bunch of the ranch people. Two tables are pushed together as they talk across the table at each other. Most of them laughing at what one person is saying.

Her eyes find mine, and instead of lingering there, I turn away from her, pissed she said no to dinner with me, but then even more pissed she's sitting at a table having a drink with someone else. "Should we stay at the bar or do you want to grab a table?" Theo asks me, probably not realizing what is going on.

"Whatever," I answer, walking into the room as he heads straight to the back, bypassing all the tables. We stand at the end of the bar. I put my hands on the top, waiting for the bartender to approach me. I feel eyes on me, but I'm afraid to look over and find she isn't looking at me; it is all in my head.

"What can I get you?" the bartender finally asks me when he makes his way over to our side of the bar.

"I'll have a beer, whatever you guys have on tap is good," I tell him as he nods and turns to Theo.

"I'll have the house blend," Theo adds, and the bartender turns away, heading to fill our orders. "So we going to talk about it, or just pretend she's not here and you are seething?"

I look over at him. "I'm not seething," I scoff. "I'm fine." I turn back to face the front instead of turning to the side and taking another look at her.

"The vein in your forehead looks like it's about to explode." He smirks as he leans on the bar, putting his elbow on it. "Dude, what is with her that has you so gone for her?"

"I'm not gone for her," I deny to him and stop when we both look over as we hear laughing and see Lilah pull Emmett up to dance as he shakes his head no. But he wraps his arm around her waist and pulls her to him anyway. My eyes quickly go from them back to Sierra as she brings the glass to her lips and takes a sip of it. The server is at their table as she leans into the new guy, I try to remember if I have seen him around or been introduced to him. Her hand goes to his elbow, and she smiles up at the server and holds up two fingers. Then she looks back at him saying something, and they laugh at something. My hands flex into fists the longer that I stand here and watch.

"Okay, so maybe we should get out of here," Theo says, and my eyes go back to him.

"What? Why?" I ask him at the same time the bartender puts the drinks in front of us. I pick up my beer and lean against the bar like Theo is, facing him. Taking a deep pull of the cold beer, forcing myself to act like I'm fine.

"Because it looks like you're about to start this brawl, and it's just the two of us and like fifteen ranch people. So I don't usually do math, but the odds are not in our favor." He brings the glass of house blend to his lips, hiding the smile, then looks at the door. He motions with his chin so I turn and sees Brock coming in, holding Everleigh's hand. "We might be three, depending on if Brock is in a good mood, but most of the time, he hates everyone, so he's a draw."

I look over and see Brock walk by the ranchers' table, holding up his hand as a hello before he comes to the bar. He looks right and left before coming toward us. Both of us watching him to see if he'll pick coming to stand with us or opting to sit in the corner by himself. With Brock it's always a toss-up. "He might be on our side," Theo mumbles, taking another pull of his whiskey. "Evening," he says to Brock, who just grunts. "Hey, Everleigh." He looks around Brock to say hello to her, which earns him an even bigger glare. "I'm just saying hello," Theo retorts. "I know she's yours." He pushes off from the bar. "You think I would be stupid enough to try to pick her up in front of you?" He shakes his head. "I like to breathe and live." He takes another sip of his whiskey, turning to the side probably to see if there is anyone else that he could go and talk to. It was supposed to be his night to let loose and I can see he's on edge.

"Ignore Grumpy McGrumpers," Everleigh advises. "He's just pissed I made him take me out tonight instead of staying home and hibernating on the couch."

"I also said we could hibernate in the bed." He turns to her, arguing his point. "I basically named every single other place in our house but here."

"Be still my heart." She crosses her hands over her heart. "He's so romantic," she says sarcastically. "Anyway"—she smiles—"how are you all doing? How was your day?" My eyebrows shoot together, and I'm actually afraid of getting throat punched by Brock if I answer. I look at Theo, who shakes his head, not willing to answer either. "Ugh, you guys are the worst." She shakes her head. "I'm going to go and sit with some girls." She puts her head back, getting on her tippy-toes before leaning in and kissing his neck before walking away.

"Great," he groans and moves between us, "now she's not even with me."

"She'll come back," I tell him, slapping him on the shoulder trying not to laugh at the big man sulking that his woman went to say hello to her friends, "or you'll find her." Theo and I both laugh while he glares.

"What the fuck are you two doing here anyway?" He looks at both of us.

"It's Friday night and we're both single, so where the fuck else would we be?" Theo fires back, looking around. "I mean, it's not like I can meet anyone at work."

Brock turns to me to find out what my excuse is. "I'm only here because it's my turn to drive or I'd be home on my couch," I confirm to him, at the same time I look over at the door and see Frankie, Dominic, and Nino walk in. "We might be able to take the ranchers now." I motion with my head toward the door.

Brock's eyebrows shoot together. "Why are you taking on the ranchers?"

"Because this one," Theo explains, looking at me, and motioning with his head, "is pining over the new girl." He points over his shoulder toward where Sierra was sitting but is now standing as she dances with Everleigh doing some line dance thing. "And the new rancher was sitting beside her, and they were talking."

"Did you ask her out?" Brock asks me.

"I did," I admit, and Theo gasps. "Asked her to have dinner with me. She obviously said no." I pick up the beer in my hand and take another pull. It feels like acid going down my throat.

"Yikes," Brock says, "maybe you'll rub off on her."

"Thanks," I deadpan and stop talking when the guys make it to us. "Hey," I say, not wanting to continue the conversation about Sierra. "Thought you guys were going back home for the weekend."

"Nah," Frankie says, "we decided to stay and work." I smile proudly, nodding my head.

"Now, that is what I like to hear." I slap his shoulder. "Drinks are on me." I squeeze his shoulder as the bartender comes to us. "But only one. I need you guys in tip-top shape tomorrow."

"I'll take a case of the house blend," Frankie jokes with him. I laugh at him, picking up my bottle of beer and looking over to see a couple of the ranchers are also up and dancing, especially the new one. He and Sierra are side by side as they laugh at themselves, trying to follow the moves.

"The worst thing you can do," Brock cautions from beside me as Frankie, Dominic, and Nino go to the other side of Theo, "is sit here watching her every move. That's like some sort of torture."

"I'm not watching her," I deny. "I'm scoping out the bar."

He throws his head back, and his bark of laughter fills the room. Everleigh smiles at him and stops dancing to watch. "I had that same look on my face when I saw Everleigh with Emmett dance once." My head nearly gets whiplash from how fast I turn my head toward him. "Wanted to rip his throat out."

"I got the message from her loud and clear," I admit. "She's not interested."

"Doesn't make it easier." He takes a pull of his own beer.

"It's fine." I shrug, pretending it's not bothering me. "How are you doing getting me more equipment?" I ask, and he side-eyes me.

"Deflection," he notes, chuckling in his glass as he takes a sip. "I'm president of that club." I roll my eyes, but he gives in and changes the subject. The two of us talk about the different cranes I'm going to need for the barn roof that has to come off. Everleigh comes over, hugging him from the back as she pants from dancing. "Having fun?" he asks her when she takes his beer and drinks whatever is left of it.

"Yeah," she replies, trying to catch her breath. I look over my shoulder and spot Sierra walking out of the bar. My eyes go to the table, seeing the guy sitting and talking to a couple of people.

"I'll be back," I state, pushing away from the bar and zigzagging my way out of the building. I turn to look to the right and then to the left, not spotting her anywhere. I turn to walk around the building when I see her leaning against the side of the bar, facing the parking lot. Her head tilts back against the building with her eyes closed.

"What the hell are you doing out here alone?" I bark at her, and she jumps, her eyes flying open as she looks over at me.

I walk toward her as she puts her hand on her chest right in the middle. "Fuck, Caleb," she hisses as I come to stand in front of her, "you scared the shit out of me." The dim light from the corner of the building lets me see her eyes just enough.

"What are you doing out here all alone?" I practically hiss at her. "It's not fucking safe. Lilah just got kidnapped."

"Well, that guy is behind bars." She straightens from the wall. "What are you doing out here?"

"I saw you come out here," I admit to her.

"So you followed me?" she asks me.

"Yes." I don't even skip a beat as I answer her. "Damn straight."

"Why?" she asks, standing straight.

"To make sure you were okay." My voice is low as I try to control my hands and keep them from doing something we both might regret.

"I'm fine." Her voice is as low as mine, her chest rising and falling faster than a second ago. "As you can see."

"Yeah, I can." I take a step closer to her, the front of our shoes touching. "More than fine if you ask me."

"Caleb," she says, and I don't know if it's a question or a plea, but the way she says it makes everything in me snap. My hands fly to her face and slide into her hair, gripping it in my hands.

The feeling is like silk in my hands. Pulling it back, I make her head go back to look at me. "You drive me fucking crazy," I admit to her, lifting my one hand from her hair and softly holding her chin in it. "Fucking crazy all the fucking time." I've never, ever felt this before. This woman has the ability to make me do things I would never do. Like pin her against a fucking building after seeking her out, even after she has shut me down more times than not. "Why is that, Sierra?" My hand moves from her jaw to the side of her neck, as my finger finds her pulse and I feel it going as fast as mine.

"I don't know, Caleb." Her eyes look into mine. The minute she says my name, no, the second she says my name in almost a moan, it's gone. Every string that I had to hold on t, to keep myself in tack, snaps. And I'm falling, free-falling off the edge of the mountain, and she's the only one who can stop me from falling.

My head advances, and she pants right before her eyes close, and I smirk, knowing she wants this as much as I do. Her parted lips give me the in I need to slide my tongue into her mouth. Her tongue slides with me, and it's even better than I thought it would be. It's fucking heaven. It's probably even higher than what heaven is. She arches her back and pushes her chest into me as her hands fly to my head, running her fingers into my hair and staying there. I push her back into the wall. Our mouths don't break apart, but instead, my head moves to the other side to get the kiss even deeper. My hand moves from her neck down her shoulder, to her arm, and farther to her hip, where I grip her. The kiss is full of heat, full of wanting, full of fucking everything. Our tongues fight with each other, wanting the other one to give in. Our heads move side to side after a couple of minutes as we try to get the kiss even deeper than it is. I let go of her mouth only to trail my kisses to her jaw. "Fuck," I murmur as I suck in the side of her neck as my tongue slides over the vein while I suck it, then going back to her lips. "Sierra," I say her name, and this time, it's her who comes in for a kiss, making me stop talking.

Twelve

SIERRA

"FUCK," I HEAR him say as he lets go of my lips, and my eyes try to flutter open, but stop when I feel his lips at the side of my neck. I should push him away to stop this madness, but instead, I move my head to the other side so he can have better access to me. His tongue comes out and my knees literally go weak. My hand lets go of his hair as it falls to his shoulder. I need to open my eyes, but his proximity makes me feel like I'm in a trance. He sucks in the side of my neck and my hand squeezes his shoulder. "Sierra." The way he says my name is like I've always wanted to hear it from a man. Like he needs me to breathe his next breath.

I finally open my eyes to look at him, and it's the wrong thing to do. My stomach flutters, my heart thumps so hard and so fast, and my breathing is coming in pants. It's as if I've run a marathon or swam a million laps in the swimming pool without stopping. My hand falls from the back of his neck to his cheek; this time, it's my turn to kiss him. He bends his knees so we stare into each other's eyes before I lean forward, lick his bottom lip, and nip at it. The groan that comes out of him surges through me. He wraps one hand around my waist, the other goes beside my head as he pushes me into the wall, and I finally take the kiss I want. My tongue slides into his mouth, and he lets me lead the kiss. Our tongues slide against each other softly at first, until he presses more into me, and I feel all of his hardness on me. We swallow each other's moans as the kiss goes from a twenty to a hundred and fifty. He now overtakes the kiss that he let me lead. He kisses the ever-loving shit out of me. Our heads move side to side in order to get the kiss even deeper.

I'm so lost in the kiss, if someone were to ask me what my name is, I wouldn't be able to tell them. The only thing I would be able to say was his name. The hand on his face moves to the back of his hair, and I'm about to lift my leg and hook it over his hip when the sound of a car alarm goes off, and it's as if you threw cold water on us. We fly apart from each other and he looks over to see the car in question. The front and back lights go on and off as the horn keeps blasting. The owner comes running out of the bar and presses his key fob to get it to stop.

The blaring horn finally stops, and the guy looks over at us. "Hey," he says with his chin up at us before returning to the bar.

"I should get back in there," I say, looking down

and trying to walk past him. I should have known he wouldn't just let me leave like that. His hand comes out to grab mine, and I ignore the way my whole body lights up, but I stop and look over at him. "We can't do this," I say in a whisper.

"What?" he asks, shocked. "Why?" He drops my hand.

I shake my head, trying to get my emotions under control. "I just can't."

"Are you with someone?" he asks, his voice sounding hurt.

"Of course not," I retort, a little pissed he would think I would kiss him if I had someone. "It's a bit more complicated than that." All he does is stand there and look at me, waiting for me to give him more. "I'm sorry I led you on and kissed you." The lump forming in my throat makes it hard for me to swallow. "I'm sorry," I finally say, walking away from him, actually almost sprinting away from him.

I walk back into the bar and head over to the table, seeing Lilah's eyes light up when she sees me. "I was looking for you." I pull out the chair, not sure my knees will hold up much longer.

"I went out to get some air." I avoid looking at her as I sit and pick up my drink. "All that dancing." I take a sip of the whiskey to stop myself from blurting out that I also kissed Caleb. Not only did I kiss Caleb and let him kiss me, but it was the best kiss I've ever had in my whole life. Like bar none, he kisses as if he has a gold medal from the Olympics for it.

"Are you ready to go yet?' Emmett comes to stand behind her and wraps his arms around her, his hands resting on her stomach as he buries his face in her neck.

"I'm ready," I confirm, not really wanting to stick around, knowing that Caleb isn't too far away. Also knowing I'm going to be spending half of my night forcing myself not to look at him, and then the other half of the night pretending I'm having such a great time. Which is going to be exhausting. We don't say goodbye to many people before ducking out. Everyone is now scattered all over the place, and it'll be hard to get to them all and make it out in four seconds, which is the time limit Emmett gave her when she agreed to leave.

"I'm going to sleep in tomorrow," she says, clapping her hands. "What do you have planned for tomorrow?"

"I have a big day tomorrow," I admit to her when I get into the truck and put my seat belt on.

"A big day?" Lilah looks over her shoulder at me. "But it's Saturday."

"Yeah." I nod at her. "I'm taking my ancestry test tomorrow." Her eyes go big. "I know," I say excitedly. "I mean, it's not like it's going to come back and be like, your mother is this person and your father is this person, but I can start to trace my ancestors, which is very exciting."

"You ready for that?" Emmett pipes into the conversation, and I look over at him. "As someone who wishes he didn't know who his mother is." He shakes his head, and it's the first time I've ever gotten anything personal out of him. Lilah reaches over the middle console and slides her hand in his. "It might not be such a good thing."

"But at least you know." He doesn't say anything. Instead, he just nods. The rest of the drive is quiet as I look out of the window, my head going back to Caleb and that fucking kiss.

When we get to the house, I don't even go in. I just hug Lilah by my car and then take myself home.

I step into the house and hear the door echo through the rooms once I close it. I make my way into the kitchen to see the progress, gasping when I see they already have everything gutted and the floors stripped. I turn and walk through the empty house as I make my way upstairs to my bedroom. I drop my purse at the side of my door before kicking off my shoes and carrying them through the bathroom and to the closet.

It takes me about twenty minutes to take off my makeup, shower, get ready for bed and brush my teeth. When I finally slide under the big thick duvet cover, I lie on my side, looking out the window at the stars twinkling in the sky. The sound of Caleb saying my name replays over and over again, followed by the images of him kissing me. "You fucked up," I mumble to myself, closing my eyes and forcing myself to go to sleep.

I'm in what is my hundredth dream of Caleb when I hear the front door open and then close. I open one eye as I listen to hear the sound of boots heading toward the kitchen. I toss the covers off myself and close the door before going to the bathroom.

I wash my hands and face before walking to my desk

and picking up the white box. "Discover your ancestry." I read the top of the box, turning it over and opening it, taking out the folded sheet of paper that gives me the directions. Once I've done all the steps, I place the vial in the box and seal it. "Step one done," I tell myself, looking at the box with the return address on it. "Now, in two to four weeks, I'll know a little bit more about myself." I get up and head toward the closet, getting ready to do step two today.

I get dressed, putting on a white bra and then a bodysuit before slipping into blue jeans that hug my hips but are loose all the way down, grabbing one of the hanging jackets. I opt to go with a rust-brown one before putting on a pair of sneakers. Tucking the box into my purse, I make my way downstairs and go toward the kitchen. I smile when I walk in, expecting it to be Theo but come face-to-face with Caleb.

"What are you doing here?" I ask him, trying not to think about the way his lips felt on me, but the way parts of my body are tingling, it's making it very, very hard. I fold my arms over my chest so he doesn't see my nipples want to be a part of this conversation.

He looks up from the nail gun to look at me. "Morning to you too." He smirks, standing up and dusting off his hand. "Fired the other guy." He looks me up and down, not even trying to hide it. "So came to do the work myself."

"It's Saturday."

He nods. "Yeah, but you want this done as soon as possible, so we'll be working weekends for the next little bit. The guys are expected to come in at ten." He stands there looking like he's about to model for a fucking photo shoot, even though I know he's been working in my kitchen all morning. "You look nice."

I shake my head. "I'm not doing this." I turn to walk away from him.

"Why not?" His question stops me from walking out of the room. "You're single, I'm single." He points at me, then himself.

"Yes, but you dated my best friend." I watch his eyes to see if he still has lingering feelings for her.

He throws his head back and claps his hands as he bursts out laughing. "I think dated is a far stretch."

"Did you take her out on dates?" I ask, and he rolls his eyes. "Did you not kiss her?"

"We dated for two months while she was secretly in love with someone else," he relays, and it whooshes through me. I can't help but be angry. It makes me picture them together.

"Regardless, I'm not—we're not—going there. It's a line that I won't cross." My voice is tight.

"I'm sorry you feel like that," he replies, looking down at his boots. "Really fucking sorry you feel like that because you drive me fucking crazy." He advances toward me and stops when we both hear the front door open.

"Hey," Theo states, coming to a stop when he looks at us, "was I interrupting something?"

"No," I answer, "I was just leaving." I give him one last look before walking out of the house.

I go to the bakery and grab a cup of coffee before heading to the post office and officially mailing the box out. My heart hammers in my chest the whole fucking time. One side of my brain tells me I shouldn't be doing this, while the other side tells me this is what needs to be done.

I walk out, heading straight to the end of the street, and see the fire station. It's different from the way it was pictured in the newspaper article. There was just one garage door, and now the one in front of me has two red garage doors.

Montgavin Fire Department is written across the building on top of two half-moon windows. I walk over to the fire station, pulling open the door to the brown brick building. An empty desk is on my left, and when I look to the right, the brown door opens, and a man enters. "How can I help you?"

"I was wondering if I could speak to your fire chief," I say nervously. "If he's available, that is."

"Yeah, who can I say is here to see him?" He waits for me to answer him.

"My name is Sierra." He nods at me before walking back toward the door. He's gone for what feels like five years, but it gives me a chance to look at the pictures on the wall.

Pictures from when the fire station first opened to when they did the expansion.

The door behind me opens, and a man walks in. He's wearing blue cargo pants, a blue T-shirt with Montgavin FD on it, and a handheld radio with a walkie-talkie on top of it. "Sierra?" he asks, and I nod. "I'm Hudson." He extends his hand to me.

"Hi, Hudson." I shake his hand. "Thank you for taking the time to speak to me."

"I can talk to you as long as we don't get a call." He smiles.

"Thank you so much," I reply nervously. "I was wondering if I could ask you a couple of questions."

"Sure." He nods. "Follow me to my office." He turns and walks down the hallway and then turns to enter an office. "Can I offer you something?"

"No, thank you." I shake my head. "I don't want to take up much of your time."

I sit in a chair in front of his desk as he puts the radio on top of the desk and then folds his hands together. "I didn't think I would be this nervous," I mumble as I open my purse and take out the folded newspaper. "Twenty-five years ago," I tell him, "I was left here in a box." I swallow down the lump that forms and blink the dryness away. "I was hoping you would be able to tell me who the fire chief was at that time." I hand him the paper, and he takes it from me. His eyes go big when he realizes I'm the kid in the picture.

"Wow," he reacts, "this story is legendary." He shakes his head. "It is even in one of the photos we have hanging in the area where the guys eat."

"Well, here I am," I say, swallowing. "I've decided I'm going to look for my birth parents." His eyebrows pinch together.

"Usually, when they give them up like that—" I hold

up my hand to stop him from talking.

"I know, trust me, I know. But I just"—I lift my shoulders—"I just have a couple of questions for the chief or even some of the firemen who were here that night on duty. I was wondering if there was any contact information for any of them that you can give me. Even a name and I can do it myself. The paper didn't really say much except I was Jane Doe and I was hours old."

"I can't give you that, but what I can do is call him and see if he'll come down and speak to you."

"I'll take anything," I say hopefully. "Anything he can give me I'll take."

"Okay, give me a couple of minutes." He gets up, grabbing the radio and walking out of the room. I pick up the newspaper article he left on his desk, folding it and putting it in my purse. I put my hands on my knees, moving my feet up and down nervously as I wait for him.

He comes back and looks down at the floor, and my heart sinks. "I'm sorry," he says to me. I let out a sigh and a tear escapes the corner of my eye, and I quickly wipe it away. "He's gotten to the age where he's extremely grumpy." He tries not to laugh, and I can see pity in his eyes. I get up, not willing to take pity from anyone. "Thank you for trying." I exhale. "I'll get out of your hair." I turn to walk away but stop. "Can I leave you my name and number if he changes his mind? Or if you talk to any of the other men who were on duty that night, and they don't mind talking to me, they can always get in touch with me."

"Of course," he agrees, turning and handing me a pen

and paper. I lean down, writing my contact information before turning and handing it back to him. "I'll see what I can do."

"Thank you, Hudson," I say softly before leaving and walking out of the office and back to the front door. Stepping out into the sunlight, I try not to let the setback bother me as I walk over to the bakery to grab something to eat. I sit at the table with my sandwich, and the phone rings with an unknown number.

"Hello." I put the phone to my ear.

"Is this Sierra?" the caller asks.

"This is she," I confirm, sitting up.

"I heard you have some questions for me." My heart speeds up, and it finally clicks that this is the fire chief.

"I do." I try to actually calm and not act like I'm freaking the fuck out, but internally I'm freaking the fuck out. "I won't take up much of your time."

"Good," he says, "here is my address." He gives me his address, and I text it to myself. "Come before dinner."

"I'm at the bakery now. I can be there as soon as I leave here."

"Ms. Maddie's bakery?" he asks.

"Yes."

"Good, bring me some donuts." I try not to smile at his request.

"Is there any kind that you want in particular?" I ask him and he hangs up the phone on me. "So one of each." I take a deep breath in and slowly let it out. "Let's get some answers."

Thirteen

SIERRA

"YOU HAVE REACHED your destination," the voice says, "your destination is on the right." I park the car by the curb and look at the little white house with dark windows. Two weeping willow trees protect it from the sun, rain, and everything from outside. A United States flag flies from the side of the open front door, but a screen door shuts out everything. "Here we go." I pep myself up as I lean over to grab the box of donuts and my phone.

I shut my car door, walking around the car and stepping onto the sidewalk, looking right and left as I make my way up the pathway to the door. Stepping up one step, I see there are two rocking chairs out here, moving back and forth softly in the wind. I look for a doorbell when I finally get to the screen door. Seeing none, I lift my hand and knock softly on the wooden side. My heart pounds fast and hard in my chest as I step back and nervously wait for him to come to the door.

"I'm coming," the voice snaps as I hear footsteps approaching me. I see him fill the doorway. He semi-glares at me, then his eyes go from me to the box of donuts in my hands, and his look softens just a touch. "Hmm," he says, "you listened."

I don't mean to but with all the nervousness I have in me, I giggle a little bit. "Of course," I respond as he pushes open the screen door so I have to take an extra step back. "I got one of everything," I tell him, extending the box to him, but I see he is holding a cane with one hand and the door with the other. "I'll carry it in for you."

"Don't need you to do no such thing," he grumbles, lifting his arm with the cane and reaching for the box. "Come in." He turns, and I must step in quickly before the screen door slams shut.

I follow him past the living room with one brown couch that seats three people. A dinner tray with remotes on it is right next to a brown La-Z-Boy. There are pictures of him in uniform on the wall from many years ago. Then another one of him in the same uniform but with a woman wearing a wedding dress beside him. Then the pictures go from black-and-white to color. Pictures of him with what must be his children and then grandchildren. I step into the small kitchen and see an L-shaped counter with a fridge and stove tucked into it and a sink facing the window in the room. A small round table with four chairs is pushed almost to the wall, facing the counter. He pulls out a chair before hanging the cane on the table and then plopping the box down right next to a glass that looks like iced tea. "You want something to drink?" He looks over at me, and I shake my head, not sure if I should join him and sit at the table or just stay standing. He sits down at the table and then looks at me. "You going to stand there all day looking at me, or are you going to sit down?"

I roll my lips, trying not to laugh at him as I pull out the chair closest to me before sitting down. "Thank you for meeting with me, Mr.—" I start, not sure what to call him because I don't know his fucking name.

"Bruce." He opens the box of donuts and looks at all of them before choosing one, taking a bite and then reaching for a napkin to wipe his mouth. "So you have questions, do you? What questions do you have?"

I rub my hand down the front of my pants, wiping the clamminess off. "Yes, just a couple."

"Well, I'm not getting any younger. So get to it." He looks at me as he takes another bite of the donut.

"In the paper, it said that you found me, but you didn't know how long I had been out there." He nods.

"We were sitting in the crew mess. A couple of the guys were playing cards. A couple were sitting around shooting the shit. It was a slow night." He looks down at the donut. "Then I heard it…" His voice trails off. "The sound of a baby crying. It was after midnight, so we all looked at each other, not sure we heard what we heard until it got louder." He looks over at me, and I can see he remembers it. "We all got up and walked toward the door. Back then, the station was smaller." He turns his eyes now as he picks up his tea. "I got to the box first, and when I looked inside, I saw you were there with just a blanket on." I can't help the lone tear. "We were pretty much in shock for a second, and then we sprang into action."

"What did you do?"

"I got the box inside," he goes on. "A couple of the guys went running around the station to see if anyone was lurking. Then we had a couple of guys drive up and down streets to see if they saw anyone. But there was no one." He taps the table with his finger. "It's like you were dropped off by angels. You were cold." He shakes his head. "We got you in a warm blanket as we called the sheriff, and then they took you away."

"Was there any talk about who my parents could be?" I sit here waiting, holding my breath.

"Not one person came to mind. Everyone we thought it could be was still pregnant or with their newborn." He stops when the front door slams shut and looks down the hallway at a woman coming in, holding a basket in her hand. Her white hair is pulled back, and only when she gets closer do I see she's in a long skirt with a sweater, her sleeves pushed up.

"Bruce," she says his name, then looks at me and back at him. "Who do we have here?" He turns to her, but she doesn't give him a chance to say anything because she gasps. "Are those donuts?" She walks over to the table, and then looks at him with a glare and then looks at me. "Did he tell you to bring these?"

"No," I lie for him, and I'm only doing it because he took the time to talk to me. "I came to ask him a couple of questions, and I didn't feel right coming empty-handed."

"I don't believe you," she retorts to me, putting the basket on the table and then closing up the box of donuts. "Here"—she holds out the box—"you take these home." I lift my hand and take the box from her.

"Woman," Bruce finally snaps, "those are my donuts. She brought them to me as a gift, and it's rude to give gifts back."

She turns to him. "You better watch it, mister," she hisses. "You have high blood pressure, and you know that sugary stuff isn't good for you. I'm not going to sit around watching you kill yourself."

"She's always been a little dramatic." He picks up his tea. "She gets more dramatic as she ages."

"I can leave," she bites out, and he ignores her. "Is that what you want?"

"Heloise," he says her name, looking at her and then at me, "meet Sierra." She looks over at me. "She's the Jane Doe we found in a cardboard box."

"Oh my," she replies, sitting in the chair beside her, putting her hand on her chest. "I thought you were his long-lost granddaughter."

I can't help but laugh, literally. "Woman, what are you talking about? We've been together since we were sixteen."

"You went away for the Navy," she snips back. "How was I to know you didn't go philandering around?"

"I'm not his long-lost granddaughter," I confirm to her. "I just found out that I was adopted." I tell her the story, and she has to wipe away the tears. "So now I'm going to try to find my birth parents."

"Honey," she advises softly, "maybe that isn't the smartest idea."

"Leave her be," Bruce interjects. "She does what she needs to."

"Hush yourself"—Heloise slaps his arm—"and focus on finishing that donut before I take it away from you," she warns him. "You do what you need to do, and we will help you in any way we can."

"Thank you," I tell her, and by the time I look around, the three of us are having dinner together. Bruce sneaks another donut in, and when it's almost seven, I walk out of the house with a smile on my face and the box of donuts tucked under my arm. Getting into the car, I turn and see the two of them standing there waiting for me to drive away. I wave at them as I pull away from the curb and head toward Lilah's house.

I don't call before I get there, grabbing the box and heading toward the front door. I walk up the steps and press the doorbell, wondering if maybe I should have had this talk with her before. I regret this decision when the door opens, and I see her face light up when she sees me. "Hey." She moves away from blocking the door to give me a chance to come in. "This is a surprise." I step in. "I called you this afternoon."

"I know," I say of my missed call when I was talking to Bruce and Heloise, "I was with Bruce."

She looks at me with confusion as I fill her in on who Bruce is. "That's incredible," she gasps. "Check that off the list."

"I know, but there is a reason I came here." I look

around. "Is there someplace we can talk privately?"

"I'm home all alone," she states, walking to the living room and sitting on the couch. "Emmett and Lucy went for a nighttime ride." She grabs the throw blanket and puts it on herself as she turns off the television. "So we are as alone as we can be."

I sit at the other end of the couch and turn to her. "Okay, I have to tell you something," I finally say, "and you are going to hate me, and it might ruin our whole friendship." I can't stop my mouth from talking.

"Ruin our friendship?" she asks and sits up, her face filling with a look of fear.

The pit of my stomach burns so hard, and I think I'm going to throw up. "There isn't an easy way to say this." I avoid looking at her as I close my eyes and take a deep breath for courage. "So I'm just going to say it." I look at her. "I kissed Caleb," I admit it, and then see her eyes go big. "I know, I know, it was wrong, and I swear it was only one time. But I crossed a line, and I'm so sorry."

"You kissed Caleb?" she asks, and I nod, waiting for her to tell me I'm the shittiest friend to ever live. "Like Caleb Walker?"

"One, how many Calebs have you dated?" I almost hiss out. "Yes, the one you dated."

"Dated is a stretch," she retorts. "I kissed him twice, and it's only because the first time was so bad I thought it was all in my head." I literally gawk at her. "News flash. It was gross. Both times." She holds up two fingers. "Gross," she whispers out the word.

"Caleb?" I now say his name because there is no way

she kissed the same guy I kissed, definitely not the same guy she kissed.

"Oh my God, is that why you look like you stole someone's kitten and are keeping it hidden in your bedroom?"

"Lilah, you dated him, which means he's off-limits." My voice rises.

"Again, dated is a stretch. We went out maybe three times and then decided we were better off as friends. I felt like I was kissing my brother when I kissed him, it was just gross."

"I'm sorry, we must have been kissing a different person because"—I shake my head—"he's hands down the best fucking kisser I've ever kissed in my whole life."

She gasps, "Wait a second, you like him." She points at me, and I close my eyes. "Oh my God, oh my God," she chants over and over again, her voice filled with glee and laughter, "you fucking like him."

"I don't know," I lie to her and then roll my eyes. "I like him a little bit. He's hot." She looks over to the side and fake vomits. "That's how I feel about Emmett, so I think it's normal."

"Emmett is hot," she defends, and now I grimace and shake my head.

"Agree to disagree," I counter. "Can you forgive me?"

"You didn't even do anything," she says. The front door opens, and then it slams back shut. We hear the sound of boots clonking on the floor. Lucy comes into the room first. "Shower." Lilah points at her bedroom. "You can say hello after."

"Ugh, fine." She walks past the couch, waving.

"Oh, hey," Emmett greets, walking into the room and going straight to Lilah, leaning over the back of the couch to kiss her lips before heading to the fridge. "I didn't know you were coming over." He pulls it open and takes out a beer.

"She made out with Caleb," Lilah announces, snickering, and I gasp at her.

"I heard"—my head whips around to him—"last night at the bar."

"Who told you?" I ask, shocked. Then I'm really fucking happy I decided to come here today and tell her instead of her finding out from Emmett.

"Someone saw you two in the parking lot," he tells me, and I close my eyes.

"She came to ask me if it's okay if she dates him." Lilah fills him in.

"I did not." I shake my head, trying not to let him know that I might have, maybe, perhaps tried to see if she was bothered by it.

He cocks his head to the side, his eyes going to Lilah. "Why would you care?" His eyebrows go up.

"I don't, but she thought I would."

"There is a code," I tell Emmett, who rolls his eyes. "You know, bros before hos, and hos before bros." He just stares at me. "Since they dated, I didn't know what to do."

"Oh, that's right, they dated." He cocks his hip.

"Don't you start with me, Emmett." Lilah gets up and puts her hand on her hip.

"You hated me."

"Never hated you." I get up when he says that as the two of them go into a standoff.

"I'm going to get going." I point over my shoulder. "Go home and open a nice bottle of wine and soak in my tub." I walk over to her. "Thank you for being the best friend a girl could ask for." I hug her. "Also, do you have a bottle of wine I could borrow?" Emmett is the one who laughs, and I look over my shoulder at him.

"She's going to be another pain in my…" he mumbles as he walks over to the cabinet and takes out two bottles and brings them to me. "Here." He hands me both. "You owe me two bottles."

"She owes us nothing," Lilah retorts. "Now, get out of here and go call Caleb."

"I'm not calling him," I scoff at her as I walk out of the house and head to my car. *Today was not a bad day*, I think to myself as I start my car. *Not a bad day at all*.

Fourteen

CALEB

I'M PATCHING UP the walls in the kitchen when I hear the sound of a car door slam shut. The soft light comes from the one light I have on in the kitchen. From where I'm standing, I can see the front door perfectly since we took down the wall that was separating the dining room and the kitchen. Opening the space up and making it an enormous fucking kitchen. When she puts in the island, it's going to be phenomenal. Her silhouette fills the glass in the door before I hear the key in the lock as the door swings open, and she's walking in. Her eyes fly around the room until they find mine, and shock fills her face. "What are you still doing here?" She looks just as beautiful as she did this morning when she left. Which was a long fucking time ago, not like I was checking my watch hourly thinking about where she was. But I did wonder where she was all day long.

I take in the box of donuts in one hand and the other

holding a bottle of wine. Then I see a second bottle of wine sticking out from her armpit. "Hello to you too, beautiful." I chuckle and turn back to the wall, not answering her question.

"It's almost eight o'clock." She turns to walk away from me, going toward the stairs. I hear the sound of her putting the bottles down before she comes back over to the kitchen. "I thought for sure you'd be gone."

"Is that why you came home so late?" I ask her as I spread the joint compound down the wall. "Were you avoiding me?"

"Obviously," she answers sarcastically, then her tone turns. "I know this is going to be shocking to you, Caleb, but my world doesn't revolve around you."

"Don't I know it," I retort, avoiding looking at her because if I look at her, I'll just want to stare at her the whole time. And I already told myself I wasn't going to throw myself at her again. I've done it three times now and nothing.

"But seriously," she huffs out, ignoring what I just said to her, "what are you still doing here?"

"Besides waiting to see you?" I wink at her before I go over the joint again. "I was able to get the painters to squeeze me in"—I turn to look at her—"but in order for them to squeeze me in, I had to make sure the joints were done. The guy we usually use for this is backed up, and I didn't want to delay this for three weeks, so here I am on a Saturday night, working, for you." She looks around the kitchen. "After the painters come in, I have the cabinet makers coming in." I turn back to the wall, my shoulders aching from working nonstop all day long. "I emailed you his name and number so you can reach out to them. I also sent you the name and number of the tile and counter guy. He's waiting for your call on Monday. He can rush anything, so it looks like this time next week, you'll probably have your kitchen up and running. Depending on what you choose for appliances."

She looks around. "That's so fast." Then her eyes come back to mine, going soft. "Thank you for rushing this."

"I didn't have any plans," I admit, but I don't tell her I was hoping to spend time with her and maybe convince her to rethink going out with me, "so it's fine." She looks around the room at the progress, no doubt probably seeing how things are going to look. "Was today stressful?"

She stops, looking around the room to turn back to me. "Why would you ask that?" She folds her arms over her chest.

I point over to the stuff that she dumped on the stairs. "A box of donuts and two bottles of wine." I chuckle as I finish the wall. "If that doesn't scream today sucked ass, I don't know what does."

"Wow." She shakes her head. "Can't a girl enjoy her night in the tub with a donut and a bottle of wine?" She lifts her eyebrows, waiting for me to answer, as I walk over and put the rest of the putty into the pail.

"Sure, but two bottles mean things didn't go well." I put down the tools, then walk over to the cloth and wipe my fingers. "Trust me, I should know."

"Old girlfriend drank a lot with you, did she?" She

makes the joke, and I can't help but bark out a laugh.

"Probably, but I also have two sisters, one younger and one older, so I know what two bottles mean. Usually, it means, one, a guy is a dick or, two, a guy did you dirty by being a dick." I fold my arms over my chest. "Are you drinking because of me? Because, baby, I have to say, I'm a sure thing, and I would never do you dirty."

She rolls her eyes. "Again, news flash, the world doesn't revolve around you, Caleb." Fuck, what I wouldn't give to kiss her. I lick my lips thinking about it. "Wait here," she says, turning, and I watch her walk back over to her purse. She opens it, grabs something out of it, and then grabs one of the bottles of wine before coming back to me.

"I'll show you something if you can figure out how to open this bottle," she bargains as she holds up the wine bottle in her hand, "since I don't have a corkscrew." She hands me the bottle, and I shake my head, turning and walking back to my black tool chest. Squatting down in front of it and opening the top, I snatch up my Swiss Army knife with a corkscrew attached to it. "That is kind of cheating, isn't it?"

"You didn't ask me if I had one. You said you didn't." I get up after I pull out the cork and then hand her the bottle. She grabs it from me and then glances around, probably looking for a glass.

When she finally realizes that she is not going to find a glass, she smirks at me. "Oh well." She holds up the bottle. "Cheers." She smirks before bringing the bottle to her lips and taking a gulp of it. "This is some good wine." She looks at the label.

"Okay, well, I held up my end of the bargain," I tell her. "What did you need to show me?" I look her up and down. "And will I be able to touch it?" My cock stirs in my pants.

"Good God." She shakes her head and then hands me a newspaper that is folded in two. The black-and-white newspaper now looks like it's yellow and black, so it must be old as fuck. I open it gingerly, seeing a picture in the middle of the article. Seeing two firefighters squatting down in the middle of them, is a small square cardboard box with what looks like a blanket in there and a small child in the arms of the big firefighter. My eyes go up to read the headline before I feel them go big as I look up at her, and she takes another swig of her wine. "In case you're wondering"—she leans in—"that's me." She points at the newspaper, and I look back, reading the article and wanting to pull her into my arms and give her a hug.

"Wow." I look at the little baby in the picture, then look at her. "You were always beautiful," I admire softly. Her eyes twinkle as she tries to hide her smile by looking down and then back up at me. But she can't fight it even if she tries and her whole face lights up as she smiles shyly at me.

"Smooth." She brings the bottle of wine back to her mouth, taking a couple of pulls. "I met that man today." She comes over to my side as she points at the fire chief, who is holding her in the faded picture.

"That's incredible." I look over at her. "You're lucky."

"Lucky isn't a word I would use"—she sighs—"but I guess you can say that." She shrugs. "That's the whole reason I moved here." She takes another sip of the wine.

"You moved all this way and bought a house to meet the fire chief?" I ask, confused.

She chuckles. "No, I'm not that crazy." She takes a deep breath in. "I moved all this way because," she blows out a deep breath, "I want to look for my birth parents."

"Whoa." I look down at the paper, making sure I read what I read before looking back at her. "What makes you think they come from here? Like, are you even sure they are from around here or maybe they drove into town and then drove back out?" I fold the paper and hold it out for her. Our fingers touch each other's when she takes it from me.

"I have no idea," she admits as she takes another gulp of wine, "but I figured I would start here and see where it took me."

"Sierra," I say. When she looks up at me, I see the bottom of her eyes are brimming with tears, and the need to hold her is so strong I don't know how much longer I can hold myself back from taking her in my arms again and kissing her just like I did last night.

"I know it's stupid," she says in almost a whisper, her voice trembling with emotion, "I mean, they dumped me in a cardboard box, for goodness' sake. What makes me think they even care where I am or what I'm doing? If they even thought about me over the years."

My hand comes up to cup her cheek, and I stop. "My hands are dirty," I tell her, looking at the white powder on it, along with some of the putty, "and I don't want to touch you with dirty hands."

"You can come with me and wash them upstairs in the bathroom," she suggests. I nod at her as she walks toward the stairs, and I follow her up the steps, the bottle in one hand and the folded newspaper in the other.

"This is my bedroom." She winks at me jokingly, opening one of the two doors and stepping in. "As if you didn't remodel it. But now I have furniture in it. Although, it's not done yet." She looks over her shoulder. "I was thinking of getting a plush rug or something." I step in and stare at the king-sized bed with the big gray headboard. The thick white cover on the bed with soft pink throw pillows makes it look like once you lie down, you won't get up. The mirrored side table adds a modern look to the room, even with the antique chandelier. "You know where the bathroom is." She points to the side and I nod, walking past her bed and to the bathroom.

I see her stuff all around one sink and walk over to turn on the water before grabbing the soap. I wash my hands and grab one of the towels, drying them off before walking back to her. I find her sitting on the little bench in front of her bed. Her jacket is tossed onto the bed so she's in just a tank top, her shoes kicked off and to the side of the bench, while she has one foot tucked under her and the other swinging as she takes a sip of wine. "You think me looking for my parents is a bad idea?" she asks me when she hears me walking back into the room.

"I don't know what to think," I answer her honestly. "Sometimes things just happen, and we have to let them.

Sort of let sleeping dogs lie or something like that. This might be one of them, just like my mother." I walk over and sit down next to her on the bench. Her folded touching my upper thigh. "She was married to this guy before my dad." She looks at me. "He died in a car accident shortly after they were married. Sad story, right?" Her hand goes to my arm, as she nods. "It gets worse, she then found out she wasn't really married to him. He had a whole-ass separate family and was living a lie with my mother. He literally was living a second life and she had no idea." She gasps. "It worked out in the end since she met my dad and then had me. You want to hear the weirdest part out of all of that?"

"There is a weirder part than that?" she asks with humor in her voice.

"My uncle Blake"—she waits for it—"he married the wife, my aunt Samantha. They have four kids together, two are from the guy who died, but we don't mention that, and two are with each other."

"Shut the fuck up." She pushes my shoulder, and I laugh.

"Theo is their son," I say and she gasps out. "Why do you want to find out who your parents are?" I ask her softly.

"I don't know." She takes a sip of wine. "I kind of want to know why. Why did they give me away? Why didn't they want me? Why go out of your way to carry me for nine months and just throw me away?" She looks down at her hands and then back at me, and I see the one tear rolling down her cheek. "Why?"

I pick up my hand and stop the tear from rolling all the way down her face, catching it with my thumb. "I don't know, baby," I say softly, "but it's their fucking loss." I lean in and kiss her lips. "You are so beautiful, you take my breath away. You are funny, smart, kind, a pain in my ass, snarky, and I know that I hardly know you, but fuck, you might just be fucking perfect."

She smiles. "You're just saying that to get into my pants." She tries to make a joke out of it.

I shake my head. "Are you going to let me into your pants, or are you going to pretend this thing between us isn't going to happen?"

"It's just—" she starts to say, and I stop her from talking when I lean in and slide my tongue into her mouth. With the taste of wine on her lips, she leans in and kisses me back. Our tongues dance gently with each other. My other hand comes up to hold her other cheek, and I want to bend her back and lie on top of her.

But with the bottle of wine in her hand, I can't, so I let her lips go. "I'm going to go before I do something you aren't ready for."

I get up, and she looks up at me. "And you're ready for it?"

"Baby," I say softly, my hand coming up to trail my fingertips on her cheek, "I was ready the second I laid eyes on you." I bend to kiss her lips. "I'll see you tomorrow."

Fifteen

SIERRA

"BABY." THE WAY he says that nickname, a couple of things happen at the same time. One, my knees almost give out, and then the second is the flutter happening in my stomach. His hand comes up, and his fingertips trail my cheek. "I was ready the second I laid eyes on you." I watch as he bends to kiss my lips. My eyes luckily stay open because it's so soft I wouldn't have felt it. "I'll see you tomorrow."

He turns to walk out of the room, my eyes going to his perfect fucking ass. "Caleb," I call his name, and he looks over his shoulder. His mouth goes into a smirk as he turns, and my feet are moving before my head can tell them not to. I swing my hips side to side, the courage courtesy of the half a bottle of wine I drank. I get on my tippy-toes, my hand going to his chest and then up into his hair before I press my chest to his. I bite his lower lip right before I slide my tongue into his mouth. One of his hands goes to the side of my neck, the other goes to my ass as he squeezes and pulls me even closer to him. His cock hardens for me, and I raise one leg and cock it over his hip. The hand on my ass now wraps around my waist as he picks me up off my feet. My legs wrap around his waist before he walks back to my bed, and instead of throwing me on the bed like I want him to do, he turns and sits down on the bench I have right in front of the bed. I unwrap my legs from around his waist as my head turns to the other side to deepen the kiss, and I get on my knees, straddling him.

I move my hips up and down, making us both moan as his hand goes to my ass, and he squeezes and moves my hips up and down. "God," I groan when I let go of his mouth for a second, but then I want it back. My hands go into his hair as I kiss him with everything I have. Fuck, this man can fucking kiss. He kisses the ever-loving shit out of me as I grind on his cock as if we're both in high school. His hands move from my ass to my sides and then up as he cups my tits in his hands. My nipples strain to get out of my bra. He pushes down one side of my bodysuit, taking the bra with him. His hand now kneads my naked breast, rolling my nipple, sending a shock right through me and straight to my clit. "Caleb," I mutter as he lets go of my mouth and bends his head to take my nipple into his mouth. My hips move up and down his cock as he pushes the other side down and takes the other nipple into his mouth. I close my eyes, my fingers in the back of his hair as he plays with one nipple while biting the other one, then sucking it into his mouth.

"Baby," he says, trailing his tongue from one nipple to the other as I look down and watch him bite it before twirling his tongue around it. I close my eyes, and my head falls back as I rotate my hips against him. I can't help but moan as he moves his hips at the same time. My covered clit moves side to side and up and down on his cock. Wanting to feel it skin to skin is excruciating.

He wraps one arm around my waist, pushing me even harder down on him, while the other one runs up my back and into my hair. He fists his hand, pulling my hair even more, giving him access to my neck. He sucks right next to my nipple before trailing his tongue and kisses all the way to my collarbone. He nibbles on it before he moves to my neck. My whole body feels like I'll explode from his touch.

Every single time I feel his tongue on my skin, I get a shiver, and then it shoots through me, and I want him to bury himself inside me. I don't think I've ever been this gone for a man before. "Caleb," I moan, my hips moving faster and faster.

"Yeah, baby," he replies softly, letting go of my hair and moving both hands so they grip my hips, helping to move me on his cock. He looks up at me, and I move my mouth to take his. Our tongues go around and around as I arch my back.

My nipple grazes his gray T-shirt and aches to be touched. It's like he knows my body because the minute I think that, his hands go from my hips to my tits, kneading them right before he rolls both nipples at the same time. His thumb and forefinger playing with them, he pinches, he rolls, and it's got me so hot and bothered I have to let go of his mouth to pant out. "Oh God," I moan, and he chuckles.

"It's Caleb, baby," he corrects, and I feel his tongue roll around a nipple before he takes it into his mouth. It's all so much—his finger, his touch, being in his arms. And just like that, I open my eyes to watch him when I come. I moan out my release, my hips moving until I'm done, my eyes fluttering closed. "Fuck," he murmurs, and my eyes spring open, "I can't wait to sink into you and make you come on my cock."

One side of my head screams *girl, same,* while the other side screams *I just dry humped him.* "Let's not get ahead of ourselves." I try not to make eye contact with him. But he doesn't let me off the hook that easily.

He cups my cheek, moving my head up so I'm looking at him. "It's going to fucking happen." His eyes hood over with lust and a little twinkle.

"I heard that zombies are also going to take over the world. I wonder what is going to happen first?" I move my hands up to cover my tits.

"I'm not a betting man"—he kisses my neck—"but you can bet your ass I'll be fucking you before zombies knock on your door. Now, I need to get home and get some sleep." He slaps one of my ass cheeks before he moves me off him, placing me down beside him before he gets up.

My eyes are at the exact level of his package. That is legit a fucking package. His thick cock can be seen straining against his jeans. "You keep looking at my cock like that, and I'm going to forget being a gentleman and fuck your mouth." I swallow, and the back of my neck heats up with embarrassment. "Now, I'm going to lock the door when I leave." I look up at him. "See you tomorrow." He bends and kisses my lips softly before walking out. My gaze goes again to his perfect ass until it disappears, and I want to run and tell him to come back. But all I do is close my eyes as I hear his boots walking through my house. I only open them when I hear the front door slam shut and the sound of his truck starting.

I lift my two feet, tucking my knees against my chest and hugging them as I listen to him drive away. My eyes look from the window to the door and see that he turned off the lights before leaving. I take a deep breath, getting up, and grab the bottle of wine I put down before walking into the bathroom. I turn on the water to take a bath, then turn toward the basin and see my lips are plump from his kisses. My hand comes up as my finger trails over my lips. "Well, that was crazy," I tell myself as I remember how kissing him felt. I slip off my clothes, fill the cup I have in here with wine, and bring both the bottle and the glass to the tub. I place the bottle beside it before stepping in, sitting down, leaning back, and sipping the wine.

"You are so beautiful, you take my breath away. You are funny, smart, kind, a pain in my ass, and I hardly know you, but fuck, you might just be fucking perfect."

His voice replays over and over in my head, words I didn't know I needed to hear when I heard them.

Slipping into bed, I turn off all the lights and lay my

head on my pillow. I've never lived with a man. The longest relationship I've ever had was seven months, and that was a stretch since he traveled for work. I've gone from living at home to living in my dorm to back to living in my house. I've forever been alone, but I've never felt as alone as I do right this minute. I've always felt like I belonged somewhere, but now, finding out I was adopted, it's like I don't belong anywhere. It is the strangest feeling I've ever felt. The pillow catches the tear before I drift off to sleep.

The next day, I wake when the sun hits my face like a spotlight in the nighttime. I slip out of bed and dress in a light-gray jogging outfit to run out and get some coffee. I walk down the steps at the same time the door opens, and he steps in, two cups of coffee in his hands. His face fills with a smile. "Morning, baby," he greets, meeting me at the bottom of the steps.

He's wearing another pair of jeans that fit him like they were made for him and him alone. His grayish-black T-shirt pulls across his chest, and from what I felt with my hands last night, it's hard as a rock. "Morning," I mumble.

"Are we going to talk about last night?" he asks me with a smirk across his ridiculous, stupidly handsome face. I can't help the way my face heats up at his question. "Or are you going to tell me you can't do this?" He steps even closer to me, and I can't help the flutter that starts in my stomach and moves south very quickly. "Because the blush on your face and your neck tells me how good last night was." He bends his head and kisses my lips.

"We are not." I shake my head, and he chuckles, making me walk, or better yet, stomp toward the door.

"I got you coffee." He holds up a hand.

"Ugh," I grunt out loud, walking over to him and taking it from him. "Thank you," I grumble, "you didn't have to."

"I know I didn't have to, baby," he replies softly, and I want him to stop calling me that, but secretly, I don't really fucking want him to. "I wanted to."

"Stop calling me baby." That is the only thing I can come back with. "And don't you take a day off?"

"I'm going home next weekend," he informs me, and I swear my vagina says *aw*, "so I'll take time off then."

"Good." I bring the coffee to my lips before my mouth decides to ask him why he's going home.

"You still going out?" he asks, and I nod.

"Yes." I turn and walk toward the door.

"Drive safe, baby," he cautions while I glare at him, and he turns to walk into the kitchen. I'm about to have the most amazing comeback when the door opens, and Theo steps in, stopping before bumping into me.

"Oh, sorry," he says, "didn't see you there."

"It's fine." I smile at him. "Have a nice day." I walk around him and out of the house.

Getting into the car, I start it, not even sure where I'm going now that I have my coffee. I head toward the bakery anyway, opting to have a bagel. I step in and order just that before heading to the side and sitting down by myself. I'm scrolling on my phone, ordering a toaster with a small fridge when I hear Lucy call my name. "Sierra." She runs over, and I see Lilah walking in behind her.

"Hi," I say, holding out my hands to give her a hug as she comes running into them, "this is a nice surprise."

"I'm meeting Saige here," she tells me, looking around, and I see Everleigh also walk in. "We're going to bake cupcakes with Ms. Maddie."

"Oh, fun. You going to keep one for me?" She nods and runs to Saige when she sees her.

I watch the girls skip to the back as Lilah comes over to the table, pulling out the chair in front of me. "Hey." She sits down. "What are you doing?"

"Ordering myself a mini fridge and toaster," I answer her as Everleigh comes over with my bagel and a couple of donuts. "Thank you," I tell her, taking the plate as she walks back to the counter, grabbing two white coffee mugs.

"I got you tea." She places the cup down in front of Lilah, who looks at it like it's gross.

"How come you have a takeout cup?" Everleigh asks me when she sees the cup as she pulls out the last empty chair at the table.

"Caleb brought me the coffee," I admit. Everleigh's eyes about come out of her sockets as she looks at me, not sure she should say something, before looking over at Lilah. "I told her," I inform Everleigh.

"She told you she likes him?" Everleigh asks Lilah, who nods with a huge smile on her face. "She was scared because you two dated." She holds up her hands to use quotations to say dated.

"I was not scared," I hiss. "It was just weird."

"I don't know why," Lilah says. "You think if I was serious about him, I wouldn't have told you?" I think about the question and shrug. "Exactly, that's like saying you're right, Lilah, like always."

"Anyway." I roll my eyes. "I told her that I kissed him"—I close my eyes—"because the last thing I wanted to do was ruin my friendship with her for it."

"Wait." Everleigh holds up her hand. "You kissed him?" She takes a sip of her coffee.

"She did," Lilah says, faking vomit to the side. "Outside the bar."

"Way to go." Everleigh holds her hand up again to high-five me. I lift my hand in return. "Also yesterday when I got home," I mumble, hoping they don't hear me.

"Excuse me?" Lilah retorts.

"I know." I throw my head back dramatically. "I know, but he was home when I got there, and he opened my bottle of wine."

"Obviously, that merited a kiss." Lilah puts her head to the side and closes her eyes as she nods.

"That's not even the worst part of it." Now both sets of eyes are on me. "I literally dry humped him," I confess embarrassingly, hiding my face from them as they both gasp and then laugh.

"That's why he got you coffee this morning." Everleigh winks at me.

"I am mortified," I admit to them. "He kissed me and was leaving, and then the wine hit me." I look over at Lilah, pointing at her. "This is your fault. You gave me bad wine."

She bursts out laughing. "I think after you get an orgasm from it, I should be saying you're welcome."

I groan, "I'm so dumb."

"You are not dumb. You like the guy, and the guy obviously likes you if he's going to let you dry hump him and get nothing in return," Everleigh states matter-of-factly. "If I give Brock an orgasm and he doesn't give me two back, I'm not doing it."

"Okay, I'm already nauseous because of this baby"—Lilah rubs her stomach—"and then this one is making out with Caleb." She points at me.

I shake my head at her. "Also, I don't know what you're talking about. That man can kiss like there is no tomorrow." I pick up a piece of my bagel and take a bite. "Literally, the best fucking kiss I've had in my whole life." She gawks.

"If he can kiss that good," Everleigh wonders aloud, "imagine what else he can do with that mouth." She smirks, and I can't help but put my hands on my cheeks to stop the redness from creeping up.

"It'll probably ruin me for all other men." I close my eyes before I look at both of them, finally admitting, "This was not on my bingo card." I rub my hand on the top of my thigh. "At all."

"Those are the best kind," Everleigh explains softly. "It sneaks up when you're least expecting it, and boom, you can't think about a day when you didn't know him." She shares those words, and my heart speeds up because whatever it is that is happening with Caleb, it really fucking feels like I've known him my whole life when the reality is I just met him.

"One doesn't fall so fast, so quickly," I refute, having the two of them look at me. "Right?"

They share a look and a smirk when they both say at the same time, making me slump in my chair, "Wrong."

Sixteen

CALEB

"YOU EXCITED ABOUT being home?" Theo asks from the passenger seat of the truck as we pass the halfway mark from Montgavin to my home where I grew up.

I have one hand on the wheel while my arm is lying on the door, the open window letting the breeze come through the cab. "It's been a couple of weeks since I've seen my parents. So I'm excited to see them and then hang with Mila and her crew. Make sure the kids remember their cool uncle Caleb."

"It hasn't been a couple of weeks since you've been home." He scoffs at me. "It's been over two months since you've been home."

"Considering that my home is in Montgavin now"—I look at the road—"I'm just visiting." He snickers, laughing, no doubt laughing about the state of play that Sierra and I are in, which is a stalemate at this point.

"The more important question of the day is." My

voice trails, waiting for him to ask me what, but when he doesn't, I just continue, "Have you decided what you are going to do after we finish Sierra's house?" I look back over at Theo, who shrugs.

"Not sure, really," he replies. "I have nothing holding me here so…"

"What the hell are you talking about? You have your house, your work with my father. Plus you are like an hour closer to your mother and father." I mention just a few things he has holding him here.

"Yeah, but they're all doing their own thing."

"You need to settle down," I tell him and he literally groans out.

"I don't need to settle down," he says, his voice tight. "Tried that. Well, almost tried that and she left." He doesn't continue his thought, nor does he say her name. Not sure he wants to think about his fiancée leaving him two days before the wedding. It broke his fucking heart and since then he's been adamant that he will never, ever settle down. He's good with one-night stands and only one-night stands. He doesn't even give anyone his number, and the exchange is first name only if that.

"Maybe you need a change of scenery." I tap my finger on the steering wheel.

"Is that what you did?" He tries to turn it around on me as if it would bother me.

"I guess so," I admit. "I had my family, but other than that, I had nothing really holding me here. Besides, do you know how annoying it was when I would show up to job sites and people would be like, 'wait, your father isn't coming?'"

"You used to have Amber." He reminds me of my first girlfriend, who I dated throughout high school and college. When we both got back home, she wanted more. I wasn't ready to make that commitment to her, so we parted ways. Now I heard she's engaged to some banker, or maybe she's even married. I don't ask about her and no one brings it up to me either.

"It was never going to work out with Amber." I tap the steering wheel with my finger. "She didn't really even want me. She just wanted the ring and all that because a couple of her sorority sisters were getting married. She wanted the Instagram life and not the real life. She was more worried about what everyone else thought about us than what I thought about us." I don't bring up the rest of it, keeping that to myself. I share everything with Theo but that part about Amber and me is going to be my secret.

"Better to know before you marry her than after," Theo declares as I turn onto his street and see his house, pulling up to it as he reaches for the door handle. He pushes the door open with his shoulder. "See you Sunday." He gets out and opens the back door. "Don't call me before." He grabs his duffel from the back seat before slamming the door.

I wait for him to be halfway down his walkway before I press the button to open the window and shout out, "That's literally tomorrow!" Walking up to his front door, he holds his hand up and flips me the bird. It was probably stupid to drive five hours to be here for less than a day, but I needed to come home and check on things. Plus, if I'm five hours away from her, there is no way I could slip over to her house and do something she obviously is not ready for.

I make my own way over to the house I took over from my parents when I came back from college. It's not far from the house they have. It is the house my father bought his first wife when they got married. After she left him with a John Doe letter, he let it sit and wanted nothing to do with it. It's the house my mother rented when she came to town. From the stories everyone tells, he hated her, she hated him, and now they are happily married.

I pull up to the house, seeing the porch swing on the side moving with the soft wind. I get out, grabbing my bag from the back before walking into the house. I open the door, the stillness of the air thick from being closed for two months. I dump my bag at the door and go over to the window of the kitchen that faces the living room, opening it before walking over to the back door and opening it as well. The screened storm door stays shut, and I can hear the ocean waves hitting the beach.

I open the fridge, seeing three bottles of beer in there with a couple of condiments. Bending to grab a beer, I twist the top off and walk to the garbage bin, tossing it in there before taking a pull of it and walking outside to the back deck that faces the ocean. I make my way down the path to the ocean, sitting on the sand and just staring out into the distance. Watching the waves rise and then crash onto the sand is almost therapeutic and I know exactly why my mother loves sitting out and watching them.

As the sun tries to peek out of the clouds, I take a pull of the beer, and my mind immediately goes to her. Sierra. We finished her kitchen late last night. Even Theo and I were impressed with how fast it went. We've never finished a kitchen in under three weeks, but it was all hands on deck for her. I think we had six men working in the kitchen at one time. But we could say that it's done, she doesn't have to have coffee in her room or eat at her desk.

I put the beer beside me as I lean back on my hands, watching the water, when I look over to see my niece, Mackenzie, running down the beach, wearing water boots with her dog running beside her. "It's Uncle Caleb!" she shrieks over her shoulder at my sister, who puts her hand to her forehead to see, and a smile fills her face. I get on my feet and squat down for Mackenzie, opening my arms for her as she runs into them. "Momma, it's really him."

"Did you think I was a ghost?" I kiss her cheek as her dog barks around my feet. Mila makes it to me then, a smile on her face. "Hey, Squirt." I look down at her, and she rolls her eyes at me.

"I'm older than you by six years." She pokes me in the ribs before she reaches out and pinches the underside of my arm, knowing I fucking hate it.

"Where is your brother?" I ask Mackenzie as I lean in to kiss her neck again and then give her a long hug, squeezing her a little bit longer than before.

"Mathias is napping," she tells me, "and Daddy is

watching him because Mom is stuck with us all week long." She emphasizes the last words and I know that she is repeating it the exact way that Mila said it.

"Mackenzie," Mila scolds her, "what did I say to you?" she asks her and Mackenzie just looks at her not sure what she is talking about. "We do not repeat what grown-ups say." The tiredness is written all over her face.

"You want to go back home and take a nap also?" I look at Mila. "I can take her and walk over to Gramps's house."

"Yes." Mila doesn't even hesitate. "See you later at Mom and Dad's." She leans over to kiss Mackenzie before turning and walking away to her house. The dog goes to her and then comes back to Mackenzie and me before going back to her.

"Take your dog!" I shout as I put Mackenzie down, and she yells for him to come with her.

"Okay, Squirt," I call her the nickname I gave Mila, grabbing my bottle of beer. "Let's go crash Grandma and Grandpop's." I hold out my hand, and she slips hers in mine as we walk over to their house.

"Don't run in the water," I instruct her when she lets go of my hand because a piece of wood washed up on the shore.

"I won't, Uncle Caleb," she assures me, running in said water I told her not to run in, but with her boots, she doesn't get too wet.

When we get to my parents' place, I walk up the pathway to their back gate. I open the gate and she runs in before me. "Grandma!" she yells as she runs past the tree house my father had made for her, past the play structure that took us four days to put up because my mother bought four of them and wanted them all put together, just like at a park. The pool is covered with a tarp since it's too cold to go swimming. "Grandpop!" she hollers his name. The back door opens, and my father steps out with a smile on his face.

His eyes go from Mackenzie to me, and his eyes and his smile get even bigger. "Sweetheart," he says to Mackenzie, who wraps her arms around his waist and he bends to kiss her head, "this is a nice surprise."

"Daddy does nothing at home." She changes the story from what she told me not long ago.

"I bet he doesn't," he mumbles. "Take off your boots. Grandma is making apple muffins."

"My favorite!" she squeals, kicking off her boots and then placing them nicely on the mat outside the door. "Grandma!" she yells, opening the door and walking in before it closes behind her.

"Look at you," my father says, coming and giving me a hug, "walking down the beach with a beer."

"I was having one beer," I tell him, putting it on the table, "when your daughter and granddaughter came walking down the beach."

"She's exhausted," he mumbles. "Her husband needs to pitch in more." I raise my eyebrows.

"You know he works, and when he gets home, he's hands-on with the kids," I remind him. "He worships her."

"Not enough." He glares at me when I try to defend

him.

My mother comes to the back door. "She said you were here, and I didn't believe her." She wipes her hands on the apron around her waist. "Look at you." She gives me a hug. "You look like you have a lot on your mind." I roll my eyes and shake my head. "Is it a woman?"

"No," I refute, and my father's eyebrows go up.

"That was a fast no, so it must be a yes." He laughs. "Who is she?"

"No one." I shake my head, not ready to talk about Sierra yet. What can I say, really? I like this woman, like really fucking like her, and she's avoiding me like I'm the plague. This whole week, she's avoided me altogether, except when she got a huge-ass whiteboard that she tried to carry up to her bedroom by herself, but stopped every seven seconds huffing and puffing. I leaned against the doorjamb, watching her trying to pull up the big box. She knew I was watching, knew all she had to do was ask me for help. But, of course, why would she? She was going to do it all by herself. Until she got to the fifth stair and thought it was going to be smooth sailing, when the box slipped out of her hand and fell right down all the stairs.

"Motherfucker," she hissed, stomping down the steps to the box, and I finally pushed away from the doorjamb and went to her.

"Need help, baby?" I asked. The glare was enough to make me go back to the kitchen and mind my business, but all I could think of was what her lips would taste like if I kissed her.

I went to the box and held the side as she came down,

her feet stomping on the steps as she grabbed the box, and we carried it up to her bedroom. "Where do you want it?"

"In the other room, but it's not finished." She tilted her head to the side, and I shook my head and laughed.

"You need a kitchen before you need a spare bedroom or an office," I reminded her as she went over to the box and flipped open the side. "Do you need help unpacking the box, or are you going to pretend you have this?"

"I wasn't pretending." She went over to her office, getting a box cutter. "I had it covered."

"It looked like it." I put my hands on my hips as I watched her cut the box on top and then at the side so it fell open to the side.

"See?" She pointed at the box. "Got it covered."

"Perfect," I said to her and turned to walk out of the room. I waited for her to say something to me, but she said nothing.

"You need to settle down," my mother interrupts my memories, "and give me grandbabies."

"Have you spoken to my other sister?" I mention Meadow. "She also can help in this project to fill your house with grandchildren."

"She's busy," my father says, "and she doesn't need"—he glares at me—"any of that."

I laugh at them protecting my sister, as Mackenzie comes out to grab my mother. The day is spent with the two of us just lounging on the couch while they bake apple muffins. We end up watching some movie that I don't even concentrate on because all I can do is think about what Sierra is doing.

We eat dinner, and I walk back to the house, showering and sliding into bed, wishing she was here with me. I don't think I've ever felt this way about a woman before. The need to constantly be around her is foreign to me. I drift off to sleep while the television watches me, waking when my phone buzzes from the bedside table. I reach out for it and open one eye, seeing it's Sierra calling. I can't help the way the smile fills my face, bringing the phone to my ear. "Hey, baby," I mumble, "did you miss me?"

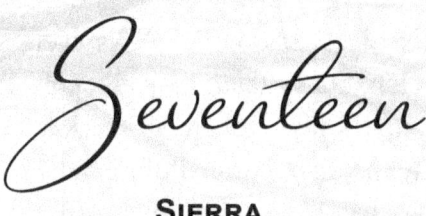

Seventeen

SIERRA

"HEY, BABY," HE mumbles, filled with sleep, and I close my eyes, "did you miss me?"

I roll on the bed, trying to focus on the wall in front of me, before wiping my mouth with the back of my hand. "Why are you so hot?" He chuckles, and my whole body shivers. "Like seriously, you can't be that hot." I close my eyes to get the room to stop moving so fast. Perhaps drinking all that wine was not a good idea.

"Sierra, where are you?" he asks, and I hear covers rustle from his end of the phone.

"I'm home in bed, all by myself," I tell him, looking down at my current state, me in the white robe I put on after my bath. One pink slipper is still on my foot as I swing my leg and it flies to the side of the room. "I got in bed tonight, and I was so horny, all I could think of was playing with myself while I thought about you. But nothing is helping me."

"Where were you tonight?" His voice rises a bit, and I can feel it fill with tightness.

"I was with the girls." I try to get up on my elbow, but then it's too hard for me. "We were supposed to have book club, but instead, they all came over here and helped me unpack my kitchen. Discussed the book while putting away the dishes and all that, but…"

"But what, baby?" he questions softly, and I groan.

"But all I could talk about was you. And your stupid kisses," I admit, wishing I could lean over and kiss him. "How good they are, how you are the best kisser in the whole world." I stop talking, taking a second to focus on making the room stop spinning. "Where were you today?"

"I came home," he replies, and I sit up in bed.

"Home?" I look around the room. "Home where? I thought you lived here."

"I came to visit my parents," he reworks the words. "If you weren't avoiding me this week, I would have reminded you. Maybe asked you to come with me."

"I wasn't avoiding you," I quickly cut him off, not touching the rest of the sentence. Flopping back down on the bed. "I was busy."

"Busy avoiding me."

"Maybe." I close my eyes. "You're so hot."

"So you spoke to your friends about me?" I can hear the smile in his voice. "Did you tell them how crazy you have been driving me?" His voice goes low. "Did you tell them how all I wanted to do all week long was kiss the ever-loving shit out of you?" His words make parts of me, actually not parts, all of me ache for him. "Tell me, baby, what did you tell them about me?"

"I told them that kissing you made me forget everything," I whisper. "I told them that when I was on top of you, all I wanted was for you to be inside me. I told them—"

"Enough." His voice is tight, almost a hiss. "What are you wearing right now?"

"Nothing," I reveal, looking down at myself, and he moans. "I'm in my white robe. I took a bath before I called you. I tried to—"

"You tried to what?"

"I tried to. With my toy and—" I groan out in frustration.

"Where is your toy?" he asks, and I move my hand over the bed covers and pick up the purple vibrator I used in the tub. It got me there, but something was missing.

"I have it here," I tell him, "it's purple."

"Tell me what it looks like."

"It's smaller than your cock, that's for sure," I tell him. "Are you going to show me your cock soon?" I don't wait for him to answer me. "I would like to see your cock soon." My voice perks up and I giggle.

"You are lucky I'm here and not at my house, or I'd be at your door right now."

"That would help very much," I tell him, "then you could show me your cock. I felt your cock. It's big." I giggle. "I bet I can't take it all in my mouth."

He moans. "Are you wet?" he asks. "I want you to slide a finger through your pussy lips and check and see if you're wet."

"I don't have to check," I pant out, "I'm soaking for you."

"Is that right?"

"Yes," I hiss.

"Someone sounds like she needs to come," he teases. "I want you to listen to me." I pant out. "You are going to do exactly what I tell you to do. Do you understand me?"

"Yes. Caleb, I have a secret," I whisper.

"Yeah, what's the secret?" he asks.

"I'm so horny," I tell him, making him chuckle.

"I'm going to help you with that, baby." I nod even though he can't see me.

"I want you to suck the tip of the toy." I do what he tells me to do, bringing it into my mouth.

"I wish it was your cock," I inform him, and I know he wants it as much as I do.

"I'm fisting my cock now, wishing it was your hand," he admits. "Now, turn on the vibrator at the lowest setting, and I want you to rub the tip over your nipple."

I move it down to my nipple that has been pebbled and achy since I got into bed and starting to think about him. Moving the tip of the vibrator over one nipple, I close my eyes. "Tell me what you feel."

"I feel achy," I respond to him, moving it from one nipple to the other. "I feel so achy, Caleb. Make me feel better."

"Move the vibrator, baby," he instructs me, "slowly down your stomach, all the way to your clit."

"Yes." I do exactly what I'm told, and the minute the

vibrator moves on my clit, I arch my back up.

"Spread those legs for me." My legs move open for him. "The next time I'm there, I'm going to eat that pussy of yours until you beg me to stop, and even then, I'm going to continue to lick it, suck it, and then fuck it."

"Yes," I pant as I move the vibrator to my entrance. "I'm about to slide it into me."

"Slide it in you," he guides softly. "Fuck, I wish it was my cock."

"Me too," I agree as I slide it halfway into me.

"Put me on speakerphone, baby, I'm going to need you to use your hand to play with your clit." I put him on speakerphone, the words a bit hazy, placing it on the pillow beside me. "Okay, baby, slide that cock inside you." I move it back inside me. "The next time I see you," he starts, and my hand moves the vibrator in and out of me, my other hand playing with my clit, side to side. "I'm going to undress you"—I nod—"then I'm going to sit you down and spread your legs. I'm going to lick that clit with the tip of my tongue before I slide it into your pussy. Feast on you." We both moan. "Finger-fuck you and eat you at the same time. Make you come on my face before I fuck you."

"Yes." I arch my back.

"How do you want me to fuck you, baby?" he asks, and I can hear his voice getting tight. "On your back, legs over my shoulders?"

"Hmm." I close my eyes, listening to his words.

"Go deep in your pussy, make it mine. Then I'll flip you onto your hands and knees, slap that perfect ass of yours as I fuck you." I can feel myself getting close to the edge. My breathing comes out in pants now. "Turn your ass red while my cock drips with your cum. But the big question is, baby"—his voice is low—"do I come in your pussy or down your throat?" Just the thought pushes me over the edge. "Fuck your throat until I coat it."

"Caleb," I say as I come on the vibrator.

"Fuck," he hisses as he moans out his own release, "came all over my fucking hand." I lie limp in the bed. "Baby?"

"Hmm," I say, pulling the vibrator out of me and putting it on the side.

"You good?"

"Oh yeah." I get on my side and sigh out. "Really fucking good." He laughs. "Thank you."

"I'll see you tomorrow." I don't know if he says anything else after that because I slowly drift off to sleep.

During the night, I get up to drink water from a water bottle beside my bed before I slide back into bed. I cover myself until the pounding of my head wakes me up the following morning. I reach out to grab my phone from the side table and come up empty. I lift my head, but the ache hits my head right away. I toss the covers off me and look around for my robe, finding it in a puddle beside the bed with my purple vibrator on top of it. Grabbing the robe first, then the vibrator, I tuck it into the side table before seeing my phone on the pillow. I snatch it up before walking down the steps to my brand-new kitchen.

I head straight to the fridge, my hand trailing the marble on the island as I walk over to the double-door, stainless-steel fridge. Pulling it open, I see half a crystal jug filled with water, so I grab it and turn to try to find a glass but find an empty cupboard since they are in the dishwasher. I open the dishwasher, grab a glass, and pour some water in it before making myself coffee. I think about having coffee in the kitchen, but with my pounding head, I walk back upstairs and straight to the bathroom to grab something for my headache. I slip back into bed as I open my iPad to check my emails, seeing I got an email from the DNA test I took a couple of weeks ago.

My heart pounds in my chest when it says "Guess what, Sierra? You've got a new DNA relative." I put the cup of coffee down on the bedside table as I click open the email.

My eyes go over the words, hoping with everything that it gives me a parent-child match, but that would be too easy, and good things aren't easy, apparently. I read the rest of the email, where it tells me that Gloria Beale is a third or fourth cousin. I take a deep breath. "Better than nothing," I remind myself, putting the iPad to the side and grabbing my cup of coffee.

I'm about to take a sip when a text pops up from Caleb.

Caleb: *Morning, beautiful. I'm heading home in a bit. Just wondering are we going to ignore last night also?*

I stare at my iPad, seeing the message now swipe up and disappear as the memories of last night come to me, slow at first. Them finally installing the fridge and stove. Then the doorbell ringing and Lilah coming in with a couple of bottles of champagne to toast the kitchen being done. Everleigh showing up next with a box of donuts to have after the pizza Autumn brought was all devoured. Harmony even decided to come and meet us to see the final product. Before we even started putting things away, we chose the book of the month, and then the wine started free-flowing for everyone but Lilah. Brock came to pick up Everleigh when she sent him a picture of her with her tongue licking her lips. She sent it and bet us a hundred dollars that he would be there in less than ten minutes. No one really thought he would come right over, but literally seven and a half minutes later and she was being carried out over his shoulder. I think he even thanked us before he walked out. The sound of him smacking her ass right before the door slammed shut made us all burst out laughing.

Lilah drove Autumn, and as soon as all of them were gone and my kitchen was clean, I went straight upstairs, where I got my purple toy out. I gasp and sit up in my bed so fast it's a miracle I don't fly out of it. "No-no-no-no-no." I shake my head, grabbing my phone and pulling up my call logs. My eyes see his name at the top and that we were on the phone for fifteen minutes. "Oh my God. Oh my God. Oh my God." I close my eyes and put the phone on my forehead. "I'm never drinking again. Never," I vow and sink back into my pillows. "Maybe he's not going to bring it up." I look at the phone in my hand as it buzzes again as well as pings on my IPad. "Ugh, what is wrong with you?" I then look down at my vagina. "And you, can't you be controlled? Jesus, you went two years without sex, and now all of a sudden, it's like the beast has been unleashed." I look up at the ceiling of my bedroom. "I'm going to ignore it and pretend it wasn't me."

I ignore the text and get up, cleaning up my room and making the bed before taking a shower to wash away the night. When I close my eyes and let the water wash over my face, I hear his voice.

"Come down your throat." I put my hands on my face as if that will make it all go away.

I pull out the chair at my desk and open my computer, scanning the email from the ancestry place before grabbing my pen and paper.

I log on to my account, my hands shaking the whole time. It feels like I'm snooping on someone's life, but it's mine. I watch the little circle go around as it accepts my username and password, every single second feeling like it's been an hour. I tap my hand beside the keyboard until my name fills the top of the screen.

My eyes go down to my DNA report, where it shows me my ancestral regions. I skip it until I see the tabs at the top that show me they have one for matches. The match for Gloria is right on top and I click her name. Which brings me to another screen and there is the message button. Holding my breath, I click it.

Hi Gloria,

Not sure if you will ever get this message or not. My name is Sierra, and I'm unsure of my family tree. I'd love to ask you questions about your tree.

Sierra

It's not a detailed message, and of course, I lie to her about trying to find my family tree. But I'll do what I need to do. I click back when it shows me I have another match, but this time, it's a third cousin twice removed. My head starts to spin at this point. On the side of the tree, it says our potential ancestry relates us to William Samuel Nortcutt and Nancy Sally, which is my fourth great-grandfather's parents.

I take a pen and paper now and start to track all the lineage to William and Nancy. When I click William's name, I find out he went by Samuel and was born in eighteen hundred and married Sally in eighteen nineteen.

I get up to walk over to the whiteboard and fill in their family tree, unsure if it will lead to anything. I'm about to go back to the computer when there is a knock on the door. I walk down the steps, my eyes on the glass door. The person is there and has his head bent forward. I unlock the door and pull it open, seeing him standing there. He has both hands outstretched on the side, holding the doorjamb. His head looks up, and I see his golden-brown-almost-hazel eyes right before his mouth goes into a smirk. "Hey, baby."

I roll my eyes and fold my arms over my chest as if his presence does nothing for me. I think I'm a good poker player because everything inside me screams that he's here. "What are you doing here?"

He takes a step in, and I have no choice but to take a step back. He grabs my hip with one hand, while his foot comes out to slam the door shut, and the other hand grabs one of my folded arms, pulling me to him. "I missed you," he answers, and I'm about to say something else to him when his mouth crashes down on mine, and just like all those other times, I forget my own damn name.

Eighteen

CALEB

"I MISSED YOU," I answer when I have her in my arms, and her body semi-melts into me. She's about to say something else, but before she even does it, I move my hand that was on her hip to her face, my mouth crashing over hers. My tongue slides into her mouth, and the minute it touches hers, she melts into my arms. Her arms loosen from her chest, and she moves one to wrap around my shoulder while the other grips my hip. I wasn't planning to kiss her as soon as I got here. But one look at her and I just couldn't help myself. When she's near me all common sense goes out the door and everything in my settles when she is near. Fuck, I didn't have any plans except to come and see her.

"Caleb," she pants out my name when she lets go of my lips and I watch her eyes slowly flutter open.

"Yeah, baby?" I say, my thumb rubbing her bottom lip. I can see she's trying to think of something to say to close this down. "I missed you."

"Stop saying that," she whispers and looks from my eyes to my mouth and back up again.

"But I did." I rub her cheek with my thumb. "I missed you"—she doesn't say anything as her arm around my shoulder runs down the front of my chest—"and you kind of missed me."

"No, I didn't," she quickly adds, trying to dislodge herself from my arms, but I just pull her closer to me. She gives up after a second and avoids my eyes when she says, "I maybe was wondering where you went."

"That means you missed me." I laugh, rubbing her back.

"That means I was curious as to where you were lurking." She pushes out of my arms, and I let her, but my hand reaches for her, and our fingers intertwine. I bend and kiss the tips of her fingertips. "I was wondering if you were going to pop up like an ax murderer." I throw my head back and laugh. "You know, those scary movies where the woman is getting ready for bed, and the guy is watching from inside the house, and everyone is screaming to get out."

"Trust me, if you're undressing, I'm not going to be hiding and lurking. I'll be front and center, sitting there watching your every move." I wink at her.

"That doesn't sound creepy at all." She shakes her head and I can't help but laugh.

"I might even have something to show you." She groans. "Something you want to see."

"No." She snatches her hand away from mine and

covers her face with both of them. "I was drunk. So it doesn't count."

"You said it, so it meant you wanted to say it. You just needed a little bit of a push." I touch the tip of her nose with my finger. "They say a drunken woman's words are a sober woman's thoughts."

"Who says this?" She tilts her head to the other side. "Who? Say their names."

"A lot of people." I pull her to me, wrapping my arm around her shoulders. She holds both my sides. My T-shirt fisted in her hands. "You look beautiful"—I softly bend to kiss her lips—"and I did miss you." I kiss her again. "And I'm really, really happy you called me."

"Does it matter that I would like to forget that phone call?" She looks up at me as she takes a deep breath in.

"You can try," I start, and her face looks hopeful, "but I'm not going to forget, and chances are I'll remind you just in case."

"Caleb." Her head goes back, and she closes her eyes.

"Love it when you call my name, baby." I kiss her nose. "Now, are you going to show me what you did to the kitchen?"

Her eyes light up "Yes." She turns in my arms and grabs my hand, dragging me behind her.

I stop dead in my tracks when I see it all together. I knew what the cabinets looked like and what tile she picked out and even the counter, but when I see it all together, it blows me away.

"This is a nice touch," I say of the base island brown-colored cabinets that she did. "Wasn't sure it would look good with the cream cabinets, but it pops out." I move over and my finger traces the white marble top with light-gray veins in it. "And the barstools"—I motion to the four barstools that she has tucked under the island—"the feet of the stools match the light fixtures." I point up to the two square brass light fixtures that hang over the island. "They match perfectly."

She moves to the other side of the island. "Just like you," she extends her hands on the island, "I'm good at my job."

"I can see that." I look over at the stove she had put in. It has four burners with a grill beside them and then another two burners. "You like to cook." I motion to the chef-like stove with two oven doors under it.

"Not really." She outstretches her hands by her sides to hold on to the counter. "But this might be my forever home"—she shrugs—"so I might as well get what I need now and not have to change it two years down the line."

"Your forever home," I repeat her words. "You've been in town for what, two weeks?"

"I sort of knew before I moved here that this was where I wanted to be," she declares. "You went home this weekend."

"I went to visit my parents," I sort of correct her. "Went to show them I was still alive and well." I stand at my side of the island. "Spent time with my niece and nephew."

"Did you enjoy yourself?" I can see her finger tapping the top of the island.

"I would have enjoyed myself more if someone was

with me"—I look behind me at the two-door, stainless-steel fridge—"in my bed."

"What's the matter, Caleb? No high school girlfriends to warm the bed?" She says the words and she tries to make it sound like it doesn't bother her, but I can see on her face it does.

"Girlfriends is a stretch but the answer is nope." I stare into her eyes. "I dated one girl in high school and throughout college," I tell her, "but she wanted to be married and have kids now." I point at the floor. "I just didn't see that with her, I guess, so we broke up."

"We broke up?" She tilts her head to the side. "Or she dumped you because you couldn't commit to her?" I see the smirk fill her face. "Is that because you are scared of commitment? That's a red flag."

I can't help but laugh. "I'm not scared of commitment, and If you must know, I broke up with her, but we ended on good terms." I end it on that, the last thing I want to do is discuss my ex and one of the real reasons that I moved here.

"I don't believe you." She folds her arms over her chest. "No one ends on good terms with their ex."

"I am good friends with Lilah." I can't help the smirk that fills my face. "I love when I prove you wrong."

"That's why I can't date you." My heart sinks. "Girl code." She rolls her eyes at me, and I can see she's really not that serious, at least I hope fucking not. "Do you want something to drink?"

"Are you asking me to stay?" I watch her walk past me to the fridge.

"Will you leave if I tell you to leave?" she asks me over her shoulder with a twinkle in her eye and I can tell she's fucking with me.

"I mean, if you want me to." I turn to watch her, leaning against the counter, folding my arms over my chest. "I did come straight here."

"You came straight here?" She opens the fridge, the shock written all over her face.

"I mean not straight straight here after I drove over the town lines. I did drop Theo off. I think I told him to tuck and roll before I kicked him out of the truck, and I came right here." Her mouth opens. "I would have been here way earlier, but my parents wanted to have family brunch, so I had to give it to them."

"I don't have much since I didn't have time to shop yet"—her voice is softer than it was just a minute ago—"so I only have a couple of bottles of beer and a bottle of red wine."

"I'll have a beer," I tell her, and she nods, grabbing it and twisting the top off for me.

"Do you want a glass?" I shake my head and reach out to grab the beer from her.

"Did you eat?" I ask, and she shakes her head.

"I had coffee this morning," she admits, "but then I…" She trails off. "Are you hungry?" changing the subject and I let her make that play. For now.

"I could eat," I tell her, "but I'm not worried about me." I take a pull of my beer. "I'm worried about you. What do you want to eat, baby?"

"Whatever it is, I want to cook it. I haven't had a

home-cooked meal in over two weeks unless I was at Lilah's house. Even yesterday with the girls all here we had pizza."

"We can cook together."

"You know how to cook?" She points her finger at me.

"I live by myself and like to eat, so I sort of have to, you know. I do watch the cooking network, so I'm basically a chef." I put the bottle of beer down beside me on the counter and move toward the fridge. "I also wash my own clothes and sometimes"—I look over my shoulder at her—"sometimes I make the bed."

"I knew you weren't perfect." She shakes her head, walking over to the counter and grabbing my beer and bringing it to her lips. "Who doesn't make their bed every day?"

"I'm just getting back into it," I tell her, looking in the fridge. "How do you feel about lemon chicken with potatoes and some corn?"

"You can make lemon chicken?" Her eyebrows go up. "If you can do that, I promise I won't say anything about you not making your bed."

"How is this, if you are going to be in my bed," I tell her, grabbing the chicken breast from the shelf, "I'll make the bed, baby." I walk over to the counter and place the ingredients on there. "Now, the question is, when are you going to be in my bed?" I wink at her as she groans, turning to wash my hands before I start opening drawers looking for a mallet. "So tell me about your day."

"Should I help you cook?" she asks, putting the bottle

of beer down. "I'll do the potatoes."

"Okay." I place the mallet down and then get three small bowls. I see that she has set up most of her dishes. Some of the drawers are empty, and she only has a handful of pots and pans.

"Things are all over the place," she mumbles as she tries to find things herself.

"This is what happens when you unpack while drinking." I cut the chicken down the middle.

"No one likes anyone who says I told you so, Caleb." She gets beside me as she cuts the potatoes in half and then in quarters.

"Depends on who you ask," I joke as I walk over to the sink to wash my hands before going to the pantry. "So did you lie in bed all day and think about me?"

"Yes." She drags out the s. "I lay in bed the whole day, wondering when you would be coming over. I was counting down the minutes and then the hours." I can't help but laugh as I grab the flour and then the breadcrumbs. "Come to think of it"—I walk out of the pantry with the stuff in my arms, finding her looking over at me with her knife down on the cutting board—"I don't know how I survived the day without you."

"Well, that's good to know." I put down the things and then lean over and kiss her neck. "Besides pining for me, what did you do?"

"I got an email." She turns back to her potatoes, and I look at her, waiting. "That is why I didn't eat anything all day," she says, her voice wary. "I found out that I have two cousins."

"Oh, really?" I look over at her.

"I mean nothing extraordinary like first cousins. But fourth cousins"—her face fills with a smile—"so I started building their family tree," she states. I stop doing what I'm doing and look over at her.

"How?"

"It's a long process. I found out that my great-great-great-grandmother was thirteen when she had her son, John, and she got married three years later. Now, this obviously could be wrong because who was actually keeping track in eighteen thirteen?" She takes a pull of the beer that we are now sharing. Her voice is getting animated while she continues her story. "So I thought, 'oh, this is easy, right? They only had one kid.' Wrong, John loved to spread his seed and populate the county because guess what?"

"I have no idea."

"He had twelve kids." She looks over at me with her eyes going big. "Twelve." Her voice goes even higher. "His son, William, was born in February, and his daughter was born in March. Which is strange because they both have the same mother, so, again, there could be errors on the dates if someone was having a bad day. Or you know when you get to work on a Monday but you forget it's a Monday and keep writing the date from the Friday before. I don't know how accurate this whole 'let's write it down in the book' is, but it's the only thing I have to go by."

I laugh at that last remark, but I'm so intrigued by everything she is finding out. "That's incredible," I say, and she shrugs her shoulder.

"I'll show you the whiteboard after dinner."

"The whiteboard in your room?" I ask. She rolls her eyes as I dip the chicken in the egg, then the flour, then back in the egg, and then in the breadcrumbs before placing it in the dish to go into the frying pan.

"I'll stay down here in the kitchen while you go up there and look at it."

"You are going to leave me alone in your bedroom?" I turn to grab a pan. "I might snoop." I step closer to her, seeing her chest rising and falling faster than it did a couple of minutes ago. Her eyes look down at the potatoes in front of her, trying not to pay any attention to me. But I can see how affected she is. "I might even try to find something that is purple."

Nineteen

SIERRA

"YOU ARE GOING to leave me alone in your bedroom?" He moves away from me, and I want to watch him, but I force myself to focus on what I'm doing in front of me. "I might snoop." He steps closer to me, his front very close to my side, and I try to ignore his smell that is now filling my senses. I look down at the cutting board with the potatoes waiting to be cut, but I know with one touch from him, I'll forget it all. "I might even try to find something that is purple."

I look over at him, his eyes light from joking with me. "I threw it away," I lie to him.

"You are lying." He tilts his head to the side and kisses my lips softly before turning back. "When you lie, you hold your breath after you say the lie."

I gasp, "I do not." I turn to face him as he walks over to the stove, putting the pan on it before looking for the oil. He finds it and puts it beside the pan before coming back to me and standing toe to toe with me.

"Do you want to go out on a date with me?" he asks. My heart soars in my chest, yelling, *Yes!*

"No," I refuse and breathe out heavily from my nose. "See—"

"Saturday," he presses, and I shake my head.

"I literally told you five seconds ago that I am not going to date you."

"Yeah, but you were fibbing." I roll my eyes at him as he walks over to the stove, and I don't bother answering him because I was fibbing.

I finish making the potatoes and go to the pantry to take out the air fryer. Seasoning the potatoes as he works with the chicken on the stove, I grab the beer when I start the air fryer and my work is done. I watch him with the chicken. "It smells good," my dumb mouth says before I can stop it.

"Wait until you taste it." He looks over his shoulder at me, a smirk on his face. I look over to the side until I can feel him look back at the pan. I turn back and watch his ass, and I can see myself gripping it in my hand and digging my nails into it. "What are you thinking about right now?" His words break into my thoughts, and I shake my head. "Whatever it is, your cheeks got pink."

"I was thinking about how I could make you cook for me and kick you out before we eat so I get it all to myself." He laughs. "Just going through different scenarios in my head." I bring the bottle to my mouth so he doesn't see I did, in fact, stop fucking breathing as soon as I said the lie.

I move around the kitchen, setting up two place settings at the island while he cooks lemon chicken. We sit side by side as I cut into the chicken with a lemon butter sauce. The minute it touches my tongue, I reach out and grab his forearm and moan. The tart from the lemon with the richness of the butter is amazing. "This is really good." I smirk over at him as I check the chicken.

"Not as good as the make-out session we are going to have after this." He leans over and kisses my cheek before going back to his chicken. "After I see your whiteboard." He sits up straight. "Wait, was that code for 'I want you to come to my bedroom and have your way with me'?"

I throw my fork down. "How did you know?" I push my stool away from the island. "Should I go up there and get ready for you to mount me?" The minute I say the words, his face grimaces.

"Never say mount me again"—he shakes his head and closes his eyes—"unless I'm on my back and holding my cock up for you, then you can climb aboard."

I take a deep breath to pretend that his words irritate me, but I swear my vagina convulses thinking of him naked on the bed, holding his cock. The images go over in my head like a movie. I pick up my fork to avoid looking at him, scared he'll see my cheeks are really pink because all I can see is him naked in my head. "So you went to visit home?" I ask him, taking my glass of wine and bringing it to my mouth to change the subject.

"Yup." He nods his head. "Went to show my parents that I'm still alive and healthy."

I laugh. "So why did you move away?"

He looks over at me. "Um."

"Is that too deep of a question?" I push him. "Okay, let's start slow. What really happened with your ex? I know that story you told me before was just sugarcoated, so tell me the real reason." I ask him and he doesn't answer me, and I gasp. "Oh my God, is that why you moved here? Did you find her with your best friend?" I put my hand on his arm. "Did she say it's not you it's her?"

He laughs. "No, it was really nothing like that." The minute he says that, my stomach tightens. "We were high school sweethearts."

"Aww," I say, "and then she dumped you." He glares. "Okay, okay, fine, tell me the story."

"Not really much to tell. I was captain of the football team."

I gasp. "You played football?"

He nods. "I did. I got a scholarship and everything." He tries to make it seem like it's not a big deal but something in his voice pulls at my heartstrings.

"No way?" I shake my head and smile.

"Yeah."

"Were you good?"

He laughs. "I was until I wasn't and it's just the way things go." His voice gets soft. "Went back home and I guess you can say that I settled." He looks at me. "Or at least that is what Amber kept constantly telling me."

"And do you think you did?" I ask him, turning to look down at my plate, moving around the food. Not really sure I want to know.

"I don't really. I had just gotten letdown from not playing football, not that it was my dream, but I thought I could have at least made it into the pros. Then I was home and I had a business degree and my dad told me to help him. Try and take over for him. Maybe this is where I would have always ended up. I guess we will never know. But when she finally resolved to the fact that this is what I was going to do, then she started harping on getting married. She probably didn't even want to actually get married; she was just following the lead of all of her sorority sisters. I"—he shrugs—"I just couldn't see forever with her and I knew that I would only be getting married once. So."

I swallow down the lump in my throat as I try not to make it sound that I feel sorry for him. "Hey, at least you had a backup plan."

"Not sure it was my backup plan," he admits, leaning back, "but I went with it."

"So how did you end up here?"

"Ms. Maddie's called in. I took the call, came here, and I don't know. I got a sense of my own person." He looks over at me. "It's not the best feeling in the world when you're taking over for your father and people are constantly comparing you to him. He's the best. But."

"I get it." I take a sip of wine.

"So," he says, "what about you? No boyfriend waiting for you at home?"

I snort. "Nope. The only thing waiting for me at home is two loving parents." I trail my voice, not sure what to say. "I feel really guilty."

"For what?" he asks me, and for the first time I admit it to him, to anyone besides me.

"I have these two amazing parents who love me and would die for me." I swallow the lump, not thinking this is where the conversation would have taken. "And here I am searching for two people who just dumped me in a box." I try and smile at him to make it as a joke and his hand comes up and holds my face.

"Looks like we both came here looking for something." He leans over and kisses my lips softly.

"What does your week look like?" He reaches for his glass of water, taking a sip and changing the subject.

"I have one client I have to finish for sure. I've already pushed her off once when I was moving." I cut my own piece of chicken. "Then I want to go to the sheriff's station." He looks over at me.

"For?"

"I want to know if they will share their files with me."

"Baby," he says softly, "it's a twenty-five-year-old cold case. I don't even think they have the file."

"Well, I'll find out." I look over at him.

"Okay, fine, I'll go with you."

"What?" I ask him. "Why?"

"Because I want to," he states, finishing his chicken. "Just tell me when you are going."

"I don't think that is a good idea."

"And I don't think it's a good idea that you go to the sheriff, who from what I've heard—"

"You mean town gossip." I finish my last bite.

"Whatever the fuck you want to call it. You are not going there by yourself, and if I find out you did, I'm going to turn you over my fucking knee"—I gasp—"and not in the good way either."

"You did not just say that to me," I accuse him, shocked.

He pushes away from the island. "Oh, I did, baby." He grabs his plate. "Now, we have to get this cleaned up, and then I have to take you upstairs"—he puts his plate in the big deep sink—"and look at your whiteboard." He uses quotation marks when he says it. "Then I'm going to make out with you. Then I have to get home. We start the barn project tomorrow, so I have to be there bright and early. Emmett is going to be a pain in my ass." I'm about to say something when he holds up his hand. "If you mention me dating Lilah one more time…"

"I'm just saying, maybe he's not keen on the fact you dated her either." I grab my own dish.

"I kissed her once." The thought makes the back of my neck heat.

"I know." I put my plate in the sink on top of his. He steps forward and his hand grabs my hip. "Also, you kissed her twice."

"And it was nothing like our kisses." He pulls me to him. "With you, I kiss you and I never want to stop. I walk into the room, and I see you, and the only thing I can think is, *when am I going to get to kiss you?* Fuck, I look at you and all I want to do is be next to you." I swallow down the lump that has somehow moved up from my stomach. "Think about that the next time you compare yourself to Lilah."

"I'm not comparing myself to Lilah," I defend myself.

"Good, you shouldn't since you would win every single time." He bends his head and kisses me. I think it's going to be a soft kiss, and that is how it starts out. Then his tongue slips out of his mouth and touches my lips, and my mouth immediately opens for him. His tongue rolls with mine as my body melts into his. "If you don't move away from me, I'm going to forget about cleaning up this kitchen."

"I don't know if I would be mad if we did that." I wrap my arms around his neck.

"Baby, you just got this kitchen. It'll take twenty minutes to clean it up." He looks around. "If you want, you can watch me and think about things I'm going to do to you with my tongue."

"You can't say things like that," I groan. "What if I get up after you leave and clean up?"

"Who says I'm leaving? Maybe I changed my mind and I'm staying." I swallow when he says those words. "We aren't going to be having sex until I take you on a proper date, but that doesn't mean I can't sleep over."

"Who says I'm going to go on a date with you?"

"Baby," he states softly, "Saturday night, you are going to get dressed up. I'm going to take you out to have dinner. I'm going to wine you and dine you, and then"—his voice goes lower—"then I'm going to bring you home and fuck the ever-loving shit out of you."

"Fine." I try not to smile. "If you put it like that, I'll go out with you."

He laughs. "Good. Now, are you going to let me clean the kitchen?"

"Ugh." I push away from him. "You were the one holding on to me and not the other way around."

"You always sass me." He shakes his head, walking to the stove and grabbing the pot. "I might have to think about ways to fill your mouth."

"Caleb," I snap his name out and stomp my foot, "do you want me to clean up the kitchen naked?"

"No," he retorts, and I take a step back, sort of insulted, "you don't have any curtains in this fucking house, and it's nighttime, and the lights are on. Everyone can see inside. Order fucking curtains, and then you can do it naked. If I can make a request, I'd like for you to do it naked and bending over. With your ass to me or your face, either works fine with me." I open my mouth to say something, but nothing comes out. I open it, close it, and then open it again. The only thing I can do is turn and stomp away from him. "I'll be up in ten!" he shouts from the kitchen, and I shake my head, wondering if maybe I can slam the door and lock him out. Then knowing I want to make out with him more than I want to prove a point.

I'm washing my hands when, ten minutes later, he comes up, his boots off, his head bent, and he's rubbing the back of his neck. "Hey," he says, walking right past me and toward my closet.

I follow him and watch him with his hands on his hips. "We can do some research during the week if you want." He looks over at me.

"You would do that?"

"One, I get to spend time with you, so I'll do just about anything, and two, I'm invested in this, so yeah, I'll do it."

"Okay, fine, I'll make out with you," I joke with him, but he stalks to me, wrapping his arm around my waist and picking me up off my feet while he takes me back to my bed. The two of us land on our sides while he attacks my mouth.

We spend most of the night making out. Fuck, his kisses, I'm pretty sure they can solve all my problems or at least a certain amount of them. He gets up at eleven. "I'm going to head home." I sit up on the bed. My shirt is halfway up from when he was feeling me up, the most he did was feel me up. Neither of us cross that line to get each other naked. "I'll close the door behind me." He looks down at me. "And I'll call you in the morning."

"Okay," I reply as he bends to kiss me again. I watch him walk to the bedroom door, grabbing his boots and slipping them on before walking out with a smooth wave before the front door slams shut. I collapse back on the bed, smelling him all over me and wanting him to come back and spend the night.

I'm thinking about doing that when the phone rings and I have to rush over to my desk to get it, seeing it's him. "Hello," I answer, putting the phone to my ear.

"Hey, baby, do you miss me yet?" he asks, his voice smooth, and it makes me shiver.

"No." I walk back over to the bed and fold my leg and sit on it at the edge.

"Well, I miss you."

"Is that why you were calling?" I lie back on the bed.

"No, I was calling to thank you for an amazing night, and I can't wait to see you tomorrow."

"Am I seeing you tomorrow?" I smile, knowing he can't see me.

I turn on my side, looking out the window. "You bet that sweet ass of yours you will be seeing me tomorrow."

I can't help but silently laugh. "We'll see about that," I say before I hang up on him and burst out laughing when his text comes through.

Caleb: Oh, we'll see all right.

Twenty

Caleb

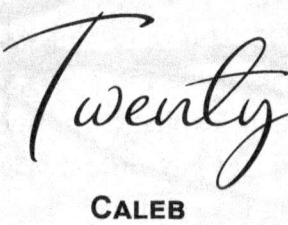

I JOG UP the steps to her front door and walk right in. The sounds of hammering and drilling fill the empty rooms. Theo looks up from what he's doing in the living room. "What the fuck are you doing here?"

"Is that any way to talk to the boss?" I put my hands on my hips. It's been three days since I've worked here. Not that I haven't been here. No, I've been here every single night to make dinner with her and then make out with her in her bed. Until I drag myself away from her and force myself to go home before I forget about fucking her before we go on our first date. Every single night I want to kick my own ass about making up the rule. But I know once I get in there, it's going to be worth it in so many different ways.

"It is when that boss is supposed to be at a barn, making sure that the roof comes off without killing someone." He moves the nail gun to the end of the shelf and starts to hit it down all along the shelf. The hissing from the gun drowns out the stomp of his boots as he finishes assembling the mantel.

"Roof is off," I confirm to him, "and everyone is in one piece." I look at the room, seeing that he's about done with the built-ins that Sierra mentioned that first time. I contacted my guy on the side and gave him a brief idea of what I wanted with the measurements and a picture of the wall, and he did the rest. I just hope that she is going to like it when she finally sees it, since I'm surprising her with it.

"So you decided to come and visit one of the job sites, or did you come for something else?" he asks, his eyebrows shooting up.

"I'm taking Sierra out," I tell him, and he chuckles. "This looks good." I do a chin jerk toward what he's doing. "Think they'll be finished by this week?"

"Probably." He takes a look at his work. "That is what I planned anyway. We're starting the bedrooms tomorrow, so I hope I timed it properly."

"Okay, sounds good," I confirm, looking toward the stairs. "I'll—"

"Yeah, yeah, get the fuck out of here. Some of us actually have to work and not just pretend," he says, chuckling and going back to work. I go up the stairs two at a time and find her door closed. I knock once before I open it and stick my head in, seeing her sitting at her desk. She turns in her white chair toward me, her face filling with a huge smile.

"You really aren't going to let me go at this alone."

She crosses one leg over the other placing her elbows on the arm rests. Her head tilts to the side and I can't help but smile.

"I really am not going to let you go there alone," I confirm to her. "You look beautiful." I tell her what I was thinking before smiling. "Now, are you ready?"

"Yes." She gets up, and I see she's wearing a pair of tight black jeans with a burnt-orange long-sleeved sweater that is tucked in the front but flows at the sides. "I'm ready."

"Are you forgetting something?" I ask her when she grabs her purse from the bed and walks over to me.

"Should I get a jacket?" she asks, and I smirk. She looks over at the window, then back at me. "It looks like it's nice outside. Is the sun deceiving?"

"You forgot to kiss me hello," I tell her, bending my head to the side to kiss her. One hand comes up to cup her jaw and the other wraps around her to bring her closer to me.

I sweep my tongue into her mouth before letting her mouth go. Her eyes flutter open. "Is that a thing now?" she asks, wiping her lip gloss off my lips before I slide my hand off of her waist and into her hand and turn to walk out of her room.

We walk down the steps hand in hand as we pass the living room. "We're out," I tell Theo, who just nods at me as I pull her out the door. I walk her over to my truck, opening the door for her.

"Oh, is this what to expect on our date?" she questions me as she gets in the truck. "The whole gentleman thing?"

"I'm always a gentleman," I remind her.

"Not really," she retorts and I gasp, putting my hands on my hips, "you made me do all the work yesterday."

"You jumped on me and straddled me. I thought my dick was going to explode in my pants." I point at her. "Do you know how painful that was?"

"That wouldn't happen if you let me take them off." She reaches for the door handle and slams the door in my face.

I shake my head and look up at the sky before walking around and getting into the truck. "Oh, also, guess who had another match today?" I look over at her. "A second cousin and he's young, so he probably has email, unlike my fourth cousin whose kids probably did it for her."

"Fingers crossed," I tell her. Another thing we've done in the last two days is try to eliminate all of John's twelve kids. Checking all the census records and then the marriage certificates is definitely cool. She also caved and hired a genealogist to see if they could help her.

We pull up at the sheriff's station and I get out, round the truck, and see her slam the truck door. "You okay?" I ask her as I see her shake both of her hands as if she's trying to fling something away from them.

"Yes or no. I don't know" "—she takes a deep breath, wiping her hands on the front of her jeans—"let's just go in there and get this thing over with."

"Or we leave and we can pretend that this never happened?" I give her a chance to turn around but she just shakes her head, so I slip my hand in hers and she doesn't take it out, so I bring it to my lips before I open the glass door with my free hand, holding it open at the top as she walks in.

We walk to the desk in the middle of the room with doors on both sides of the receptionist. "Hi," Sierra greets her cheerfully and I hold her hand tighter in mine. "I was wondering if there was someone I could talk to about a case from twenty-five years ago."

"I can maybe get someone for you." The receptionist turns to grab the phone in her hand, leaving it dangling. "Do you know what type of a case?"

"It would have been the abandoned child who was left at the fire station." I see something in her eyes click and then she quickly hides it, nodding at us and looking away.

"Sheriff Hadley," she says into the phone, "there is someone here about a Jane Doe case from twenty-five years ago." She looks back up at Sierra and me. Sierra looks down at her feet and I rub her thumb with mine. "He'll be right out," she tells us.

A couple of seconds later the sheriff comes out, wearing brown jeans and a white buttoned shirt, his gun holstered at his side. A cream-colored cowboy hat on his head, his beady eyes trained on us. "How can I help you two?" His voice is gruff and nothing about him screams helping the community.

"My name is Sierra," she starts, letting go of my hand and extending it to the sheriff, who looks at her hand for a second before taking it, and already I don't like him. "I'd like to ask you about this case," she says, opening her purse and taking out the newspaper clipping and handing it to him. He grabs it from her and reads it before looking back up at her. "That's me and I was wondering if there was a case file I could read."

"There isn't," he declares, handing her back the paper and he's about to turn around and head back to his office.

"How do you know if there is no case file?" I ask him, and his eyes go to mine. "You know every single case file you've ever had?" I watch him just look at her. "How isn't there a case file?" I ask him confused, "A child was left in a box."

"I remember this case exactly. The child was left *unharmed* in a box." His beady eyes stare into mine.

"Unharmed because they heard her crying, but it was cold." You can see he doesn't like to be spoken back to.

"Look"—he sighs and then his voice goes low and tight—"we did what we needed to do, which was take you to the hospital for a wellness check, and then called Child Protective Services. There was no need to do an investigation."

"So no one asked the hospitals if someone had given birth to a child and then just dumped their child off?"

"For all we know, you could have been birthed at home and then they discarded you there." His tone is tight.

"She wasn't discarded," I cut in and his eyebrows rise. "So basically, unless she died, you weren't doing an investigation." I nod and grab Sierra's hand. "Well, this answers your questions. Thank you for nothing." I turn and nod to the receptionist and then walk out with her behind me.

"This is why I didn't want you to come with me." She pulls her hand from mine.

"And why is that?"

"Because you went all protective on me and I didn't need it." She shakes her head and places the article in her bag.

"You're damn fucking right I was going to go all protective on you. That guy was a fucking idiot and he wasn't going to answer one fucking question you had."

"You don't know that," she says softly.

"Baby," I placate, pulling her in my arms, "he wasn't going to answer any question that you had."

"He didn't even try to look for who left me." She lays her head on my chest, wrapping her arms around my waist. "It's like no one fucking cared." Her voice quivers with emotion. "Well, I guess no one did care." I hear her sniffle and close my eyes, knowing if I knew who her parents were, I would probably punch the shit out of her father.

"Baby, you're killing me," I admit to her. "I don't know why they did it, but I have to believe that it was for a reason."

"Is being an asshole a reason?" She pulls away and looks up at me. I see her eyelashes wet with tears.

"I don't like to see you cry," I tell her, bringing my hand up to her cheek. "In fact, I'm going to say it's my least favorite thing in the whole world."

"Can you please stop saying all the right things?" She rolls her eyes and brings her forefinger up to her eye and uses it to wipe away the tear. "Then it makes me feel bad when I have to tell you things that will hurt your feelings."

I can't help but snort out a little laugh. "Good to know." I kiss her lips. "Now, let me get some food in you, and then I'll take you back home."

"Okay," she agrees softly as we walk over to the bakery and have lunch outside, sitting at the picnic table.

"Have you thought about hiring a private investigator?" I ask her when I take a bite of my donut.

"Not really."

"Why don't you reach out to one and see what they say?" She shrugs.

"I guess there is no harm in doing that," she concedes. "How does one look for a private investigator?"

I shake my head. "I have no fucking idea," I answer, making her throw her head back and laugh.

"That's the second sexiest thing that you do with your mouth," I tell her, and she stops laughing and smiles. "Actually, not really. It might be the fourth."

"The fourth?" She leans her elbows on the table. "What are the first three?"

"Well, the first sexiest thing you do with your mouth has to be when you moan out my name." She looks down at the table, shaking her head. "The second sexiest thing you do with that mouth is kiss."

"Okay, what's the third?"

I look around to make sure that it's just her and me. "The third sexiest thing you are going to do with your mouth is swallow my cock." Her cheeks turn a tint of pink. "Actually, that might be scratched up to number one." I close my eyes. "Fuck, I'm hard thinking about it."

"Caleb," she hisses and looks around, "you are not."

"Want to come over to this side and check?" I wink at her, and she rolls her eyes. "I can't fucking wait for our date."

"Who says we're going to have sex on our first date?"

I lean into her. "Technically, it's like our sixth date by then."

"How do you count that?"

"One was when I cooked you dinner on Sunday. Two was when I came over on Monday and we had dinner again, cooked by me. Yesterday, I brought burgers over."

"But you didn't cook for me."

"Still a date, I brought food. Tonight, we'll be having dinner, so that's four."

"I get it, I can count, but Friday, I'm busy."

"Really?"

"Yeah, really, I'm getting ready for the date, so I have to do certain things."

"You do those things on Saturday morning. I'm not giving up a make-out session so you can shave your legs."

"Caleb, it's more than my legs." She laughs.

I lick my lips. "Oh yeah, tell me what other parts you plan on shaving."

"I will not."

"Can I guess?" I whisper. "Does it start with a p and end with a y?"

"Nope."

I glare at her. "Liar." I point my finger at her. "Okay, we can leave now, my cock has gone down." I stand, and she laughs again.

"I didn't know we were waiting for it to deflate."

"Can we not talk about my cock and the word deflate in the same sentence?"

"We don't have to talk about your cock at all." She crushes her shoulder into my arm, and I hang my hand around her neck. "You're the one always talking about it."

"That's because you keep dreaming about it." She laughs as she slaps her hand on my stomach.

"Tonight, can we make out without our T-shirts on?"

"No." I shake my head and stop when we get to my truck.

"What? Why?" she asks when I open the door. "It's just skin."

"My cock also has skin, and if you take your top off, all I'll want to do is fuck your tits while I pinch those nipples." My eyes go to her shirt, then up again. "Bet I can make you come just from playing with them."

"Don't make fucking promises you can't keep, Caleb," she snaps angrily.

"You better not make any plans for Saturday night until Monday morning because you'll be naked the whole fucking time." I shut the door, her shocked face looking out the window. "The whole time!" I shout.

Twenty-One

SIERRA

THE PHONE RINGS as I'm sliding on my black leather miniskirt, and I look down to see it's Lilah calling. I don't know why, but I get nervous when I see her name. "Hey," I answer, pressing the green button and putting it on speakerphone.

"She lives," Lilah huffs out.

"I'm alive," I confirm to her. "Or we're both dead, and our ghosts have found each other."

"I would not be surprised in the least if we're ghost friends. But I'm going to have to hang around and haunt Emmett for the rest of his life, so you might have to be stuck here with me for a while."

"Why are we haunting Emmett?" I ask her as I zip up my skirt and look at my reflection in the mirror.

"Because I love him," she states, her voice sounding like I just asked the dumbest question. "Anyway, where the heck have you been? I've been calling you all week long."

"I know, I'm sorry." I hang my head. "It was a bit crazy this week and…"

"And you've been spending all your free time with Caleb." She snickers. "What is wrong with you?"

"I don't know," I admit, "I just feel—"

"Oh my God, it was a couple of dates. I have food in my fridge longer than I dated him," she groans. "So you need to stop this bullshit and tell me, did you guys do the deed?"

"No." I shake my head and look at myself in the mirror. "But tonight is the night, he's taking me on a date." I take a deep, deep breath. "A real proper date." I put my hand on my stomach to quiet the butterflies that have suddenly come on full force.

"Ohhhh, the tea is hot," she teases me.

I laugh at her. "That is not what that means. The tea is piping hot when you have gossip the other person doesn't know."

"You going on a date with Caleb is gossip I didn't have. I did have the gossip that he's at your house every single night."

"From who?" I gawk, shocked, before walking over to my shoe rack, deciding to take out the big guns tonight. The stiletto heels that kill my feet and pinch my toes but make my legs look sexy as fuck.

"From everyone who is watching," she announces as I slip a foot in one shoe and regret my choice already.

"That's creepy. But, yes, we've spent every single night together, making out and doing nothing else." I try not to groan out in frustration, but I fail.

"That has to be the longest foreplay of life."

"You are telling me this? I've never been so on edge in my life." I slip the other shoe on. "But tonight is the night, and I'm going to get lucky."

"Well, we can talk about it tomorrow. Let's meet for coffee."

"I can't," I tell her sadly. "Apparently, I'm going to be naked until Monday morning. His words not mine, but"—I cross fingers on both hands—"fingers fucking crossed he's serious."

"That's gross." She acts like she's going to throw up.

"You literally wanted to get together tomorrow to discuss it."

"Yes, but that's one night. Now I know it'll be all weekend long."

"I said fingers crossed," I remind her when the doorbell rings, and I look over my shoulder. "Got to go. My date is here."

"Get it, cowboy." Lilah laughs.

"Pregnancy has taken all your cool points with it."

"I know"—she pretends to cry,—"it's very sad. Yesterday, I called the vagina a cooter to Lucy, and she looked at me, and I thought she was going to vomit on my shoes."

"Oh, Jesus." I rush out of my bedroom, not having a chance to take a final look at myself before I hear the door open. "I'll call you Monday, and we can have an emergency meeting about getting your cool card back."

"Thank you," she replies. "Have fun tonight, and be

safe."

"Thanks, momma, now I gotta go. He's here, and I have to make a grand entrance that has him eating his tongue, or whatever that saying is," I whisper and then hang up on her.

"Baby!" he shouts from the door. I take a big deep breath before I start to walk toward the door. The click-clack from the heels sound on the hardwood floor as I close my eyes for one last time before making my grand entrance, of sorts. I tuck the phone in my purse, which only has my ID and lip gloss.

"I'm ready," I say when I get to the top of the U-shaped stairs, looking down at him. My mouth waters with how fucking hot he is. He's wearing black jeans that fit him just as perfectly as all the other ones. I take the steps down toward him, my eyes going to his package and seeing that it's something I'm going to enjoy unwrapping later. His long-sleeved black button-down shirt opens at the collar, showing me his neck. His sleeves are rolled up until the middle of his forearms, showing me his tats and the silver Rolex I've only seen him wear one other time.

"Holy fucking shit," he swears when I get to the bottom step and walk to him, "you can't go out like that." He points at me, and I look down at my own outfit. Did I go all out? Yes. Did I choose what I thought was my sexiest outfit that wasn't lingerie? Also yes. Did I want to forget he said he was taking me out on a date and come down naked wearing just the shoes? Also yes. Was I going to torture him until he snapped? You bet your fucking ass I was. "You can't go out in that."

I look down at the black leather miniskirt I bought a while ago, probably hoping for this moment right here. The slit on the side shows you even more leg. The white lace top leaves very little to the imagination, and if we were staying home, I would wear it with no bra underneath to really push his buttons. However, since he's taking me out, I paired it with a white satin bra. The long sleeves are cuffed at the wrists and then fall out around my fingers. "What's wrong with what I'm wearing?"

"Nothing, but I'm not okay with people using you to beat their cock when they go home." He shakes his head and licks his lips. He takes a step toward me, reaching out and pulling me to him. "We are going to be keeping those fucking shoes on later while I fuck you."

"Promises, promises," I grumble when I'm flush with him. With my heels, I don't have to move my head back to see him. I put my hands on his chest as I smell the musk of his cologne. His hands go to my ass and pull me even closer to him, feeling his hard cock on my stomach. "Is that something in your pocket or are you happy to see me?" I kiss his jaw before I nip it.

"We have to go, or else I'm going to forget about everything I said I was going to do and fuck you right here on the dusty fucking floor." He moves away from me, grabbing my hand and literally dragging me out of the house with me laughing the whole way.

He locks the door before turning and making his way down the steps, his hand still gripping mine. He opens the door of the truck, and when I'm about to take a step to get into the cab, he turns me and pins me against the side of the truck. I gasp out in shock, giving him enough time to cup my face with one hand, cup one ass cheek with the other, and slide his tongue into my mouth. The kiss isn't soft, it's hard and full of passion. We attack each other, our heads going side to side as we try to take the kiss even deeper than we are. This whole week leading up to this moment has been the longest week of my life. I felt like every single time he touched me, I would explode. It would be soft touches while we cooked together or even when we would make out in my bed, which we did a lot of. He kept it to the point that I wanted so much more, but he teetered on the edge, and I was fucking done with it.

"Let's get this date on the road," he urges when he lets go of my mouth, and I have trouble opening my eyes.

"Let's get that cock out of those pants and into me." I brazenly turn, cup his cock through his pants, and rub it up and down. It's the first time I've ever touched it and it's as big as I thought it was. "Shall we?" I wink as I grip the handle of the passenger side door before getting into the cab. "What are you waiting for?"

"I'm going to remember that later"—he sounds like he's growling—"after you beg me to let you come, and I deny you." He slams the door, and I watch him walk around the front of the truck and get in. "Ready?"

"Are you ready?" I ask, putting on my seat belt.

"Baby, I feel like I've been waiting for this day my whole fucking life," he declares, looking into my eyes. I wish I had a snarky comeback, but I don't. I have nothing except the pounding of my heart filling my ears.

I swallow when he pulls away from my house. "So where are you taking me?"

"I'll tell you where I'm not taking you," he states, turning when he gets to the end of the street, "and that is somewhere is where people can't see what's mine and only mine."

"Caleb." I shake my head, trying to laugh off his comment, but nothing comes out, except for the heaviness of my breath.

I look out the window at the trees going by. "In case I forget to tell you later"—I turn to him—"you know, because I'm going to be busy getting into your pants…" I laugh nervously. "This is the best first date I've ever been on."

He pulls to a stop. "There is more of that to come, baby." He puts the truck in park, and I'm so mesmerized by his gaze, I can't look away. "The way you feel right now, I'm going to make you feel it all the time." I nod, not sure my words would come out without my voice quivering.

He gets out of the truck, and I look out my window at a house. My eyes go big as I open my own door, and I'm about to step down when he's there to hold my hand while I do it. Nothing would ruin this date like me falling flat on my face. "I know I said I would take you on a date. And this is a date. But I wanted it to be intimate and, let's face it, no matter where we went, someone we know would be there, and I wanted it to be just about you tonight."

I shake my head. "You just want to make sure that your mouth doesn't ruin this date."

"Baby"—he wraps his arm around my waist—"my mouth is going to be so busy making you moan, there is no way it's going to ruin this date." He kisses me, and I want to bypass all the things he has planned and go straight to the bedroom.

He slides his hand in mine as we walk down the concrete pathway to his house. We walk up the three steps to his tan double door with two big windows. Its blinds are closed so you can't see in, but you can see a glow from the light he must have left on. I look to the left while he gets his keys out and see two rocking chairs in front of massive windows, their shades also closed, but you see darkness coming from them. He opens the door. "Welcome to my home." He holds out his hand for me to go in, and I smile as I step up and into his house and stop when I see what the glow was.

All along the right side of the wall are different-sized glass vases filled with candles. "Oh my," I say when he steps in behind me and closes the door.

His hand goes around my waist, pulling me to him as he bends his head and whispers in my ear, "I wanted it to be romantic for you." He buries his face in my neck, and I put my hand on his arm around my waist, turning to look at him. The way the candles light up the entranceway makes his eyes feel like home. "I wanted you to feel how honored I am that you went out on a date with me."

"I kind of didn't have a choice." I smile at him, trying to tame the way my heart is beating and not letting him see this is the most romantic thing anyone has ever done for me. No one has ever gone to the trouble with me. Sure, I've been on first dates, but no one has done this.

He slides his hand in mine. "You always have a choice." He moves my hand to his mouth, bringing it to his lips before he leans over and kisses me on the lips. He pulls me down the hallway, and we step into the great room, and I can't help but gasp.

On every available surface is flowers. All different shades of white, all kinds of flowers. It smells like a flower shop. The lights are very dim, but it's also the candles scattered around the room that gives it the romantic glow while soft music plays in the background. "This is a little bit of a—" I start, trying not to allow my voice to quiver as I let go of his hand and do a circle in the room with a big U-shaped couch. It looks cozy as fuck as it faces the fireplace that has flowers draped across it and hanging down on the sides, vases of water and candles mixed in. The big television over the fireplace is off, but you can just picture sitting down and watching a movie while you snuggle on the couch.

"It's too much, right?" He laughs, and I just shake my head. "I thought it was, but then I was like, maybe it isn't enough."

"It's enough." I smile. "It's perfect."

"The only thing perfect in this room is you," he states. He comes over to me and pushes the hair away from the side of my face, his fingertips trailing up my cheekbone. "You are the most beautiful woman I've ever met."

I put my hands on his hips, more to steady myself than

anything else. "You say that to all the girls," I joke with him and try to laugh, but the way my heart is beating and the way my chest tightens, it comes out in pants.

"I haven't said that to any other person than you," he assures me. His eyes stare into mine as he licks his lips, and I want him to kiss me more than I want anything else. "Are you hungry?"

I nod, and he turns and walks with me to the table set up between the couch and the big island in the kitchen. "Sit." He pulls out a chair. "Would you like some wine or champagne?"

"I think we should do champagne, don't you?" I ask. "Celebrate me getting the D, finally, after stringing me along all week long."

He throws his head back and laughs. I get up on my feet because I want to kiss the side of his neck that is exposed. His eyes widen when I stand and kiss him. "All week long, Caleb," I mumble, turning and pushing him back into the chair I just got out of. "It was torture." He falls into the chair, and his legs open for me to stand between them.

"You aren't the only one who was tortured," he replies as he looks up at me. I put my hands on the side of my thighs, moving my skirt up a bit so I can straddle him. His hands go to my ass when I sit down on him. I can feel his hard cock under me, and I'm done waiting.

"How much torture was it?" I ask before I put my hand on the side of his face and open my mouth to kiss him and swallow his words. My tongue slides in with his as we kiss. The kiss starts off slow, but then heats up about two seconds later just like it always does. His hands go from my ass and roam up to my back, pulling the shirt that is tucked in it out. His warm hands touch my back, making my hips press down into him.

He groans as I let go of his lips, moving my hand from his face, crisscrossing it in front of me and peeling the shirt off me. Leaving me in a white lace half-cup bra that really doesn't hide anything. "Fuck," he hisses, one of his hands going to my ass while the other one pushes the cup down, and he holds my tit before bending his head and taking a nipple into his mouth. I place my hand behind me on his thigh before I grind into him. "I wanted to take my time," he says when he lets go of my nipple to roll it.

I put my forehead on his. "I think we've gone slow enough, don't you?"

His hand moves from my ass to the other side as he pulls the other cup down, holding my tits on the sides as his thumbs move over my nipples softly, making them achy. "I don't want to rush you."

I pant out as I grind up and down on his covered cock. "You aren't rushing me."

I run my hands up and down his chest, feeling his heart beating as fast as mine. "I don't think you understand this, Sierra. There will be no one else after me." His words drain the air from my lungs. "Not one other person will touch you like this again."

The back of my neck tingles, as well as my whole body, when I grip his shirt in my hands. I move it up his chest and pull it over his head, tossing it to the side where my shirt is. "I've never seen you without your shirt," I tell him, ignoring what he just said, "but my fingers know every inch of you." I kiss down his chest, then slowly move off his lap. "Stand up for me," I ask, and he does, and I finally take in all that is Caleb, all the ridges of his body. The way his chest is defined, but not too much. It's just fucking perfect, like him. His arms are covered in tattoos all interconnected. An angel on his forearm and then, on the other side, the picture of a football from when he was in college. His tattoo on the right side of his chest with the saying, "A man is not finished when he is defeated. He is finished when he quits." My nails drag down his chest to his belt. He takes a step back. "Caleb," I say, "do you want me?"

"More than I want my next breath," he whispers, and I stare at him as my fingers work his belt. Our chests rise and fall as if we are racing. "I don't think—"

"You don't think what?" I ask as I unzip his pants, itching to get my hands and mouth on him.

"I don't think that I can." He trails off when my fingertips move over the elastic to his boxers.

"There will be no one else after me," I repeat the words he said to me not too long ago. "Not one person will touch you like this again. It's going to be just me." I step into him and run my nose on his bearded jaw. "Are you okay with that?"

"Take what you want, baby." I smirk as I push his boxers and jeans over his hips.

"I want you to sit back down and watch me suck your cock." He pushes his pants all the way down to the floor, kicking off his boots and then stepping out of them, leaving him buck-ass naked. I decide we are going to spend the whole fucking weekend naked. "Oh my." My eyes trail his thick thighs right up to his cock, making my mouth water. "Sit." He does, and I crawl to him. Taking the base of his cock in my hand, he hisses. "Answer me"—I move my hand up and down, his cock is so thick I can't close my hand—"how many times did you come this week thinking about me?" I watch him as I take the tip of his cock into my mouth, and his head goes back.

"Every fucking day, twice a day," he hisses out as I lick him from the base to the tip. "Twice today."

"Twice?" I ask him before I take half of his cock into my mouth, letting it go and moving my hand up and down.

"Woke up hard thinking of you riding my face," he informs me as I swallow half his cock again. My mouth strains to open around him. "Then took a shower before I came to get you and thought about sinking my cock into you." I moan around his cock, the vibration making his hips jerk up and pushing his cock deeper into my mouth, hitting the back of my throat. "Touched the back of your throat," he says to me as I work my hand and my mouth. "Got to open it up so I can slide down it."

"I don't think I can take you all in," I admit, "but I'm going to fucking try." I try to take him deeper into my mouth, spreading as wide as I can as his hips move with me now.

"Attagirl, swallow me down." I grip the base of his cock tighter in my hand, moving it frantically up and down. "I'm not going to last," he blurts, and I look up at him, watching his jaw get tight. "If you don't want me to shoot down that throat of yours, you better move." When I don't move, I see his eyes twinkle. "Going to come down your throat now, and then spend all night covering you in my cum." I lose his eyes as my pussy clenches. "Every inch of you will have my cum," he grits between clenched teeth while the first rope of his cum hits the back of my throat, and I swallow whatever he has to give me. I only let go of his cock when he's done, and his body relaxes in the chair. I stand and step between his legs, but he pushes me away only for him to stand and wrap his arm around my waist, picking me up and turning me. "Time for me to eat my meal"—I try not to smile—"bed or table?"

I look at the table that has all the decorations on it. "Bed would be easier."

"Yeah," he agrees, walking through his house, "I'll fuck you on the table later."

"Don't make me promises you can't keep, Caleb." I push his buttons as he walks back toward the great room and to his bedroom. I look over his shoulder and gasp.

The bedroom is masculine with the king-sized bed in the middle, but he has fairy lights hanging from the ceiling all around the bed. "Wanted to fuck you under the stars," he tells me, "this was the easiest way." I'm about to say something to him but he throws me on the bed. "Spread your legs. I'm about to make you see a whole lot of stars, baby."

Twenty-Two

Caleb

"NEED YOU NAKED," I tell her when I step to the side of the bed and see her get up on her elbows, "or with your skirt around your waist, either way."

"I want to feel all of you on me." She sits up and bends her hand backward to the clasp of her bra as she unclips it, tossing it to the side before lying down on her back. She lifts her hips as she reaches to the side and unzips the skirt before she discards it. "As much as I want to get your cock into me"—she does the same with her lace panties, tossing them over, and she's finally naked in my bed—"I'd like to feel your mouth on me."

"Fuck," I groan, watching her lie there on my covers, her feet on the bed and legs open for me.

"Put your money where your mouth is, Caleb." She bends one arm and props it under her head. "Make me see stars."

I put one knee on the bed before moving between

her legs. My hand comes out and runs through her slit. "Already wet for me." I watch her eyes close as my fingers graze her clit. "How many times did you play with yourself thinking about me?" I move my middle finger in slow circles around her clit.

"None." She moves her hips up a bit, wanting more. "I was saving it all for tonight."

"So you didn't play with yourself?" I ask, rubbing my finger down and sliding my middle finger inside her. The wetness makes it easy to bury it all the way to my knuckles. She heaves out, "Not once did you fuck yourself thinking about me?"

"Not this week." She opens her legs even wider. "I was waiting for you to make me come."

"Is that so?" I ask, taking my finger out of her and sucking it in my mouth. "You taste like what heaven would taste like." I bend my head and slide my tongue through her slit until the tip of my tongue flicks her clit. "Fucking heaven." I get down on my stomach and devour her pussy, sucking it into my mouth. I hold back her legs as I watch her face while I lick her pussy, until I suck her clit into my mouth. Her back arches off the bed. "You're going to watch me make you come with my mouth and my fingers," I tell her before sliding two fingers into her, "then you are going to watch your pussy take my cock."

"Yes," she pants as I move my fingers in and out of her as I suck her clit. She gets up on her elbows to watch me.

"Your pussy is gripping the fuck out of my fingers." I feel her G-spot. "It's going to strangle my cock." I move up, my tongue trailing to her nipple, taking it in my mouth as I fuck her with my fingers before moving back down. My tongue slides in with my fingers, tasting her wetness on my tongue. I bite down on her clit while she moves her legs back and tilts her hips toward me.

"Caleb," she moans as she moves her hands to her tits, where she pinches her nipples, "I don't think I'm going to—"

"You're going to come on my fingers," I command, feeling her pussy get tighter and wetter. "Drip down my wrist." My finger runs over her G-spot. "You're going to come, and then I'm going to fuck you." We both groan. My tongue flicks her clit. "I can't wait to sink my cock into you." That's the last thing I tell her before she explodes onto my fingers, her pussy pulsating around my fingers as she drips down my hand. "That's my girl." My fingers ride out her orgasm until her elbows give out, and she lies back. I kiss her once before getting on my knees. "Condom."

"I'm on the pill, and I'm clean"—she grips my cock—"please tell me—"

"Got my physical before I came to town," I grind between clenched teeth as she rubs my cock up and down her slit. "Never been without one, though."

"Good, first time for both of us." She places me at her entrance. "Fuck me, Caleb."

I groan, moving her leg over my shoulder. "I want to get deep into you." I put my hands beside her side as I look down at my cock. "Watch your pussy take my cock," I tell her as her eyes fly between us, and we both watch as I slide my cock into her so slow it's agony. "Fuck, you have me like a vise."

"Enough with the teasing"—she moves her hips—"and fuck me like you promised to fuck me."

"So fucking greedy." I pull out and slam back into her as my mouth covers hers. "Your pussy was made for me," I declare and all she can do is pant.

"Good, now fuck it good," she demands, and I lose control. I wanted to go slow, wanted to take my time, but I don't. I slam into her over and over again as hard as I can, the sound of skin slapping filling the room. "I'm going to come," she states as if I can't feel her.

"I know." I look down at her pussy, her finger now playing with her clit. "Need to ask me permission to touch *my* clit," I scold her.

"Can I touch *your* clit so I can come all over your cock?" She barely gets the words out before she explodes all over me.

"Fuck, I'm going to come," I tell her as I try to keep it at bay until she's done before I pull my cock out of her and come on her landing strip. Her eyes go wide as I empty on her.

"Why did you do that?" she asks, looking down at me.

"So I can do this," I tell her, taking my cum and rubbing it all over her pussy. Side to side, down and into her before coming back up and rubbing both of us into her. "Next time, it's your tits." I bend down to kiss her mouth, turning her to the side. Her chest crushing against mine as I slide my tongue into her mouth. Her leg hooks over my hip, and I can feel the heat from her pussy. I move my hips and slide back inside her again.

"Already"—she lets go of my lips—"umm, is that normal?" I bury myself inside her. "Did you take anything?" I laugh as she snuggles into my neck.

"I've been waiting for this for the whole week." I pull out and then slide back into her. "Thinking of all the ways I was going to fuck you."

"That's interesting"—she meets my thrust—"me too." She pushes me so I'm on my back. "And this was one of them." She puts her knees beside me, my hands going to her ass, and then I bend to suck her nipple into my mouth as she rides me. "It's so good," she pants as she rises and then falls down on me, both of us groaning out, when she moans, "Feel so full."

"Take what you need, baby," I urge her. She moves her hands behind her, putting them on my knees as she lifts up and puts her feet flat on the bed.

"Now you watch," she demands as she lifts her hips up and down on my cock.

One of my hands comes up, and I suck the thumb into my mouth before moving it to play with her clit. "Open for me to play with you at the same time you take my cock." I move my hand down into her slit, taking more of her wetness before running it back up to her clit. "Every single time I touch your clit, your pussy clenches me." She wants to say something to me, but she is too far gone. She rides my cock as if it's the last thing she'll do in her whole life. Up and down, her pussy getting tighter and wetter with each rise and fall. She comes twice before I grab her by her hips and take her off my cock. "On your back," I order, and she does as I say. I straddle her chest, pinching her nipple, while my legs push her tits together so I can fuck them. "That's my girl." I smirk at her. I fuck her tits until I aim for them and come on them. "That was fucking hot," I state, my hands coming up, but she pushes them aside as she takes my cum and rubs it into her skin. "Fuck, I just came twice, and my cock is still rock hard."

She licks her fingers clean from my cum before sliding out from between my legs. "I'm going to need some food." She moves off the bed, and I'm assuming she's going to cover herself up, but she heads straight for the door.

"Do you want a robe?" I ask, and she stops, looking over her shoulder at me.

"How are you supposed to fuck me if I bend over if I'm wearing a robe?" She winks and then walks out of the room.

"Yes," I shout, "how indeed?" Hearing her laughter, I get off the bed and head to the bathroom to clean up.

I'm making my way into the kitchen when I see her moving around in it. "You look good here in my house."

"That's only because I'm naked." She looks over her shoulder at me. "I'm sure if I was dressed…"

I stop beside her, pushing her hair over her shoulder and bend to kiss her clavicle softly. "Never had a woman in my kitchen before." She rolls her eyes at me.

"I find that hard to believe." She places one hand on my chest.

"Not like that. I've had women in my house before. But not one that I wanted to cook for," I say, picking up her hand and kissing the inside of her wrist. "This is intimate. It's domestic. Walking into the kitchen and I saw you and for the life of me it's like you've always been here. Like you were born to be here. It feels like we've been doing this forever." I wrap a hand around her waist and pull her to me. "So while there have been women in my house. It's never this. Never like this."

"You never cooked for anyone?"

"No." I shake my head. "It was always a night out. Or they would come over after."

"So a booty call." She laughs. "That is so, so romantic."

My hand moves from her waist to her ass. "Maybe I was more closed off than I thought I was."

I smirk at her as she kisses my neck and moves away from me.

"I'm glad I got to open you up." She winks at me, taking one of the grapes and popping it into her mouth.

"So how many men have you cooked for?" I ask her with a glare, and I don't even know if I want her to answer me or not. "We talk about me all the time. What about you?"

She laughs. "I did cook for this guy one time." She holds up her hand and the glare gets even more glarey. My eyes into slits so much I can barely see out of them.

"We were dating for about six weeks. He always took me out and finally he asked me to cook for him."

"He had to ask you to cook a meal for him?" My interest piqued.

"He did." She nods. "I think I was twenty. I don't even know but I do know that I knew how to cook two things perfectly. Ramen noodles."

I bust out laughing. "You mean the noodles that you put in water and then empty the packet of flavor?"

"I sometimes used to add frozen veggies to that." She folds her arms over her chest. "Anyway, second thing was." I wait for her to say something gourmet like steak and baked potatoes or something. What I'm not expecting her to say is "mac and cheese."

"Like homemade, grate the chest and do a roux or like blue box, pour noodles in and add butter and milk with the fluorescent cheese?"

She slaps her hand on the counter. "There is nothing wrong with that mac and cheese," she says angrily. "Anyway, according to him, a woman is supposed to dazzle him in the kitchen, and well, let's just say there was no dazzle, so he ghosted me." I open my mouth. "For three weeks until I ran into him in a bar and confronted him and his new girlfriend."

"Of course you did." I grab her hips, pulling her to me.

"I wasn't just going to let him get away with it, Caleb!" she shrieks. "He broke my heart."

"He broke your heart?" I ask her and she rolls her eyes now.

"No, but he bruised my ego." She pushes away from me. "So it's the same thing." She turns, going to the fridge.

"Not the same thing at all." I watch her. "So how did

you learn to cook?"

"I took a couple cooking classes." She shrugs, and my eyes go to her ass. My feet moving to her, taking her ass in my hand and seeing her eyes lust over. "You better stop looking at me like that or I'll forget I need food, then fucking," I tell her.

"I don't think I'm that hungry now anyway," she says, dropping to her knees in the middle of my kitchen.

"IF THIS DOESN'T scream walk of shame," Sierra deadpans when she gets out of my truck the next night, "I don't know what does." She's wearing exactly what she was wearing when I picked her up here the night before.

I shake my head, getting out and making my way to her, sliding my hand in hers. We've spent the last thirty hours having more sex than I thought was humanly possible. If we weren't fucking, we were sleeping and vice versa. It wasn't just me; she wanted it as much as I did. "This wouldn't have happened if you stayed at my house until tomorrow."

"Oh, because coming home on a Monday morning wearing a leather skirt and lace top with you doesn't scream I got banged all weekend long." She looks over at me as she squats down to pick up the stack of papers at her door.

"I wasn't the only one who did the banging." I put my hands on her hips and kiss her neck, loving that she smells of my body wash. "You banged me just as many times."

"I did, didn't I?" She lets us into her house. "Got to say though, I thought I'd have to ice my vagina after that one time."

"You said you were fine." I put my hands on my hips as she walks toward the kitchen, putting the papers down.

"I was fine, but your cock is like a miniature baseball bat." She snickers as she looks through the papers and sees a white envelope with her name typed in bold black letters in the middle of it. She turns it over and then looks at me before sliding her finger under the flap and ripping it open. She takes the white paper out that is folded in three, putting the envelope back down before unfolding it and then looking back up at me.

"What is it?" I ask, and she turns the paper toward me with the same typed letters from the envelope. "Stop looking."

I look at the letter, then at her, seeing her eyes going back to the letter before she says, "It seems they don't want to be found."

Twenty-Three

SIERRA

I WATCH HIS eyes read the letter I just read before he looks back at me, and I quickly look back down at the letter, trying to calm myself down. "It seems they don't want to be found."

"Baby," he says softly, and I fold the letter back and put it in the envelope, before tearing it in half and walking over to the trash bin and tossing it inside.

"No," I say, shaking my head, "no, fucking no, Caleb."

"But—" His voice goes low, and I look at him.

"I deserve to know who I am," I tell him.

"You are beautiful, amazing, independent"—I roll my eyes at him—"sassy, and a pain in my ass sometimes." He comes to me and takes me in his arms. "You are strong and fierce and you suck a mean—"

I put my hands on his mouth. "I don't think I can repeat that to anyone when they ask me what I'm good at."

He glares. "If you do, I'll have to put you over my shoulder and rush you to the courthouse and marry you." I think my eyes about come out of my sockets as he kisses my nose. "Unless you'd be willing to come with me."

"Are you insane?" I push away from him, but he only tightens his arms around me even more.

"That's why I'll have to carry you over my shoulder," he jokes with me and buries his face in my neck, and I sink into him, feeling his heat all around me.

"I'm not going to stop."

"I know." He kisses my neck. "It's probably the grouchy sheriff."

"Whoever it is, I'm not going to stop." I lay my cheek on his head, trying to brush off the letter, but deep down inside, I'm freaking out.

"Let's get ready for bed," he mumbles, grabbing my hand and turning off the light.

"You're sleeping over?" I ask as he walks up the steps with me trailing him.

He turns on the lights in my bedroom, letting my hand go. "I'm not just going to drive you home and make you do the 'walk of shame' and then leave." He uses his fingers to do the air quotes. "If people will shame you, I might as well spend the night so they can really know we banged."

I clap my hands together, laughing. "We could just be sleeping."

"We could"—he kicks off his shoes—"but we're not going to be." He winks at me before he bends one arm, grabbing the back of his shirt, ripping it over his head, and tossing it to the side. The minute I see his chest and tattoo, my stomach gets that flutter. At first, I thought it was because I didn't really eat, but then the same thing happened every time I saw it. He's, without a shadow of a doubt, the best I've ever had. I can't get enough of him, and from the way we went at it the last day and a half, neither can he.

"Well, it's good to know I'm going to get lucky tonight." I walk to him, putting one hand on his stomach, the heat of him soaring through me before I kiss him. "And maybe tomorrow before you leave." I kiss the side of his neck before walking into my walk-in closet. He doesn't follow me as I undress and put my stuff to be dry-cleaned aside before grabbing a pair of a dark blush-pink satin shorts and matching tank top.

I walk back to the bathroom, turning on the faucet and doing my skincare routine. When I walk back into the bedroom, his clothes are thrown on the bench in front of the bed and he's sitting down with his back to the headboard as he flips the channels on the television. "Comfy?" I ask, pulling the covers back and getting into bed.

"What the fuck are you wearing?" I look over at him as I fluff my pillows to lie against.

"My pj's." I look and lie back as I turn to watch the television and see what he's stopped at.

"Why?" I look back over at him, seeing the perplexed way he's looking at my top and then back up at me. "If we're in bed together, it has to be naked."

"Is that a rule?" I ask. "You're not naked." I reach out

under the blanket, thinking I'm going to encounter his cotton boxers, but instead, my hand lands on his hard cock.

"Naked." He tosses the remote to the side of the bed before covering me and pushing me on my back. "How am I supposed to just slide into you if there is a barrier?"

I smile at him, raising one of my hands up to touch his face. "Did anyone ever tell you how beautiful you are?"

"Well, not besides my parents, who have to say that because they made me." He bends to kiss the tip of my nose gently. "I've been called hot and all that, but never beautiful."

"Well, you're hot also," I confirm as he smiles back at me, "but you are beautiful."

"I figured I would have to be to land the most beautiful girl in town." He kisses me, his tongue sliding in with mine. My legs open for him as he plants himself in the middle of them. "This is why you have to be naked," he explains when he lets go of my lips and moves the kisses down to my neck. "I could have slid right in."

"I will never come to bed with you with clothes on," I declare as his hands frantically move to take off the satin pj set I'm wearing, leaving me naked. He wastes no time sliding into me. My back arches up as my legs wrap around him as if he was made for me. "Yes."

"See?" he says, resting his forehead on mine as he fucks me.

"You were right." I hold on to his sides as he moves into me faster. "You were so right." I bite his jaw, and ten minutes later, I've come five times, and he's just come on me again.

"You know that I shower, right," I deadpan once he's rubbed it into me, "and it gets washed away?"

"Yeah"—he gets out of the bed, and his cock is hanging sideways, still at half-mast—"but until then, you have my mark on you."

I shake my head, getting out of bed with him. "That makes no sense."

"To you because you aren't a guy, you don't get it." He slaps my ass as we make it to the bathroom, where I open the shower door before starting the water, then closing it.

"Men are weird," I mumble, watching him lean against the counter and fold his arms over his chest and cross his feet at the ankle. "Women don't do any of this."

He laughs. "You forget, I grew up with two sisters." He mentions his sisters as I open the shower door again and check the water to see if the temperature is right, before stepping in. "You guys might not leave marks, but they're always there."

"Like how?" I turn and let the water cascade around my back.

"Showing up by accident where we are," he relays, and I roll my eyes.

"That's called stalking"—I point at him—"and I have never done that."

"But you would with me." He pushes off from the counter and comes to the shower. "Although, you wouldn't really have to because if I'm out, you're with me."

"Not if it's boys' night." He steps in, and I move out of the way so he can get some water on him.

"What if I want you there?" he asks softly. "Not the whole time, but what if it's boys' night, and I wanted you to come by and see me, would you?"

"Probably not," I reply, even though my head screams yes at the same time I say the words.

"But if you did, you would come in and kiss me, wouldn't you?" He grabs the loofah from the hook that is hanging and puts shower gel on it. "So everyone would know I'm yours."

"I could not kiss you and then you would be free for the pickings," I joke with him, earning me a glare, "and so would I."

"Trust me"—he stands in front of me—"everyone is going to know you're mine."

"Relax, there's no need to duel at dawn for me," I joke with him, making him laugh. He washes me down and I wash his back before sliding into bed naked.

I wake up when his alarm rings, my eyes fluttering open as he reaches over and turns it off. "What time is it?" I ask from my side of the bed.

"Seven thirty." He tosses the cover off himself and I turn on my back, stretching as I watch his ass walk to the bathroom.

"Can I wear a robe to go downstairs and make coffee, or do you want me to do that naked?" I ask him, and he glares at me over his shoulder, the sleep still in his eyes. "I'm just asking, I don't know the rules."

I get up and grab a robe from my office chair before

walking downstairs to the kitchen and starting the coffee. Ten minutes later, he's walking down the steps dressed in his clothes from yesterday as I take the milk out of the fridge.

"Do you want some breakfast?" I ask, and he grabs the cup of coffee I hand him, shaking his head and taking a sip. "Aren't you going to be hungry?"

"I'll be okay until lunch," he assures me at the same time as the front door opens, and we both look over to see Theo walking in.

"Well, well, well." He looks from me to Caleb. "I see the date is still going strong."

I can't help but laugh, grabbing my own cup of coffee and bringing it to my lips. "Do you want coffee?" I ask Theo.

Caleb snaps out, "No," taking another sip of his coffee. "You make coffee for me and me only. He can make coffee for himself if he wants coffee."

"That's rude," Theo says. "What if I wanted her to make me coffee?"

"She can't make you coffee. She's already making me coffee," Caleb grumbles, and I gasp.

"Oh my God, is this some sort of 'you can't touch her she's mine' talk?" I ask, making them both laugh.

"I know you're his," Theo states. "Everyone knows that you're off-limits." I open my mouth in shock. "Why do you think no one makes eye contact with you?"

"I thought they were just scared of me." I put my mug down. "What did you say to them?"
"Didn't have to say anything to them." He comes to

stand next to me. "I fired one guy for overstepping, and then I was here day and night."

"I thought that was to finish the job." I look at him and then Theo, seeing him shaking his head, looking down, and laughing. "Good to know." I grab my cup. "Now, I'm going to go up and get started with my day." I tilt my head back and he bends to kiss my lips.

"I'll call you later, baby," he says softly.

"Maybe I'll answer," I threaten him, "or maybe I won't." I walk past him and then Theo. "Please make yourself at home."

"He's not going to do that either!" Caleb shouts at my back as I walk upstairs to my room. Ten minutes later, I'm sitting at my desk, still in my robe, when he comes into the room.

"Okay, I'm leaving," he informs me, and I look over my shoulder at him coming to me.

"Yeah, you said that already," I remind him.

"I know, but I didn't get a proper goodbye." He bends his head and kisses the ever-loving fuck out of me. "Now, it's goodbye." He winks before he walks out of the room, and a couple of minutes later, I'm touching my lips where his kiss still lingers.

I don't have a chance to sit around and think about it when my phone rings, and I see it's my mother calling. "Hey, Mom," I answer, putting the phone on speaker as I get up and walk to my closet to get dressed.

"Hey, sweetheart, did I catch you at a bad time?" she asks.

"No, just getting ready for the day."

"What have you been up to?" she asks, and I can tell she's nervous about the question.

"I've met the fire chief on duty where I was left. I also did a DNA test and found out that my great-great-great-grandfather had twelve children, so that will be a big family tree to work through." I don't tell her about the note telling me to stop searching, not really wanting to worry her.

"No closer relatives?" Her voice is soft and she sounds sad for me.

"Sadly, no," I reply, slipping on a pair of loose jeans, then searching for a shirt and finally grabbing a long-sleeved cream one.

"I do have a list of hospitals and private clinics in the area, and I think I'm going to reach out to them. I had to have been born somewhere."

"I'm just worried," she confesses to me. "I don't want you to get hurt or feel like you aren't wanted or loved." I hear her sniffle.

"I've been thinking about it the past couple of days"—I pick up the phone—"and just because I find my birth parents doesn't mean I have to go and meet them. Maybe it's going to be okay just knowing that I know."

"Whatever you decide to do," she encourages, "we will be there supporting your every move."

"Thanks, Mom." I close my eyes. "I love you."

"Not as much as I love you," she returns with a lightness to her voice.

The conversation doesn't last much longer since one of my clients calls me. I work past lunch, and finally, at three o'clock, I take out the pad of paper I made with private clinics on it first.

Two of the four are out of business, so I will make a note to see if I can find any information about them before I dial the third. The receptionist answers with a cheery voice. "Hi, I'm wondering if you could help me," I say, nervously tapping my finger on my desk. "I was given up for adoption twenty-five years ago and was wondering if you had any records of births from that year."

"Those are confidential," she says, "but you can go to the county office and ask for the records."

"Thank you so much," I reply and disconnect the phone with her, searching up the county records office and then dialing the number. I listen to the woman answer the phone before I speak, "Hi, I was wondering how I would be able to get the birth records from September twenty-fifth, twenty-five years ago."

"You make your request through email," she answers. "It might take a day or so for someone to get back to you." She goes on to give me the email address, and by the time we hang up, the email has already been sent.

The phone rings as soon as I hang up with her, and I see it's Caleb. "Hey," I say, putting the phone to my ear.

"Hey," he replies and I hear the truck door slam. "I got an emergency call and I might be really late."

"Oh no." I try not to sound disappointed. "Everything okay?"

"Yeah, there's flooding in someone's basement, so we have to head over there and drain it," he explains. "Not sure how long I'll be."

"Why don't you do what you need to do and then go home, and we'll see each other tomorrow?"

He groans, "I don't want to, but I also don't want you waiting up for me." I smile. "I'll come by tomorrow morning bright and early."

"Oh goodie," I joke with him, "I can't wait." I hang up the phone and decide to make a frozen pizza and get into bed.

I drift off to sleep around ten, maybe even earlier. I don't even know how long I've been asleep before the sound of a window breaking wakes me up, and then the sound of a thud on the floor. I throw the covers off me as I get up and slip my pink slippers on, grabbing my phone and rushing to the stairs. The front window has a huge hole in it, and when I look into the empty room, I see a brown object in the middle of it. My legs move before my head can stop them, shaking as I make my way to the object, seeing it's a rock when I get closer. My hand comes out and picks it up, seeing the words "LEAVE" spray-painted in red. The rock falls out of my hand and lands with a thud in the middle of the floor where I just picked it up from.

My hands shake as I pull up his number and call him right away. He answers after half a ring. "Sierra," he says my name, with worry in his voice.

"They threw—" My voice hitches. "Someone threw a rock through my window."

Twenty-Four

CALEB

MY PHONE RINGING in the middle of the night has me springing up in my bed. Nothing good comes from the-middle-of-the-night phone calls. My heart speeds up with a million different scenarios running through my head. My parents are number one. When I see it's Sierra, I'm already out of bed when I press the green button. "Sierra," I say her name with worry in my voice.

"They threw—" Her voice hitches and I feel like my body has turned to stone. "Someone threw a rock through my window." Nope, I was wrong. That sentence makes my body turn to stone and fill with rage at the same time.

"I'm coming." I tuck the phone between my shoulder and my ear. Rushing around to my chest of drawers and pulling out a pair of jeans. "You are going to hang up the phone with me and call the police." I can hear the whimper coming from her side of the phone. "I'm on my way. I want you to call me back after you get off the phone with the police."

"Okay." Her voice is shaky. "Okay."

"I'll be there in ten," I tell her as she disconnects, and I call Theo as I slide on a T-shirt.

"What?" he answers with a grumble.

"Someone threw a rock through Sierra's window," I inform him as I put on my socks and then my boots.

"Ugh," he says, and I can hear him moving on his side. "Meet you there. Try not to kill anyone until I get there, please." I grab my keys and a baseball hat before rushing out the door.

She calls me right back at the same time that I'm pulling away from the driveway. "Baby," I say and all she can do is cry.

"I'm okay," she says, clearing her throat. "I'm just."

"I know, baby," I tell her. "Where are you?"

"I'm in my bedroom."

"Is the door locked?" I ask her and she gives me a hmm. "Okay, I'm around the corner," I tell her. "The police are right in front of me. I'm going to let you go," I say when I pull up to her curb and see her looking out the window.

I turn my car off right in back of the police cruiser. Opening my door and getting out at the same time that Theo arrives, he doesn't even turn off his truck before he's walking beside me. "This is going to go way easier if you aren't breathing fire from your nose like a bull." He looks over at one of the officers getting out of his car.

"That's a dragon," I retort as the front door opens, and she stands there in her robe with tears running down her face. "Baby." I wrap her in my arms as she tries to remain strong, but I can feel her shaking.

"I'm fine," she declares, dislodging herself from my arms. "Theo, what are you doing here?"

"Making sure this one"—he points at me with his thumb toward me—"doesn't end up in the back of that." He then points over to the police cruiser. "And to help with the window."

"Hello," the deputy says, breaking it up, "I'm Deputy Sheriff Lincoln Burke." He looks at me, then at Sierra. "This is Deputy Phillips." He motions to the man standing next to him. "We got a call about a window."

"Yes," Sierra says, "I was sleeping, and someone threw this through my window." She walks into the house, and I follow her as I look at all the pieces of glass in the living room. Theo follows me in, taking a sweep of the room before walking to the back of the house and then to the garage.

The deputy puts on his gloves before he touches the rock, then I see the red paint across it with the word *Leave*. "The fuck is that?" I roar at the same time Theo is coming back into the room.

"Here we go," he mumbles, putting down the piece of plywood he's carrying, and coming to my side in case he has to contain me.

"You did not tell me you were threatened, Sierra." I say her name with my teeth clenched, and when I look over at her, she closes her eyes and then opens them. "This is the second time this has happened." I look at Deputy Burke, trying to literally rein in the rage that is going through my blood. "Yesterday, she got a white paper that said stop looking, and now this."

"I'm sorry," Deputy Burke replies. "Can I get a little context?" He looks at me, then at Sierra.

"Yes," she answers softly. "Twenty-five years ago I was left in a cardboard box at the local fire station. I came to town to look for my birth parents." She tells the deputy the whole story. I put my arm around her shoulders. "I don't know who did this or if they are the ones who even sent the note. I've spoken to a couple of people about it. I spoke with Sheriff Hadley about the case, but there was no case. But today, I called the county to have all of the birth records for my birth date."

"Do you have the note?" Deputy Burke asks, and she shakes her head.

"No, I tore it up and put it in the garbage. I didn't think anything of it." She exhales deeply, and I bring her even closer to me.

"I'm guessing you have no cameras," Deputy Phillips states, looking around.

"She'll have them up tomorrow," I inform him. "She has an alarm, but that doesn't mean shit."

"I'm going to have to take the rock." Deputy Burke looks at her. "Tomorrow, we'll have someone coming by to ask your neighbors if they heard or saw anything."

"Tomorrow? Why not now?" I ask, and he looks over at me. "Didn't it just happen? Shouldn't you, I don't know, process something?"

He smirks as he looks over at Phillips. "Why don't you do a sweep of the property and see if there is anyone or anything out of the ordinary?" he tells the kid who just nods his head and walks toward the front door. "It's the middle of the night. Chances are no one saw anything and the suspects are long gone. But tomorrow morning when someone shows up to ask questions, they are going to be able to talk to them and see if anyone heard anything. Hopefully someone has cameras, but until then we won't know." He looks at me. "I know you're pissed, but if we go knocking on the doors, chances are they are going to be pissed and not want to help with anything. We are going to call it in and patrol will be circling the area tonight and tomorrow." He gives me a tight smile. "This is a quiet neighborhood. If someone heard anything, I can almost bet that they would have called it in already. We'll call you if we hear anything."

"So you aren't doing anything?" My arm falls from around her shoulders. "They could do this nightly if they want."

He's about to say something when Deputy Phillips comes back in. "Nothing," he says, "no footprints in the back, none in the garden." He points to the window. "They either came to the porch to throw it or just stopped their car and threw it in from the grass."

"We're chasing a ghost." He looks at me. "She didn't see anyone or anything. Not a make or model of a car." He looks at Sierra. "I wish I could help more."

"Thank you," she says softly as he turns and walks out of the house.

"Well, that went better than I expected," Theo observes, going over to the other side of the house, grabbing the broom. "Thought his head was going to explode when he told you someone would be by to ask your neighbors."

"Not now." I put my hands on my hips, then look at Sierra. "Someone threw a rock through your fucking window." I point over at the window. "*Someone* didn't throw it. *They* did it." I wait for it to register on her face before I continue. "Your birth parents did this, or whoever the hell they are."

"We don't know that," she says softly.

"Sierra, listen to yourself." I try to keep my voice calm. "It wasn't just someone. They left you a message. Actually, they left you two messages. One was a calm one, but this"—I point to the busted window—"this was crossing the fucking line. And let's just say for whatever reason it was a stranger, they would just throw the rock, not leave a fucking note on it—"

"Caleb," Theo interrupts, "this isn't helping anyone."

"It's helping me," I snap at him. "It's one thing for them to send you a letter, but this"—I shake my head—"this is a bit extreme."

"I agree," she admits. "I don't know what else to tell you." She shrugs her shoulders. "I'm in shock, and to be honest, I was scared, but now I'm at the point where I'm getting really fucking pissed off."

"Oh, good," Theo snips, "there are two of them." He sweeps up the glass before he gathers it in the dustpan and then goes for a cardboard box.

Once he is away from us, I look at her. "How are you doing?"

"I'm not talking to you right now," she returns, and my eyebrows shoot together.

"What? Why not?"

"Because you're an ogre, and instead of making me feel better about all of this"—she points at the window—"you are making me feel bad about it."

"Yup, that sounds about right," Theo interjects, coming back into the room. "Now, if you two excuse me, I'm going to need you to help me put up that piece of wood on the window so I can go home and sleep."

"This isn't finished," I warn her, and she looks past me like I didn't just tell her something.

"Thank you so much for coming out and helping, Theo," she says softly. "It was very nice of you." She then turns to me before she stomps up the steps. "You can see yourself out."

"I don't know a lot about a lot of things," Theo starts as she gets to her bedroom door and slams it, "and I may be rusty when it comes to women and relationships, but that woman does not like you."

"She one thousand percent likes me, or else she would have told you to take me with you." I shake my head and walk over to the plywood. I hold it up while he nails it into place. "I'll call Mitchell tomorrow." I mention the guy who does windows. "Thanks for coming to help."

He nods at me, shaking his head. "Good luck with that one." He motions with his chin to the upstairs where Sierra is.

I lock the door after him before shutting off the light and walking up the steps. Opening the door, I find her in her bed, looking at the door. "Did I not tell you to see yourself out?"

"You did." I kick off my boots and then toss the baseball hat onto the bench in front of her bed. "You calm down yet?"

She sits up and folds her arms over her chest, and I see she's wearing the same thing she tried to wear to bed yesterday. "Me calm down? You need to calm down."

"I'm sorry," I finally say and she just stares at me, not sure what to say to that. "I shouldn't have flown off the handle like that, but I was very fucking worried."

"Well—" I don't give her a chance to say another word.

"Tomorrow"—I shake my head and pull off my T-shirt—"more like in four hours, we are going to call someone and get fucking cameras all around this fucking house." I unbutton my pants and remove my jeans, keeping on my boxers before walking to the side of the bed. "Now, I know we said we sleep naked, but I'm fucking exhausted."

"*We* didn't say anything about sleeping naked. You were the one who said it." She watches me get into bed with her.

"Turn off the lights, baby," I urge softly, and she reaches to turn off her bedside table lamp, bringing the room into darkness. I get on my side, reaching for her and bringing her to me. "Tonight scared me," I admit to her, my voice soft.

"It scared me too," she confesses as she buries her face in my neck, and I'm finally able to relax with her in my arms. Kissing the top of her head, it takes a while to find her asleep, but she becomes heavy in my arms. I spend most of the night listening to her breathing until sleep finally takes me.

I ARRIVE AT the barn a little later than I like, and Emmett and Charlie are waiting for me. "You look like shit," Emmett states the minute I get close enough to them, a sly smile on his lips.

"Yeah." I shake my head. "Someone threw a fucking rock through Sierra's front window last night."

Charlie immediately stands up straight, the smile on Emmett's face quickly erased. "I need to get her cameras."

"I have someone," Charlie offers, pulling out his phone from his back pocket. His fingers fly across the screen. "I'll call them."

"I think it's her birth parents," I admit to them. Charlie's fingers stop moving, while Emmett hisses from beside me. "Two days ago she got a letter telling her to stop looking and then the rock that was thrown through her window in the middle of the fucking night had the word Leave in red spray paint across it."

"Shit," Emmett hisses, "that's not good."

"Yeah, tell me about it." I put my hands on my hips. "Police can't do shit either since there is no evidence anywhere."

"Shocking," Charlie says. "We'll get the cameras up

today, and if they come back to fuck with her, we'll catch them."

"You talk to her about dropping this whole thing?" Emmett asks me and I look over at him.

"What do you think?"

"Yeah, thought so," he replies. "Does she have someone who she is with during the day?"

"For now," I answer, "Theo. Except he is going to be finished working there in the next two weeks."

"What about at night?"

"I'm moving in with her," I tell them and their eyebrows go up.

"She know about this?" Emmett asks me, trying not to laugh.

"She will when I bring my stuff over to her house and unpack." I look over at the barn.

"Sounds like a solid plan." Charlie tries not to laugh.

"Only got one plan," I explain to him, "and that is to make sure she is fucking safe." I nod at them. "The only thing I care about is her being safe. I can deal with her being pissed." They don't say anything else because I walk away from them and toward the barn, not willing to admit to them that I'm so fucking gone for her it's not even funny.

Twenty-Five

SIERRA

I WALK DOWN the steps with the empty coffee cup in my hand, looking over at Theo, who is in the living room with the broom in his hand. He looks up and smiles. "Hi. Mitchell just left." He points over his shoulder at the new window.

"That was fast," I observe once I get to the bottom of the steps. The movement from outside has me looking at the front door.

"Caleb had a couple of words with him." Theo snickers, and I can just imagine. "The guys are almost done putting up the cameras too."

"Cameras? As in plural?" I walk to the front window, seeing three people on my porch.

"He's got four in front," Theo starts to say, "four on the side, and I think four in the back."

I gasp out, "Isn't that…"

The front door opens and my head whips around

to look at Caleb. "Hey," he greets, looking at me, then looking at Theo. "Everything good?" he asks, putting down the black duffel bag he was holding in his hand.

"I'm great," Theo replies, "but I don't know if I'm the one you should be worrying about."

He looks at me with a confusion filling his face. "Can you explain to me, please?" I try to remain as calm as I can, but today has been a roller coaster of emotions. I've been on fucking edge all day long. Even though Theo has been here with me, every single noise made me jump. "How did one door cam equal out to, I don't know, a thousand?"

"It's not a thousand," he defends himself. "There is one at the door, which you need, and another on top of the garage. Then I got two more in the front at the corner and a couple in the back."

"So a thousand. I don't think I need all of that."

"Better safe than sorry," he says, then turns to Theo. "You going to head out?"

"I am now." He scoops up the dust that was made putting in the window. We don't move from our spot as Theo goes to the garage to grab his things. "Call me if you need me." He opens the front door. "Actually, scratch that, I don't want to hear from you." He walks out and slams the door behind him.

"What's with the bag?" I ask him, my eyes going to the duffel.

"My stuff." He picks up the bag and starts to walk to the stairs, avoiding looking at me.

"What stuff?"

"Clothes"—he walks up the steps—"shaving shit, shower shit." He gets to the top of the stairs and looks down at me. "I'm moving in."

"Um, excuse me?"

"Until this is all fucking over and you aren't scared out of your skin, I'm moving in." He starts to walk toward my bedroom, and even though what he just said sounds really, really nice, we should have maybe discussed it.

"Um, shouldn't you have asked me before you just showed up here with your stuff?"

He tosses the bag gently into the bedroom before turning and coming back down the stairs and straight toward me, grabbing my face in his hands and bending to kiss my lips. "If I tell you to pack your shit and move in with me, will you do it?"

"No."

"So this was the only way that it was going to happen." His thumbs rub my cheeks.

"What if I don't want you to stay here?"

"Then I'll sleep in my truck in the front." My mouth hangs open. "Bottom line, I'm not fucking leaving you by yourself."

"Caleb, they are just—"

"You said you aren't going to stop," he cuts me off. "So this is what we have to do until you get the answers to whatever it is you are looking for."

"You can't be sweet and annoying at the same time." My voice comes out soft and he laughs before he bends and kisses me just as softly. "It's an either-or situation."

"I'll work on that," he quips and then he's interrupted

by the doorbell. He walks over to the door, opening it. The guy with the camera equipment is there to talk to him, so I walk over to the kitchen. Placing the mug in the dishwasher, I walk over to the fridge and open it, spotting the steaks I bought two days ago. I take them out.

"Where is your cell phone?" he asks, coming into the kitchen. I reach into the back pocket of my jeans and hand it over to him.

"What's your code?" He looks down and then looks up at me.

"You don't even know my birthday and you are moving in with me?" I put my hands on the counter. "Do you not see how fucked up that is?"

"You can either tell me or I put in random shit and lock you out for five hundred and fifty-four days." He smirks at me. "I know it was last month, so I have what, thirty tries."

"Zero, nine, two, five," I grind between clenched teeth, as he pulls out a stool and starts doing something on my phone.

"I'm making dinner tonight, but I hope yours doesn't taste good." I turn back to the fridge and take out the ingredients I need to make one of my favorite meals.

"Baby," he says, not even looking up, "I'll love whatever it is. I'm starving, I didn't have lunch."

"Why not?"

"I was dealing with stuff," he mumbles as I grab the garlic and an onion.

"Weren't we all." I place the ingredients on the island before walking over to get a cutting board.

"What stuff were you dealing with?" he asks me as I grab a knife and start going over to my spice drawer and grabbing the paprika, parsley, and salt.

"I got the list of births for the day I was born, and from the look of it, everything looks normal." He looks up now. "So I was thinking, if I wanted to get rid of a baby, what would I do?" I open the steaks and start seasoning them with the spices and some olive oil. "I would either have it at home so no one would know, or have it at a private clinic where they don't really have to issue paperwork." I look up at him as I rub the spices into the steak with my hands. "There are four private clinics that were open and two are now closed."

"So you think it's one of those?"

"I have no idea, but I'm going to go and speak with Bruce and see if he remembers anything."

"You should check and see if there are any forums on the clinic also," he suggests. "Sometimes you can get a doctor's name or something and then work with that."

"I hadn't thought about that," I admit to him as he pushes away from the island and comes over to me.

"I got it all downloaded." He shows me my phone. "The app is there. I also installed it on my phone. As soon as it detects motion, it starts recording."

"There goes me trying to sneak all my other men into the house." I knock his shoulder with mine, laughing. When I look at him, all he does is glare at me. "I was kidding. Jesus, you live here now. How am I supposed to be able to do anything?"

"Sierra," he says my name, his voice tight, "I'm going

to go upstairs and take a shower and then come and help you make dinner."

"You better not leave your dirty clothes on the floor in the bathroom," I tell his retreating back as he jogs up the stairs.

I turn to start making dinner, and when he comes back downstairs, I'm almost done. He wraps his arms around me, pressing his front to my back as he buries his face in my neck. The wetness from his hair makes me scrunch up my shoulder. "I cleaned up my mess." He kisses me. "It smells amazing. What are we having?"

"Creamy garlic pasta with steak," I tell him and he stands up.

"You did all that in twenty minutes?" he asks me, looking around.

"I did." I nod and plate up his food, the two of us eating side by side.

"That was so good," he compliments after his third plate.

"You don't say." I grab my plate and start to stand.

"You cooked, I'll clean. Go take a bath," he urges and I lean over and kiss his lips. "I'll be up after I'm done."

"Okay, maybe this living-together thing is going to be okay for a while." I kiss his neck before walking upstairs and taking a bath.

I slide into bed with him, as if I've been doing it forever and not that we just started doing it. The following morning I'm getting dressed when my phone rings, and I look down to see it's Bruce. I called him last night after dinner but left him a message on his answering machine.

And not the one where it's in the phone; no, this one was an old-school one.

"Hello, Mr. Bruce," I answer him, putting it on speaker.

"Hello yourself," he booms out, "you called and left a message late last night."

"It was six thirty." I try not to laugh.

"I get up early." The gruffness to his voice feels somewhat like a hug. "What do you want?"

"I was wondering if I could come over and ask you a couple of questions."

"Are you going to bring me something sweet?" he almost whispers.

"I can but—"

"But nothing, I'll be waiting for you this morning." He doesn't even give me a chance to answer him, he just hangs up.

"Who was that?" Caleb asks, walking into the room as I grab a pair of brown dress pants that are tight on the hips but loose all the way down.

"That was Bruce," I answer as I button the pants and look over at his side of the closet. Which made me stop in my tracks yesterday when I came upstairs. I knew he was "moving in" but I've never had a man live with me before. His stuff mixed with mine, I thought would look out of place but it's the complete opposite. "I'm going to go over there and talk to him about the private clinic."

He looks at his watch. "Okay, let me get a couple of things in place and I'll come with you."

"What?" I stop getting dressed to look at him. "Don't

you have to work? I thought you were going to the barn today?"

"I'll send Theo, get him out of this house. He might like it."

"You don't have to do that." My voice is just above a whisper.

"I know I don't have to, I want to," he says. "I'll be waiting downstairs." He turns and walks out of the room, and I have to squat down and exhale because the tightness in my chest gets even tighter. Besides my parents, there hasn't been anyone in my whole life who has tried to take care of me like he does. Who has gone above and beyond to make sure I'm okay, and I'm not sure what to think or feel. Can I fall in love with a man in less than a month? That's insane, right?

I swallow down the lump before getting back up and sliding a knit, long-sleeved brown sweater on before pairing it with my brown boots, and then making my way downstairs. "Thank you," Theo calls from the front door, "I never thought I would leave this house." I shake my head, laughing as I walk with him to the front door, with Caleb following me.

"It's literally almost done," I tell him. "You said I could move my office downstairs this weekend."

"I know, but it feels like forever," he says, walking out and down the steps to his truck. "I may never come back."

"He's so dramatic," Caleb mumbles as he takes my hand and leads me to his truck. I get in, trying not to laugh. We stop and get donuts, and when we pull up at

Bruce's house, the screen door shows you that the front door is open.

I get out with the box of donuts as Caleb walks beside me, and then I see Bruce walking toward us. "Who did you bring?" He pushes open the door as we walk up the stairs.

"This is Caleb." I turn toward Caleb and smile. "We brought donuts."

"He your man?" He moves aside so we can step in.

"Yes," Caleb answers for me as I roll my eyes.

"He's something," I mumble and then hear the sound of footsteps.

"Is that why you were trying to rush me out of the house?" Heloise questions with her hands on her hips. "Why you lying liar who lies."

"I did no such thing, woman," Bruce defends, grabbing the box from me. "How was I supposed to know she was going to show up and bring donuts?"

Heloise shakes her head. "Hello, dear." She looks at me. "Ignore my husband with no manners, please come in," she invites, going to Caleb. "I'm Heloise." She extends her hand to him. "I've heard about you."

"From who?" Bruce says. "Say their name."

She rolls her eyes and walks away from him, but he is quick to follow her. "They seem nice." Caleb puts his arm around my shoulders, bringing me to him and kissing my lips.

"They really are," I tell him, then hear the arguing coming from the kitchen. "We should get in there."

"Should we?" he asks, following me into the kitchen.

"Sit down," Bruce says, looking at the chair beside him as he bites into a donut. Caleb pulls the chair out for me before walking over to the chair beside me and sitting down.

"Can I get you two anything to drink?" Heloise asks from the kitchen as she makes two cups of coffee. We both shake our heads as she comes over, handing one to Bruce and then sitting down in the only empty chair left. "So what is this visit about?"

"Well," I start and I wipe my sweaty hands on my pants, "I was wondering if you guys know anything about the Hope Springs Medical Clinic."

Heloise snorts. "That thing?" She shakes her head, taking a sip of her coffee. "It was horrible. Doctors performing things they had no right performing. Taking money from the insurance companies and the patients. They got shut down or something like that."

"I think I was born there."

"Makes sense," Heloise says, looking over at Bruce, who is just eyeing me.

"Why do you say that?" he asks me. I explain to him what I found out and he looks down at his donut. "There was chatter while it was still up and running," he finally says. "No one could get proof of what was going on, but things were definitely not on the up-and-up."

"Do you know anyone who used to work there by any chance?" I ask, holding my breath until he nods.

"Meredith Casey," he says her name, "she worked labor and delivery." I feel Caleb reach over and grab my hand in his.

"Do you think she would talk to me?"

"I'll give you her number and also call and tell her you'll be getting in touch with her," he offers. "Surprised she went to work there to begin with. She was retired when it opened up."

"Do you think they kept the medical records somewhere?" I ask, my heart beating hard as I feel like I'm one step closer to the answer.

"They should or at least they did, but then the main pipe valve broke," he shares and the little bit of hope I had sinks down. "Everything was damaged and then they threw out what was covered in mold."

I take a deep breath in. "Interesting." I look over at Caleb.

When we walk out of the house a short time later, I have the piece of paper in my hand. When I get into the truck and he drives away from the house, I pull out my phone. "Here goes nothing," I tell him, dialing the number and then putting it on speaker.

It rings three times before the answering machine picks up. "You've reached Meredith, leave me your name and number and I'll get back to you."

"Hello, Meredith, my name is Sierra. If you can call me back at 561-715-4499. Thank you." I hang up the phone and then look over at Caleb. "And now we wait."

Twenty-Six
CALEB

"I'M GOING TO be done by the end of next week," Theo says when I walk into the house a week later. "We are finishing up the bedrooms upstairs and it'll be all done."

"It turned out so good," I praise, looking around at the living room with all the built-in cabinets she wanted made.

"She got a bunch of stuff delivered today and she's getting more stuff delivered tomorrow," he whispers to me, "so have fun with that." He doesn't even try to hide his smile as he whistles picking up some of the tools.

"What are you doing this weekend?" I ask him before he walks to the door.

"Going home," he answers, "show my face, try to see if your father has work for me."

"We just got seven new clients this week," I remind him, "and you have to admit you're starting to like it here."

"I will admit no such thing." He opens the door. "I haven't gotten laid once since I've been in town."

"What about last weekend?" I remind him.

"That is very different. She was from out of town and house-sitting the house next to mine." He puts away his stuff in his toolbox before unclipping his tool belt.

"I mean a win is a win, isn't it?" I watch him look back at me.

"You can hit up the bar on Thursdays instead of Friday and Saturday. There are a lot of business people that now come through the town and head to the distillery."

"Unlike you"—he walks over to pick up the nail gun, undoing the hose before he puts it down and starts to roll up the hose—"I like to take my time when I have sex. Not be like a school kid on a weeknight."

"You need to decide if you are staying for good," I tell him and he looks down at his boots, not answering me before walking to the side.

"I'm leaving, Sierra!" he shouts toward her office.

"Have a nice weekend!" she shouts back as he salutes me with his hand and then I walk from the front door to her office, which she moved into a couple of days ago. Took Theo, me, and two other guys an hour to bring down all her stuff, including the whiteboard.

I walk toward her new office space, leaning against the doorjamb as I take in what she's done in the last two days. I see her standing and looking at the whiteboard. I look over at the bay window, which now has two beige chairs, side by side, with a round glass table between them with a vase with green flowers. A matching footstool is in front of one of the chairs with a plush gray cover. "This is new." I point at the sitting area and she looks over her desktop at me.

"It is." She looks over her shoulder at me and smiles, making me want to take her in my arms and hug her. "Isn't it pretty?" I nod at her and walk in, going toward the chairs. "If you sit in those chairs in those dusty-ass pants"—she doesn't even turn around to threaten me—"you will lose all access to coming into this room from this day forward."

I detour from the chairs and toward her, standing beside her as I look at the board. "What is that?" I point at the part of the board that has red writing on it.

"Those," she says of the writing, "are some of the names I got on some of the message boards I searched up." She folds her arms over her chest. "That was a good idea you had there."

"I've been known to have a couple of good ideas." I smirk at her.

"Sleeping naked isn't that great of an idea," she mumbles. "Two of these doctors have lost their licenses because they were billing for procedures that never happened."

"Any word from the nurse yet?" I ask her and she shakes her head. "It's almost been a week, so why don't you try to call her again?"

"I didn't want to be pushy," she states, walking over to her desk and sitting down in the white chair, "but it's been long enough, right?"

"I think so," I tell her as she presses things on her

phone and the sound of ringing fills her office.

"We're sorry; you have reached a number that has been disconnected or is no longer in service." She gasps and disconnects the phone.

"That is no coincidence." She slaps her hand on her desk. "That was done on fucking purpose." The burn in my stomach starts when she shakes her head, looking down, then back up at me, and I see the big tears in her eyes.

"Baby," I say softly and she just keeps shaking her head.

"No, they aren't going to win." I don't cut her off, knowing she needs to vent right now. "I'm not backing down."

"Okay." That's the only thing I can say before going to her and holding my hand out to her. "Come on."

She puts her hand in mine as I pull her up to her feet. "Where are we going?"

"First things first," I say, bending to kiss her lips, "we should always kiss hello." Her mouth goes into a smile as she puts her hands on my chest, and I wrap one arm around her waist. "Second, let's go take a bath."

"Oh, that sounds really, really good," she admits to me.

"Why don't you go get a bottle of wine"—I kiss her jaw—"and I'll get the bath started for you."

"Meet you in the bathroom," she replies, dislodging herself from my arms.

"It's a date." I follow her out of the office and go up the steps, two at a time, until I walk into the bathroom. I take a look around to see what I'm working with. "Don't come in the bathroom yet." I go searching for things to make it romantic, and all I come up with are five candles.

I shake my head and start the bath before filling it with her favorite bubble bath, and then I go to light the candles when I see they aren't even real, so I switch them on. "Can I come in now?"

"Might as well," I huff out as the door opens and she steps in carrying a bottle of wine and two glasses. "You have the best taste in the world," I tell her as she looks around, "but not a romantic bone in your body."

"I'm romantic," she gasps. "Tomorrow night I'm going to romance the shit out of you." She walks over to the side and pours two glasses of wine. "Prepare to be romanticized."

"That's not a word." I shake my head.

"I think it is." She turns and peels her sweater over her head, leaving her in the dark burgundy lace bra I saw her put on this morning. She undoes the button on her jeans, and I know she's wearing the matching panties. "Are you going to stand there all night gawking at me, or are you going to get naked and show me your package?"

"My package?" I bend to untie my boots before kicking them off and then tear off my T-shirt, tossing it into the basket in the corner. "What do you like about my package?"

She walks to me, holding both glasses of wine as she places them on the little table she has on the side of the bathtub where she has two rolled white towels. "I like the shape of it," she says as I take my pants off, making my "package" spring free. She walks to me, standing in front of me naked. My hands are not able to stay by my sides and instead I grab her hips, her hands going to my cock. "I like that it's the perfect size, even though sometimes it's hard to walk the next day." I smirk before I bend and take one of her nipples into my mouth. "I love that you are always, and I mean always, in the mood." She moves her hand up and down.

"You act like you don't want it as much as I want it." I move to her other nipple.

"You want it more than I want it." Her voice trails off after I bite down on the nipple and then suck it into my mouth.

"Get in the tub, baby," I urge her as she steps away from me and lifts one foot into the tub and then the other. She moves over to the water, shutting it off before falling to her knees and then putting her back to the end of the tub. I walk over to her, standing behind her head, leaning down, and kissing her lips. My hand moves into the warm water running down the middle of her chest and to her pussy. Her legs automatically open for me as I slide my middle finger through and into her.

Her tongue moves faster when I add another finger. I move my fingers out of her and to her clit where I make small circles. "You've got a greedy pussy." My lips hover over hers as I slide two fingers into her. Her tongue slides back into my mouth. "Every single time," I say as her hips start to move up and down to meet my fingers.

"I am going to—" she starts to say but my mouth swallows her words. I know her body better than I know my own. I know what she wants when she wants it. What she needs when she needs it, and even how she needs it. I pick up the pace, her pussy getting tighter and tighter as I finger-fuck her.

Her hand moves over mine to her clit as she rubs it side to side. "There we go," I tell her as she moans out her release. "Strangling my fingers," I hiss out, not stopping to fuck her until she's done, "going to strangle my cock soon."

"Yeah," she agrees, turning, and the water goes everywhere. My fingers slip out of her, and when I go to stand, she's on her knees, one of her hands going to my cock to grip it and pulling it to her, while the other hand is on my hip. I watch her mouth swallow my cock, and I can't help but close my eyes as I take in the heat from her mouth. She moves her mouth to the tip of my cock before taking more of it inside her. She moans as if she's won her reward and not the other way around. "This is the cock I want."

"Oh yeah." I watch her lick the base of my cock all the way to the tip.

"I always get what I want," she declares as she twirls her tongue around the tip, "and right now"—she looks up at me—"I want your cum dripping down my chin." She takes me to the back of her throat. "So fuck my face."

"Fuck, baby," I hiss as my hands come up to hold her head, "got to give my baby what she wants. Open that throat, baby," I urge as I push more of it to the back of her mouth, "and take me as far as you can go." I move my hips back and then thrust up. "I'm not going to stop,"

I tell her, pushing even more into her mouth. "Not even if you are gagging and choking on my cock. You are going to swallow it." Her moans vibrate right through me as I fuck her face. I want it to last, but with her mouth on me and the way her hand is working my shaft, the way her eyes look up at me, it's not as long as I want it. "Get that chin ready," I order her as she lets go of my cock but keeps her mouth open for me to shoot my cum into her mouth. "Fuck," I hiss, working with her hand on my shaft, as I aim for her face. She swallows what goes in her mouth until I'm done, and then she takes her hand and rubs the cum dripping on her chin, adding it to her mouth.

"It's a shame to waste it," she states, winking at me. I don't know if she's the one who jumps out of the tub or I grab her and pull her up, but the way I want to fuck her I'm not doing it in the tub. I take her over to the vanity, bending her over and rubbing my cock through her slit that is wet from when I made her come. She lifts one of her legs to give me better access to her. I slide into her, and she arches her back. "That feels good," she moans, "always so fucking good."

"Always so fucking good," I repeat as we fuck in her bathroom. I fuck her as hard as I can, and she takes it. She takes it all every single time. "Every fucking time."

Twenty-Seven

SIERRA

I FEEL LIKE someone is giving me the biggest bear hug I've ever gotten in my life. My eyes slowly drift open and I look at the semi-dark room. Light from outside starts to come in from the side of the curtain. I feel him right at my back as his body embraces mine.

His one arm is under the pillow while his other arm is wrapped around me, his hand holding my breast and making me smile. One leg tangled in the middle of my legs as his face is buried in my hair.

I take an extra second to bask in it before I slowly start to disengage myself and try not to wake him. By the time I finally slip out of bed, I feel like I've run a marathon because I'm panting hard. On my way to the bathroom on my tippy-toes, I grab his T-shirt he put on last night when we finally went downstairs to eat food after we fucked in the bathroom.

Sliding it over my head and then untucking my hair

from the back of it, I go to the bathroom before walking over to the sink and washing my face. When I walk back to the bedroom, I find him still softly sleeping, and I take a second to watch him. He's, without a doubt, the best man I know. It's also, without a doubt, when I realize what I feel for him isn't some sort of crush. It's the real fucking deal. The minute my mind realizes what my heart is thinking, my stomach drops, and my hands start to get sweaty. I feel almost sick thinking about the fact I fell in love with him so quickly. Fuck, I love him.

I put my hand to my stomach, turning and making my way out of the bedroom and downstairs. They finished the stairs this week, and they're more beautiful than I thought they would be. They stained each step in the garage and then just put them in. I look over at the empty living room, seeing all the built-in custom shelves Theo made me, and I'm still in awe. All my furniture is coming today, and I could not be more excited.

The house is finally going to be my home. I take a deep breath before turning and walking toward the kitchen. Turning the lights on, I go over and start the pot of coffee. I went all out on the most beautiful coffee maker that grinds up the beans right before it makes the coffee. I press the button for my latte before walking over and grabbing the milk. Pouring it in the milk frother, I then press the middle button to get it warmed up before I put it back and decide to start making Caleb breakfast.

I snatch up the bacon and then the sausage, putting it on the island before going to the oven and opening the bottom drawer to grab one of the baking dishes. I work peeling the potatoes, then slice and place them on the parchment paper, my mind trying not to think about what is going to happen once this is all over.

Where is this going to leave us? He moved in here to take care of me, but when I find out who my parents are, is he just going to go back to his house? Will we even see each other daily? The thought of not waking with him in the morning and not going to bed with him at night is something I don't want to think about, yet it's the only thing I can think about.

I take a sip of my coffee before I start on the pancakes, opting to make regular and blueberry. I'm at the stove, pouring the batter in the pan, while the smell of bacon is now filling the kitchen, when I hear footsteps coming toward me and smile softly to myself.

I hear him right before I feel his arm wrap around my stomach, and he buries his face in my neck, inhaling deeply. "You snuck out of bed," he accuses me, his voice still heavy in sleep.

"I did," I confirm. "Thought I was training for the *American Gladiator* contest to get out of your grip, though." I take my hand with the spatula and flip the pancake.

"You could have woken me up." He kisses my neck gently, pressing me tighter to him. "We could have made breakfast together."

"I wanted to do it for you. Start the day with romance. I was even thinking of bringing you breakfast in bed to show you how romantic I can be."

He snorts before his head moves from my neck. "You

are lying right now."

Flipping the other pancake, I turn to look at him, seeing him wearing his boxers and nothing else. My mouth literally waters as I look at his body. "I'm going to romance the fuck out of you tonight."

"Are you?" He turns and walks toward the coffee machine, and I admire his ass, which, besides his cock, might be my favorite part of him.

"I feel you staring at me," he notes, not even turning around.

"I'm admiring the view." I use his words back at him every time I catch him looking at me.

"If you stayed in bed, you could have admired it more closely," he points out, and I shake my head, turning when I hear the oven timer beep.

"Bacon and sausage are ready." I pull the dishes out of the oven and place them on top of the stove.

"Do you want scrambled eggs or poached?" I ask, and he shrugs. "That isn't an answer, Caleb."

"I'll eat whatever you cook." He takes a sip from the coffee, leaning back on the counter.

"That isn't what I asked you," I huff out. "Scrambled or poached?"

"If I had to choose"—he puts the mug down beside him—"I would pick scrambled."

"Good." I walk over to the fridge. "Was that so hard?"

"Yes," he says. "Can I do anything to help?"

"Yes." I look over at him as I grab a mixing bowl. "Go sit down."

I motion with my head while I start preparing the

eggs. "What are your plans for the day?" I ask him as I take a serving platter out and start putting everything on it.

"I'm off this weekend," he tells me, "and I heard from a little bird that you are getting furniture today."

"A little bird?"

"Theo," he tells me, and I shake my head.

"Snitch," I grumble under my breath. "So you are going to just stay here and wait with me."

"I figured, if anything, we can keep each other busy." I look over at him just in time to see the smirk and then his wink.

We sit side by side as we eat breakfast, and when I'm about to start cleaning up, he pushes me out of the kitchen. "The rule is the rule—you cook, I clean. Or if I cook, you clean."

"But it'll go faster if I help, and then we can keep each other busy." I move my eyebrows up and down twice. "If you catch my drift."

He laughs at me, holding my face in his hands and kissing my lips. "Go get ready for me."

"What does that mean? Get ready for me?" I ask, trying not to smile big but failing. "Should I, like, get naked and take my toy out? Should I wait for you in the shower?"

"If you don't get your ass out of this kitchen, I'm going to fuck you on this floor." I look up to the side, thinking that I'll win either way in that scenario. "Get upstairs." He laughs. "It'll take me no time at all since you like to clean as you go."

"It's easier," I tell him, turning and walking toward the stairs. "I feel you staring."

"Enjoying the view, baby," he compliments, and I move his shirt higher, showing him my bare ass. "That ass is going to be red by the time I'm done with it."

I literally stop in my tracks, turning on the bottom step and facing him, folding my arms under my chest. "Don't make promises you can't keep."

"Really?" He puts his hands on his hips. "Okay, then." He smirks and turns around to walk back into the kitchen.

I'm making the bed when he comes into the room. He puts one hand on my hip and the other between my legs, and making the bed is a thing of the past.

"That," I say, heaving, "might be the best sex I've had." I'm on my stomach, looking over at him on his back, his hand on his chest as he looks at the ceiling.

"Might be." He looks over at me, his hand at his side comes out to rub my ass. "When I smacked your ass, I thought your pussy was going to strangle my cock."

I smile at him. "I wasn't expecting it, and then—"

"Yeah, and then," he teases me as he turns on his side and kisses my neck, "and then I couldn't stop."

"I should get up," I say but don't move. "They said they were going to be here between nine and ten thirty, and it's already…" I look at him. "What time is it?"

He does an ab curl, grabbing his phone from beside the bed. "Nine forty-five."

I turn on my side and get out of bed. "I'm going to need to shower," I state, going to the bathroom, "alone."

I point at him. "Listen for the truck."

Fifteen minutes later, I'm walking out of my closet at the same time as he's getting out of the shower when the doorbell rings. "In record time," he says, and I roll my eyes at him.

I run down the steps, opening the door and seeing the big truck in front of my house. Two guys wait at the truck while two guys are on the porch. "Hi," I say, "bring it in."

It takes them an hour to unpack the living room furniture and then another hour for the dining room. The big table was the biggest challenge for them since it was so heavy. Three hours later, I'm closing the door and looking around at the state of my house. Everything is piled in the middle of each room. "Now the magic happens," I tell Caleb, who is looking from one room to the other.

He's about to say something to me when my phone rings from the kitchen. I run to get it, seeing it's an unknown caller. I put it on speakerphone as I head back into the living room with Caleb. "Hello," I answer, and it takes a full minute for the voice to come out.

"Is this Sierra?" The woman's voice is low, almost as if she's whispering or she's afraid.

"This is she." I look at Caleb, trying not to show that I'm a little freaked out. "Who is this?"

"You need to stop what you are doing."

"Who is this?"

"Doesn't matter," she replies, and I feel Caleb beside me.

"Is this Ms. Casey?" I ask, but she doesn't answer.

"You need to stop what you are doing before you get hurt." Her voice trails off.

"I am not going to stop looking until I find out everything," I announce, my voice coming out shaky at the end.

"You've been warned," she says before she disconnects, and the phone goes back to my screen picture.

"That had to be her, right?" I look up at Caleb, who is looking like he wants to throw something across the room. The anguish on his face makes me take a step back. "Are you okay?"

He shakes his head, and I don't know why, but something inside me turns to stone when he says the next words. "This is over."

Twenty-Eight
Caleb

"THAT HAD TO be her, right?" she asks. All I can do is look at her and then back down at the phone in her hand, and then back up at her. My body locks up, and the rage creeps in. She takes one look at me and takes a step back. "Are you okay?"

I shake my head. "This is over"—the blood drains from her face—"fucking over, Sierra."

"What are you talking about?" I know I should calm down. I know I should sit and maybe count to, I don't know, a hundred, but it's just all too fucking much.

"I'm talking about all of that." I point at her office where the fucking whiteboard is. "I'm talking about you going around asking questions that maybe you shouldn't."

She looks as if I just slapped her in the face. "If you think I'm going to let a couple of phone calls and—"

"And a rock through your fucking window." My

voice goes higher and higher. "And then a fucking note in your mail. Honestly, Sierra, it has to fucking stop, and it stops now, right here. You promise me this is over. You gave your DNA, and you are in the system. If they want to find you, they will find you, but your search for them is over."

"No, it's not." Her voice is low as she shakes her head. "It's not over."

"I'm not going to sit here and watch you get dragged down." The words come out of my mouth before I can even process them.

"Then you should go." She doesn't even miss a beat.

"Sierra," I say, my heart feeling like it's literally being shattered in my chest, begging her to choose me, holding my breath.

"You should go," she repeats. I take one more look at her before I walk to the front door, grab my keys from the table, and walk out. Better yet, storm out, slamming the door behind me.

I take five steps and stop, ready to turn around and storm back in there, but my feet have other plans. I go to my truck and get in, driving away from her house. The whole time wanting to turn back around and go to her. Instead, I make my way over to my office, parking in the driveway. The front door is locked since it's the weekend. I put the key in the door, opening it before the alarm starts beeping. I put in the code, then walk toward my office, tossing my keys on my desk and sitting down.

Looking at the stack of papers I've been neglecting, I lean back in the chair and look up at the ceiling when my phone rings.

I reach around to my back pocket, taking it out, hoping it's her telling me to come back so we can talk about this, but it's not. It's my father, and he's FaceTiming me.

I exhale and press the green camera button and wait until it connects. "Hey, buddy," he greets with a smile on his face, and I see he's sitting at home in the kitchen. "Why are you at work on a Saturday? I thought you were taking the weekend off, finally," he jokes with me. I look at the side, trying to come up with an excuse to get him off my back, but I know he'll probably see right through me. I exhale deeply before looking back at him. "What's wrong?" he asks immediately, and I look up, trying to get a hold of myself. "Are you okay?" The worry in his voice makes my mother come into the screen.

"I'm fine," I reply, and then I shake my head. "I don't know, Dad."

"Why don't you start at the beginning?" he urges softly, and I wish I was sitting in front of him instead of on the phone.

"I met someone," I finally tell him and shock fills his face and my mother's eyes go big.

"Since the last time you were here?" my mother asks me the question.

"No, I met her before I came home, but things have sort of progressed since."

"Sort of progressed?" my father repeats my words.

"Okay, fine, they progressed but—"

"But she doesn't like you," my mother interjects with pity in her voice. "She's not worth it if she doesn't know how amazing you are." She looks at my father, who side-eyes her. "What? He's perfect."

"He's not perfect"—my father puts his arm around her—"but he's pretty close."

"I'm not perfect," I confirm to them, "and I think I might have fucked it up even more than I could explain."

"Why don't you start at the beginning?" my father suggests. "Let us be the judge of that."

"I don't know if I can be an impartial judge in this." My mother shakes her head. "In my eyes, she's going to be wrong, and he's going to be right."

"Why don't you try?" my father encourages her.

She shrugs. "I can try, but you hurt my kids, and you earn yourself an enemy for life. I will cut a bitch. Remember that little shit who tried to copy Mila's social studies paper? I almost drove my car into their house."

"She was seven, and we spoke about that already."

"I'm just saying"—she holds up her hands—"I can only be me."

"Noted," my father responds, then looks at me. "What stupid thing did you do?"

"I guess I should start at the beginning," I tell them. "On her twenty-fifth birthday, she found out she was adopted." The way my mother gasps out loud, I have to give her a minute. "Yeah, not only was she adopted but she was abandoned. They left her in a cardboard box at the fire station, wrapped in a fucking blanket."

"Oh my God," my mother says, "you were wrong." She shakes her head. "I don't know what it is, but she's not wrong and I am sorry I said she was."

"Go on," my father urges, his glare at me.

"So she moved to town to find out who her parents are."

"Nothing wrong with that," my father states.

"I agree one hundred percent." I swallow. "But ever since she started looking for them, she's been threatened."

"What do you mean she's been threatened?" My father's voice comes out sharp, very much a dad voice, like "you better tell me this right now, or else." So I fill them in on everything, and I mean everything. I don't keep anything from them. From the talks with Bruce to her fucking whiteboard and tracing her ancestry, I lay it all out for them, including just storming out on her.

"Oh, honey," my mother whispers when I finally stop talking, "you were one hundred percent"—I wait for it—"wrong."

"What?" I say, shocked.

"You are wrong, honey," she repeats, then looks at my father. "He got that from you."

"But she's hell-bent on putting herself in danger," I try to defend myself.

"She's not trying to put herself in danger." My mother quickly defends her. "She has no control on how others deal with things. The only thing she can control is how she is dealing with this."

"But," my father interrupts, "he's just protecting her."

"By storming out of the house and leaving her alone?" My mother rolls her eyes and shakes her head. "Come on, Caleb, put yourself in her shoes." I listen to her. "She has no idea who she is. You don't know what it feels like waking up in the morning and wondering who you are."

"She knows exactly who she is. She's—" I think of a word to do her justice, but there's only one word I can think of. "She's everything."

"You can't ask her to choose between finding out the truth about herself and you." My father sighs.

"I don't want to make her choose."

"But you do, you just told her that." I close my eyes. "Telling her it's over isn't you being supportive."

"I don't want her to get hurt!" I roar out. "The thought of her being hurt is just too fucking much."

"And there it lies," my mother declares, "he's in love with her, and this is how he acts." I stare at her in shock.

"In his defense, I don't think he knew he was in love with her." My father argues my side as if I'm not sitting here.

"I just want her safe," I whisper. "I want her to have everything she wants. I just want her to do it by not putting herself in danger."

"So you don't leave her." My mother hits the counter in front of her. "You stand beside her and brace for whatever comes her way, holding her up. You don't leave her to be knocked down with no way to get up." She pushes away from the counter. "I thought I raised you better." She shakes her head. "You get off your stubborn ass and go see her—"

"I think you need to decide," my father cuts in by inching forward, "if you want to be the one helping hold her up. If you don't, then walk away." I grit my teeth. "But if you do, get ready to brace the fucking storm that is going to come to her."

"What if I can't protect her?" I ask the question that scares me the most. "What if I do all this, and I can't protect her from this and then I lose her?"

"What if you don't?" my father retorts. "What if you can protect her and you don't lose her?" He smiles sadly. "It's up to you to decide what you want to do. But be honest with both of you. Tell her how you feel and how scared you are." He trails off. "Now, I'll let you go because you have some thinking to do. You call us tomorrow, yeah?"

"I will." I nod. "Thank you, guys."

"It's what we are here for," my father says. "Love you, son."

"I mildly like you right now, I'll know more tomorrow when you call us back," Mom snaps and then hangs up on me.

I turn to the side, looking at the stack of papers, already knowing what my answer is. Also knowing I have to be sure before I go to her, because my father was right. I'm scared something is going to happen to her, and I'm also scared I won't survive it.

Twenty-Nine

SIERRA

I PICK UP the last box in the garage with living room written on it before turning and walking up the two stairs back to the mudroom. I go through the family room, which is still empty since I haven't even started to decorate it yet, toward the living room in the front, which I've now named my reading room instead of the living room.

Placing it down among all the other boxes, I try not to let my mind drift to the fight Caleb and I had a couple of hours ago. I'm ignoring how mad I am that he just doesn't get it. I start to open the box when I hear a car door slam shut. My eyes go to the front door at the same time my heart speeds up, going a mile a minute. My breathing starts to come out in pants as I hear the footsteps on the steps.

My eyes fixate on the door, hoping it's going to open and he's going to be standing there. Hoping it's him and he'll come in and hug me and I'll feel safe. Every single second feels like an eternity. Every single second the hope that it's him goes higher and higher. Until it crashes and burns when the hand comes up and knocks at the front door.

I blink away the tears and the sting in my nose as I walk over to the door and pull it open. I smile big when I see it's Lilah standing there with a bottle of champagne. "Surprise." She walks in when I move aside, giving her space. "I come with gifts for you"—she holds up the bottle—"and gifts for myself, but they're in the truck." She holds out the bottle for me to grab before rushing back out the door and heading to her truck. I watch her reach into the passenger side, grabbing two boxes. She grabs the big pink box I know has either cupcakes or donuts in it, and then grabs another smaller one before shutting the door with her hip. She walks back up the steps toward the house. "I'm so excited for you to open this." She holds up the small one in her hand.

"You didn't have to do that," I tell her as I close the door behind her and she looks at the furniture in my library.

"Can I come here and read?" she asks me, stepping into the room and looking at the built-in cases I had built and painted a deep moss green, with a black ladder that moves from side to side against the big wall.

She puts the box of sweet treats down on one of the moving boxes before she makes her way over to the chair I have next to the window in the corner. She turns and sits down in the big oversized, light-beige chair with a matching footstool. The small round bleached wood table is empty beside the chair. "Me reading right here"—she puts one hand on the armrest—"with my tea on this table." She points at the table.

"I bought an amazing pitcher vase for that table," I tell her, "and the throw blanket I got for that chair is like cashmere but heavy."

"Say less." She smiles at me. "Now, I know you already have lots of books for these shelves, but I couldn't help myself." She gets up and walks over to me, giving me the present in her hand.

I put the champagne bottle by my feet and grab the present from her. "You know you didn't have to, right?" I repeat what I told her earlier.

"Oh, trust me, this was so worth it." She claps her hands together. "I'm not even going to lie, I got one for myself."

I laugh as I peel off the wrapping, knowing it's a book. I see it's one from Parker Cooper, and I gasp because it's one that isn't even out yet. "Oh my God." I look back at her. "How?"

"Charlie's cousin, Gabriel, is married to her cousin, Zara," she explains. "When she came to visit the last time, she caught me reading one of the books and was like 'this is my cousin.'" I put the book to my chest, my mouth hanging open. "I know, so I told her how we started talking and she got a kick out of it. Then a couple of weeks later, Autumn comes into the office and hands me two books."

"You kept it from me all this time?" I glare at her.

"Trust me, the hardest part was not reading it and waiting for you," she tells me.

"I can't believe this," I say, looking down at the book.

"Look inside," she prompts me, and I open the book. I think I scream when I see it's signed to me.

Sierra,

A good friendship is built on good books.

Thanks for choosing mine.

Cooper Parker

"This might have to go in a glass box," I inform her, and she laughs.

"After we read it," she states, and I grimace. "We won't break the spines," she quickly adds, "and we will have to take notes on a different paper for our favorite quotes." I smile at her. "I can't wait for book club. Now let's get you unpacked." She looks around. "Where is Caleb?"

"Um, he's out." I look away from her. "He's going to be back later." I put the book down on the table by the chair.

"Everything okay?" she asks softly, and I shrug one shoulder.

"We had a difference of opinion, you could say." I try not to sound upset. "It's fine. It'll be okay," I quickly say. "Nothing a cupcake and a bottle of champagne can't cure."

"That means you don't want to talk about it." She points at me.

"Not really," I admit, "especially since I don't know what to say about it." I fill her in and tell her what happened.

"I can see both sides," she says sadly and I nod.

"Okay, enough of this," I tell her, "let's unpack and make this library the envy of all libraries." I change the subject.

"It's so pretty," she says when we unpack the last box. "I'm so jealous."

"Well, how about we trade?" I look over at her sitting in the big chair. "You come over with the baby. I get snuggles and you get to read."

"Where do I sign?" she chirps and her phone starts to ring.

"Yes," she answers, picking it up and putting it to her ear, sounding annoyed but the smile on her face says she's not annoyed in the least, "I'm leaving now." She rubs her small baby bump. "I'll see you soon. I love you too." She smiles even bigger. "Okay, bye." She hangs up and then looks at me. "I'm sorry." She gets up. "Lucy is staying at Autumn's tonight."

I hold up my hand to get her to stop talking. "Please don't say whatever it is you are about to say." I close my eyes and squish up my nose and she laughs. "Go and get back to your man." She comes over to me and gives me a hug. Then I walk her to the door and watch her walk to her truck before I wave at her and close the door. The sun is setting outside and I see a couple of the stars are already out twinkling in the sky.

I close the door, lock it behind me, and look at the library, sighing happily at all we have done. I pick up the glass of champagne and the glass of water that is on the round table in front of the big couch. I take it to the kitchen and then go back to sit on the couch and stretch my legs out. I put my hand across the back of the couch and I'm going to lay my head down on my arm when I hear the sound of footsteps, and then the door opens.

I sit up as I see him standing there. His hair looking like he's been running his hand through it all day long. He looks over at me, a sadness fills his face. "I'm sorry," he says, walking into the room wearing the same jeans he wore the first time we met, but this time he's wearing a blue-and-red plaid button-down shirt, his sleeves rolled up. "I shouldn't have walked out on you."

"You shouldn't have." I sit up on the sofa now, putting my feet on the floor.

I'm about to say more when he looks down at his feet, and then he looks back up at me. The anguish written all over his face takes my breath away. "The thought of you getting hurt in all of this"—his voice is pained—"it's just, I can't even fathom to think about it." I put my hand under my neck. "What if they are horrible people who want to hurt you?"

"Then I'll deal with it." I stand. "But I have to do this"—I swallow—"for me, if no one else. I deserve to know. I'm going to find out who I am." I point at myself. "Whatever it is. If they want me or not, I need to know who I am, because regardless of anything, I still have a piece of me missing, and it's theirs, whether they want it or not."

"Then we'll deal with it." He points to me and then to himself. "I'm going to be there every single step of the way, and I'll support you no matter what," he declares, walking into the room. I tilt my head to the side. "I know I didn't exactly handle that as I should," he starts to say, and all I want is to be in his arms right now, "but you have to know, the thought of them trying to hurt you, it was just too much for me."

"What happens the next time they try to strong-arm me?" I fold my arms over my chest to stop myself from going to him.

"Besides me losing my shit and wanting to hunt them all down?" he seethes, his teeth clenched together. "I will follow your lead." I'm about to say something. "I'm not even going to lie, I'm not going to like it. And I'm going to probably need a minute to calm myself down, but I promise to never storm out on you again."

"I'll hold you to that," I finally respond.

"Good, now get your ass over here." He points at the floor in front of him.

"Why are you still over there?" I don't want to give in to him, but I also just want to touch him.

The two of us move at the same time. His hands go to the side of my face and in my hair as he tilts my head to the other side and kisses me. My hands go to his chest as I feel his heart beating as fast as mine. His tongue slides into my mouth. I groan, and he moves us back to the couch. His hand moves my shirt up and over my head, pushing down my bra before he bends his head, taking a nipple into his mouth. I groan as he unbuttons my jeans and rids my legs of them and my panties before pushing me onto the couch. I reach behind me to unclip my bra and toss it to the side. "Lie back," he urges, and I do. I lie back, putting my head on the pillow as he drags my ass to the edge of the couch. Kneeling between my legs as he kisses my left thigh and then my right. He trails his tongue from my thigh up to my stomach and then toward the other thigh. His eyes stare into mine as he licks up my slit. My hand goes to the back of his head as my eyes close, and I feel his tongue flick my clit.

He sucks in my clit as he moves one hand to my nipple, where he rolls it between his fingers and the other one goes to push back my leg. His tongue slides down and into me as he moves his face side to side back up to my clit. His tongue flicks my clit before he sucks it into his mouth and then bites it. He moves his hand from my leg to my pussy, rubbing it up and down. "Going to make you come on my fingers, then you are going to come on my cock," he announces, sliding two fingers into me, "then I'm going to turn you over and come on your ass."

Thirty

CALEB

I WATCH HER eyes lust over when I tell her I'm going to come on her ass. I move up over her as my mouth devours her. She tries to get the kiss to go deeper, her hands going to my pants and unbuttoning them. She slides one hand into my boxers and grips my cock, working it up and down. I let go of her mouth as she plays with my cock. "I'm so fucking hard for you." I kneel beside her as she takes my cock into her mouth. My hand goes between her legs to finger her. "That's my girl," I praise as my knuckle hits her ass, "open that throat for me." I close my eyes as my fingers fuck her, and she sucks my cock. Every single time, I think it can't get better, yet every single time, she shows me that it can.

"I'm not coming down your throat," I tell her, pulling my cock out of her mouth as she groans. "I told you where I'm going to come," I remind her, getting off the couch. "I want to watch you play with yourself." I direct her as she lies back on the couch naked, her pussy glistening from my tongue and then my fingers. "You are going to listen to everything I say, and after, I'm going to make you come hard," I inform her, licking the fingers that were just inside her. "Slide your hands down your chest, making your nails graze over your nipples," I instruct her, watching her do it while I unbutton my shirt. "Move your hand slowly down your stomach until you get to your clit." My eyes are glued to her hands, watching every single movement. "Move your middle finger over your slit in little circles." I undo the last button before shrugging it off my shoulders. "Then move that finger down and inside you." She does everything I tell her and my cock gets even harder, so hard I have to grip it in my hand in a fist. "In and out, baby," I tell her as she does what I say, "add another finger."

"Yes," she pants out, adding another finger. Her hips come up to meet her fingers, going faster and faster now. I kick my boots off, then my jeans as I see her eyes close and her breathing starting to come in soft pants. Once I have my pants in a pile on the floor next to her clothes, I walk toward her. My hand comes out to play with her clit while she finger-fucks herself. "Yes," she says again, her eyes fluttering open. I can see she's almost there by the way her chest rises and falls, the way her hips are moving more frantically than before, her fingers trying to get deeper. I know she's fucking there, and I know I should let her have it, but I'm greedy for it. I want to be the one who brings her all the pleasure. I want to be the one who makes her come. I move her hand away from her as I bend to suck her fingers into my mouth. "Caleb," she whines, "I was right there."

"I know." I bend my legs to make sure my cock lines up with her. Moving one leg over my shoulder, I rub my cock up and down her slit before sliding into her. I move in and out of her. My lips hovering over her as I fuck her. "Fuck, baby," I swear as I thrust into her, "you are so wet"—I pull out and move my hips—"so tight." I move my hand up to grab her tit. "Fucking mine," I declare as she meets my thrusts, faster and faster. Our eyes locked on each other, I can feel her getting tighter and tighter. I can feel myself get closer and closer to the edge. I grip her waist in my hands, pulling out of her and flipping her onto her knees. "Hold on," I warn her as I slam into her. She holds on to the back of the couch as I pound into her from behind. My hand goes to her clit and works it at the same time as I fuck her. Her hand joins mine as she comes all over me. Her juices gush over my cock, leaking out and down my balls. "You just soaked me," I grit between clenched teeth, holding on until she's done before pulling out and gripping my cock. She looks over her shoulder at me as I come on her ass. My hand moves up and down my cock, shooting my cum on her.

"You know that I can't move now," she announces, pushing her ass into my cock, "or I'll drip cum all over my brand-new couch." She moves her hand to her ass, rubbing my cum into her skin. "Is it all in there?" she asks, and I nod as she then licks her fingers clean. "I need a shower." She moves to me, kissing under my chin before walking toward the stairs.

"You know what else you need?" I turn toward the stairs and follow her up there. "My cum down your throat." I chase her as she laughs all the way to the bathroom. The shower takes us so long that the water turns ice cold by the time I get out, leaving her moving from one foot to the other to rinse off the soap.

"I'm freezing," she grumbles, coming out of the shower, and I wrap her in a white towel.

"What do you want to eat for dinner?" I ask as she dries herself off. I watch her, and it suddenly dawns on me that she might not be here for the long haul.

"What just happened?" she asks, noticing right away. "You went from all smiling to pale and looked like you were going to throw up."

"What are we doing?" I wrap a towel around my waist as she wraps one around her chest.

"I thought we were going to check what we were going to eat for dinner," she answers softly.

"After that," I start to say, trying not to freak out but scared as fuck she's just going to leave me. "And then what?"

"Dessert." She laughs.

"No, Sierra," I say, "I mean, after you find your parents, what is going to happen?" I put my hands on my hips. "Are you going to stay here, or are you leaving and going back to your old house?"

"What?" she whispers.

"I just started the business here," I say, and confusion is written all over her face. My mouth just spews out words, and I don't even know if I'm making any sense, really. "I can't just up and leave, and now with you and starting this thing with you. I don't even…" I close my eyes, trailing off. "I'm in love with you." The gasp that leaves her lips is hard for me to hear, and her hand goes to cover her mouth. "Yeah, so I'm really wondering what is going on here?"

"You love me?" she asks, and now I'm the one who is confused by it.

"Did I not just say I did?"

"Yes, but you also were ranting, so I just let you go, but you said it." She points at me. "You said you love me."

"Yeah, I did," I acknowledge. "I also told my parents about you today."

"Oh my." She puts her hand on her forehead.

"And I want you to come and meet them."

"But—"

"Do you not feel the same way about me?" I ask, the floor feeling like it's being pulled from under my feet. "It's fine if you don't. I just wanted you to know how I feel about you."

"I'm staying here," she says, "because even though I didn't grow up here, I feel like this is my home." She smiles as the tear escapes the corner of one eye. "And with you, it just solidified it. This is where my home is supposed to be." She smiles through the tears. "I haven't told my parents about you, but I will. Tomorrow." She walks to me. "I love you, Caleb." She puts her hands on her hips. "And for the rest of my life, I'm going to have to live with the fact that you said it first, and that really fucking pisses me off." I can't help but laugh, pulling her to me. "Unless, if you really love me, you would say I said it first."

I bend down to kiss her lips, but right before, I retort, "Not a chance in hell, baby." I rub my nose to hers. I said it first, my lips hovering over hers, saying, "I love you."

I WALK INTO the bathroom and see her standing at her side of the sink, the hair dryer going as she brushes her roller brush through it. "You want to go out tonight?" I ask her, and she looks at me in the mirror.

"Go out?" she asks me. "Where?"

"How about we head over to the bar?" I say. "We can also get something to eat."

"Okay," she says, "I'll be ready in about thirty minutes. Be ready to be romanticized."

I chuckle. "Okay, baby, whatever you say." I turn and head over to the closet, slipping on a pair of jeans and a T-shirt. I'm snapping my watch shut when she comes into the closet, and the robe is flying away from her legs.

"Wait for me downstairs," she tells me, and my eyebrows pinch together. "I want what I'm wearing to be a surprise."

"Okay"—I turn to walk out of the closet—"but wear something I can tear off easily under it."

She gasps. "You will not rip any of my things off." She shoos me away with both her hands. "Go away."

"Fine," I say, walking back to her and holding her

face in my hands as I kiss her lips, "I can't wait for me to be romanticized." My hands move from her face around to her ass, squeezing it and pulling her into me. "Is that code for we're going to do nasty things to each other tonight?"

"You always do nasty things to me." She pushes me away.

"Don't pretend you don't like it," I say, turning and walking out of the room. "Maybe we can take out the purple friends, and I can."

"Caleb!" she shouts my name. "Get out!"

"Fine." I try not to laugh as I walk down the steps and head to the kitchen, turning off all the lights before going to the living room and walking over to her library. Scanning the names of the books before taking them down and reading them back. I hear the sound of her clicking on the way down the stairs. I put the book down and head toward the entrance. I see black boots first and then legs, a lot of fucking legs. Before the blue jean skirt hits the middle of her upper thigh, I see bare skin and her shoulder all out. The black top looks like it's wrapped around her neck.

"Before you do anything," she says, stopping at the bottom step. "This is wrapped around my neck"—she points to the top—"so it has to be taken off gently over my head."

"That's good to know," I tell her. "Now go and change and put something else on."

She laughs, and I don't move. "I'm not kidding with you." I shake my head. "I'm not going out with you looking like a sex kitten."

She laughs as she puts her hand on my abs. "It's all for you." She kisses under my jaw. "I take it you approve of this outfit."

"I don't approve at all," I say between clenched teeth as she walks past me and to the door. "I'm rethinking this night out," I say as she walks out the door, and I follow her. The door slams shut behind me and automatically locks. "Let's stay in. We can cook, and then I don't know. Read a book." She stops and turns on her heel, laughing as she reaches for the truck handle.

"You want to read a romance book with me."

"If that will get you to stay home"—I put my hands on my hips—"then yes, yes, I do."

"Okay, tomorrow you can read one of the dirty parts, and we can reenact it." She taps the tip of my nose before she climbs into the cab of the truck and slams the door closed.

I put my hands on my hips and look up at the sky. "Give me strength," I mumble to the universe as I walk around and get into the truck. "Are you sure about this?" I ask her one last time, hoping she will change her mind. But she just smiles big at me and nods her head. "Great," I say, making my way over to the bar. I park in the almost full parking lot, knowing that every single second we are inside this bar, I will be glaring and threatening anyone who looks at her.

She hops down off the seat and meets me at the back of the truck, slipping her hand into mine. "This is going to be so much fun."

We walk into the jam-packed bar, looking around to see if we see anyone we know. "Oh, Brock and Everleigh are here," Sierra says, dragging me through people and toward their table. "Hey, guys," she says, seeing two empty chairs, "are these taken?"

"Yes," Brock snaps.

While Everleigh says, "No," with a huge smile on her face. Then, she holds out her hands to the two empty chairs. "Please sit."

"Or not." Brock leans in. "You can go and have a drink at the bar."

"Brock," Everleigh hisses his name, "that's not nice."

"It's date night, and I'm socializing." He looks at her and then turns to glare at us. "And now you've invited people to sit with us where I will have even less of your attention."

She puts a hand on his cheek. "I promise you will have me the whole night to yourself."

He grunts, and only then do I pull out the chair for Sierra to sit down before I sit next to her. "If it makes you feel better"—I look at Brock—"I don't want to be here either."

"It doesn't." He picks up his drink and brings it to his lips.

"Okay, can we get this romantic thing going"—I look around—"so we can hurry up and leave?"

"Romantic thing?" Everleigh asks us, making Brock groan.

"If they wanted us to know, they would explain it to us." He leans back in his chair. "Mind your business, woman."

"It's called socializing, Brock," she hisses at him. "Now explain this romantic thing."

"Caleb says he's more romantic than I am, so I am spending all night romancing him." She puts one of her shoulders up and shakes side to side.

"You know how you can do that." Brock looks at her. "Stay home and get naked."

I point at him as Everleigh gasps, "That. I would like to be romanticized like that."

The waitress comes over, and we order a round while the music starts to get a touch louder, and people start getting up beside their table to dance.

"They should just make a dance floor," Sierra says as the waiter puts her drink down in front of her. "It would be fun to watch everyone dance."

"No, it wouldn't." Brock quickly crushes her dreams. "I remember when no one wanted to come into this bar. It was fantastic."

"It was not," Everleigh says. "They almost went bankrupt."

"Okay, minus that." We all laugh as we talk about how it was the last couple of years. We order burgers, while Brock and Everleigh order a couple of small plates to share.

By the time I look around, more people have arrived, and a couple have even come over to say hello to us. Everleigh and Sierra are going on and on about this show they are both watching, and I'm about to just push away from the table and drag her out of there. Her hand has been on my leg the whole night, rubbing it softly up and down.

The music goes soft, and she cuddles up to me, her mouth going to my ear. "Will you dance with me?" she asks me, and I don't answer her; instead, I push away from the table, holding out my hand for her.

She slides her hand in mine as we move to the side of the table, and she wraps her arm around my neck. "Have I told you that you look beautiful tonight?" I wrap an arm around her waist and pull her even closer to me.

"No," she says. "You were too busy telling me how much you hated my outfit."

I chuckle when I look over and see that Brock and Everleigh are now dancing on the other side. "I love you." I bend and kiss her lips.

"How much?" She looks up at me.

"I'm in a bar dancing with you instead of having my face buried in the middle of your thighs." I wink at her. "That's how much."

"Okay"—she turns in my arms—"we're out." She holds up her hands at Brock and Everleigh. "We're going home." She shrugs. "He's much more romantic than I am."

Thirty-One

SIERRA

THE PHONE RINGS beside me on my desk, and I look down, seeing his name flash across the screen. I press the green button before leaning back in my chair, "Hello."

"Hey, baby"—his voice goes soft—"whatcha doing?"

"I'm about to have tea with the queen," I joke, and the way he chuckles makes me smile even more.

"Oh, I didn't want to interrupt tea with the queen. I was just calling to see how your day was going."

"It's going good." I smile as I look out the bay window. "I finished a redesign of one of the contracts I got a couple of months ago. So it's been a relaxed sort of day. But now I guess it's better since you called." I smile, thinking of him.

"Is it?" he questions. "Do you know I'm always the one who calls you?"

"What?" I shake my head. "That's not true. I call you all the time."

"Name once," he pushes, and I look up at the ceiling, trying to think back. He's right, I don't think I've ever just called him. "I've been busy."

He chuckles, and it makes my stomach flutter and certain parts of me tingle, parts that after almost two months should stop fluttering already. "Which is why I call you every day, just to say hello."

"No, you call me every day so you can be 'I'm the one who always calls you,'" I mimic his voice horribly.

"I'll be home around five," he says, laughing. "We can argue then."

"You just want to argue with me so we can have make-up sex," I point out.

"Baby," he murmurs softly, "don't make me hard when I'm on my way to meet my guys."

"Goodbye, Caleb," I snap, "I love you."

"Love you too, baby," he replies softly, and I hang up, putting the phone beside my keyboard.

It's been two weeks since I told him I loved him, or better yet, he told me he loved me, and it's been smooth sailing ever since. Mind you, nothing has been happening with my birth parents. No more mysterious phone calls, no more notes telling me to leave. Nothing. It's been crickets. I guess no news is good news. I'm about to get up and maybe go start making dinner, when my phone rings. I look down, thinking it's him again, but instead, it's an unknown caller.

"Hello," I answer, putting it on speakerphone.

"Is this Sierra?" the male voice asks me.

"This is." I sit up in my chair, looking down at the

numbers, counting how long we are on the phone, ticking by.

"Hi," he says, "my name is Brendan Frisby." I try to place his name but come out blank. "You hired me through the DNA site to trace your ancestors. I'm a forensic genealogist."

"Oh, hi," I reply, suddenly getting nervous.

"I'm calling you today because I have some news." The hair on the back of my neck starts to stand. "I've been working on your DNA matches, and I've found a close relative."

I close my eyes. "How close?"

"I will email you right now, and we can go over the tracing at the same time," he states, and a ping shows me a new email has come in.

My hand hovers shakily over the mouse as I click on it and open the attachment. The top of the tree has my eyes hovering over it. "I have traced your ancestors back to the eighteen hundreds." The names are totally new to me and not at all the ones I have on the whiteboard, which is weird.

"These aren't the names I have on my board," I tell him.

"That would probably be your paternal side, which is what I'll be working on next, but I did your maternal side." If I thought I was going to throw up before, it's nothing like how I feel right now.

"If you go down the tree, you'll see that you have a parent relation with one of two people." My eyes roam to the bottom of the tree. "Chester had five sons," he starts to talk about my great-great-grandfather as he works his way down the tree, but my finger is already moving the document down to the bottom. "Frederick had three kids, two sons and a daughter." He is just talking, and I'm not even following him at this point. "Your grandfather's name is Rob Dyson." I think I gasp out, or maybe it's in my head. The only thing I can hear is the way my heart is thumping in my ears. "Rob had three children: Peter, Fiona, and Sonia." My eyes blink a couple of times as I look at the names at the bottom. "Now, you are either Fiona's or Sonia's daughter."

"Oh my God," I whisper, putting both hands on my cheeks, "are you sure?"

He laughs. "I am. None of them have anything in the system, but their cousin did, so that is how I started tracing it back."

"I'm—" I try to catch my breath. "I don't know what to say. Thank you so much."

"You are very welcome. I'll be starting on the other side tomorrow."

"I don't know how to thank you," I say.

"Well, I have even more news for you," he replies, and I laugh.

"I don't know how much more you can possibly have."

"I reached out to Tina, who is the second cousin, and she gave me both phone numbers. She also said if it comes out she gave it to me, she's going to deny it."

I think I stop breathing when he says that. "The information is in the email that you probably didn't read."

I belly laugh now, out of nerves, out of happiness, out of everything. "Guilty."

"Figured you wanted to get to the end of the story and not read the beginning."

"Next time, I'll start at the beginning," I assure him.

"Sounds good. I'll call you once I finish on the other side."

"Thank you so, so much," I say as he hangs up the phone. I stare down at the phone and then go to the email and see the numbers there. I don't know how long I sit at my desk; I don't even feel the tears that run down my face. I don't feel the way my body shakes. I feel nothing.

I pick up my phone and dial his number. "Oh, now you want to call me because I pointed out the obvious."

"They found her," I whisper, and then the sob rips out of me. "He found her."

"Baby," he soothes, and I can hear him running on his end, "breathe for me, yeah?" I hear the sound of his truck door slamming shut and then turning on. "I'm going to be there in four minutes."

"He found her." It's the only thing I can say over and over again until I hear the front door swing open and his boots on the floor. He finds me in my office, the phone to his ear now moving down. "He found my mother." I can see the exact moment he registers what I just said. "He found who my mother is." I get up, and his hands are there to hold me up because my knees give out. I bury my face in his neck as he wraps his arms around me.

"That's amazing," he murmurs in my ear. "It's going

to be okay." He kisses the side of my head. "Tell me everything."

I tell Caleb everything that Brendan found. "So now it's either Fiona or Sonia who is my mother."

He holds my face in his hands. "Well, what are you waiting for?" He smiles as his thumbs dry my cheeks. "You've been waiting for this for a while."

"I know." I look down. "I'm scared."

"There is no need for you to be scared, baby," he assures me softly. "You got this."

"I got this," I repeat his words. "Who should I call first?"

"Sonia," he says, "start there."

I sit back down in my chair, and he squats beside me, holding my hand as I dial her number. "I'm so nervous," I admit to him as I dial the number and press the green button before I lose my nerve. The sound of ringing now fills the room, and I look over at Caleb, who holds my hand in his and brings it to his lips.

"You got this," he whispers right before someone picks up the phone.

"Hello." The female voice fills the room, and I feel like I'm going to throw up.

"Hi, I'm looking for a Sonia Dyson." I try to get my voice under control and not have it come out shaking.

"This is she." I want to say her voice is warm, but it's not. It's the sound of a voice that I would hurriedly rush to get off the phone with. It's filled with attitude and something else I can't put my finger on. "Who is this?"

"My name is Sierra Davidson," I say, and she interrupts me before I finish.

"I don't know anyone by that name," she snaps, "and if

you are calling to sell me something, I'm not interested."

"I'm not calling to sell you anything," I reply quickly before she hangs up on me. "I was wondering if"—I look over at Caleb to gather the strength—"if by any chance you gave up a child for adoption twenty-five years ago."

"Who is this?" Her voice goes down into a whisper. "Who gave you this number?"

"I'm looking for my birth mother."

"Stop looking." She doesn't give me a chance to finish. "You need to stop looking. We don't want you looking into things." My blood runs cold. "We're not interested in having anything to do with you. Forget this number. Forget my name. Just like I have tried to forget you." I don't say anything else because the phone disconnects.

My mouth opens but then quickly closes. "That—" Caleb stands up, not sure what to say. I can see his jaw getting tight.

"Well, that answers that," I say, trying not to feel crushed. I shake my head. "I did my part."

"You did," he agrees as I look up at him, the tears making it hard to see.

I get up, trying to be as strong as I can be. "There you have it," I state, and he wraps his arms around me while I sob out. In the comfort and strength of his arms, I let go of the pain from finding out I was adopted, from the pain of finding out my birth mother wants nothing to do with me.

He rubs my back. "It's her loss, baby," he soothes softly. "It's her fucking loss."

Thirty-Two
CALEB

"IT'S HER LOSS, baby." I rub her back, pushing away the rage I have inside me. "It's her fucking loss."

"I guess so," she says, defeat filling her voice, and if I thought I was angry before, I was wrong. Now I'm not only angry, I feel like I could murder someone with my bare hands.

"Why don't I go and draw you a bath?" I offer as she pulls out of my arms.

"I don't want to have sex with you right now." She smiles through her tears, and I see she's trying to be strong.

"Baby." I kiss her lips, tasting the tears. "You're the one who is always jumping me."

"Did I jump you this morning when I woke up to your face in my crotch?" She puts her hands on her hips.

"Yes," I confirm. "You were wiggling your ass in your sleep. You basically said 'eat me, Caleb.'" She rolls her eyes. "So I did."

"I wiggled my ass in my sleep." She takes a deep sigh. "This fucking sucks."

"It does," I agree with her.

"I mean, I didn't think she would welcome me with open arms." She shrugs. "But I didn't think she'd tell me to take a hike."

"I'm sorry, baby." She blinks away the tears, or at least she tries to blink them away. "You are better off. She doesn't deserve to know how amazing you are."

"You're just saying that because you love me."

"Damn right, I do." I smile at her. "I love everything about you, and even if I didn't love you, I knew you were amazing before I fell in love with you. I knew you were hot." I hold up a finger. "I knew you had a wicked sense of humor." I add another finger. "I knew you were a pain in the ass with all that attitude you had." I shake my hand at her with three fingers held up. "I also knew you are the type of woman who takes all things thrown at her and gets back up."

"I am that person," she states proudly. "It's her loss," she finally says. "I'm fucking amazing." I try not to laugh. "And I'm kind, and I'm loyal."

"You are all fucking that," I agree proudly, "and you're mine."

"I'm yours." She nods. "Now I'm going to go upstairs and get into a bath, and my man is going to pour me a glass of wine and make me my favorite meal."

"Um," I say, "yeah, I am. I just need you to tell me what your favorite meal is, and I'll make it."

"Shrimp scampi." She tells me something that I would have never guessed, not in a million years. "I took out the shrimp this morning."

"Then I'm going to get on my phone and find a recipe and make my woman her favorite meal"—I kiss her—"after I deliver a glass of wine to her as she takes a bath."

"You're very, very smooth." She winks at me as she starts to walk away.

"I'm the only one with romance in this relationship." She stops walking and looks over her shoulder at me. "I'm still waiting for you to romance me."

"I was going to romance you"—she turns on her foot—"and you went and stormed out of the house, so you lost it. Then I took you to the bar, and instead of me romancing you, you mentioned your face in the middle of my thighs and it was all too much to fight."

"That was two weeks ago"—I smirk—"and you haven't tried since."

"Um, Saturday night"—she taps her foot—"did I not romance you?"

"You were semi-drunk from the bar, and telling me 'I'm going to suck your dick so hard when we get home' isn't considered romance." I hold up my hand. "Even if you did it when you got home. Something I think you would have done anyway."

She gasps. "But I did." She shrugs. "Now I'm walking away from this conversation before we start fighting and then have to have make-up sex on my desk—" She stops. "Again."

I look down at my feet, trying not to laugh at her as

she goes. Going straight to the fridge and pouring her a glass of wine, I take it to her upstairs. I find her in the tub as the water is filling it up. She looks over at me as she leans back. "Today sucked," she declares as I hand her the glass of wine, "and you only brought me one glass and not the bottle." She shakes her head. "Rookie mistake."

"I realized my mistake the minute you said today sucked." I kiss her lips. "I shall get you the whole bottle."

"And then don't forget to tell me I'm pretty."

"You aren't pretty, though," I call over my shoulder. "You're gorgeous, and anyone who doesn't see it needs to have their eyes checked."

"Smooth." She takes a sip of the wine. "Very fucking smooth."

"Also I'll break anyone's face who looks at you. So." I wink at her as I jog back down to the kitchen, grabbing the bottle and bringing it back to her, before pulling up a recipe. She comes down just as I put the pasta in the water.

She sits on the stool with half of the bottle of wine gone. When we slide into bed, she snuggles into me and falls asleep.

When I get up the following morning, I slide out of bed, trying not to wake her before going down to start the coffee. I'm in the middle of making her a bagel when she comes down the steps. "Morning." She comes over and wraps her arms around my waist. "You snuck out like a bandit."

I kiss the top of her head. "It's like a thief in the night."

"Either or," she grumbles before moving away from me and making her own coffee.

"Are you taking today off?" I ask as she prepares her coffee and then takes a bite of the bagel I just finished buttering.

"Yes." She nods. "I'm going to go down to the local high school."

"For what?" I ask as she takes a sip of her coffee.

"I'm going to go check out some yearbooks and see if maybe she was from around here. I'm going to go out on a limb and guess she was pregnant when she was sixteen or seventeen, maybe just turned eighteen."

I shake my head furiously before she finishes, knowing exactly where she is going with this. "Baby."

"I know her name now," she says softly. "I want to put a face to the name. It's like this unfinished puzzle piece."

I close my eyes and put my head back. "Sierra."

"I still have a father and, unlike my mother, maybe he wants to know me," she explains. "Half the battle is done." She doesn't give me a chance to say more. "He also has a choice, and maybe his choice is going to be exactly like hers, but I need to hear it for myself."

"Sierra," I say her name again, this time trying to sound calmer than before, but probably not. "Do you know how hard it was to see you in that much pain yesterday?" I ask. "Do you know what it did to me to hold you in my arms and watch you cry and mourn the mother who you thought you were going to meet? Do you have any idea how much this is killing me right now?"

"I'm sorry, Caleb." She puts her cup down and comes

over to me as I look down at the bagel in front of me.

Her hands go to my hips. "No," I say. "How would you feel if the roles were reversed?" I ask her, putting my hands on her shoulders. "If you saw someone hurting me and me suffering from it, what would you do?" I look into her beautiful eyes, falling more and more in love with her. Wanting and needing to protect her with everything I have. "Tell me, Sierra, what would you do?"

"I don't know," she answers softly. "I would feel helpless, and I would do whatever I could to make sure you knew you were loved." She moves her arms from my hips to around me. "I would make sure you knew every single second that it didn't matter what anyone said, that you have someone who is happy to have you at home. Who will go above and beyond to make sure not a second goes by that you don't know how special you are. That is what I would do."

"Nothing I'm going to say is going to change your mind, is it?" I ask her and she slowly shakes her head side to side.

"Okay, let's eat breakfast and then head on over to the high school."

"You are going to come with me?" she asks, shocked I'm giving in so easily and equal parts shocked I'm going with her.

"I'll be there to either help you walk," I tell her, "or carry you. Either way, you aren't doing this alone."

The smile fills her face. "You are so getting lucky later."

I chuckle. "Baby, every single day I get to come home

to you and lie by your side is me being lucky."

"Okay, enough of that, or we won't even leave today." She gets on her tippy-toes and kisses my neck, moving back over to her coffee.

We get dressed side by side, her in a pair of black tights with a thick, knitted, long-sleeved charcoal turtleneck sweater. Me in a pair of black jeans and charcoal T-shirt, the whole time not saying a word. Neither of us says anything as I open the truck door for her when we leave the house. When we get to the school, we walk side by side, and she takes a deep breath when we walk into the building.

Opening the door at the same time the bells ring, we look right and then left, seeing kids coming out of the classrooms and rushing to get to the next one. I spot one of the teachers walking down the hallway and give him a chin up. "We're looking for the office?" I ask as he holds a book in one of his hands.

"Up those stairs." He points at the five stairs to the side. "It's the second door on the right."

"Thank you." I nod, sliding my hand in hers as we make our way over to the office.

The big sign hanging in front of the open door says "Main Office." We walk in past the seating area where four chairs are lined up against a wall with windows that show out of the room.

There's a long desk in the middle of the room, with two desks behind it facing each other. Two office doors are on each side, right behind the desks. There's a binder opened up at the far end of the counter with a pen and white paper.

The woman sitting at the desk takes one look at us before pushing away from her desk and coming over. "Hi, may I help you?"

"Hello," Sierra says, "I was wondering if by any chance there is a library where we can go and check out old yearbooks."

"You would need to sign in"—she points over at the book at the end—"and I'll take you there."

I walk over to the book and sign us both in, and she hands us both visitors' badges. I clip mine to my shirt when she clips hers on hers. "This way," she urges, walking out of the office and down the same hallway to the end where the library is. "You need to hand in your badges before you leave."

"We will," Sierra says. "Thanks for all your help."

We walk into the library and head straight to the counter. "How can I help you?" asks the woman working behind the counter.

"We were looking to see if we can check out yearbooks from twenty-nine to twenty-five years ago," Sierra answers, and the librarian whistles.

"Those are going to be in the archives for sure," she states. "May take me a couple of minutes to get them."

"Do you need any help?" I ask her and she smiles over at me.

"If you want, I would never say no to that." I nod at her and give her my own smile.

"Lead the way," I tell her and she walks around the counter and heads toward the back room.

I follow her as she takes her keys out of her pocket and opens the door before turning on the light and stepping in. "They are all dated by year," she says of the boxes that are facing us piled on shelves. She holds open the door for me as she steps into the room, and you can smell the oldness of the room. "It will most likely be in this area," she says, looking at the second shelf. "Yup, this is from twenty-five to thirty years ago." She calculates the years written on the box. I grab the small footstool they have, walking over and grabbing the handle to the brown box before stepping down. The inch layer of dust on the top of the box shows you this hasn't been opened in the longest fucking time. "You can take that box and look at it on one of the desks."

I follow her out and see Sierra standing there pacing back and forth in front of the door. "I'll be at my desk if you need anything."

I look over at her. "You ready for this?" I ask, putting the box on the table. "It's literally like opening Pandora's box."

She takes one look at me and nods, rubbing her hands together. "I'm ready."

Thirty-Three

SIERRA

I LOOK AT the box that has dust on it, my heart hammering in my chest, my knees just a touch weak, and my palms are clammy. And I don't even know if there is anything in the box that will help me. Nothing. I just know this box might hold some answers, but nothing in life is this sure.

When I woke up this morning, something pushed me to go check the local high school. I don't know why, but it was like a force I couldn't really explain. So now here I am with the box in front of me, and it feels like I'm really lifting the cover off Pandora's box. "I'm so nervous." I laugh. "It's crazy, right?"

"A little bit," Caleb replies with a sly smile. "Do you want me to open the box first?"

"No." I shake my head and pull up the top of the brown box, seeing the old yearbooks stacked in two piles. "I don't think we should start twenty-five years ago since she was having me, so maybe twenty-six years ago."

I grab the one on top that is just twenty years old, placing it beside the box and then going one by one until I find the one that is twenty-six years old. "It smells old," I tell him as I crack open the book. The pages are glossy and some stick together. "How different it was back then," I say as I look at the first page of the whole school outside taking a group shot. "Lots of bucket hats." I laugh as I search the crowd, trying to see if my face pops out.

I turn the pages. With each page, I feel like someone is going to jump out at me, but nothing happens. We see the pages for the graduates first, a couple of pictures of different groups of friends. A couple of pictures of activities that had been happening around the school year: a barbecue, a Christmas one, a ski trip. My eyes roam over the last names, and when I get to D, there is nothing there. I move along to eleventh grade, checking for anyone with the Dyson name and also come up empty. I go until the ninth grade and then close the book. "Well, one year done," I say, trying not to feel defeated.

"Baby, the chance that you'd find it on the first try was slim to none." He puts his arm around me, and he pulls me to him as he kisses the side of my head. "Nothing has come easy this whole journey, you really thought you would open the first one and boom, it would be there?"

I feel the dryness in my eyes as I blink and turn to look at him, staring at me. "I know it was crazy, but I did think I would open it and it would be there."

He shakes his head, grabbing the next one and opening it up, as I place the one in my hand to the side.

He opens it up and isn't like me when he looks for the Dyson name. He doesn't take a second before he goes to the graduating year, seeing no Dyson, and then going to the rest of the grades. It takes him a full minute to place it on top of the other one and then he grabs the next one.

"Every single time we place one on the side, it feels like a lid is being shut," I tell him, and he smiles.

"I'm sorry, baby," he responds, picking up the next one. He then fans the book until he gets to the graduating class and comes up empty, and then stops when he gets to eleventh grade. "Holy shit!" he exclaims and I look over at the picture his finger is on. It's Fiona Dyson. I gasp when I see her. Our features are very similar. We each have the same color hair and her eyes are blue, whereas mine are a green hazel. "Do you think?" he asks as I take the book from him, my eyes fixated on her as she smiles at the camera.

"I have no idea," I answer him. "I spoke to Sonia and she said we know who you are. So it could be." I turn the pages to the younger grade and then finally, three years later, I find Sonia. She looks very much like Fiona. Her hair is a darker color—almost like a chestnut—and her eyes are brown, but they have the same shape of eyes, which are mine, along with the same nose.

"It makes no sense that they were here this year and then gone," Caleb notes, grabbing the yearbook after the one in my hand, and he finds the page. "Here she is again," he says, "so they left town after this year."

"How are we doing here?" The librarian comes over and smiles at us.

"Amazing," Caleb answers her. "I was wondering how one would get a copy of a certain yearbook?"

"That would depend on if there are any extras," she says. "Usually we print twenty extra, just in case you have a student who forgot and then those go into storage."

He grabs the one in my hand and then closes it so she can see the year on the front written in silver. "We were looking for this one."

"Let me check in the storage room," she tells him.

"Would you like me to help you?" he offers her and she smiles bashfully at him.

"That would be lovely," she says, turning and walking toward the room.

"If she wasn't seventy," I start to mumble, "and I was confident in what a catch I am, I would seriously wonder who else you are flirting with all day long." He chuckles, giving me a kiss before leaving and walking out of the room.

I look down at the picture of her, it's the younger her. The next picture the year after shows how much she changed in a year. I find Sonia and she looks even younger with braces on. My hand hovers over her picture.

It's a couple of minutes later when I see the door open, the librarian walking out first followed by Caleb, who holds the book up in his hand. "We found one," the librarian says.

"We did," Caleb confirms, "and she gave us fifty percent off since it's been a long time, so instead of thirty-five dollars it's seventeen fifty."

"Oh." I put the box down before going to my purse.

"I gave her a twenty and told her to keep the change for all her help," he mumbles when he gets closer to me.

"My hero." I smile at him.

"Let's get these packed back up, so I can put them back and then we can leave." I nod at him as he places the books back in the box in the same order, then turning and following her back into the room. I hold the book to my chest as if it's my most prized possession.

He comes out of the room followed by the librarian, who locks the door behind her. "Thank you for all your help," Caleb tells her as he puts his hand at the base of my back and ushers me out of the room. We stop at the office where we both hand in our badges before we walk out.

"So, successful?" he says, slipping his hand in mine.

"I would say so," I tell him. "I wonder where they went to after."

He shrugs as he opens the door for me and kisses me before I get up and in. He buckles the seat belt around me before he walks around. His phone rings as soon as he sits down. "Yeah," he answers, putting it to his ear. "I'm just finishing something up." He starts the truck. "Give me twenty." He hangs up.

"Everything okay?" I ask him as he pulls away from the school.

"Yeah, that was Theo, asking me to go see him for something."

"Why don't you drop me off at the bakery? I'll have a coffee and then walk home." I look over at him as he just nods.

We pull up to the bakery, and as he parks I lean over to kiss him. "Thank you for today," I tell him. "I'll take care of you tonight." I wink at him before reaching for the door handle and letting myself out.

I slam the door and head toward the bakery, pulling open the door and immediately being hit with the smell of baked goodness. I look around and see that some of the tables are taken by a couple of people before walking up to the pink display case and looking at the donuts they have in there. It's Everleigh's specialties, but she changes them almost monthly. "Hey," Everleigh greets, walking out of the back room, wiping her hands on the apron around her waist, "this is a surprise."

"It is." I smile at her. "I was out with Caleb and he got a call, so I told him to just drop me off here."

"What can I get you?" she asks.

"I'm going to have a latte with some cinnamon on top," I tell her, "and then give me whatever donut you think I should try."

"We have a new one this week," she states, grabbing a plate and then white wax paper. "It's called Fall into Apple." She places the donut on a tray as I look at the little pieces of apple crumble on top of the donut covered in white drizzle icing. "It's as if an apple pie and an apple crumble had a baby." I laugh at her. "Go and have a seat, I'll bring you the latte." She motions with her chin as I grab the tray and head to the corner of the room, pulling out one of the cast-iron pink chairs, before placing the tray on the table and sitting down. I place the yearbook beside the tray, looking around as Everleigh comes over and places the latte on the tray. "What do you have there?" she asks, pulling out the seat in front of me and sitting down. "I think Mom is in here," she says, laughing as she opens the book.

I gasp. "Really?" She looks at me with her eyebrows pulled together.

"Yeah, I think so. Mom!" she shouts for her mother, who comes out of the kitchen a couple of seconds later.

She looks around the room, spotting Everleigh sitting with me. "Must we shout?" she scolds her, coming to the table.

"Sorry, I was too lazy to get up and come and get you," she admits. "Look at this." She holds up the yearbook and Ms. Maddie's eyes go big.

"Isn't that a blast from the past," she declares as she grabs it and opens it, seeing the teachers first. "I had this teacher, and I think he's still teaching." She points at one of the guys, laughing, then goes through a couple more. "This is like four or five years after I graduated," she says. "What are you doing with it?"

"Did you know the Dyson family?" I ask, and she nods.

"I graduated a year before the brother did," she says. "I want to say his name was Kevin, but I could be mistaken."

"What happened to them?" I sit practically at the edge of my seat.

"There was talk about one of the sisters falling in love with someone from the wrong side of town and the father was having none of it, so he up and moved everyone away," she relays.

"Which sister?" My hands are practically shaking.

"I think the older one," she hesitates, not sure. "He was from up north somewhere."

"Do you know where they went to?"

"I want to say Jefferson County, but I'm not really sure." She shrugs. "The mom came from big money," she fills me in. "Her father owned the newspaper in town, along with a couple of them from all over the United States."

"Well, that makes sense now," I mumble, thinking the story of me being left was only run once and nothing else after that. "I think he sold it a couple of years ago, but I'm not sure." She looks up from the book. "What's with all the questions?"

I smile at both of them, the tears escaping without me even knowing. "Fiona Dyson is my birth mother."

Thirty-Four

CALEB

I'M GOING DOWN the ladder in the barn when I hear a truck door slam. Looking over at the open door, I see her running inside.

Her blond hair is flying in the wind. "Hey," I say when I get to the last step and turn toward her, "this is a surprise."

"I know," she warbles, and I see tears running down her face.

"What happened?"

"I found him," she says between sobs. "I found my father."

"What?" I ask. "I left you two hours ago, and you were going to start working for the day."

"I know, but you know yesterday, when I came home from the bakery and Ms. Maddie told me she thought they moved to Jefferson County?" I nod as she continues. "So this morning, I went online and searched up their alumni and just wrote on the message board, asking if anyone from the graduating class had their yearbook and if I could ask them something."

"Okay."

"Well, one girl messaged me back maybe ten minutes later." She puts her hand on my chest. "And I asked her if she could send me a picture of Sonia and Fiona Dyson," she explains, and she takes a deep breath in, "and she wrote his initials in her yearbook."

"Who did?" I ask as she takes a second to catch her breath.

"Fiona," she says, "my mother is definitely Fiona."

"How do you know for sure?" I rub my hands up and down her arms. She holds out her phone, and I look down to see Fiona Dyson, her yearbook quote next to her name, "Nothing is what it seems to be. Love will prevail all, or that is what you keep telling me. C.B."

"The girl who sent me the picture," she adds while I stare at the picture, "said there was some gossip about the two of them running away with each other. But she wasn't sure."

"Does she know him?" I ask her and she shakes her head.

"He was a year older than Fiona, but like she said, no one really saw them together. She came to town in the twelfth grade and didn't really have a friend group she hung out with and then the next year everyone went off to college. She said she pretty much stayed to herself."

"Baby, do you know how many C.B.'s there are?"

"I know. I called the forensic genealogist and gave

him the initials, and he thinks his last name is probably Boston. My great-grandmother married an Edward Boston and they had a couple of kids so…" She closes her eyes. "I'm so freaking close."

"You are so very close, baby." She smiles at me. "Are you going to call Fiona now?"

"No, I called Sonia. For sure she will tell her, if she wanted to get in touch with me, she would have."

I breathe a sigh of relief not to have to watch her live through that again. "Are you still okay with going to meet my parents this weekend?"

"Yes," she almost shrieks, "of course I am. I'm a little nervous but…"

"What are you nervous about?" I laugh.

"I'm sleeping with their son."

"I'm almost thirty." I try not to laugh. "I think they are going to be okay with me sleeping with you."

"You say that now." She leans up and kisses my lips. "I'm going to head back home and try to work," she says, but then her phone rings, and she looks down. "It's him."

"Baby, there are so many hims in your life, you are going to have to be more specific."

"It's Brendan." I raise my eyebrows. "The genealogist." She presses the green button and then presses the speaker button. "Hey, Brendan." I listen to her fake voice. "This is a surprise."

"I've been doing a bit of digging around," he says, "since you called me, and I think I found your birth father. His name is Carl Boston." She goes almost lax in my arms. "The ages add up, and from the information I found online, he's got his own business in woodworking. I've sent his information to you. Let me know if you need anything else."

"I will, Brendan," she replies. "Thank you so, so much for all your help." She disconnects.

"Could this be it?" she mumbles as she opens an email. "Carl Boston," she says his name again. "CB Woods."

I look up, my brain going through all the names I know in the area and gasp. "He did your library cabinets," I whisper, and her eyes go even bigger.

"What?" she asks me as I take my phone out of my pocket and pull up the emails I had going back and forth with him.

"Carl Boston." I turn my phone to her so she can see the invoice. "Wow." I shake my head. "What a small world." I look back at her. "What are you going to do? Will you call him?"

"I don't know. I feel like I have to, but then again I'm not sure I'm ready for the other side. He might not want anything to do with me."

"I'll call him," I tell her. "I've been talking to him about other jobs, so it won't be…" I trail off. "I have no idea. What if he didn't know?"

"Oh my God," she says, putting her hand to her mouth, "what if she never told him?"

"Only one way to find out," I declare, and she nods as I start to dial the number. "I'm so nervous," I admit. She rolls her eyes and stops when he answers the phone after one ring.

"Hey, Caleb," he answers right away, "how're you

doing?"

"Hey, Carl," I reply, "I'm good." I close my eyes. "Listen, I'm calling, and it's going to be really strange, but I have a couple of questions to ask you."

"This sounds serious." He laughs. "If you are calling to ask me to build you one of those sex contraptions where you tie a woman up, I'm going to have to say you are not going to get it from me."

I look at Sierra, who rolls her lips and tries not to laugh out loud. "Nope," I say, "definitely not calling for that."

"Then nothing can be strange," he replies. "Whatcha got for me?"

"I was…" I try to think about how to word this, but there aren't really very many ways to do this, so I shoot straight. "I'm wondering if you ever dated a Fiona Dyson?" I ask and you can hear the silence through the phone and it's deafening.

"What is this about?" he quickly says, his voice going tight, the humor now gone.

"I know this is going to come out of left field, but my girlfriend, her name is Sierra."

"Okay," he responds, and I can tell he's not following.

I look at the phone, and before I say anything else, Sierra starts. "Hi," she says softly, "I'm Sierra." Her voice is a whisper. "I'm searching for my birth parents who gave me up for adoption twenty-five years ago."

"I'm sorry, come again?" he says.

"Twenty-five years ago, I was left at a fire station. I've been tracking my DNA, and well, I traced it back to either Fiona or Sonia Dyson."

"You were left at a fire station," he repeats the words, and it feels like each word stabs him in the heart. "I thought you were…" His voice trails off. "I had no idea."

"I don't want anything from either of you," she explains. "I just want to know where I come from."

"Your mother," he says and his voice quivers, "was the love of my life." I can feel it soar through him, whatever happened between the two of them, he never moved on. "The two of you were the loves of my life." You can hear the anguish in his voice. "Where are you right now?"

"I'm…" She trails off, and I cut into the conversation.

"You built her the shelves for the library." The gasp that comes out of him fills the phone.

"Is the delivery address on the bill?" he snaps out.

"It is," I confirm to him.

"I'll be there as soon as I can." He hangs up, and I look over at Sierra, whose eyes go big.

"Where is he even located?" she asks.

"About forty minutes from here," I tell her, and she puts her hand on her stomach. "Do you think he's coming to my house?"

"I have no idea," I tell her, "but we should go just in case he does."

"Are you coming with me?"

"You think I'm going to let this man come into your house without me being there?" I shake my head and walk out of the barn with her. "Keys." I hold out my hand for her keys.

"What about your truck?" she asks as I open the

passenger door to her car.

"We'll come back and get it later," I tell her as she gets into the car, and I walk around to the driver's side.

We don't say a word to each other as I drive back to her house. We walk in, and she goes straight to the couch and collapses on it. "Maybe he's not coming here." She looks at me. "Maybe he just wanted to google my house and see where I live." I don't say anything because I know this is her nervous energy coming out of her. "Maybe he just wanted to get off the phone with you, and now you're blocked, and you are going to have to get a new wood person."

"Sierra," I say, but instead of saying anything more, I walk into the kitchen and take the bottle of whiskey Autumn gave her when she came to visit last week. I pour her a shot, turning back and heading to the library room and handing it to her. "Here."

"It's not even noon," she retorts, and I raise my eyebrows. "Yeah, good call," she concedes, taking it and downing the shot and then hissing and trying to cover her cough. "Smooth," she pants out. "So gross, I never want to do that again."

"Noted. Should I call him, and ask him where he is?"

"No," she snaps. "What if he was just wanting to get off the phone?"

"What if," I say when the sound of a car door shuts, and I look over at her. "Should I go and check?"

"No," she whispers, her eyes going to me and then to the door, "that would be creepy. What if it's my neighbor?"

She is about to say something else when the doorbell rings, followed by a frantic knocking. "I don't think it's your neighbor."

Thirty-Five

SIERRA

I'M ABOUT TO tell him it's probably all in our head when the doorbell rings, followed by a frantic knocking. "I don't think it's your neighbor." He looks at me.

"Should I answer it?" I ask, and he shakes his head.

"No fucking way," Caleb retorts. "We are going to have a couple of words before he walks in here."

"Do you think that's really necessary?" I ask.

"It's nonnegotiable," he declares as the bell rings again, followed by the knocking. "He's not coming in here until we talk."

"Okay," I concede, knowing I would probably do the same thing if the roles were reversed. I sit back down on the couch as he walks over to the door and it opens. "Carl." He's about to take a step out when he moves back because Carl has walked into the house. Or better yet, he's stormed into the house.

"Where is she?" he asks, and I watch him from the

side. His voice sounds like it's trembling as I take a step to the side to take him in. He's a touch taller than Caleb, and his shoulders are definitely broader than Caleb's. His hair is salt-and-pepper, and I have to wonder if he had black hair before or brown. The beard that covers his face is a lighter color than the salt-and-pepper hair he has.

"Before you speak with her," Caleb warns, "we need to set up ground rules."

Carl looks over his shoulder, and he must spot me because he gasps, his hand going to his mouth in shock. "Holy shit!" he exclaims. "It's true!"

"Hi." I finally walk toward them, making sure I stand behind Caleb. "I'm Sierra."

"Oh my." He runs his hands through his hair over and over again, frantically walking back and forth in front of us. "I can't." He shakes his head, his breathing coming out in pants. "This is." He pulls his hair. "I can't fucking believe this." The tears brim in his eyes. "I can't." He looks like he's about to have a full-blown panic attack.

"Carl," Caleb says, walking toward him, "can I get you some water?"

"I don't know." He looks up at the ceiling. "They said—" His voice trembles, and I can see the heartbreak in his eyes as he walks to me. He stands in front of me. His hand comes up, and we can both see that it's trembling. He palms my cheek. "You are so fucking beautiful." He smiles through the tears, and his eyes shut as he sobs. "You take my breath away, you are so beautiful." He pulls me into his arms to hug me. I can't help but feel like

I'm being hugged for the first time. "Jesus," he hisses. "You are fucking beautiful," he repeats it over and over again.

I don't know how long I stay in his arms, the two of us just holding each other. Then I feel Caleb beside me, rubbing my back. "Perhaps we should sit down."

"That would be good," Carl agrees, letting me go but grabbing my hand to keep me close to him. "My legs are about to give out."

I laugh as I move with him to the library. "Do you want water?" I ask him as he looks around. "Juice, coffee?" He shakes his head. "Whiskey?" He chuckles.

"I'm good," he assures me. I sit down, and he follows my lead. His hand immediately goes to hold mine as Caleb stands on the side of the couch, giving us our moment. "I want you to know that I never knew, or else I would have taken you," he starts, and I can't help the tears that run down my face. The feeling of knowing that at least someone wanted me makes all of this up-and-down worth it. "Your mother," he begins and shakes his head, "I loved her with everything I had, and I wanted to give her the world."

"How did you two meet?" I ask, and he smiles sadly.

"I was walking home from my job at one of the ranches nearby. It was summer, and she was stuck on the side of the road. Her tire was flat. She was trying to change it, but the lug nuts were just too tight. So I helped her." He smiles. "She was the most beautiful woman I had ever laid eyes on. I asked her to have dinner with me the next day. She showed up, and I knew she was the one for me. Knew I wouldn't ever find someone who would take my breath away. Still is to this day, the love of my life."

"But she moved."

"Yeah, her parents found out we were dating. It wasn't a good look. Her grandfather was a newspaper tycoon, and I was the kid from the wrong side of the tracks, with barely any schooling and no prospects. My parents were hardworking people, but we still lived paycheck to paycheck, and that wasn't what they envisioned for their daughter. So they moved her away."

"But you never stopped?" I ask, and his smile gets even bigger.

"Never," he admits. "We snuck around for over a year. I would work eighty hours a week just so I could buy a car and get gas money to go see her for a couple of hours on the weekend." My heart breaks for both of them. "Losing your mother and then losing you. I knew there was no way I could ever love anyone as much as I did you guys." He brings my hand to his lips. "I never moved on." I don't know if I gasp or if Caleb is the one who gasps, but the whole room goes silent. "But now you're here."

"Now I'm here." I smile at him, the tears running over my lips to my chin. "And—" I'm about to say something else when the doorbell rings.

"I'll get it," Caleb states, and he walks away from us, but Carl is on his feet.

"I should have told you," he starts to say, but then stops when I look over at the woman who is now standing in the middle of my foyer and the living room. Her eyes go to Carl first and then to me. "Fiona," he says, and before I can say anything, she falls right there in the middle of my foyer.

"Holy shit!" Caleb catches her right before her head hits the floor. Carl rushes to her while I stand here frozen in my tracks.

"I've got her," Carl assures him, taking her in his arms and carrying her over to the couch.

"I'll get her a cold rag," Caleb offers, rushing to the bathroom upstairs.

"I'll get her some water," I say, running out of the room and toward the kitchen, grabbing a water bottle and then walking back into the room. She's lying on the couch, a pillow under her head with Carl putting the cold rag on the back of her neck.

"Fiona," he says her name as he brushes the hair away from her face. Her eyes flutter open as she tries to focus. "Hi," he says, smiling down at her, "you fainted." He fills her in as she looks up at him. Her hair is very different from the picture I found of her. It's more brown with soft blond highlights.

"Carl," she says his name as if he hung the moon and the stars, "tell me it's not true."

"Someone needs to tell me what is going on," Caleb interjects. "Please fill us in. What is she doing here?" He points at her.

"When I got off the phone with you, I called her." Carl fills us in as Fiona sits up on the couch, her eyes going past Caleb and to me.

"Oh my God," she gasps, "it's true."

I look at Caleb and see he's about two seconds from going Hulk on both of them. My hand reaches out to grab his arm. "It's okay," I assure him. "I'm okay, I promise, and if I'm not, I will let you take me away from it all." I kiss his lips before I turn back to my birth parents.

"I called you last week," I tell her, and her face goes even whiter than it was before.

"No, you didn't." She shakes her head. "There was no way in hell you called me last week."

"I mean, I called Sonia. Surely, she would have told you I was looking for you."

"She would one hundred percent not tell me that," she rebuts. "Oh my God, she's alive."

"What?" I shriek. "What are you saying?"

"I went into labor," she starts as she looks at Carl, who is squatting beside her now, his hand still holding hers, "my mother didn't want me giving birth in town because it was a secret. No one could know I was pregnant. For six months I was tucked away and hidden from everyone for them to make sure that my secret didn't get out. I didn't even go to the doctor, he came to the house. When my water broke, I thought this was it. I would go to the hospital and get someone to call Carl. Except it wasn't really a hospital, it was this private clinic. We got there, my mother, my sister, and I were ushered in. Not one other person besides the doctor and two nurses were there. I thought it was strange but then the contractions started, and I told them I wanted to do it naturally. They gave me an IV and the next thing you know I'm waking up two hours later…" She trails off as if she is remembering it.

"They told me you were dead," she says the words like they pour out of her soul. "They told me you were stillborn." I take a step back as if she struck me. "I begged to see you. To hold you. To tell you how much I loved you, but they refused. My mother and sister were adamant it wasn't something I wanted to see. They stood beside me as I picked out a fucking casket for you to be buried in. It was the size of a bread box. My sister told me she would take care of everything for me." She puts her hands on her stomach. "I forced my mother to give me a phone and then I called Carl. He was waiting to come and take me away with him. Take us away with him. But I couldn't face him. It was my fault you had died." The pain in her soul is like it had just happened and not twenty-five years ago. "I blamed myself, it was my fault you died." She shakes her head. "I couldn't do it, I couldn't face anyone. I told my mother to take me away and I never looked back. My body healed, my heart—" She shakes her head. "Every single year on your birthday, I would spend in bed. Reliving the nightmare of never holding you. Never being able to tell you how much you were loved." The sound of her wailing now fills the room.

"Those motherfuckers," Carl growls from beside her, his body shaking with the same emotions she has.

My head is spinning as I listen to her story. Shock fills me, and I'm about to say something when the doorbell rings. "It's like Grand Central Station in here," I mumble, going to the door. It happens so fast I don't even know it's happening. One minute, I'm pulling open the door, and the next minute, my name is being roared out by Caleb, and then everything goes black.

Thirty-Six

CALEB

"IT'S LIKE GRAND Central Station in here," Sierra mumbles from beside me and moves away from me, heading to the door. I turn back to see her birth parents on the couch, her father now sitting beside her mother as she sobs in his arms. The whole story has been mind-blowing to say the least.

The next couple of seconds happen so fast, I don't even think I know what's going on. Sierra opens the door, and she has one hand on the doorknob while she looks up at the guy who is there.

Something pushes me toward the door. I don't know what it is, and I can't explain it, but the minute I get close enough, I see his hand straighten up. It takes me half a second to register that he's aiming a gun at her. The look on his face is filled with rage. "I told you to stop looking." It's the only thing he gets to say before I roar out her name.

"Sierra!" I rush to her, wrapping an arm around her waist and pushing her to the side when the gun goes off. There is chaos all around me as I cover her body with my own.

"Fuck," the man swears, looking down at us, his gun aimed at us.

"What the fuck are you doing?" Carl shouts, and the man turns to look toward them.

"Are you crazy?" Fiona shouts, coming to stand next to them, and I look down at Sierra, whose eyes are closed.

"Sierra, baby," I say as wetness fills my chest, and I look down to see she's bleeding. "She's been shot." I get off her, looking down at her to see that she's been shot in the shoulder.

"Don't think you'll get away with this, Peter!" Fiona yells her brother's name, as I pull my phone out of my pocket and dial 911, leaving it to the side.

"We need some towels!" I shout to them, and Peter aims his gun at all of us.

"Move and I'll shoot you all." His brownish-blond hair that was perfectly coiffed when he was standing outside the door is now becoming disheveled, just like he is. He waves the gun around, and Carl now looks like he's about to charge him, but he steps half in front of Fiona.

"You had to go and fuck everything up!" he screams at Sierra. "We took care of this shit twenty-five years ago."

"What are you talking about?" Fiona asks.

"You think we were going to give you the inheritance

with that no-good piece of shit, who was just with you because all he saw when he looked at you was dollar signs?" He points the gun at Carl. "You went and got knocked up like a stupid slut instead of listening to us when we told you to walk away from him."

"You think I gave two shits about the money?" Carl retorts, trying to push Fiona behind him.

"She's bleeding!" I yell, taking off my shirt and pushing it on her shoulder to stop the bleeding. "For fuck's sake, we need help." I look over at my phone to see that I'm connected to 911 and hoping like fuck they get here fucking fast. "She's been shot. We need to get her help. If anything happens to her—" I stare at Peter, who just puts his head back and laughs.

"Good. Hopefully, now she really fucking dies, and we don't have to deal with this shit anymore." He shakes his head. "The minute the kid was born, we had to get rid of her. I told them we should have just dumped her in the garbage like she was, but fucking Sonia didn't listen to me. No, she took her and dumped her off at a fire station, for fuck's sake." The more he talks, the more rage fills me, my eyes going to Sierra's beautiful face as I plead with her silently to open her eyes. "The number of people we had to pay off to keep your fucking secret was insane. Doctors, nurses, journalists, police chiefs, the list went on and on, all because you couldn't keep your fucking legs closed."

"I loved him," Fiona declares. "He was the only thing that mattered. I didn't want any of the money. I wanted nothing but him and my daughter, and you guys just took that away from me."

"So irrational." Peter shakes his head, the hand holding the gun starting to get really fucking shaky. "I was supposed to get it all…me." He points the gun at himself. "I was the oldest, but you"—he points at Fiona—"you with your feminist bullshit and how it's not fair, so our grandfather then changed his fucking will to include you and your kids. Your bastard of a child would get it all because she was first in line. There was no fucking way I was going to allow that to happen." He shakes his head, and we can hear the sirens now, far off in the distance. "It ends today!" he roars. "It should have ended twenty-five fucking years ago." He points the gun at Fiona. "You ruined this family"—there is a frightening look in his eyes as he sneers at her—"for nothing."

The sound of the sirens getting closer makes me close my eyes for a second before I open them back up and look down at Sierra. "Hang on, baby," I whisper before I see movement in my peripheral vision. Carl charges at him like a bull, leaving Fiona open, but it takes him less than a second to knock Peter off his feet. His shoulder going straight to his stomach, his arm moving high, and the sound of the gun going off. I see Fiona's eyes go big as she looks down and puts her hand to the side of her stomach.

Blood oozes through her fingers. She takes her eyes away from her hand to Sierra, and the tears flow down her face. "I love you, baby girl," she says before her legs give out on her, and she falls to her knees.

The sound of sirens now fills the whole house. The red

lights flash through the windows and the open door. "In here!" I yell. "They're here, baby," I murmur, wanting to shake her to make her wake up. I look over to the side and see Carl on top of Peter, his fists flying one after another on Peter's face.

The police come in first, guns drawn and I see it's Deputy Burke. "Drop your weapons," he orders, and I look at him.

"One weapon," I inform him, and he looks over at me. "On the floor over there." I motion with my chin toward the gun that fell from Peter's hand when he was tackled. One of the officers behind him comes in and kicks it aside while the firemen come in with the first responders.

"She was shot," I tell them as they come over to me, "and so was she." I motion toward Fiona, who is lying by herself. "Carl!" I shout his name, but he's in another world.

Deputy Burke rushes over to Carl, side tackling him to get him to stop hitting Peter. His fists are bloody. "Sir," the woman paramedic says, "can you move your hand?" They look down at my shirt that is covered in blood. I move out of the way to let them treat her, falling on my ass as I take a look around the room. Ten minutes ago, it was a tearful reunion, and now it's probably going to be the scene of a crime.

I look up, seeing a fireman in front of me, and he holds out his hand to me. "Let's get you up and in a shirt so you can go with her to the hospital." I reach out my hand for him, and he pulls me up.

"Is she—" I ask the paramedic beside Sierra.

"I think she'll be fine." He smiles at me. "It looks like it went right through."

"I'm going to have to do a sweep to make sure it's all good," the fireman tells me, and I nod at him.

"Her blood pressure is going down," a frantic voice says from Fiona's side. "We need to get her out of here before she codes."

She's loaded on a stretcher as Carl gets up and walks over to her. "I'm here, Fiona," he says by her ear. "Don't fucking leave me again." He grabs her hand, bringing it to his mouth.

"Sir, you can't go with them," one of the officers says to Carl.

"He'll be okay," the officer who came in first says. "I'm Deputy Burke." He looks at Carl. "We are going to have questions for you."

"I'll be at the hospital," Carl replies. "I'll answer them all there." Deputy Burke nods at him and then comes over to me.

"We have questions for you as well," Deputy Burke says to me. "I'm assuming you are going to the hospital."

"Really nothing to say," I say to him. "He came in here." I motion to Peter, who is mumbling on the ground. The officer getting him to sit up as a paramedic checks him out. "He shot them. I'll answer whatever questions you want, but I'm not leaving her."

"I'll come by the hospital when we finish up here," Deputy Burke relays and walks away.

I run out of the house beside Sierra when I look up and see Theo running toward the house, fear written all over his face. "Fucking shit, Caleb," he hisses when he spots me and then looks at Sierra. "What happened?"

He stops mid-run when he looks at the female paramedic. "Oh my God, it's you," she says at the same time he whispers, "You," pointing to her and then he shakes his head and turns back to me.

"Meet me at the hospital. Get me a shirt," I instruct him. "Call Lilah, we're going to have to call her parents," I tell him. "My phone is somewhere inside." I motion with my chin toward the house as I get into the back of the ambulance. I sit on one side while the female paramedic sits on the other side. She keeps looking at Sierra and at the house where Theo just went into. The door shuts and her eyes go back to Sierra as she works on her.

Sierra moans out, and my hand reaches for hers as she moves her head side to side. "Baby," I say softly, not realizing there are tears now running down my face. "Baby," I call her again. "I'm here, baby, you're going to be fine."

"Burning," she says, "it burns." She licks her lips.

"I love you," I state, letting out a sigh of relief from hearing her voice, "more than anything, baby. I love you."

"I love you too," she whispers. "What happened?" she asks, and I look over at the paramedic.

"We'll get into that later," I tell her. "You need to save your strength."

"Okay," she gives in. "I'm just going to close my eyes, but don't leave me." She looks back at me.

"Not for a minute." I smile at her as she closes her

eyes, and I look at the paramedic. "That's good, right? That she woke up."

She smiles and nods as I sit with my back against the cold steel side and close my eyes. I open my eyes, and the paramedic hands me a blanket to cover myself up with. I wrap it around my shoulders and look down at her the whole time. We get to the hospital, and they take her out, and I follow, walking into the waiting room and seeing Lilah there with Emmett. Her face is white and streaked with tears when she looks around and finally sees me and rushes to me. "What happened?" she asks.

"You need to call her parents," I tell her, and she nods.

"I already called them on the way here. They're on their way. Is she going to be okay?" Lilah asks, putting her hand on her stomach.

"She's going to be fine," I assure her. "She has no choice." I look over to see Carl standing there, looking at the door they just wheeled Fiona in.

I walk away from Lilah, who turns in Emmett's arms, as I walk to him. "How is she?"

"She coded in the ambulance," he says, his voice monotone. "If I see him, I'm going to kill him." He looks over at me. "Have nothing to live for anyway."

"You have your daughter to get to know," I remind him, "and her mother to take care of." He looks at me. "They're worth it."

Thirty-Seven

SIERRA

I OPEN MY eyes and then shut them again for a second before I force myself to open them again. I look around and see I'm in a hospital room. The door is closed and a machine is working on the side. The IV in my arm pinches me as I see the chair next to my bed and Caleb sitting in it. His head is back, his eyes closed, and his hands folded on his chest. I lick my lips as I try to lift my arm, but the burning in my shoulder makes me hiss out.

Caleb's eyes fly open, and he looks at me. "Sorry, I didn't mean to wake you."

"You're up." He sits up, and I close my eyes again.

"I need water," I tell him, trying to swallow, but my mouth is so dry. He gets up and walks out of the room, and I rest my eyes until I hear the door open, and he walks back in. "Thank you," I say, grabbing the plastic cup he is holding in his hand, but he continues to hold it, putting the straw in my mouth. The cold water hits my tongue right away, and I take a couple of sips. "That was good."

He turns to put it on the brown hospital table before he sits on the bed beside me. "You scared the shit out of me," he mutters, his hand coming up to cup my cheek. "I was so fucking scared. Never do that to me again."

"Okay," I reply softly. "In my defense, I didn't want to do it in the first place."

He smiles. "You have been in and out all night." I'm surprised by his words.

"What happened?" I ask, thinking back to when the memories start to get fuzzy.

"Before we get to all that, I have to go and get your parents"—he gets up from the bed—"and my parents."

"Our parents are here?" I ask, shocked. "Like my parents and your parents?"

"Yes." He nods. "The waiting room was busting with all our friends. All of them left when they found out you were going to be okay, except for our parents. It's pretty great but a little bit too much." His hands go by his head. "I'll be right back." He walks out of the room, and I can hear the rushing of footsteps when the door opens. My mother is the first one in, followed by my father.

"Oh my gosh," she says, rushing to my side while my father follows her. "We were so scared." My mother holds my face. "So fucking scared." She uses the f-word and then gasps. "I didn't mean to swear, but don't fucking do that again."

I try to smile at her as I look over at my father, who is holding my mother's shoulders. "Your mother is happy you're okay." He tries to hide the tremble of his voice by clearing his throat. "I told her you were going to be okay, but she never listens to me."

"Oh, hush"—my mother swats at him—"she was shot. I never thought that would ever come out of my mouth. I know someone who was shot."

I look over at the side, seeing Caleb standing with his parents who I've met on FaceTime a couple of times. My heartbeat starts to pick up. "Um, hi." I hold up my hand as much as I can, but it falls beside me. "Sorry, I would be more chipper, but getting shot is exhausting."

"Sierra," my mother gasps, "too soon." She wipes her eyes, then looks at my father and face-plants her head in the middle of his chest. "She gets that from you."

"Of course she does."

"Can I meet Caleb's parents now?" I ask them, and they move aside. "This is really not how I wanted the first meeting to go with the two of you." I try to sit up in the bed but that just is too much energy. "I had a dress picked out and everything."

His mother comes forward first with a smile and tears, of course. "It's so good to finally meet you," she says, and I look over her shoulder at Jensen, who Caleb looks exactly like.

"Thank you for coming. You really didn't have to."

"Of course we did," she refutes. "We're practically family." I look at her, then at Caleb, who looks up and avoids my eyes.

"He did tell me the two of you were moving in together," my mother interjects.

"They already live together," Jensen adds, and my father quickly looks at Caleb.

"This is fun," I note, "but can we talk about me getting shot?"

"What do you remember?" Caleb asks, coming over to sit by the bed. His hand wraps around mine, bringing it to his lips.

"I remember my birth mother telling me about what her family did to her." I look at him. "Then I remember opening the door to a man."

"That was your uncle." He fills me in on everything he knows, the silent sobs coming from my mother as she listens to the story as Jensen holds Hailey in his arms. His jaw is tighter with each passing second the story goes on. My mouth hangs open. "I don't know how to tell you this next part," he says softly, "but Fiona was shot."

I sit up in bed, ignoring the way my arm burns. "What?"

"She's going to be okay," he assures me, and I shake my head and turn to the other side of him, tossing the blanket off me and moving to the edge of the bed.

"Baby"—he rushes to the other side—"can you relax for a minute?"

"No." I shake my head. "You can either take me to her, or I will call the nurse and get her to take me."

He exhales a heavy breath. "Let me get you a wheelchair." He looks at my parents and then his. "Don't let her get out of that bed."

I want to fight him on it, but my body is going to give out mid-step if I try to fight it off and walk to her. "Is she okay?" I ask the four of them, and they all nod at me.

"She came out of surgery a while ago, but she hasn't woken up," my mother shares. "You look so much like her."

The only thing I can do is nod at this, knowing it must be very hard for her to come face-to-face with my birth mother.

Caleb comes back a couple of minutes later with the black wheelchair in front of him. "The nurse is going to come in and disconnect you from all of your things," he tells me, and a second later, the nurse comes in.

She takes the monitor off my finger and the two on my chest. She hangs the IV bag on top of the pole on the wheelchair. "She is good to go." She nods at him and then at me as Caleb picks me up and places me in the wheelchair.

"Should we put a blanket on her legs?" he asks the nurse, who looks at me. "Is that a no?"

"If it will make you feel better," I give in to him, "then sure." He places the blanket over my legs.

"See, compromising already," Jensen jokes, and my father chuckles as Caleb pushes me out of the room and into the dimly lit hallway.

"Are you guys coming?" I look over at my parents, who haven't moved from their spot.

"We don't want to intrude," my mother says, standing tall and trying to be strong.

"Mom," I retort, "you're as much a part of this as I am." She nods when I hold out my hand to her.

I hold my mother's hand as Caleb wheels me down

the hall two doors. He stops the chair and then walks in front of me, as he knocks and then opens the door. "She forced me to bring her." He sticks his head into the room before the door is pulled open, and my birth father, Carl, is standing there. His eyes go to my parents as he nods at them, and I have a feeling they've met, and then they come to me.

"You're up." He smiles at me, his eyes filled with brand-new tears. "I was coming by to check on you in a couple of minutes."

"How is she?" I look past him and toward the bed where Fiona lies.

"Doctor said it's a good thing the gun was a twenty-two." He runs his hand through his hair. "Missed all the organs, and she got shot in the side." He moves to the side so Caleb can wheel me in.

"What happened?" I look at the two of them, who share a look. "You might as well tell me because I'm bound to find out. Someone got shot in my house. I'm sure there will be a police report out there somewhere."

"She's not going to let up," my father concedes. "She's tenacious." He looks at Carl, who smiles sadly at me. My heart hurts for him, thinking I was dead all these years. I can't even fathom what that would feel like.

"Fine." Caleb fills me in on everything that was said while I was unconscious. My mother shakes her head side to side in shock.

"Where is he now?" I ask, my head reeling from everything that happened today.

"He's being held at the local jail," Caleb replies. "Carl

broke his nose and busted his lip open, but it's nothing that will cause him to stay in the hospital."

"So they did all of this for money?" I ask, looking at Carl.

"It's the root of all evil." Fiona's voice comes out hoarsely, and we all look at her.

"Fiona," Carl calls, rushing to her side, "you're okay." He grabs her hand and tries not to disturb her. The tears just pour down his face. The way he looks at her, you can feel the way he loves her. "You're okay," he sobs quietly, taking her hand in his and kissing it. "I'm sorry."

"I'm the one who should be sorry." She tries to clear her throat, and I look up at Caleb, not wanting to ruin their special moment.

"I'm the one who should be sorry. I didn't protect our child." She tries to move her hand to wipe her tears, but it quickly falls down beside her hip. "I should have protected her."

"I'm fine," I interrupt softly. "I grew up with the best parents that I could ask for. They loved me unconditionally, and not once did I feel that I wasn't theirs, not once." I look at my mother, who puts her hand on my shoulder, and I put my hand on hers.

"But you were mine," my mother says. "You were ours."

"I'm still yours." I try to steady my voice. "I'm here because of my parents"—I look at my mother and my father—"and because of you two. This is my story." I look at them. "Our story is just beginning." I look at Carl and Fiona. "That is if you'll have me. Have us."

"That's the question we should be asking you," Carl replies, then looks at Fiona. "Will you"—he swallows—"allow us to be a part of your life?"

"I never forgot you," Fiona declares. "You were never forgotten. And I'm not about to forget about you now. I'll take whatever it is you want to give us." She looks at my mother. "Thank you for raising her when I couldn't. For loving her with us."

My mother lets go of my hand and walks over to the bed. "No, thank you two for creating the perfect child." Fiona and my mother share a look. "Nothing I can give you can replace what you lost. But we can fill in the gaps."

"I'd like that very much," Fiona says, then she looks at Carl. "We would like that very much."

I look over at Caleb, who comes to squat beside me. "Oh, by the way," he mumbles, "I may have told them we were engaged." I gasp. "I had to think of something. They wanted to know how we were related."

"And you went with engaged?" I roll my eyes. "I better get a big ring." I look over at Fiona and my mother. The two of them try not to laugh as Fiona closes her eyes. "It's going to be okay," I assure them between my own tears. "Everything is going to be okay."

Two weeks later:

The knock at the door has both of us looking at each other. "Are you expecting anyone?" I ask Caleb as he walks to the front door.

"No," he says over his shoulder before opening the door and seeing Theo standing there.

"Hey," Caleb says, moving aside to give room for Theo to come in. "This is a surprise. I thought you were going to visit your parents this weekend."

"Yeah," he says and I can see that he's going through something when he looks at me, then at Caleb, running his hand through his hair. "No." He looks up. "Fuck, I don't even know how to say this."

"You're scaring the shit out of me," Caleb snaps at him and I stand here, my heart pounding in my chest thinking he's in trouble. "Just say whatever it is."

I don't know what I'm expecting to hear, but from the shock and gasp out of Caleb's mouth, it's not what he's expecting either. "I'm going to be a father."

Epilogue One

CALEB

Five months later

THE DOORBELL RINGS as soon as I walk out of my bedroom and slip on my suit jacket. "Come in!" I shout, and the door opens, and my parents walk in. My father is wearing a blue suit, while my mother wears a satin dress that goes just past her knees.

"Are you ready?" my father asks, following my mother in as she looks up at me with a big smile.

"You look so handsome," she compliments me when I get to the bottom step, pulling out my sleeves from my black suit jacket, "just like your dad." She leans into him, and he wraps an arm around her shoulders.

"You look beautiful, Mom." I kiss her cheek.

"If we don't leave now, we might be late." My father looks at his watch. "Or at least late in Sierra's mind, and she has enough to worry about today."

"Then let's go," I urge, walking to the front door, following my parents. My father opens it, and my mother stops as she looks over.

"You know what this house is missing?" She steps outside, looking over her shoulder.

"If you say kids"—I close the door behind me before turning and locking it—"I'm going to tell you that you have to take it up with Sierra."

"No, not kids." She walks down the two steps toward the walkway. "Even though that would be lovely." I nod, following them as I tighten the tie around my neck. "A dog."

"Mom." I stop in my tracks. "I like the kid idea more."

"You always had dogs growing up." She looks over at me while my father opens her car door.

"Yeah, and you know what sucked about all of that?" I open the back door of the car. "Saying goodbye to them."

"So dramatic." She rolls her eyes at him. "You can't have kids without a dog. That's just cruel."

I slam the door as she looks over her shoulder while she reaches one hand for the seat belt. "Brewsky was your shadow from when you were five until you were seventeen."

"Mom, I love you"—I stop when my father gets in—"but can we not talk about this today? There is enough going on without bringing up a dog and children."

"It's the circle of life, Caleb." She turns back to face the front. "You have to give us grandchildren."

"Again, talk to Sierra."

"I can't talk to her today," my mother huffs out. "She's

already going through it."

I pull out my phone and send her a message to give her a heads-up.

Me: My mother wants us to get a dog. The answer is no.

I press send, not thinking she has much time to get back to me with her doing her hair and makeup for today. But I'm shocked when I see the gray bubble pop up with the three dots.

Sierra: Why can't we get a dog? I want a dog.

I look up, ignoring the conversation my parents are having in front of me when I answer her.

Me: We can't get a dog because when they die, it's traumatic, and our kids don't need to go through that.

Sierra: Wow, instead of thinking how amazing the experience would be for the children with a dog, you just go to the bad part of it.

Me: Yes, I've lived through it, and it sucks.

Sierra: We're getting a dog.

Me: Aren't you busy doing other things? You have time to argue with me about a dog?

Sierra: I always, always make time to argue with you. It's my favorite pastime.

Me: That's because you want to get in my pants.

Sierra: Like that's hard.

Me: I'm getting hard thinking about it.

Sierra: Got to go. Love you.

Me: See you soon.

I put the phone in the inside pocket of my suit jacket and look out the window. It's been five months since that fateful day. I want to say it was uneventful, but the roller coaster that came after was something straight out of a movie. The first thing that happened is Sonia rushed to the hospital but was escorted right out when Fiona called security on her, and then told both her and her mother—in no uncertain terms—they were both dead to her. She would never, ever forgive them for taking Sierra away from her. Never.

The second thing that happened was her uncle Peter pleading not guilty by reason of temporary insanity. They went through all the steps, and in the end, they found he knew exactly what he was doing. He's being held without bail since he purchased a plane ticket to the Bahamas while he was being held for attempted murder.

The third thing that happened was we found out Sierra was worth millions, like tens of millions, from her great-grandparents as the firstborn grandchild. She wanted to refuse the money, but her mother said it was the least of what they owed her.

"I can't believe they're getting married," my father says as I look out the window. We are on our way to Fiona and Carl's wedding. It's still strange to say, but when you are with them, you can feel the love pouring out of them. The minute she was discharged from the hospital, he took her home to his house, and she never left.

"I can't believe they are having another baby," my mother says. "She was shocked. She thought she was starting premenopause and boom. Baby."

The two of them moving in with each other right

away was something else, but then they have moved to be closer to Sierra, buying a house a street over and fixing it up. Even though they didn't want to push Sierra to do anything she didn't want to. They wanted to be close when she was ready. Right away, she included them in everything. We had Sunday meals together every single week. That with the fact she and Fiona would get coffee a couple of times a week. Each time, Sierra would come home and tell me how she was getting to know her. Each time, it was as if they were almost the same person. Her adoptive parents were just as included and made it a point to come down for Sunday dinners every week even though the drive was over three hours. They made a weekend trip out of it most times and were now looking to buy a home near us. It's like one big happy family, and as long as Sierra was happy, I didn't really care.

We pull up to their home, parking on the street as we make our way around back where the ceremony will be held. I spot Joseph and Carl standing together. Both of them are in black suits. Carl with his hands in his pockets while Joseph talks to him. "Hey," I say to them, "how is everyone doing?"

"He's nervous," Joseph states, slapping Carl on the shoulder.

"I'm not nervous at all. Never been more sure of anything in my life. I just want to get this show on the road and finally make that woman mine."

"Good things come to those who wait," Joseph teases, and my father laughs at them.

"I'm going to go in and see if I can help in any way,"

my mother says, getting up on her tippy-toes and kissing my father.

"Do me a favor, Hailey," Carl says when she takes a step up, "tell her to get her ass out here."

My mother hides that she is trying not to laugh but fails. "I'm never going to tell a bride that," she retorts, then looks at me. "Are you coming with me?"

"I wasn't going to," I tell her and share a look with the guys.

"Good, you tell her that message from me," Carl says, and I throw my head back and laugh.

"You think I'm going to tell my girlfriend's birth mother to move her ass?" I shake my head. "There is not enough money in the world for me to do that." I walk up the steps onto the covered porch and into the house.

"It's almost time," Marian says.

"You are going to be late." Sierra knocks on the door. "Isn't morning sickness supposed to leave after three months?" We walk down the hall toward the voices.

"Knock-knock-knock," my mother says and knocks on the open door. "How is everyone doing?" She stops and looks at Sierra. "You look beautiful," she exclaims, walking over to her and giving her a kiss on the cheek, "and so do you!"

"She's in there. I'm not sure if she's going to vomit or not," Sierra tells my mother. "I'm just saying we walk down the aisle, and if she has to throw up, she runs back inside."

I lean against the doorjamb, taking her in. Her eyes come to me, and she smiles before making her way over to me. She's wearing a lilac one-shouldered dress that hugs her curves perfectly. It's like the dress was made for her. A slit down on the right side shows her leg, with a sash that hangs down on the side, trailing her when she walks. "Aren't you so handsome," she coos when she gets close to me, putting her hand on my chest and fixing my tie. "So very, very handsome."

"And you look more beautiful than you did yesterday." I wink at her.

"We have to talk," she says softly, coming even closer to me. "We're getting a dog."

"Sierra." I stand now. "I don't want a dog."

"But my mother said she always wanted to get me a dog, and then Fiona said she would have definitely gotten me a dog to be my best friend and talk to." I roll my eyes. "And that's what I want to give our kids."

"Shouldn't we work on getting the kids before the dog?"

"No, it's even better if I'm pregnant and then bring the baby in. It'll protect them." She looks up at me, a smile on her face.

"Fine"—I look over her shoulder—"we'll get a dog, but when our kids are depressed because the dog died, you're going to handle that."

"Deal." She gets on her tippy-toes and kisses my lips lightly.

"Now I'm not going to say what was said to me"—I look down at her—"but if Fiona doesn't get out there soon, Carl is going to come in and carry her out."

"Fiona," Sierra calls over her shoulder, "Carl is done

waiting and is about to bring everyone inside to have the wedding here."

"I'm ready." She opens the bathroom door and steps out. "How crazy is this, getting married at forty-three?" She holds up her hand. "The question is, how crazy is it being pregnant at forty-three?" She laughs and puts her hand on her stomach.

"I don't even want to think about how that happened," Sierra teases, "but I always wanted a brother."

Fiona looks at her with all the love one can look at another person with. "All this time, we never moved on, and now this. I'm standing here about to marry the man I've loved my whole life with our daughter beside me. If someone told me this was going to happen, I would have told them that they were lying." She wipes the bottom of her eye with her thumb. "Let's get me married."

We share a smile, and a couple of minutes later, I'm walking out of the house with my mother and Marian. "She's coming."

"Everyone get into place"—Carl claps his hands—"especially you, Joseph." He looks at Sierra's dad. "I need you to make all this legal."

I stand here in the front row, watching Sierra walk down the aisle, first stopping in front of her birth father and giving him a hug. He kisses the top of her head, and when she turns to walk toward me, he stops her. "I want you standing beside me." He takes her hand and wraps it around his arm. "That's my wish—to marry your mother with you beside us."

"Then this is where I will be," she confirms with her

own tears in her eyes as they look down the aisle at her birth mother walking down. The whole thing takes less than ten minutes, with them just wanting to share their vows and nothing else.

He walks her down the makeshift aisle as Sierra comes over to me. "When are you going to make a decent woman out of me?" She puts her hands on her hips, and I just look at her. "You are getting the cow for free."

"Yeah," my mother pipes in, "when are you going to do the right thing?"

"You're asking me this?" I point at myself. "You haven't even said yes to my proposal."

"You haven't even gotten me a ring," she barks out. I look over at her parents, knowing it was going to come later tonight, but now that she's all up in a mood, I have to do it now. I reach in my pocket and pull out the black ring box.

"I got you a ring." I hold it up, and now she shuts up. "Of course, I had this whole plan, but well, you are you, and nothing with you goes to plan." I get on my knee in front of her, and she puts her hand to her mouth. "Sierra, when I met you, I felt the earth shift underneath me." I smile at her. "And you ran so far and fast away from me, it was hard for me to keep up with you. But I couldn't let you go. No matter how many hurdles you made me jump over, I knew you were the one."

"That's called stalking," Theo interjects, walking into the backyard, making everyone laugh, "and I said it wasn't a good idea."

"Either way, I had to make you mine," I tell her

when she stops laughing at Theo and looks back at me. "I want to have kids with you, grow old with you, and now, apparently, I want to get a dog with you. Marry me, Sierra."

"Well, you are getting me a dog"—she rolls her eyes—"so I guess I will." She walks to me and holds my face in her hands. "I wasn't running that fast or that far if I let you catch me." She kisses my lips. "And I'll let you catch me each time."

Epilogue Two

CHARLIE

A Special Day

"Landon William." I hear Autumn yelling our son's name from the barn, and I look over at him as he pretends he didn't hear her. Walking over to the hay, he puts his pitchfork in it before walking over and dumping it in the stall. "Landon William Barnes." Now she uses his full name and even he stops for a second, unsure of what to do. It's one thing when she yells his first and middle name, it's a totally different ball game when she uses his whole name.

"Son," I say and he looks over at me, "is there a reason your mother is hollering your name right now?"

"I might have," he replies, looking out the barn door, hearing the sound of footsteps coming closer, "maybe? Perhaps." He starts talking faster. "I'm supposed to be in the shower right about five minutes ago."

I'm about to tell hm to run out the back door and miss her, when my wife is in the middle of the back door with her hands on her hips. Her blond hair is piled on top of her head, the blue jeans have holes in the knees and are a touch baggy around her hips. The smile on my face goes from ear to ear each time I see her. "You." She points at our son.

"Mom," he says and she just shakes her head, telling him to stop talking, giving him the look she gives him when she doesn't want to hear another word from him. Something our children push at daily.

"I don't want to hear anything from you. The only thing I want to see is your ass walking out and going to the house and you getting in the shower. Why is it the only one ever listening to me is your brother, Casey?" She isn't really asking him the question as much as telling him to get his ass into the house.

"Momma," our three-year-old daughter, Anabelle, says from beside me, with her plastic pink shovel my father keeps sending her, "you said ass." She wipes her cheek with the back of her hand, smearing dirt across her little face. Her blond curls are wild on her head, her eyes just like her mother's. She looks like the stamp of Autumn, but she's one hundred percent a Barnes with the daredevil activities she does for fun.

"You"—she points to Anabelle—"you are supposed to be in that house also, putting on your dress. I just gave you a shower and did your hair."

"Oops." She giggles and drops her shovel by her feet. "I go now," she singsongs, skipping away, wearing shorts and a T-shirt with her worn cowboy boots. As if she doesn't have to be given another washdown before putting on the dress.

"And don't be wearing those boots into the house, young lady," Autumn warns, walking deeper in the barn to stand beside me, turning her glare to me. "And you."

I raise my eyebrows when she aims that look at me. "What about me?"

"You should be in there with them." She points over to the empty doorway where our children just escaped. I take off the gloves I was wearing to carry in the bales of hay, tucking them into the back pocket of my jeans. "We have to be at Brady's house in thirty minutes."

"I'll be ready in thirty minutes," I assure her, closing the distance to her and wrapping one of my arms around her waist. "It takes me fifteen minutes to shower and then another five to dress." I kiss her lips and she melts into my arms. "We have ten minutes to sneak something else in there."

"Oh good, just what I want to hear. Ten minutes to rock my world." She rolls her eyes and pushes away from me.

"Last Saturday night it took you less than two minutes for me to rock your world," I remind her, "and then I had to muffle you the rest of the night."

She folds her arms over her chest. "We are going to be late." She avoids talking about last Saturday night, but I can see the pink tint on her cheeks. "And it's a big day for Wyatt."

"Fine." I put my arm around her shoulders as I walk

with her toward our house. "But tonight…"

"Yeah, what about tonight?" she asks softly as we walk up the back steps to our house. Anabelle's red tricycle with a pink basket is tossed to the side, right next to Casey's scooter.

"Well, after we put the kids to bed," I begin once we are standing right outside of the storm door, "why don't you and me grab a couple of blankets and come outside to watch the stars?" She puts her hands on my chest, and even though we've been together for all these years, she still makes my heart speed up. She still makes me smile every single day. These days the smile comes when it shouldn't, which gets me in lots of trouble.

"Charlie Barnes," she says my name softly, "are you asking me to have sex with you on the swing?"

"I never said anything about us having sex on the swing." I turn my head to the side and kiss her neck. "But I was hoping it would lead to that."

"What am I going to do with you?" She moves her hands from my chest and up around my neck.

"I have a couple of thoughts about that." I put my hands on her hips and pull her closer to me. "But there is really only one big thing I want you to do." She rolls her eyes, thinking I'm talking about my cock. "Not that." I shake my head and I just look into her eyes. "I want you to love me for the rest of my life." The smile now fills her face. "I want to love you for the rest of my life."

"Okay, that I can do." She gets on her tippy-toes and kisses my lips softly. "But if you don't get your ass in that shower," she whispers in my ear, "there will be no swing sex for you."

I let her go, turning to walk into the house. "Say less." I wink at her. "Love you."

She shakes her head as she looks at me. "I love you too, Charlie."

"Wow." I kick off my shoes and they get mixed with the pile of shoes our kids have on rotation. "I felt that emotion all the way to my soul."

She's about to answer me when we hear the kids calling our names. "Ugh," she huffs and walks into the house toward the sound of their voices.

I follow her but stop at the table filled with pictures that span the last almost ten years. Jennifer's picture is in the middle of it all. Even after all this time, Autumn refuses to tuck it away. "Thank you," I say silently, then look toward where voices are ringing out from, "for leading her back to me."

Brock

"Okay, I want all of you," I shout from the kitchen island as I put the juice away that was left on the counter, no doubt by one of the boys when they were called in to shower over an hour ago, "in the truck in five minutes." I close the fridge and hear the sound of movement all around the house. "Do I make myself clear?"

"Yes," Everleigh says, coming into the kitchen dressed in a long white dress filled with pink flowers. The top of her dress is tight and the straps look like she tied it on the top of her shoulders. "I heard you," she confirms, walking to the sink with two coffee cups in her hand. Every Saturday morning, I get out of bed and make her coffee. The two of us have coffee in bed before our children wake up and demand attention from us. It's something we started after we had our third child. Skye, our second child, is usually the first one up, as if she is going to miss out on something. Our sons, Bax and Brantley, sleep like the dead. I can't wait to see them sleep away their days once they hit their late teen years. Saige usually ventures out of her room when she smells food, typical for her since she's in full-blown mid-teen years. "The whole block heard you." She looks over her shoulder, her black hair brushed loose and swaying side to side.

I walk over to her, putting my hand on the ledge of the sink, boxing her in. My cock nestles perfectly in the crook of her ass. "I like this dress," I whisper in her ear, "gives me easy access to do things to you."

"Yeah?" She looks over her shoulder at me, smirking. "Like what sort of things?" I move one of my hands to the middle of her legs, and I'm about to show her when I hear the sound of footsteps coming toward us. My hand moves to her hips as I lean in and kiss her neck.

"Eeww," Skye groans, walking into the kitchen, "are you guys making out again?"

"Yes," I answer her at the same time that Everleigh says, "No," moving away from me and my hold on her.

"It's gross." She goes over to the fridge and pulls it open to grab a bottle of juice. "I was over at Rickie's house"—she mentions her best friend—"and her parents didn't even talk to each other the whole night."

"That's because her parents are on the verge of getting divorced," I state, making her gasp and earning me a slap on my abs.

"Stop saying that," she says between clenched teeth.

"What?" I lean against the sink. "It's not like it's a surprise."

"Saige, Bax, Brant," Everleigh shouts, "we are going to be late!"

"I'm here," Saige announces, walking into the room wearing a white summer dress with little purple flowers, "and I'm ready."

"You look beautiful," Everleigh tells her, smiling at her and earning her own Saige smile. It's been four months since she moved in full-time with us, opting out from going back and forth. Something her mother didn't like or approve of, but Saige was of the legal age to decide who and where she wanted to live. I was happy to have all my kids under one roof, but no one was happier than Everleigh, who felt guilt every time we had to celebrate something without her. Celebrations were usually pushed off until Saige could be with us.

"Bax!" she shouts for our son, who comes running into the room followed by his brother, the two of them thick as thieves. Both of them with our black hair and brown eyes. They look identical and exactly like me. "Let's go." She motions with her head toward the door.

The six of us usher out of the house and head toward the minivan we had to get to fit us all. "Are you okay?" I hear Everleigh ask Saige, who just shrugs and walks toward the car.

"What's up with that?" I stand at the door, watching the kids argue about who is going to sit in the back row. Saige doesn't even bother, instead she just gets in and heads to the back.

"Wyatt is going to ask Lucy to be his prom date tonight"—I look up at the blue sky—"and even though she says that she's fine with it—"

"She's not." I look at Everleigh, who gives me the same shrug Saige just gave her.

"The three of them are all best friends, and she thinks she's going to be left out now," Everleigh explains.

"Great," I reply, "I warned you."

"You did not." Everleigh turns to me. "When did you warn us?"

"When I said I don't think her hanging around with Wyatt is a good idea." I point at her.

"She was ten."

"Well, look at where we are now." I raise my hands to the sides. "Where I said we would be."

"You are so annoying." She walks ahead of me and down the steps to the car. "You are also going to be nice and not go and give him a talking-to."

"Why not?" I ask her.

"Remember Rio?" She mentions Saige's first boyfriend, who asked to take her to the movies.

"His name was Rio," I grit. "I already didn't like him. Plus, he was two years older than her. You know what he was thinking about in that movie theater?" I ask her. "Getting under that dress, that is what he was thinking about, trust me, I should know, I was him once."

"Wow." She shakes her head. "You have to trust her."

"Oh, I trust her." I point to the back of the truck. "I just don't trust all the penises around her."

Everleigh inhales deeply. "For today, I'm going to have you dial down the crazy, please."

I stare at her. "I can only be me." I walk around the minivan, looking over at her. "It's who you fell in love with."

"Great," she says, trying to hide her smile, "good to know you've evolved."

I get into the minivan and start the car, looking in the rearview at my oldest, who has her earbuds in and is looking out the window. I make my way over to Brady and Harmony's place, pulling up to their house and seeing people have already arrived.

I get out and the kids jump out of the van, the boys running to the backyard where everyone is. I stop Saige before she can leave. "You going to be okay?" I ask her and she just gives me a smile. "Yeah, you'll be fine." I kiss the side of her head. "You'll be better than fine."

She turns and walks to the backyard and then turns to walk backward. "Does that mean I can go to prom with Austin?" She mentions one of the newest mechanics I just hired, right out of high school.

"Saige"—I point at her—"under no circumstance are you allowed anywhere near my shop."

"Come on, Dad," she replies, "we work together." She grins before walking into the backyard.

"Well, that was one way to tell you," Everleigh goads

from beside me and I look over at her. "You have no one but yourself to blame for this, you were the one who said a girl should know her way around a car." She walks past me toward the yard. "Hey," she says, turning and walking backward, just like my daughter did, "love you."

"Yeah," I mumble, making her laugh. "You can show me tonight."

"You bet," she confirms, and the smile on her face is the smile I first fell in love with all those years ago, sitting by a creek, watching her dip her toes into the water. "Tonight and every night after."

Emmett

"How is this?" Lucy asks, walking into the kitchen and showing us her third dress option for the day. "What about this one?" She turns to give us the full effect and I look over to Lilah, who nods her head.

"I still like the second one," she states. "The yellow is so nice on you."

"Okay, I'll try that one on again," she says, running back to her bedroom.

"Lucy, we are going to be late, and it's Wyatt's special day," Lilah reminds her softly and Lucy grumbles that she'll be a minute.

"What the fuck is all the fuss?" I bring the cup of coffee to my lips and take a sip. "It's just a barbecue with the family."

"Well," Lilah admits, tapping her finger on the counter, "it's a bit more than that."

"Yeah, sure, it's a big deal," I state, "but at the end of the day, it's just us getting together. We do it almost every single Sunday."

Lacey walks into the room dressed in shorts and a T-shirt. "Dad, I don't have school tomorrow, can I come to the barn with you?"

"Yeah," I agree, looking at our daughter. She looks like me, but she has Lilah's eyes. She also has her soft heart, thank God. "Go and get your brother out of his room and tell him we are leaving in one minute."

Lacey laughs. "Lucy isn't even done getting dressed." She points over her shoulder to where the kids' bedrooms are. I never in my life thought I would have a house filled with kids. Never in my life knew this is what my I was missing until Lucy came into it, and then made me see loving someone else was okay. She taught me how to be a better man, how to be a father, and got me ready for the other two. My life now consists of my three kids, who I would die for, and a wife, who puts up with me and loves me unconditionally. I make sure every single day I never let her regret loving me. Some days I succeed, some days I don't.

"Lucy!" I shout. "We are leaving, and you are going to be wearing whatever it is you are wearing and it'll be fine."

"Dad," she groans out my name. "It has to be perfect."

"Yeah," Logan agrees, walking out of his bedroom dressed in jeans and a T-shirt, "it has to be perfect." He rolls his eyes at Lucy and her teenage dilemma.

"Go sit in the truck," Lilah tells him.

He looks at me. "Can I start it?"

"No." I shake my head. "Last time you did that, you smashed the front of my truck into the back of your mother's."

"I wanted to see if I could reach the pedals." He rolls his eyes. "Fine, I'll go and sit outside and die in the heat."

"You'll survive," I tell his retreating back. "Lucy, we are leaving."

She comes back out from her bedroom, this time dressed in another dress. It's yellow and is tight around the waist with what looks like little pink flowers or maybe it's cherries. "How is this?"

"That's the one," Lilah praises, putting her hands to her mouth, "it's perfect."

"Good," I add, "now get in the truck."

"Dad," Lacey says, "it has to be perfect for when Wyatt asks Lucy to prom."

My head goes back as if someone just punched me in the face. "I'm sorry, what?"

"Lacey," Lucy shouts out, "you are so annoying and such a blabbermouth!"

"It's not like he's not going to know." Lacey tries to defend herself. "He's going to be there."

"Lacey," Lilah orders, "go outside and wait with your brother."

"Wait, so you are going to prom with Wyatt?" I ask her, then look over at Lilah, who is pretending to look around instead of at me, and I know she knew this all along and didn't tell me.

"Yes," Lucy admits. "Wyatt told Elijah, who then told

Lucas, who then mentioned it to—" I hold up my hand, not caring about how the food chain went. "He's going to ask me out today and then to prom."

"Go out?" I shake my head. "That's not happening."

"But, Daddy," she sighs out.

"If you say you love him"—I put my hands flat on the island—"you aren't even going to the barbecue today."

"Emmett," Lilah starts softly and I turn to her, "this is a big deal."

"No, it's not." I shake my head. "A big deal is getting into the right college." I turn back to point at Lucy. "And getting your degree to become a social worker. That's the big deal."

"She can do both." Lilah laughs and then stops when I look over at her. "They've been in love." I raise my eyebrows at the word. "They've liked each other"— she changes the word love to like—"since they were in middle school."

"I told you it was weird that he was hanging around her."

"It's not weird. They like the same things and their families are always together, it was inevitable."

"Yeah," Lucy chimes in, "Lacey said she is going to marry Bax."

"Lucy," Lilah says, "why don't you go outside and make sure Lacey and Logan are okay."

"Can we go and you guys have this discussion later on tonight?" Lucy asks. "I don't want to be late."

"Then you should have thought about that before you changed five times," I snap at her. "Go and wait outside."

She turns to walk out. "Actually, you don't have to. I forbid you to date him."

"Okay," Lucy replies with a sly smile, just like Lilah gives me. She may not be her mother, but the two of them are thick as thieves.

"I'm not joking," I warn her retreating back, then turn back to Lilah and see the same sly smile. "She's too young to date."

"She's going off to college next year," Lilah reminds me. "She'll be able to date and do all those other things you don't want to think about her doing."

"Fine, she's not allowed to go off to college. She can get her degree online." Lilah laughs. "They do that nowadays."

"They do." She puts her hands on my hips. "It's going to be okay," she soothes softly. "She's a good kid. We raised her to be a strong independent woman."

"I did no such thing," I gruff out. "Wyatt."

"You helped raise him," she reminds me. "He spent every single moment that he wasn't in school in the barn. You know he's a good kid."

"Doesn't mean I have to like it," I mumble out and she nods.

"Noted." She kisses my chin. "Now, let's go before we're late." She walks away from me and I inhale and look up at the pictures all around the house. Pictures that show us growing from the three of us, to the four of us, to the five of us. Every single memory there in some form or another. "You're a good dad," she declares and then smiles even bigger, "but an even better man."

"Yeah." I walk to her. "It's all because of you guys," I tell her honestly. "You all make me want to be a better man." I hold her face in my hands. "Never thought I would be so filled with love that I would be unable to breathe. Thank you for showing me how good it could be."

"Thank you," she retorts, "for knocking me up"—she winks at me—"and saving me, of course." I can't help but laugh. "And showing everyone else that I was right about you all along."

"Not everyone, I'm sure there are still a couple people out there who hate me." She laughs. "But you don't, and our kids don't, so that's all that matters."

Brady

"Hey," I say to Charlie when he gazes into the backyard and looks around, coming straight to me, his hand outstretched to shake my hand, "thanks for coming."

"It's a big day," he comments, looking around the yard. "How is Wyatt?"

"I think he's good," I answer him and then look over to see him sitting on the step just looking out. "Might be a bit strange for him." I motion with my chin. "I'm going to go and see if he's okay."

"You got this," Charlie assures me, slapping my arm as I make my way toward my son.

I walk and stop when I see Brock and Everleigh walk into the backyard. "Hey," I greet, looking around and seeing their kids running rapidly into the yard, looking for the rest of the kids to go and cause havoc with.

"Hey, you two," I say. "Thanks for coming. It means a lot."

"You're welcome," Everleigh replies. "It's a big day for you guys."

I look over toward Wyatt and see Saige is now sitting with him. "It is," I agree. "I'm just worried about him."

"Don't be," Brock assures me. "He's going to be fine."

"Yeah," I agree, "I'm going to go and make sure."

They nod at me as I inch forward and am stopped again by Caleb and Sierra. "This is such a special day," Sierra states, coming to kiss my cheek. "We're honored to be a part of it."

"You okay?" Caleb is the first one today to ask me that.

"More than okay," I tell hm, "just worried about…" I trail off when Harmony makes it to my side.

"Are you good?" I ask her as she wraps her arm around my waist and smiles up at me.

"I'm good," she confirms, "but he's being quiet." She motions with her chin toward Wyatt.

"I'm going," I say, kissing her and walking away from her and our friends. I don't let anyone interrupt me before I get to Wyatt, who is talking to Saige.

"Hey," I say and he looks up at me, "can I borrow him for a minute?"

"Sure," Saige replies, getting up. "I'll be over there." She points to where everyone else is.

I walk up the steps and sit next to him, not the first time we've sat on these steps. I think back over the last years, remembering every single memory, playing over and over in my head on loop. "What's going through your mind right now?"

"I don't know," he answers me, leaning forward and putting his elbows on his knees as he watches everyone in that yard who has come here for him, "a bunch of different emotions, really."

"Listen," I say and he looks over at me, his sandy-blond hair, which is getting darker as he gets older, is pushed to the side, "we don't have to do anything you don't want to do." I smile at him. "It's a fucking paper and doesn't mean anything. In my heart you are my son, that is the only thing that really matters."

"It's not just a piece of paper," counters the little boy who turned into a man right before my very eyes, "it's more than that."

"It really isn't." I try to not let it be a big deal in case he wants to change his mind. "It's literally going to be the same. You, Whitney, your mom, and me."

"Yeah, but," he starts to say and then I see his bottom lip tremble; the last time I saw that, he was telling his mother he wanted to live in this house, "but it's so much more than that."

"Wyatt," I comfort, putting my hand on the back of his neck, "it's just another day."

"Do you think I'm worthy enough to have your name?"

"What the fuck?" I squeeze his neck. "Why would you even think?"

"I want to make you proud."

"You make me proud every fucking day you get up and start your day. You are the best son and big brother anyone could ask for."

"I never want to be like him."

"You are already not like him." I slap my hand onto his chest. "You even caring right now, in this minute, you are more of a man than he will ever be. I don't care what your last name is or whose blood runs in your veins. In here…" I point to his chest. "In here you are mine and you are a Thatcher."

"I am," he proclaims. "Down to my bones, I'm a Thatcher and I promise you I'll make your name proud."

I don't answer him because I can't. I just bring him closer to me and kiss his head. "Every fucking day," I tell him when the lump goes away.

"Mom is crying." Whitney skips over followed by Brantley, who stands beside her.

"Again," Wyatt says, standing up. "I'll go this time." He walks down the steps as Whitney skips away with Brantley chasing her. "By the way"—he looks over his shoulder at me—"going to ask Lucy to be my girlfriend."

"Oh, good God," I groan, looking to see Emmett arriving and coming straight our way. "Something says he knows."

I get up, ready to step in front of him. "You." He points to Wyatt. "We need to have a couple of words."

"No, you don't." I chuckle. "Go and find your mom."

"Okay, Dad. Hi, Emmett, thanks for coming," he says with a sly smile as he walks away.

"Do you know our kids are going to start dating?"

Emmett questions and he puts his hands on his hips. "He wants to date my daughter."

"I heard," I confirm, walking down the steps and looking over to see Wyatt didn't find his mother, but instead, he found Lucy.

"That's all you have to say about it?" he hisses.

"He spends more time with you than he does with me these days," I point out to him. "If he's a dick, you have no one to blame but yourself." He rolls his eyes. "But that's not the type of man he is, because I didn't raise him like that." We look over at our kids and see them smiling at each other. "It's going to be fine."

"It fucking better," he huffs, turning and walking away at the same time that Harmony comes over.

"What is all that about?" she asks and I just smile down at her.

"Wyatt and Lucy becoming a couple," I tell her. She wraps her arms around my waist and then looks up at me smiling, before looking at our backyard filled with all of our friends and family. My father, still alive and kicking in a chair, is talking to Mr. Mendelson and Oliver about something, the three of them laughing.

"It's about time, don't you think? He's been in love with her since middle school," she reminds me of something that only the three of us knew because we saw the way he looked at her and said he needed to be sure before he took that step. Well, he waited long enough. "It's time." She looks up at me. "It's time to finally celebrate." She just smiles up at me big, making my chest expand. "Thank you for giving me the life people dream of."

She steps away from me and into the throng of people as we celebrate Wyatt Cartwright becoming Wyatt Thatcher.

Caleb

I PARK IN the driveway, turning off the truck, and then getting out. The two of us move like sloths up the steps to the front door. "I swear if you ask me what I want to eat for dinner," Sierra says as she unlocks the door, "I'm going to vomit on your shoes."

"Good to know." I slap her ass as she steps into the house and we hear the sound of the dog barking from his crate.

"I'm coming, my boy." Sierra dumps her purse on the first step, like she always does, before walking to the side and opening the black crate we have for Maxwell, our dog. "Hi, my boy, did you miss us?" she asks him as she scratches his golden neck, the back of his body shaking side to side with glee that she is home. It's supposed to be our dog, but make no mistake about it, he will choose her each and every time.

"We were gone for three hours." I look at her and she gets on her knees and lets Maxwell lick her cheek before getting up and walking over to the back door. "He's fine."

I pull open the fridge to grab a bottle of water as she opens the door, and then looks back at me. "I'm going to go out with him."

"He can go and pee by himself," I tell her, but she's

already out the back door as I watch through the window at her walking over and sitting on the step. I'm about to go out there when she turns back and rushes into the house. "I think I'm going to be sick." She runs to the bathroom and shuts the door behind her.

Maxwell runs back into the house, ignoring me and going to sit outside the bathroom door. I walk over. "Move," I say to the dog, who literally doesn't budge, snarling at me as I knock at the door.

"I don't feel so great," she states and then I hear her throwing up.

"Can I come in?" I ask her and she groans and shouts.

"Don't you dare." She has enough time to order me before she gets sick again.

I stand here looking at the closed door with Maxwell sniffing under the door and whining, before lifting his front paw and scratching at the door to let him in. "If I'm not going in there, neither are you," I tell him.

"Baby." I use my forefinger knuckle to knock on the door. "Can I come in now?"

The sound of the toilet flushing answers my question, along with the sound of the sink running before the door is pulled open. "Hey," I say softly, seeing her face is pale, "you don't look so hot."

"Wow," she fires back, "just what you want to hear for your man. You look like shit."

She walks past me and toward the steps, walking to our bedroom. Maxwell is right behind her. I follow her, and when I walk into the bedroom, she is lying on her back with her head on the pillows and Maxwell is there on the bed beside her, in my spot. "Off the bed." I point with my finger to the floor and he literally just takes a deep sigh as he licks his lips and then closes his eyes, resting by her. "What did you eat?" I ask her.

"Nothing really, my stomach was all up and down today."

"Again?" I ask, putting my hands on my hips. "Shouldn't you call the doctor? It's been over two weeks with you feeling like shit. I think we can scratch off you having the flu."

"We can definitely scratch off me having the flu," she retorts. "I have this whole plan to tell you," she says and I just stare at her, "but, well, obviously it's the way it goes with us." She opens her side table drawer. "I was going to have Maxwell wear a shirt." She sits up now grabbing something. "But, well, this will have to do."

"What the hell are you talking about?" I ask her, confused by what she is saying.

"I'm talking about…" She gets up and walks over to me. Maxwell sticks his head up, ready to tear out of the room if Sierra leaves. "You and me"—she stops in front of me, a white thing with the blue tip in her hand—"having a baby."

"Um, what?" I ask her as she holds up the pregnancy test with the letters pregnant on it.

"I'm pregnant."

"Are you sure?" I ask her, grabbing the test from her and looking down at it.

"As sure as that is," she declares and then tries to take it away from me. "I was going to put this in a frame with our baby pictures in it. You know, be romantic about it, but again it's like the universe is against me showing you that I'm more romantic than you are." I chuckle before grabbing her face in my hands and kissing her. "Eeww, gross. I peed on that stick and now it's on my face."

"We're having a baby." I can't help but wrap my arms around her and spin her around. Maxwell is barking at her shrieking. "A baby," I say, putting her down. "Oh my God, I'm going to be a dad." I can't help the way my voice goes high with anticipation. "I love you."

"You better," she huffs out, "I'm carrying your child." I look down at the test again, making sure it didn't change. "I swear if this kid comes out looking like you and only you, I'm not having another one."

"I don't know," I counter, "I say we try until we get one that looks exactly like you."

"Yeah, right." She pushes my shoulder.

"You did it," I tell her and she just looks up at me. "You made literally everything I've dreamed up come true."

"Well, I am pretty awesome"—she flips her hair behind her shoulder—"but you kind of helped with this one," she declares, putting her hand in the middle of my chest. Her engagement ring with the eternity wedding band under it on her finger. "You gave me a dog, so I had to give you a kid."

I can't help but bark out with laughter. "I love you, today, yesterday, tomorrow, always."

www.ingramcontent.com/pod-product-compliance
Lightning Source LLC
LaVergne TN
LVHW031934110725
815950LV00014B/133